PUSHKIN PRESS

THE EVENINGS

'As funny as it is ultimately profound… should cause many readers to revise their opinions of *The Catcher in the Rye*. In all fairness to Salinger, *The Evenings* is so much better'   *Irish Times*, Books of the Year 2016

'Fascinates the more you read of it… A fantastic novel'
Sunday Telegraph

'*The Evenings* is packed with the minutiae of life: luckily, the minutiae are fascinating… Reve isn't the kind of novelist to give you a straightforward answer but the journey is quite a ride'   *The Times*

'This much lauded book, finally available in English, [is] the perfect January read'   *Spectator*

'Hats off to Pushkin Press and the outstanding translator, Sam Garrett, for making this odd, orphaned masterpiece available at last to an English-speaking readership'   *Times Literary Supplement*

'Fascinating, hilarious and page-turning. The publication of this novel marks the exciting introduction of a wonderful writer to an Anglophone audience'   *Publishers Weekly*

'It's like BS Johnson and Kafka wandering the crepuscular streets of 1940s Amsterdam together – in a good way'
Observer, Best Fiction of 2016

'Reve's keen eye for absurdity manages to cast the mundane in a new, albeit macabre, light'   *Financial Times*

'This 1947 Dutch novel, considered the Netherlands' greatest in the 20th century… is a savage novel, full ⟨…⟩   *Daily Mail*

'Hilariously gloomy… a Dutch ⟨…⟩

GERARD REVE (1923–2006) is considered one of the greatest postwar Dutch authors, and was also one of the first openly gay writers in the country's history. A complicated and controversial character, Reve is also hugely popular and critically acclaimed. His 1947 debut *The Evenings* was ranked as the best Dutch novel of the twentieth century by the Society of Dutch literature. This is its first translation into English.

SAM GARRETT has translated some 40 novels and works of non-fiction. He has won prizes and appeared on shortlists for some of the world's most prestigious literary awards, and is the only translator to have twice won the British Society of Authors' Vondel Prize for Dutch–English translation.

GERARD REVE

THE EVENINGS

A Winter's Tale

Translated from the Dutch
by Sam Garrett

PUSHKIN PRESS
LONDON

Pushkin Press
71–75 Shelton Street,
London WC2H 9JQ

Original text © 1946 Erven Gerard Reve

Published with De Bezige Bij, Amsterdam

Translation © Sam Garrett 2016

First published in Dutch as *De Avonden* in 1946

This translation first published by Pushkin Press in 2016
This edition first published in 2017

N ederlands letterenfonds
dutch foundation
for literature

The publisher gratefully acknowledges the support
of the Dutch Foundation for Literature

1 3 5 7 9 10 8 6 4 2

ISBN 13: 978 1 782273 01 1

Set in Monotype Baskerville by Tetragon, London
Printed in Great Britain by the CPI Group, UK

www.pushkinpress.com

I wrote *The Evenings* because I was convinced I had to write it: that seems to me a good enough reason. I hoped that ten of my friends would accept a free copy, and that twenty people would buy the book out of pity and ten others by mistake. Things turned out differently. It's not my fault it caused such an uproar.

GERARD REVE, 1948

I

I T WAS STILL DARK, in the early morning hours of the twenty-second of December 1946, on the second floor of the house at Schilderskade 66 in our town, when the hero of this story, Frits van Egters, awoke. He looked at the luminous dial of his watch, hanging on its nail. "A quarter to six," he mumbled, "it's still night." He rubbed his face. "What a horrible dream," he thought. "What was it again?" Gradually it came back to him. He had dreamt that the living room was full of visitors. "It's going to be a glorious weekend," someone said. At that same moment a man in a bowler hat walked in. No one paid him any heed and no one greeted him, but Frits eyed him closely. Suddenly the visitor fell to the floor with a thud.

"Was that it?" he thought. "What happened after that? Nothing, I believe." He fell asleep again. The dream went on where it had stopped. His bowler pressed down over his face, the man was now lying in a black coffin that had been placed on a low table in one corner of the room. "I don't recognize that table," Frits thought. "Did we borrow it from someone?" Then, peering into the coffin, he said loudly: "We'll be stuck with this till Monday, in any event." "I wouldn't be so sure about that," said a bald, red-faced man with spectacles. "Would you care to wager that I can arrange the funeral for this afternoon at two?"

Frits awoke once more. It was twenty minutes past six. "I've had enough sleep," he said to himself, "that's why I woke up so early. I still have more than an hour to go."

He dozed off eventually, and entered the living room for the third time. There was no one there. He walked over to the coffin, looked into it and thought: "He's dead, and starting to rot." Suddenly the cadaver was covered in all kinds of carpenter's tools, piled to the coffin's rim: hammers, drills, saws, spirit levels, planes, pliers and little bags of nails. All that stuck out was the dead man's right hand.

"There's no one here," he thought, "not a soul in the house; what am I going to do? Music, that always helps." He leaned across the coffin to turn on the radio, but at that same moment saw the hand, bluish now and with long white nails, begin to stir. He recoiled in fear. "I mustn't move," he thought, "otherwise it will happen." The hand sank back down.

Later he awoke, feeling anxious. "Ten to seven," he mumbled, peering at the watch. "I always have such horrible dreams." He rolled over and fell asleep again.

Parting a pair of thick green curtains, he entered the living room. The visitors had returned. The man with the red face came up to him, smiled and said: "It didn't work out. It will have to be Monday morning, at ten. We can put the box in the study till then." "Study?" Frits thought. "What study? Do we have a study? He means the side room, of course." Six men lifted the coffin to their shoulders. He himself walked out in front, to open the door for them. "The key's still in the lock," he thought, "good thing, too."

8

The coffin was extremely heavy; the bearers moved slowly, with measured strides. Suddenly he saw that the bottom of the box was beginning to sag and swell. "It's going to burst," he thought, "that's hideous. The corpse is still intact on the outside, but inside it's a thin, yellow mush. It will splatter all over the floor."

By the time they were halfway down the hall, the bottom was sagging so badly that it had begun to crack. Slowly, out of that crack, appeared the same hand from which he had recoiled. Gradually the whole arm followed. The fingers groped about, then crept towards the throat of one of the bearers. "If I scream, the whole thing will fall to the floor," Frits thought. He watched as the bottom sagged further and further and the hand drew closer and closer to the bearer's throat. "There's nothing I can do," he thought. "I can't do a thing."

He awakened for the fourth time, and sat up in bed. It was seven thirty-five. The bedroom was cold. He sat there for five minutes, then stood up and, turning on the light, saw the windowpanes covered in flowers of frost. He shivered as he made his way to the toilet.

"I should start going out for a little walk in the evening, before bed," he thought while washing himself at the kitchen sink. "It would make me sleep more soundly." The soap slipped through his fingers, and he spent quite some time feeling around for it in the shadowy space beneath the counter. "We're off to a roaring start," he mumbled.

"But today's Sunday," he realized suddenly, "what a piece of luck." Then he added to himself: "I'm up far too early, how stupid of me. But no, for once my day won't be ruined by lying around till eleven." While drying his face he started to hum, then went into his room, dressed, and combed his hair in the little mirror that hung beside the door, above one corner of the bed. "It's ridiculously early," he thought. "I can't go in yet. The sliding doors are still open."

He sat down at his little desk, picked up a white marble rabbit about the size of a matchbox and tapped it softly against the arm of the chair. Then he put it on top of the pile of papers from whence it came. Standing up with a shiver, he returned to the kitchen, opened the bread bin and took out two soft white rolls, the first of which he stuffed into his mouth in a few bites. The second he held clenched in his teeth as he went into the hallway for his coat.

"A brisk, invigorating walk in the morning air," he murmured. As he crossed the landing and passed the downstairs neighbours' door, a dog yapped. He pulled the street door closed behind him quietly and followed the frozen canal to the river, which was covered along both banks with a dark layer of ice. There was not much wind. The sun had barely risen, but the street lights were already out. The gutters of the houses were lined with rows of gulls. After kneading the last of his roll into a little ball, he tossed it onto the ice and scores of birds descended. The first gull that picked at it missed. The piece of bread slid, fell into a little hole in the ice and sank before another bird could peck at it.

Church bells rang once. "An early start, this will be a day well spent," he thought, turning right along the riverbank. "It's cold and early and no one's out yet, but I am."

Crossing the big bridge, he skirted the southern railway station and walked back beneath the viaduct. "It's wonderful, taking a walk so early in the morning," he said to himself. "You've been outside, you feel chipper and your spirits are high. This will be no wasted and profitless Sunday."

As he came into the hallway again, the kettle was singing on the stove. In the living room he found his mother setting the table for breakfast. "You're up bright and early," he said. "Your father is in one of his moods," she replied. "He wanted to get up early and make a day of it." Frits looked at her closely. Her face was without expression.

His father came in from the kitchen in his vest and trousers; the braces dangled to the floor. His face was still wet.

"Good morning, Father," Frits said. To speak these words, he felt as if he first had to clear his windpipe of a stone, which now fell at his feet. "Good morning, my boy," his father replied. They sat down at the table.

"I must not let my attention flag," he thought, "I must observe closely." From the moment his father began to eat, he kept his eyes on him. "He chews without a sound," he thought, "but the mouth opens and shuts each time." He looked at the back of his father's neck and felt rage rise up. "Seven warts," he said to himself, "why hasn't he had them removed? Why not get rid of them, at least?"

His mother poured tea. She slurped softly as she drank. His father raised the cup only halfway to his mouth, then stretched his neck, puckered his lips and drank loudly. "Have you had a look at the fire, dearest?" his father asked. "Yes," Frits's mother replied, "it's sputtering away."

When they were done his father went to the bedroom to finish dressing, then returned, book in hand, and sank into a chair by the fire with a deep sigh. Frits watched him as he sat down. "Why such an enormous sigh?" he thought. "Why act as though you're a pair of bellows?" He looked at the head of black hair, combed back and drab in spots, the thick lips curled in a tired smile, and the brown hands with their short, thick fingers which, after some tentative fumbling, slowly turned a page.

Frits himself sat on the divan, close to the window. He leaned over to turn on the radio and dialled through the programmes. "Bach, a sonata," he murmured, clasping his hands behind his head as he leaned back and listened. His father was sucking at his pipe, blowing out slow, thin jets of blue smoke.

"Frits," his mother called from the kitchen, "what did you do with the attic keys?" "I never had them," he said as she came into the room. "Who did, then?" she asked. "Not me, that's for sure," he said. "Weren't you the one who fetched coal yesterday?" she continued. "It was you, wasn't it?" "No," he said, "not me. You probably went upstairs and left them lying on the table." He got up and went into the kitchen. His mother followed. "Are you sure they're not on the sill?" he asked, lifting the curtain and groping along the length of the windowsill.

"You're the one who had them," his mother said. "If you don't bring them back, the fire will go out. You had the keys yesterday, you were the last one to fetch coal."

He looked at her: the thin face, the grey hair, the slight growth of hair around mouth and chin, the arms that never stopped moving. "Help us," he thought. "The voice is too loud; whither lieth succour?" His father came into the kitchen in stockinged feet. He was holding the book in one hand, his index finger stuck between the pages. "What is it now?" he asked. "Calm down, you two." "Don't you get yourself in a state," Frits's mother said. "Who's the one making noise here?" "All that harping and carping," his father said, "what on earth is it good for?" He turned around and disappeared into the hall, his head bowed.

"Go and see whether the key is still in the door," his mother said. Frits climbed the stairs to the storage rooms that lined the attic floor, looked at the lock and saw the key, one of two on a little wire ring. He opened the door and picked up a paper sack of anthracite. Downstairs in the kitchen he tossed the keys onto the windowsill with a jingle. "I suppose now you didn't bring any coal down with you," said his mother, who had just come in from the living room. "Yes, in fact I did," he said. "Here's a whole sack full." "That's not the way you do it," she said. "You have to empty the sack into the scuttle first, upstairs. Otherwise I get all that dust in here."

As they came into the living room his father leaned over to the radio, which was playing a fugue for violin and harpsichord, and turned it off. "All that nagging," he said, "can't we have a little peace and quiet for once?" He dropped into his chair with a faint sigh, opened the book and read on. Frits looked at the clock on the mantel. It was twenty minutes past ten. "The morning rushes by," he thought. "But on any other Sunday I'd still be in bed, so little time's been wasted." He went to his bedroom, pulled one book after another from the shelf, flipped

13

through them and put them back where they belonged. "It's too cold in here," he mumbled. Returning to the living room he took a newspaper from the rack and sat down by the window. Outside he saw passers-by walking quickly, their faces stern and tense. The sky was a solid grey, with a dirty, yellow tint to it. From the divan he could see the street. In the two hours that he sat there, paper in hand, without reading a word, there passed in various directions: four soldiers; two women, each with a pram; a young couple, the husband carrying a child; a boy with a girl on the back of his bicycle; and a group of children herded along by two gentlemen. He watched as the neighbour tried to lure his dog, which was refusing to enter the house, with coaxing and with threats. "I just sit here and sit here and don't do a thing," he thought. "The day's half over." It was a quarter past twelve.

His parents put on their coats. "Be sure to answer the bell if it rings," his mother said. "We're going out for a little stroll." She looked out of the window as she spoke. "We'll have to be quick about it, though: you'd almost think it was going to snow. Come, Father, hurry up. See you in a little while. And don't forget to lock the door behind you if you go out."

"Lock the door behind you if you go out," Frits echoed to himself a few times. As soon as his parents had picked their way down the stairs and he heard the street door close behind them, he turned on the radio. The announcer was reading the time: twelve twenty-four. Taking an oval, nickel-plated tobacco box from his pocket, Frits rolled a cigarette and ran through the luminescent scale of frequencies without finding anything to his liking. He turned off the set, walked down the hall to the side room, where papers and open books were strewn across the writing table, opened a wooden tobacco box and transferred a pinch to his own, which he slid into his pocket.

On his way to the living room he paused before the big mirror in the hall, twisted his mouth to the left and to the right, then lifted the upper lip and pulled down the lower, rolling them inside out. After that he viewed his face from the side, fetched the circular shaving mirror from the kitchen, held it up beside him and used both mirrors to examine his head from above, from behind, and then in full profile. Turning off the light in the hall, he opened the door to the side room. "As seen by daylight," he said quietly. After having examined his head from every angle once more, he combed his hair and turned the light back on. "Let us assess the effect created by daylight in combination with an incandescent lamp," he said to himself. "Very like a giant turnip," he said out loud then, "yet with tell-tale signs of sagacity."

He sighed, hung the shaving mirror back on its peg beside the kitchen window and went to the living room. It was almost one o'clock. He sat down on the divan. "We're more than half-way," he thought, "the afternoon started an hour ago. Valuable time, time irretrievable, have I squandered." He turned on the radio, but even before it had warmed up he turned it off again, stood up, opened the sliding doors and entered the back room. Pushing aside the floor-length curtains, he pressed his face against the window. His forehead left a greasy spot on the pane. He pressed it to the glass once more and looked down.

In the garden of the house to the right, a little corgi dog was performing its duty beneath a rhododendron. Three coats were hanging out to dry on the line. On the concrete walkway of the house immediately below theirs, a white-haired man was chopping blocks of wood. Occasionally, a blow of the hatchet would cause a piece to catapult through the air.

Frits sank his canines into the wooden strip between the panes, touched his tongue to the glass, then turned and walked to the kitchen. There he took a handful of kindling from a paper bag in the corner, laid the pieces of wood on the kitchen table and opened the window soundlessly. Immediately after each blow of the hatchet, he tossed a piece of kindling far off into the garden, at various spots: on the gravel, onto the ornamental rocks, or against the plank fence: forcefully each time, with considerable noise. After retrieving the fourth piece of kindling, the man stopped and studied the wood quizzically. Frits threw one more piece, as far to the left of the walkway as he could, closed the window and sighed. "The empty hours," he murmured, turning away.

As he entered the hallway he heard his parents on the stairs. "Have you been eating sweets again?" his mother asked as she came in. "Goodness gracious, here's what I've been waiting for," she continued, quickly draping her coat over the stand and rushing to the toilet. Breathing heavily, his father moved slowly to the living room door and opened it with a hard shove. It was one thirty.

"Shall we have a bite to eat?" his mother asked. "What will it be, coffee or tea?" "Makes no difference to me," his father said. "It's so cold out," she went on, "there's a real Middenweg wind blowing." "East wind, you mean east wind," Frits said. "Please don't use terms unfamiliar to the uninitiated." "What would you two like?" she asked again. "Tea or coffee? There's still some coffee left." "Tea, make it tea," Frits said. "Coffee," his father said at almost the same instant. "I'll just make coffee, then. All right, Frits?" she decided. "You'll have some anyway, won't you?" "I'll take mine with only hot water, no milk," Frits said. "No," she said, "I'll be serving no black coffee in this house."

By then she had set the table and cut the bread. "Who'd like a pickled herring?" she asked. "No, please, no," Frits said. "And you, Father?" "Uh, no, I don't really feel like it," his father replied. "They've been lying on that plate in the kitchen for three days," Frits said to himself, "they've turned green. Even the chopped onions have gone brown."

"Then I suppose I'll just have to throw away the fish again," she said. "And you two will start whining about why I never buy pickled herring. So I'll buy them and then they'll just lie there, and the long and the short of it is that they'll wind up in the bin again."

"All right, bring them on," Frits said. They sat down at the table. "It's a wonder to behold," his father said, "how poorly they clean fish these days." "That's right," his mother said, "they know you'll buy it anyway." "Do you have a clean knife for me?" Frits asked after he had cut his herring into pieces and eaten it. "I'd like some jam." "If it's a clean knife you want, get one yourself," his mother replied. "The day is two-thirds finished," he thought, "and now I'll have a filthy taste in my mouth for the rest of the afternoon."

After eating, they remained seated for a while. "Time to relax and have a smoke," Frits said. He had just started to roll a cigarette when his father pulled out his case and offered him a cigar. "That looks good," he said, taking one.

"Make a cigarette for me, would you?" his mother asked. He rolled a thin one and handed it to her. She stuck the cigarette a fifth of the way into her mouth, right in the middle of her lips. Puffing shallowly, she pulled the cigarette out of her mouth each time, using thumb and forefinger, and exhaled even before the smoke could quite fill the oral cavity.

"The way you smoke is both incredibly clumsy and ridiculous," Frits said. "First of all, one should always hold the very tip of the cigarette between the dry, outermost part of the lips. Secondly, you must then move it to one corner of your mouth, not take it out all the time. And if you do, then only between index and middle finger." "Make it sound like I'm joking," he thought, and went on in a shrill voice, creasing his face into a smile. "Like this," he said, pulling the cigarette from her mouth. It remained glued to her upper lip.

"Ow," she cried. "Ow!" "Come now, stop this," his father said, suddenly blowing a huge cloud of smoke. "She has to learn sometime," Frits said. His mother stubbed out the cigarette and laid it in a groove in the ashtray.

While she was clearing the table, his father went and lay on the divan, then sat up again to remove his shoes. He remained seated like that for a moment, staring into space, then stood up and walked to the bookcase. Just as he reached it, he slipped; his left leg shot out, but he regained his balance. "Goodness!" his mother cried, "oh mercy!" "It's nothing," Frits said. "Don't start bawling right away."

His father took a book from the shelf, went back and lay on the divan, running his free hand through his hair. "Oh heavens, the fire," his mother said. She peered into the stove, then said: "It's burning nicely now. Mind, you two, that you leave it exactly like this. With the kettle just a little in between." She demonstrated how to balance the aluminium kettle against the top of the stove door, to keep it ajar. "Otherwise it will all burn up within the hour," she said, going into the kitchen.

Frits looked at the clock. "All is lost," he thought, "everything is ruined. It's ten minutes past three. But the evening can still make up for a great deal." His father was feeling around with his right hand between the divan and the wall. "What are you looking for?" Frits asked. "Mmm," his father replied, "I'm looking for something." "Did you drop it?" Frits asked. "My lighter," his father replied. His mother came in. "Have you lost something?" she asked. "Yes," his father said, "yes, I have." "What has your father lost?" she asked Frits. "The lighter," he replied, "it rolled back behind there."

"Get your lazy bones off that divan," his mother said, and once his father was standing she pulled the divan away from the wall. Something hard fell to the floor. Frits bent over, felt around, found the little copper contraption and handed it to his father, who was bent over the divan, ready to lie down again. "Move it back first," his mother said. Frits pushed the seat straight against the wall. His father turned and sat on it, relit his cold cigar, and lay down.

Seating himself before the window, Frits watched the ducks waddling across the ice on the canal. He leafed through a railway timetable he'd found on the mantel. His mother sat beside the fire, knitting something in white wool. "Needles ticking like a fast clock," he thought. Forty-five minutes passed in this way. He moved to another chair, beside the divan, in front of the radio, and looked at his father. "He's asleep," he said to himself, and turned on the set. Suddenly the kettle began singing in the kitchen. "Make that noise stop," he thought, "for God's sake, make it stop." His mother hurried into the kitchen; a moment later the whistling stopped. She came back with tea. "And now, dear listeners, 'La Favorite' by Couperin," the announcer said. When the music had begun, his mother said: "That's not a violin, is it? But it's not a piano either. It must be a harpsichord. Is that a harpsichord?" "A glorious instrument, isn't it?" Frits said. "I forgot to turn off the gas," she said quite suddenly. "Would you do it for me?" He went to the kitchen and turned off the burner. When he came back, the radio was silent. His father was sitting half-upright, leaning on one elbow. The clock said twelve minutes to four.

When the doorbell rang, Frits went to open it. "Who's there?" he shouted. There was no reply. "Who's there, goddam it!" he bellowed. "Whoever it is, I feel like giving them a sound thumping," he said out loud. A young man with black hair and glasses rounded the corner of the final landing.

"Oh, it's you. Hello," Frits said with a smile, which vanished immediately. "See, things can get even worse," he thought. The visitor was of slender build, his red, bony face dotted with pimples.

"Well, well, Mr van Egters," he said, "how are you today?" "Fine, thank you, Mr van Egters," Frits replied, "and you?" They entered the hallway together. "Is Ina coming too?" Frits's mother asked after pecking him on the cheeks. "As chance would have it, Mother," the young man said with a smile, "Ina isn't feeling well. The only purpose of my visit is to say that we won't be coming to dinner." He shook his head. "He's already grown a little balder," Frits thought.

"Oh goodness," his mother said. "Is she feeling poorly?" "Not well at all," the young man said. "If you wait a moment, Joop, I'll make something for you to take with you," she said, going to the kitchen.

"How are things here?" Joop asked. "How do you think?" thought Frits. "How do you think?" he said. For a moment, no one spoke. "Since Joop has left home, Father" he went on in a jovial tone, "I find that I get along with him swimmingly." Joop smiled. His father turned on the radio and found a waltz. He patted his right knee to the rhythm.

His mother poured them tea. "Have a macaroon," she said to Joop. "We've had ours already."

It was growing dark. Frits turned on the light, which caused a grinding noise to come out of the loudspeaker. "Ben Beender and his orchestra, with 'On the Ice'," the announcer said. His father clicked off the set.

"Our toilet's frozen," Joop said to Frits. "Christ," Frits said, "is it frozen solid, or just blocked with ice? If it's the latter, maybe something can be done about it." "What do I care," he thought, "what difference does it make to me?" "Well, that's probably all it is," Joop said. "Do you have something thin, something strong but flexible?" Frits went into the hallway and searched through the broom cupboard, until he found the top section of a fishing rod. "Will this do?" he asked, coming back into the room. "No," Joop answered, "that would be a pity. It's a good rod." Frits put the piece back where he'd found it. "That was easy enough," he said to himself. "Why do I think that way?" he thought then. "What right do I have to be so blasé?"

His mother came into the living room, carrying a pan. "Listen," she said to Joop, "here's some meat and gravy. There's a little apple sauce in a jar, in there, between the endives and the potatoes. If I wrap it all in some newspaper and put it in here"—she held up a wicker shopping basket for him to see— "it won't spill and it won't get cold." Joop put on his coat and coughed. "You're going awfully bald," Frits said. He eyed Joop's scalp, the hairline already in full retreat along both sides of the forehead. "You say that with a certain glee, I note," Joop said. He left, carefully balancing the pan in its bag. "Say hello, and give my love to all," his mother called after him.

"At least that's over with," Frits said to himself. "All this coming and going, the doorbell never stops ringing." His father crossed to the stove, seized the handle and opened the door with a clatter. "He's going to make a mess," Frits thought, "and all I can do is watch. Why can't I stop watching?" His father rapped his pipe hard a few times against the metal sill: charred tobacco fell between door and stove to the floor. Then he slammed the door with a clang.

His mother set the table and brought in the food. "Some of the potatoes might be a little hard," she said as they sat down, "but I can't help it. If you know of a better place to eat, I won't stop you." "There isn't a single glassy one in the bunch, as far as I can ascertain," Frits said. "Careful with the gravy," she said, "don't drown your food in it. I can make more, but it will only be waterier." "The gravy is exemplary," Frits said, "it's absolutely heavenly. In fact, you don't even need much of it, it's so nice and rich." "The gravy *is* good," he thought, "it really is excellent." "Father, does it meet with your approval as well, if I may be so bold?" he asked with mock affectation, his head tilted to one side. "It tastes fine to me, I have to admit," his father replied.

After dinner his father went to sit by the stove, in the same spot where Frits's mother had done her knitting that afternoon. Frits put on his coat and came into the room. "Where are you off to?" asked his mother, who was clearing the table. "Why not spend a nice, quiet evening at home?" "I'm fidgety," Frits said, "I need to get out. I think I'll go to see Jaap Elderer tonight, or else Louis." Confirming the presence of tobacco and rolling papers in his box, he slid it into his coat pocket and left.

It was cold outside. A south-easterly wind was blowing hard. Not a single star could be seen on the firmament. At the river he turned left and followed the granite embankment. Crossing a bridge with heavy stone balustrades, he walked along the other bank, past a broad, busy street, turning at last onto a quay with warehouses at the start of it. At number seventy-one, having first climbed a flight of seven flagstone steps, he rang the bell beside a door with a wrought-iron grille before the glass. At the first pull of the bell handle he heard a dull rattle: only after a slight delay did the clapper sound two clear, penetrating notes. He waited thirty seconds, rang again, then went back down the steps. "The chances of this evening's success have been significantly reduced," he said quietly. "These are trying times."

He took the same route for his return. Close to his own home he entered the portico of a tall, broad house by the riverfront and rang the bell. When the door swung open, he shouted up the stairs: "Egters, in the flesh." High above him someone was leaning over the banister, peering down. "I reiterate: Egters, Van," Frits shouted. "Well, all right then, why not?" the person upstairs shouted. "It's probably better than nothing." When Frits arrived upstairs he was met by an extremely tall young man with thin, blond hair slicked back. The young man wore no jacket, and had his sleeveless jumper on inside out, without a tie.

"I came by out of boredom," Frits said. "A busy day, sometimes one needs to get away. Forgive me for imposing on your own hectic schedule, your studies, your labour of exploration. What are you working on at the moment?"

The windows in the room they entered were bare of curtains. It was, without actually being cramped, not a large room. An oversized paraffin heater was lit in one corner, yet the air was in no way stale. Along the wall to the left was a table, on the other side an upright fold-down bed, and between these two chairs.

"Photography," said the young man, picking up a book from the table. *Experiments with Film Sensitive to Colour*, Frits read. "And are you making headway in this, Louis?" he asked. "Sometimes I believe I am," the young man replied, flicking a breadcrumb against the wall. "Shoo, puss," he said, giving a whack to the head of the black-and-white dappled cat that had jumped onto his lap. The animal leapt to the floor and crawled under the chair by the window where Frits had just seated himself. "They're learning," the young man said. "But Louis, I thought the cat you had here was black," Frits said. "There are any number of them," Louis said, "oh yes, any number indeed." "How large a number might that be, pray tell?" "Five, I think," Louis said. "And they have the run of the place?" Frits asked. "Doesn't anyone else live here?"

"No," Louis said. "When Kade is in his studio, his wife brings food for him and the cats. They have a room of their own. They're not allowed to go into his studio any more, not since they shat on a pile of drawings." "Ah, I see," Frits said. "When you go into their room," Louis went on, "they're all sitting there on the table, pretty as you please." "You should turn down the heater a bit," Frits said. "I see it flaring up yellow." As Louis was trimming the burner, Frits looked at the frost flowers on the windows, examining the ice crystals that had risen in twin sheaves, like a bird's feathers. "Excuse me for just a moment," Louis said, standing up and moving to the table. "I want to finish jotting this down; after that I am at your beck and call."

"Fine," Frits said, but it didn't register. His eyes traced the outlines of the frost flowers and he poked his index finger against the ice again and again, leaving a little round hole each time where it melted. "That's been a while," he thought, looking over his shoulder at Louis, who was bent over his book. On his wrist he wore a large, flat watch with a broad grey strap. A pencil dangled from his lips.

"I must have been twelve or thirteen," Frits thought. "We were on the balcony. Who else was there? Louis, Frans, Jaap, Bep and a couple of the others, I can't remember their names." He closed his eyes. "I can still see it," he thought. "They were walking back and forth, on the fourth floor, balancing on the rail. It wasn't much broader than my hand. And the others just laughed and laughed. How could they laugh?" He opened his eyes, looked at Louis, and closed them again. "To have such courage," he thought, "what a blessing. Or did they simply fail to see how dangerous it was? Perhaps that was it. I felt nauseous, and there was this pain behind my eyes; that was me. And a sort of tickling at the base of my spine. Afraid I was, afraid I have remained. So is it." He sighed. "If only I were Louis, or Frans, that's what I used to think," he said to himself. "And merely watching, and being discontented."

"I need to find an envelope," he heard Louis say. Rummaging through folders and piles of paper, the young man then seemed to find something that caught his eye, for he started reading it attentively.

"Yes," Frits thought. "And that business with the flowerpots. Dropping them on someone from the fourth floor and then, at the last moment, yelling: look out! So they could jump aside just in time. It's a miracle no one ever got hurt. I can't explain it." He listened to the silence, in which he heard his own watch ticking. "Or that time on the footpath," he said to himself. "The four of us picked a fight with six others, they were all just as strong as we were. But they ran away. We caught one of them, took him along, tied him to that pole and left him there, and it was already growing dark. Louis didn't care."

Suddenly he heard the rustling of paper. Louis had finished, turned his chair to him and said: "Well well, Mr Egters." "Allow me, if you would, to inquire as to the state of your well-being," Frits said. "As per usual," Louis replied, "as per usual." "By now, of course, it has been demonstrated beyond a shadow of a doubt," Frits said, "that you do not inhabit a sound body. One suspects a family with a great many haematological disorders. Describe, if you would, the symptoms anew." "How can I say things like this?" he thought, "why can't I make it stop?" "They are known to you by now," Louis said. "Does the headache give you no respite?" Frits asked. "No," Louis said, "I'm sorry to have to disappoint you on that score." "As soon as you work, or read, or write, it returns in force, isn't that correct?" Frits asked. "Even at this very moment?" "Certainly, even at this very moment," Louis said.

"So are we to conclude that you are headed for your demise, that it is all going steadily downhill?" Frits asked. "And that you are waiting patiently for your final repose?"

"Well, in the long run it does get a bit annoying, I must say," Louis answered, slowly wrinkling his brow. "When it goes on for years, never changing, then at a given point"—here his voice suddenly took on something airy—"you start thinking that the

27

end might not really be so terrible after all. In the long run, you see, one starts to have doubts."

Frits looked at Louis, at the eyes glistening colourless in his head. "It's like they've been steeping in hot water for ages," he thought. The room had grown hot again. For the second time that evening the cat sprang onto Louis's lap, and again he smacked it. "He acts like it's a casual slap," Frits thought, "but this time it was a calculated movement. The knuckles of the right hand precisely against the beast's head." The animal did not jump away immediately. Louis drew his arm back a bit further and this time administered a more powerful blow. The cat sprang away with a cry. "It sounded just like: 'mama'," Frits said. They laughed.

"Do you like cats?" Louis asked. "Do you?" Frits asked.

"I asked you first." "No," Frits said, "in fact, I consider them creatures without a soul." "For the love of me," Louis said, "I can't understand why anyone would keep such animals in their home."

The chastened beast was hunched up beneath the fold-down bed by the door. Its tail and a few whiskers were the only things sticking out from under the curtain. "Render kindness unto animals, and consider the birds of the air," Louis said with a grin. "A dog, though," he went on then, "I can almost imagine that." "One with big, faithful eyes," Frits said, twisting his face into a grin that produced a yawn.

"Have I ever told you that crazy story about the dog in Bloemendaal?" "No," Louis said, leaning forward. "A house in Bloemendaal," Frits said. "A big old house, a mansion. This old man lives there, alone. All alone. One day the neighbours say: we haven't seen him for ages. You know how that goes, one story leads to the next. They start poking around outside the house. Not a sound. Everything's locked, they can't get in."

"No, of course not," Louis said.

"So they call the police," Frits continued. "Two plainclothesmen come, punch in a window, open the door and go inside, very carefully. Not a sound. Completely silent, not a sound. They walk across the thick, soft carpet. Then they get to the foot of the stairs. There, on the first step, is the old man's head, staring at them. They're scared stiff. They draw their revolvers, examine the head, then start climbing." He paused for a moment. "Well, go on," Louis said.

"Some ways up the stairs," Frits went on, "they find an arm, and on the landing half of a foot. At two other locations they find more body parts. So they move on, step by step, and start searching the top floor. Finally, they hear this hideous shriek, as if people are slowly being torn to pieces. They find a little bedroom and go into it. On the floor, beside the bed, amid a bunch of torn bedclothes, they find the rest of what they needed to complete the picture. And in the corner is this big, black dog. How do you like that?"

"It's incredible," Louis said slowly, "really stupendous." "The man had fallen ill," Frits continued, "and I think his housekeeper had taken a week's holiday. So he must have fallen ill right away. That's what showed up in the investigation, the post-mortem. Once he was dead, the dog had nothing to eat, all the cupboards were closed. So what else could he do?"

"It's an exquisite story," Louis said. As he spoke he kept his pencil rotating across the table, first holding it upright, then letting it slide between two fingers and thumb, then tumble round. "It's a real corker, it almost reminds me of the story about the doctor and those two children." "How does that one go?" Frits asked.

"It's perfect," Louis said, "so completely realistic, nothing contrived about it. A father had this son, a little boy, and sometimes he picked him up by the head. So one time he does it again and—pop!—the neck breaks. Dead. They call the doctor, the doctor says: The child's dead, how did it happen? I don't know, the father says, we were horsing around. But something strange must have happened, the doctor says. No, not at all, says the father, all I did was pick him up—like this—and he picks up the little boy's sister, his twin sister, by the head, to show how it went. Pop! Her neck broken too. So at least they knew how it happened. Good one, isn't it?" They laughed.

"What does that studio look like, anyway?" Frits asked. "We must keep talking," he thought, "conversation mustn't lag." They got up and went into the hall. Passing the kitchen, they entered the last door on the right and came into a room with canvases leaning against the walls on all sides. Five piles of portfolios lay on the floor in the middle of the room. "What's that?" Frits wondered, walking over to view a little panel he'd seen on the mantelpiece. "That's quite something," he thought. The miniature showed an old woman sitting at a window, seen from the perspective of a sitting room. "Paralysis," he murmured. The woman's mouth sagged crookedly, her tongue and bottom lip stuck out slightly.

He examined the little triangular crack in one of the windowpanes. "How sharp, what craftsmanship," he thought. "It's amazing."

"Are you coming?" Louis asked. He was holding the door by the knob. "Quickly," he said, "otherwise one of them will sneak past you." Further down the hall he opened another door. In a somewhat smaller room, four cats were sitting up straight on a table, their tails curled around their front legs. A shadeless table lamp was on above the fireplace. "Turn off the light for a moment, just to rattle them," Frits requested. Louis flipped the switch. In the darkness, eight green eyes stared at them. Through the mica windows of the stove came a pale, red light. "There's a fire going in here," Frits said. "Of course," Louis said, "otherwise they'd get cold."

Once they were back in his room, Louis lowered the bed. "I'm going to grab some sleep," he said. He undressed and climbed into bed in his underwear. Frits picked up a green vase from the windowsill, held the opening to his ear, ticked his nails against the glazing and sat down. He looked at his watch. Nine fifteen. "The evening is half-finished," he thought.

After a few minutes of silence, Louis said: "It's about time you were going." "Excuse me," Frits said. "We'll be leaving now." "Turn off the light on your way out, would you?" Louis said, holding out his hand. "Mr Egters, the pleasure was all mine."

"Looking at this dispassionately," Frits mused once he was outside, "one could say: we still have half the evening left. Yet

31

that would be an unfounded representation of affairs. The evening has been wasted, nothing can alter that."

When he arrived home, his father was sitting at the table, reading. "Any news?" he asked in English. "No, nothing," Frits replied. The room reeked of pipe tobacco. His mother's clothes were hanging over the arm of a chair beside the stove. "Ah," he said to himself, "home again." His father was staring silently into space. His right hand lay on a little book. Slowly he turned his gaze on Frits. "Please, don't let him say anything," Frits thought. From the back room came the occasional stifled gasp. "It's both muted and unclear," he said to himself, "it's not loud enough for me to hear. I can't hear it." He pulled off his shoes and socks, placed them behind the stove and slipped out of the room. In the kitchen he brushed his teeth. He heard the sound of someone stumbling about in the living room; a moment later the light went out. He heard the reading light in the bedroom click on, then, thirty seconds later, click off again. "This is the earliest I've gone to bed in weeks," he thought. "The Lord is my shepherd," he said out loud, then burst out laughing and had to cough.

He examined his teeth in the shaving mirror, holding his breath to keep the glass from fogging. Then he went into his bedroom, saw that the window was open a crack and shut it, closed the curtains and undressed. He removed his underwear as well and, after taking the mirror down off the wall and placing it against a table leg, looked at himself naked. He changed the lighting by pulling the desk lamp all the way up and turning the shade to one side. After this examination he moved the mirror

32

in such a way that, by taking a few steps back, he could view his entire person.

Mirror in hand, he went into the hall. He shivered. Careful not to make a sound, he flipped on the light switch and examined the latch on the front door. "Locked," he mumbled, then lifted the heavy hall mirror from its nail and leaned it against the door. He stepped back and then forward again, each time arranging the mirror in a slightly different way. When his whole body came into view, he sucked in his stomach and held the little mirror in his left hand so that he could see himself fully, first from the side, then from the back. Hanging the big mirror back in place, he turned off the light and returned to his bedroom. "A loss," he mumbled softly, "a dead loss. How can it be? A day squandered in its entirety. Hallelujah." While uttering this final word, he studied the movement of his lips in the little mirror as he hung it back beside the door. He put on his underwear, climbed into bed and presently fell asleep.

He was walking down a road through a forest. "Stupid of me not to have put on my shoes before I left," he said to the two ladies on either side of him. His feet were bare, and the twigs and sharp stones on the narrow wooded way forced him to proceed with caution. "Such a glorious summer," one of the ladies said. "That's exactly the point," he replied. "In fact, there's no way to be completely certain that it's summer at all. Just look at that beech tree." He pointed to a thick beech which, though all the trees around it bore green foliage, was itself decked in autumnal hues of brown and yellow. "How can that be?" he thought, "what possible reason could there be for that?"

33

A little later they found themselves in a busy neighbour-hood, on their way up the stairs to a flat on an upper storey. At the top of the stairs they were met by a grey-haired lady dressed in black. As she was pouring them tea, he made the rounds, introducing himself to the others present. After having shaken hands with two old ladies, he arrived at a divan. Seated on it were three young men, all leaning back. Two of them wore black evening attire; the third had on a pair of grey overalls. Frits approached them and saw that the heads of the two dressed in black were white as milk, as though made of plaster or gypsum; their faces were immobile, their eyes stared expressionlessly at the ceiling. Their hands, too, were of the same mineral composition, and left crumbly trails on the divan's upholstery.

"There's no getting around it," he thought, and shook their hands, which they had slowly lifted to meet his. Each time the arm fell back like a block of wood. Their torsos never moved.

Then he was standing in front of the third. "He's the size of a child of eight or nine," he thought, "but why does his head look so horrible?" The head was almost as big as the torso, and perfectly flat on top. It was white as well, made of the same chalk-like substance. "That neck, terrible," Frits thought. The head began rocking back and forth on a neck thin as the hose of a vacuum cleaner. The eyes, thick and bulging, moved independently of each other in separate directions. When Frits held out his hand, the creature raised its right arm. It did not end in a hand, but in a black pincer. "Help," Frits thought, "where can I find help? What must I do?" He awoke in a sweat. "Did I hear something go bump?" he thought. "No, it's nothing," he said to himself. He arose and went to the kitchen for water. It was one thirty. He remained standing for a moment, listening to the silence, then crawled quickly under the covers. A few moments later he was asleep once more.

II

A T FOUR THIRTY in the afternoon of the next day, he cycled home from the office where he worked. The weather had taken a turn for the worse: banks of cloud crossed the sky at a steady pace; a few drops of rain were falling; a moderate, mild wind blew from the south. Head tilted slightly to one side, he cycled slowly through the heavy traffic.

"If the driver of one of these cars makes a mistake," he thought, "and I am killed, the news will produce sorrow at home, a great outcry. Imagine there are no parents, then it will be sad tidings for the family at large. But what if there is no family either, who will worry their head about it then? Who?" He felt a pang in his chest and tears came to his eyes. He glanced over his shoulder. "The tail light is working," he said to himself. Dusk settled in.

"When I get home later, my father is going to ask whether anything new and interesting happened today," he thought. By then he was on the broad street of shops close to his house. Along the pavements, strings of pedestrians hurried by.

"They are on their way home, just like me," he thought. "Up in the morning, back again in the evening. One morning they should all just stay at home. Have their family call in, say they have the flu." "No," he thought then, "not everyone can have the flu, that might seem suspicious. Four types of illness, divided up a bit cunningly, not that everyone calls in with the same excuse. They can stay at home, wear a dressing gown and read by the fire. Eat shrimp at lunchtime. Meat, potatoes and salad greens for dinner; rice pudding with berry syrup for dessert. It's been three days since Mother asked why I don't join an athletic club," he said to himself. "That is exceptional."

On the canal in front of his house, a group of children were busy testing the ice. A girl on the bank was holding the hand of a little boy, who stamped on the ice with both feet. At last she let go of him and he took several steps towards the middle. Frits, who had dismounted, walked over to them, holding the handlebars in one hand. The boy clambered quickly onto the bank. "You'd better not do that," Frits said, "it's thawing fast." "But that never happens so quickly," the girl said. "She answers me, because one must reply to even the stupidest of remarks," he thought. The boy hopped back onto the ice.

Frits opened the door, humped his bicycle up the stairs and rested it on its back wheel in the storage cupboard. At that moment the door to the side room opened and his father, wearing a black woollen dressing gown, entered the hallway. "Good afternoon," Frits said. "Well," his father asked, "anything new and interesting to report?" His face was creased in a smile. "No, nothing like that," Frits answered. "What was that?" the man asked, sticking his head out, the better to hear him. "Business as usual," Frits said. "What?" his father asked. "The same as always," Frits said, loudly now, almost shouting.

His father, silent, crossed the hall in front of him. Frits hurried into the side room and turned off the gas fire, then followed his father into the living room.

His mother was at the table, darning socks. He greeted her, sat down on the divan and turned on the radio. A tango was playing.

"Did you remember to turn off the fire?" she asked. "No, I don't believe I did," his father answered, rising slowly to his feet. Frits felt as though he had a handful of dry flour in his throat that was keeping him from swallowing. "I've already done it," he said, the first words coming out hoarsely. "No task too great, no job too small. We are at your service. House calls by appointment." He crinkled his face into an expression of good cheer. A silence descended.

"I don't know if it's the weather," he went on, "but today I feel extremely fit." "When are you going to join an athletic club?" his mother asked. "I've written to them and signed up already," he answered. His father stood and shuffled out of the room on his slippers.

"Today that man threw away one guilder and sixty cents' worth of postage stamps," his mother said. "How did that happen?" Frits asked. "God knows," she said. "I found five ten-cent ones in the rubbish bin. It's like he's started to lose his senses. I think he threw them in the wastepaper basket first." She got up and went to the kitchen.

Frits turned off the radio, which was now airing a lecture, and rolled a cigarette. Flicking his lighter, he realized it was empty; he went to replenish it in the kitchen. While he was busy

38

filling it, his mother said: "Have you noticed how he's wearing that new suit to rags? There's not a crease left in it; I believe he wipes his hands on his trouser legs."

"Tom ta tom tom, tom ta tom," Frits sang to himself, "nothing's good, but everything's fine." He screwed the top back on the lighter, blew on it to dry the wick of dripping fuel and went to the living room. His father, who had returned by then, unscrewed the stem of his pipe and cleaned the metal bore with scraps of newspaper, which he then crumpled and tossed into the coal scuttle. He viewed his handiwork, then wiped the stem on the sleeve of his suit. "Why, if he has to wipe things off on his clothing, doesn't he use his jumper?" Frits thought, "his jumper is dark anyway." He looked at the blue woollen sleeve sticking out from under his father's jacket.

When the table was set, his mother came in with a platter of cod. "There might still be a bone in it here and there," she said, "but I got most of them out." There were potatoes, grated raw celery root, boiled endives and pink custard. After dinner Frits washed his hands and face and ate a bit of toothpaste. "The proven remedy for dried cod," he mumbled. It was a quarter past six.

"What is the weather like?" his mother asked. "Normal," Frits said, "not so very cold." "When it's cold like this," she said, "I don't much feel like leaving the house; Father and I were planning to go out this evening, to Annetje in Haarlem." "That's true," Frits said, "you told me this morning." "What's it like outside now?" she asked, "is the wind very cold?" "It's blowing, but it's not a cold wind," Frits said. "But what do you

39

call cold?" she asked, "is it that humid cold?" "The air is moist," Frits said, "but the wind is actually quite sultry."

"Let's go anyway," his father said.

"Then I'll be sure to wrap a scarf around my head," she said, "and if it's too cold for me, if it makes my head hurt, we'll come back. We may be back by ten thirty, eleven o'clock." His father fetched the coats.

When they had left he remained standing before the bookcase and rummaged through a pile of newspapers. He listened to the ticking of the clock and the sounds in the flat above. Suddenly his eyes focused on the masthead of a newspaper and he read the date. "Of course," he murmured, "that is today."

After checking his watch against the clock on the wall, he went to change. "A blue shirt goes well with this suit," he said, tying his necktie before the mirror. "We must take care not to neglect our appearance." In the living room he laid a note on the table; written on it in red pencil were the words: "The gymnasium is celebrating its twentieth anniversary. I'm going, just for fun." "We shrink from nothing," he said out loud. "It would be childish not to go. One must face one's torments head-on. I'll drop by Joop's first."

When he stepped outside the same soft, tepid wind was blowing. He first followed the route he had taken the night before, turned left after five minutes and walked along a stretch of public garden to a canal, which was crossed by a little wooden drawbridge. Here he rang the bell of a lopsided house, the old double door of which bore a layer of peeling paint. A sash was thrown open on the second floor and Joop's head appeared. "A fine thing to behold," Frits called out, "you would do better to place that head on the sill, better than a geranium any day." "Catch!" Joop shouted. Frits caught a ring of keys, unlocked the upper door, turned the latch of the lower one, then made his way up a set of steep, twisting stairs. Joop led him into the living room.

The room was a commodious one, with three very large sash windows. The curtains were too narrow to cover them entirely. The ceiling rested upon heavy beams painted grey. There were posters on the walls, a miniature lime tree in a wooden tub in one corner and seats at each window. On the mantelpiece Frits noticed a bucket, directly beneath a dark spot on the ceiling.

A young woman with a rosy complexion and black hair came out of a back room. "Hello, Ina," Frits said, "I almost forgot that it was this evening." She walked over to a large mirror and began brushing lint from her dress. "Please, do have a seat, Mr van Egters," Joop said. He took a box of cigarettes from a drawer and presented them.

"Oh, but you are becoming quite bald," Frits said. Joop did not reply. "Listen, Joop," he started in again, "without meaning to be nasty, your scalp is really almost bare. It will not be long before you can count your hairs on the fingers of one hand." Joop smiled, keeping his lips pursed. "I'm not going bald all that quickly," he said. "But it seems as though you can barely wait." With index and middle finger he felt at the deep indentations along the hairline. "I'm afraid you are," Frits said. "Do you count the hairs in your comb each morning? If you did you would see that there are more of them each day. Slowly but surely. I would be horrified to know that I was going bald. I would lose all desire to live. But please don't misunderstand me, I don't mean to discourage you."

"Is he at it again?" Ina asked, arranging her petticoat.

"I believe," Frits said, "that your particular lack of interest in the malady is due to your not fearing it. Women, indeed, tend not to go bald. But still"—he turned to Joop, who had started leafing through a book—"are you listening? But still, I once knew an old woman who had perhaps twenty hairs on her head. They called her Old Scurfyscalp, because of the way her scalp flaked off in sheets. Like cheap primer."

"The only reason this comes up is because I never know what to say around here," he thought. "I will go on. There's no stopping it now."

"How are things with you otherwise?" Joop asked. Frits was silent. "Anything new to report?" "No," Frits said. "Except that someone at the office told me they had set a man's newspaper alight in the train." "What?" Ina asked. "Look," Frits said, "a man is sitting in a train compartment, reading his newspaper. Fully unfolded. The man across from him holds a match to the bottom of it. They told me so, and I could see it before me quite clearly. First a bit of smoke, then a huge flame. Try to imagine: suddenly, with a smack, the reader crumples his newspaper into a wad. Startled within an inch of his life." "Well, well," Joop said.

"But speaking of baldness," Frits went on, "it is a nasty business. One sees it quite often. It seems to be all the rage." Ina poured them tea. "Do we still have time for that?" Joop asked. They lapsed into silence. "There are countless antidotes for baldness," Frits went on, "but few are effective. There are, however, many known methods for disguising the vacuity." "My, my," Ina said, "aren't we in a talkative mood this evening?"

"What do you think?" Joop asked. "Why don't we just take a taxi? Listen, Frits, if you weren't such a bounder you would treat us to a taxi." "The hell I would," Frits said, "what a waste of money." "But it's true, isn't it?" Joop continued. "You earn so much money anyway, right?" "I wouldn't dream of it," Frits said.

"Go on, then, tell us something more about baldness," Joop said. "No, I've forgotten everything now," said Frits. "Listen, Ina," he asked then, "does it truly bother women so much when their husbands have a bald head?" "I wouldn't know," she replied, "you would have to ask those women."

Frits looked at his brother, who was holding his cigarette in such a way that the glowing tip pointed straight up. "You and I, we get along swimmingly," he said. Joop said nothing, only looked at his cigarette as a wan smile drifted across his face.

"Interesting, that," his brother said at last. "I'm starting to believe that it was all very terrible." "No, not that," Frits said. "Do you remember that jam jar?" "No," Joop answered.

"Don't you remember," Frits asked, "how I kept marine animals in a jar full of methylated spirits? That must have been, I think, fourteen years ago." "So now I get to find out a bit about you, from the sound of it," Ina said to Joop. "Well, go on," Joop said.

"We were still living in Cementwijk," Frits said. "That jar of mine with the sea creatures in it, you threw it from the second floor, it shattered on the street. We lived across from a green-grocer's then. The jar broke into little shards and it left a spot on the street." "Sea creatures in spirits?" Joop asked. "I don't remember that."

"I brought them home from Zandvoort," Frits went on. "With that German fellow. The one who stayed with us, the one who had peptic ulcers. He toasted his bread on one of those electric things." "Yes, yes, I remember that," said Joop.

"He had never," Frits continued, "seen the open sea. Mother suggested that he go to the beach, and I was allowed to go with him. It was in early autumn, a Wednesday, because I had no school that afternoon and it was not a Saturday. He looked at the sun, which was going down, and his mouth fell open a little, so that it glistened on his gold teeth. We'd had a few days of stormy weather just before that, so there were all kinds of things on the beach. He just stood there staring, so I went looking for starfish and crabs and put them in my beret. He examined them, as I recall, with a great deal of interest."

"How is it that you are able to remember things like that?" Ina asked. "It is a gift," Frits replied. "I kept all that junk in my hat. On our way home we went into one of those fancy shops close to the tram stop. Chocolate bars cost four cents back then, in all different flavours, but you also had those huge bars, too big to even stick in your pocket. Those cost fifty cents. I was terrified that he was going to buy a fifty-cent one, but I didn't dare tell him that."

"And which one did he buy?" Joop asked. "The big ones," Frits said. "Two of them, fifty cents apiece. He handed me one and removed the wrapper, pulled back the silver paper. I bit off a piece of it, but I didn't like it. Strange, isn't it?"

44

"But you were talking about that jar," said Joop. "Well," Frits said, "at home I put them in a jam jar, covered in methylated spirits, because Father said that was every bit as good as alcohol. A few days later the spirits had already turned red. I thought it was from the animals' blood. I held it up to the light each day."

Ina poured them more tea. "And why did I toss that jar out onto the street?" Joop asked. "That is the question," answered Frits. "We're off to a good start, I must admit," he thought.

"I'm afraid you're putting a twist on things here, though," said Joop. "I remember something about a jam jar. Thrown against the wall. But you were the one who did that."

"At your service," Frits replied, "that was me, indeed. But that was a different jam jar. It was around the same time. I was keeping freshwater mussels in a jar, on a bed of cotton wool and dried burdock. On a water lily stem. That jar I threw at the head of Eli Hogeweg. When you had visitors in the evening, you would torment me in my bed. Because I was already in bed by eight thirty. You would make the bed rock back and forth. You and Eli did that and I took the jar of mussels and threw it past Eli's head, against the wall. It was thrown past his head on purpose, it was meant to go past, but still, he was startled beyond measure. He thought I had been aiming for him. But that was absolutely not the case."

"A child's petty tribulations," Joop said. "Isn't it time yet?" "No," said Ina, "not yet." "It depends on what one calls petty," Frits went on. "Do you recall shooting my books to pieces? You and Jozef Pijp? With the air gun? All the bindings shot to tatters. That wasn't even so long ago." "Yes," Joop said with a smile. "Let's get going."

"The weather is no problem," Frits said once they were outside. Ina walked between them and offered them each an arm. "How about if you run on out ahead," Joop said as they passed the public garden, "and see if there is a taxi."

"Indeed," Frits thought. "It was only a matter of time. What must be, must be." He hurried ahead at a trot and hailed a taxi, which had just pulled up to the stand. "Now he's shifting to second," he said as they drove away, "eases up, accelerates, eases off the gas, uses the clutch, shifts to third; Ina, you do know that I'm going to start driving lessons in two weeks, don't you?" "You don't say," she said.

Traffic was light and the car hummed calmly over the asphalt. Within a quarter of an hour they found themselves before the entrance of a tall building with two large wings. "There is no going back," Frits thought. "Let us adopt an impassive or, if need be, even cheerful expression."

After he had paid the driver, they crossed a darkened court-yard to the entrance. Along the way Frits paused for a moment and, his gaze travelling upwards, examined a low, squarish tower where the southernmost wing merged with the body of the building proper. "We're a bit on the early side," Ina said. Passing through a little corridor, they entered a large hall. "We're there," Frits said to himself. He took a deep breath. There were two tables where tickets were being sold. He allowed the crush to lead him to the table where Joop and Ina were not standing, and bought one for himself. At the foot of the stairs, where

46

the ticket-takers stood, they met up again and climbed past a banner reading "Berends Gymnasium, 1926–1946" and then, in a hall even smaller than the one below, found themselves before the entrance to an auditorium. "Here it comes now," Frits thought. They hung their coats in the foyer. Frits lingered, paid a visit to a water closet and saw, when he came out, Ina and Joop disappearing into the crowd. "One down," he said, peering cautiously around him.

Suddenly he heard someone cry "Frits!" and, when he looked towards the sound, the same crow-like voice called out again: "Van Egters!" A short, thickset young man with dark, pomaded hair parted slightly off-centre came up to him. "By Jove," he said, "so you've shown up too!" He slapped Frits on the shoulder and shook his hand, almost forcing him to reach down. "Were he any shorter, I should have to bow," Frits thought. "Of course," he said, "and I see that you have not left this earthly vale either; it has been a very long time." They lapsed into silence. The boy squinted his little eyes and rubbed his hands together. He was wearing a black formal suit, a bow tie and shoes with a sharply tapered toe. "He's going to ask questions," Frits thought. "Let me bring myself into readiness." He kept a close eye on the other.

The moment the boy's mouth began to move again, Frits said right away: "Henk, how have you been lately?" He said it with such haste and urgency that drops of saliva flew from his lips. "You speak in all humidity," the young man said with a grin, wiping his face with the back of his hand. "I was just about to ask you the same thing. It's not something you can

47

tell in short so quickly. You would say: strange, inadmissible practices. You would have found some weird word for it, van Egters; god-oh-god, I'll never forget how we laughed about that seal. It's an elderly seal."

"You're not up to much, I take it?" Frits asked hurriedly, when the other paused for a moment. "Student emeritus, I suppose. Dropping in on a class now and then for the sake of form, and otherwise waiting till every day's a Sunday and the fair has come to town?" "A feeble attempt," he thought, "awfully feeble." "Am I not right?" he asked.

The other burst out laughing. "All right, Egters," he said, "but I *am* registered. Officially, I'm studying medicine. Christ, what a tough subject that is."

"That is one of the few faculties for which I feel respect," said Frits. "As if there were anything for which you actually feel respect," the boy said, tapping him forcefully on the chest with his fist. "I'm not in any hurry," he said. "You are not overextending yourself," Frits said, "I was not worried about that."

Swept up in the crowd, they approached the entrance to the auditorium. "I also do a bit of business on the side," the young man said. "Last week I went to Brussels. God-oh-god, did I ever have a good time. It would have been right down your alley too." "Does it pay reasonably well?" Frits asked. "At times," the other replied, "but the market fluctuates. The life of a businessman is no bed of roses, Mr Egters." As he spoke these words he raised his hand, waggled it, and winked. "And what are you up to these days?" he asked. "Do you have any

48

idea why these people are being so pushy?" Frits asked. "Maybe I'll get away with it," he thought.

"Hey, Frits," the other insisted, "what are you doing at the moment?"

"I'm keeping my eyes open for something good," Frits replied. "At the moment I'm working in an office." He held his ground against the throng, shifted to the left and saw how the young man drifted further and further away from him. "See you later," the other shouted. "So far everything is, indeed, going the way I'd expected," Frits mumbled. "We shall see."

He was pushed into the auditorium. It was a long, high room with bare walls, the ceiling of which rose to a point like a dome. Each of the big chandeliers bore three glass globes. The walls above the podium were decorated with stylized murals with Greek lettering. Everywhere was the din of yellow wooden chairs scraping across the parquet floor.

The auditorium was not yet full. The crush at the entrance ebbed rapidly. He remained standing at the back of the room, looked around for a moment and then walked slowly down the centre aisle. He saw a man with thin white hair approaching and slid, as though with purpose, into an empty row. "It's Vogel," he thought. "Why am I hiding?" When the man had passed, he walked back slowly towards the exit.

"Egters, why are you wandering around here like a little lost lamb?" a voice beside him asked. A slim young man reached out once he had turned around, and shook his hand. Frits smiled and looked closely at the handsome, bronzed face with its deep-set, dark blue eyes. "Look for the brand when you buy toothpaste,"

49

he thought. "Wandering?" he replied, "I'm not wandering. It's bound to be a nasty business this evening, don't you think, Wim?" The young man looked at him for a few moments before replying casually: "Why's that? It could be quite nice." "It has been so long since we've seen each other," he went on. "How are things with you?" "I'm doing well enough," Frits said. They fell silent. Frits stared at the floor in front of him. "I'll see you later," the boy said, and walked on.

"I should have known what I was getting into," Frits thought. The door was closed and everyone took a seat. He quickly found a place in one of the back rows, which was empty.

The crowd grew quiet and a piano started in on a few robust bars. "The alma mater," he thought, "here it comes." All stood and began to sing. "'Sumus','" he thought, "I still know that much. But how does the rest go? I can't understand a word they're saying. Sloppy articulation."

A boy with thick spectacles stepped up to the lectern. Around his neck, on a black and red ribbon, he wore a medallion. "I wish all of you a warm welcome," he said in a feeble voice. "Now I would like to hand over the floor to our principal, who will open this commemorative evening." A man with a fat, fleshy face approached the lectern. "The mouth is droopier than ever," Frits thought. "He could survive quite well without a comb." He listened and looked at the big, bald head that swayed to the left and then to the right at the end of every sentence. The words were loud and easily understood, but they did not get through to him. He looked at the windows, the ceiling, the doors and the seat of his chair, then stuck his thumb in his mouth.

When the principal was finished, a man with thick, grey hair took the floor. He wore a pair of dark, heavy spectacles and spoke in a muffled, nasal voice. "Shh, shh," the audience demanded. By the time the second speaker was done, fifteen minutes had passed. The evening's programme started with an old Dutch play featuring bright costumes.

After that the boy with the medallion moved up to the lectern again and said: "The following is a Greek one-act play. It was found written on a roll of papyrus during an Egyptian excavation. I would like to draw your attention to the following passages." He began reading aloud from a sheet of paper. "I'll be damned if I understand a bit of it," Frits thought. "I forgot to buy a programme, at least that's a penny saved." The performance began. Frits leaned forward and looked at the floor. "There is not a single word of it that means a thing to me," he thought. "Still, I applaud." When it was over he clapped his hands long and loudly, like the others. It was intermission. Everyone hurried to the hall, where lemonade was sold. Frits was one of the first ones there. Taking his bottle, he withdrew from the crowd and leaned against the banister. The hall filled quickly, and little groups of people chatting formed everywhere.

He strolled through the upstairs corridors, gazing at the classroom doors and sucking lemonade through his straw, then walked back. In the hall, Joop and Ina were talking to a fat man in a brown, neatly pressed suit. Frits bit the insides of his cheeks, came closer, held out his hand and said: "Good evening, Mr Wening." The one so addressed looked surprised, then quickly seized the hand held out to him and adopted a pensive expression.

"Frits van Egters, younger brother of Joop van Egters," Frits said. "The failure." "Oh," the man replied, his fat, red face holding on to a smile. "Well," he said to Ina and Joop, "it's like I was saying: whether they left two years ago or ten years ago, there is no difference; funny, that. Once you know someone, that never changes. Ina remains Ina, but I have no idea exactly when it was. When did you two graduate, when was that?" "In thirty-eight," Joop said. "Both of you?" the man asked.

"We were in the same class," Joop replied. "An idyll, pure and true," the man said. Rocking his corpulent frame forward, he raised his eyebrows, producing a crease in his shiny forehead and a quiver in his smooth, pasty blond hair. "Well, well," he said with half-bated breath. He moved his right hand without raising it all the way.

"We heard that you were leaving—leaving the school," Ina said. "Oh really?" the man asked, "who told you that?" "We just heard," said Ina. "I must admit, my child, that it is news to me," he said in an amused tone. "No," he went on slowly, "those are the little disappointments of life: I'm sure I will never leave here again."

Frits was still standing beside him. He listened to the voice, saw the eyes in their startled motion and observed the awkward movements of the arms. He began shuffling cautiously backwards, turned slowly on his heel and sloped off. He almost collided with an already partly bald young man wearing a pince-nez. The man was tall and lanky of frame and sported a pair of thin little moustaches. "How are you?" Frits asked, "Kasper Sterringa, what a pleasure." He waited, examining the man's immaculate evening attire. "My, my," the other said. Frits held out his hand. When the other man held out his, he shook it immediately. "We're standing a bit in the way here," Frits said. "Is that all I can come up with?" he thought; "wait, I can always tell him about that photograph." "Weren't you at that soirée at the Hermes Pavilion, back in May?" the pince-nez asked. "I thought I saw you there, but you didn't see me." "No, that can't be," answered Frits, "I wasn't there." "I know something I can ask him," he thought. "Have you ever heard anything from Sal Jachthandelaar?" he asked.

"No," the pince-nez said. "He's dead, of course," Frits said. "No, no, what I meant was yes, I have," the other corrected himself, "he made it to Switzerland and from there to England. His family is dead. He became a pilot over there." "Well I never," Frits said. "He was at the airfield in Valkenburg recently," the other continued, "but I haven't seen him since, not for a few months."

"I am extremely pleased to hear that," Frits said. "Really, that gives me great pleasure." "Another question," he thought.

"What are you doing at the moment?" asked the pince-nez. "I heard that you're studying to become a notary," Frits said. "Yes, I'm in my third year already," the other said. "I still have to get my master's, otherwise the work's only half-done. What about you?" Frits took a deep breath, opened his mouth, closed it, opened it again and said then in a flat voice: "I work in an office. I take cards out of a file. Once I have taken them out,

I put them back in again. That is it." He closed his mouth, squinted a bit through his left eye and looked at the floor.

"You're still the same madman you always were," the other said with a smile. "I can never figure you out. Do you still tell those crazy stories? You always had something silly going on." "Only that story about the photograph," Frits said blandly. He counted the tiles in the floor. "What's that?" the other asked. "Well," Frits said, "at this school they were going to take a photograph of the whole class, but the little poor boy wasn't allowed to be in it, he looked too ragged. The teacher told him: listen, Pete, when that picture has been taken, later they will say: that's Wim, he's a bank manager these days; his father was a manager before him. And that is Klaas, he's a notary. His father was a notary too. And that is Eduard, he's a doctor now. And that one there is Joop, he is a clergyman. So, Pete, when the photographer comes in I want you to go stand over there. Do you understand? All right, so the little poor boy does that and the picture is taken. A few days later the photographer sends them the picture. Who wants to order one? the teacher asks. Most of the children do. Pete too." "It really is very old and corny," he thought. "The teacher is surprised," he went on. "She asks him: Pete, what do you want a picture for? You're not even in it. I know, teacher, he says. So why would you want to have one? she asks. I'll keep it, he says. Then later, when I'm grown up, I can say: this is Wim, he became a manager. And that's Klaas, he's a notary. And that is Eduard, he's a doctor. And that's our teacher, she started coughing up blood and died at an early age."

54

The pince-nez laughed loudly. When his mouth opened, Frits saw that threads of saliva had formed between his jaws. A lady gestured to him and he left, after quickly shaking hands with Frits, who turned and walked down the stairs to the less crowded hall below. "Jesus, that's Tafelmaker over there," he thought, "that's all we need. Now we've had it." A young man came walking over to him. He wore a dark-blue worsted suit. "A bit baggy," thought Frits. The boy's forehead was acned; the nose was thin and white, while the cheeks exhibited an unnatural blush, like a Californian apple. The brown hair was flattened and heavily pomaded in long, wavy rows. "Spaghetti head," Frits thought. "Hey, old Frits!" said the boy, thumping him hard on the shoulder. "Well, well, old seal," he said. "Here we go," Frits thought. "Can you still give yourself a hump?" he asked. The other turned, bent over a little and, after moving his shoulder blades back and forth, succeeded in moving one of them into a position that caused a high, pointed hump to appear beneath his clothing. "Ha, Ba, Bariba," he sang, tapping one foot loudly. "Ha, Ba, Bariba." "That's very good," said Frits. The other suddenly hurried off. "An evening well spent," Frits thought. "A profitable way to pass the hours."

He saw Joop and Ina coming down the stairs with their coats on, and stopped them. "Are you two leaving already?" he asked. "It's only nine thirty." "Yes," Joop answered with a smile, "otherwise we won't get to bed on time." "Before you know it, you'll be going to bed at eight," Frits said. "It only gets worse when you give in to it." "I need my ten hours of sleep,"

Joop said, "here's the programme." They walked on and left the building.

Intermission was over. He took the same seat and looked around as the auditorium filled. The programme resumed with a short concert in three parts. When that was over, it was ten minutes to ten. The next number was Schubert's Impromptu. The fragile, plangent music got off to a slow start.

"I am twenty-three now," he thought. "Twenty-three years old. My first year, that was in thirty-seven, or was it thirty-six?" He gave his left earlobe a gentle pinch. "The second year," he whispered. The pianist reached a slow passage, during which he fingered the keys carefully, with long pauses.

"Right, then," Frits said to himself, "on to the third." He leaned over and put his face in his hands. "The fourth year, the fourth," he thought, "what was that like? How was it? Can everything be understood? Why didn't they send a letter right away?" He closed his eyes, which he had kept half-shut the whole time, all the way. The music arrived at a loud and rapid passage. "Still, I must be able to remember and know precisely why it went the way it did," he said to himself. "Everything can be understood, when a body puts his mind to it."

The music ended. He stood up and walked out of the auditorium while the applause continued, threw on his coat, ran down the stairs and was outside. Standing still, he heard violins being tuned. He spat on the ground and strode home.

He could see no lights in the windows. He looked at the house front. "No one knows what a human abode encompasses," he said quietly. He climbed the stairs slowly and entered the hallway. All was dark. "They are at home," he thought as he turned on a light and saw his parents' coats on the coat stand. He brushed his teeth, went into his room and sat on the bed. Then he slid aside the curtain that hung before the lowest shelf of his bookcase and looked at a long row of books and blue, green, orange and grey notebooks. He remained staring at them for a long time.

"I should get rid of this rubbish," he said softly. "Out the door, gone completely. Not a trace left." "Who would be mad enough, who is insane enough, to actually go to something like that?" he thought. "I am," he said aloud. "I, Frits Egters." He shivered. "How many hours of sleep does a person need?" he thought. "Eight hours at most. Six, in the long run, is insufficient, but enough in exceptional circumstances."

He pulled from the row a thin, flimsy book with a brown cover, opened it and read: "In compiling this syntax, I have adopted a mode of categorization less than common. I did so with an eye to the second book of translation exercises by Graning-Kok. In translation it is desirable that the student grow acquainted as quickly as possible with the accusativus cum infinitivo, the gerundium, the gerundivum and the ablativus absolutus. That is why, in seeking connection with the aforementioned book of translation exercises, these constructions have been dealt with first. For the rest, I should note that I have attempted to be concise. Finally, in this foreword I must not neglect to mention the support received from—"

Frits began tugging on the halves of the book, trying to tear it in two, but stopped. "Why is it that I don't go on pulling?" he

57

thought, bit down softly on the binding and placed the book back on the shelf.

He twisted the desk lamp in such a fashion that the light spread across the ceiling, and viewed his hair in the mirror beside the door. Using his fingers, he parted it and regarded the pale scalp. Then he took a swig of cod liver oil from a bottle on his desk, undressed and promptly fell asleep.

He thought he heard music, but as soon as the notes became almost distinct, the wind would rise up and blow away every sound. A little later he was walking beside the river.

In his hand he held a bouquet of flowers, wrapped in paper. Across the water, a large, white swan came swimming towards him. The animal climbed with difficulty, yet quickly enough for all that, up the steep embankment and waddled in his direction. It was a normal swan, of the kind one sees in parks. The feet, however, were stuck in a pair of ladies' shoes, but this did not worry him.

He tried to say something, but his voice was gone. Still, he felt no apprehension. The animal had now come quite near him, it stretched out its neck, picked and tore the paper from the bouquet and began snapping at the flowers. They were sturdy, white chrysanthemums. Each snap caused new damage. The white petals blew away into the river. Where they touched the water's surface they formed a snowstorm.

Sometimes the bird bit an entire flower off its stalk and spat it out. Soon the bouquet was bare. Frits tossed it on the ground.

Then the bird's head came closer and closer. First the head grew bigger, then only the eye. In a twinkling it was already as big as his own head. He looked into it and grew very calm. He knew that, should he offer no resistance, this would be his demise, but he had no desire to struggle against it. The animal would kill him, but the sight of the eye, now so large that he saw himself reflected in it, gave him a feeling of satisfaction: it made no difference to him.

He awoke, rolled over and tried to recall the dream, but could not. He remembered only that there had been a swan in it, fell asleep once again and dreamt no more that night.

III

TUESDAY AT NOON, during the three quarters of an hour between morning and afternoon shifts, he left the office building, hurried down a few alleyways and, arriving at a large square, found the entrance to the warehouse known as "The Hornet's Nest". He had the lift take him to the second floor, sauntered through the book section, descended one floor and then climbed back up again. In the objets d'art department, he picked up a metal beaker. "This is not silver," he thought, "but some cheap, stainless metal. Perhaps even copper with a coating of chrome." He turned it over, the price was on the bottom: eighteen guilders and seventy-five cents. He viewed the handle. "This is clumsily tin-plated iron, simply soldered on," he thought. When a salesgirl approached he returned the beaker to its spot and walked on.

Atop a table lined with green velvet he saw a smaller beaker without a handle. "It's almost a vase," he thought, "for the brim sticks out too far. One wonders whether it is a drinking cup at all." Picking it up in one hand he saw on the bottom that the price was nine and a half guilders. The metal was covered with spots. "Twenty minutes of my time gone already," he thought, and left the shop quickly. The sun was peeking from behind the clouds; it was not cold.

He crossed the square at an angle and made his way down a narrow street. Passing through a set of revolving doors he entered the large shop, located in its entirety on the ground floor, that was known as "The House of Gifts". He worked his way hurriedly past the displays, from the household items to toys and from there to the fur department, and saw at last a host of glistening objects on a table bedecked with gracefully crinkled green felt. Here lay metal tea strainers, letter openers, teaspoons and beakers too. "They're the same ones," he murmured, picking one up. "The same handle too," he thought. The price was eight-and-a-half guilders. Beside it was a taller, narrower beaker that cost eleven guilders. He had been inside for six minutes and slipped quickly out of the door. Cutting through two alleyways he arrived at a broad street and suddenly, in the window of a bicycle shop, he saw a pile of aluminium saucers and a stack of beakers of the same metal. The price of the former was one guilder and twenty cents, while the beakers cost one guilder and ten cents apiece. In the shop he asked to see one of each, and noted that the material was sturdy, well polished and of purest aluminium. He bought them and stuck them in his briefcase.

He had ten minutes left. He ambled his way along a canal, entered a grubby street, turned into a sandwich shop and said to the assistant, who was standing before the display: "I'll have three chocolate bars." "The sixty-cent ones or the forty-cent ones?" the man asked. "Two sixties and one forty," said Frits. The man looked around cautiously, opened a tin, took out what he had asked for and dropped them into Frits's case.

At the very end of the break he walked into the office and sat down at his desk. "Pim, look at the bargains I've found," he said to a woman of about thirty, seated at a desk by the window, "good material, too." He showed her the beaker and saucer and mentioned the price. "It's for the little son of a friend of mine," he said. "I didn't know you were so practical," she replied. "He's celebrating his first birthday," said Frits, "what better present could you give? And I'll put two chocolate bars upright in the beaker. I'll wrap it nicely in pretty, thin paper with a coloured ribbon round it. And I brought this for you." He placed the forty-cent chocolate bar on her desk. "That's awfully kind of you," she said. "It's very expensive chocolate," Frits said. "They had the cheaper kind as well, but I thought: it's for Pim, so the best is only barely good enough." "That's terribly kind of you," she said.

When he arrived home that afternoon, he found the house deserted. After eating a few biscuits from a tin he found in the sideboard, he took a spoonful of jam, a lump of butter from the pot with the same spoon, and shook some chocolate sprinkles onto his hand. Having eaten this, he turned on the radio. "The four- and five-year-old, in other words," a woman's voice said. He turned off the set, went into the kitchen, put the pan of meat on the gas and waited until the layer of fat had melted. Then he took a few slices of brown bread and ate them, after first dipping them into the steaming gravy, one by one. He replaced the lid and slid the pan back to where it had been, at the back of the range.

Shortly afterwards, at five thirty, his mother came home and put their dinner on the stove. "God only knows where that man has got to," she said to Frits. "He went into town at nine thirty this morning without saying a word." "He will show up," said Frits, "let's not bother about him and just eat at the usual time."

At six o'clock his mother put dinner on the table. His father arrived in the nick of time. They ate pea soup, meat, potatoes and kohlrabi. Just as they had all filled their plates, the lights went out. "Where are the matches?" his mother asked. "I have matches," said his father, and lit one. He remained seated, staring at the flame, and when it was burned out he placed the matchstick on the edge of his plate. It was dark again. "If you keep sitting there like that, the light will come on quickly enough," Frits's mother said. "The pixies will see to that." "What do I have to do?" his father asked, rising from his chair. "Give me a token." "Not a gas token, it's not a gas lamp," she said. "You need an electricity token, a guilder." Turning her chair around she took, by the light of his father's second match, a large, shiny token from a box atop the sideboard and handed it to him. When the second match went out, his father, picking his way in utter darkness, stumbled into the hallway. They heard him entering the side room, but no further sound reached them. Frits kept his eyes closed and clasped his hands between his legs.

His father returned. "I found the meter," he said, "but where does the token go?" "The top right—you have to lift the little iron latch and after you've put it in, you turn the knob on the right," said Frits. His father left once more, colliding with the living room door, which he had left ajar. At last they heard the click of the mechanism and the fall of the token. The light came on. "And that is what they call an intellectual," his mother said.

Once they had eaten their pudding, Frits said: "Today I bought something at a most reasonable price for Jaap's little Hans, whose birthday it is today; he is one year old." He stood up and produced the saucer and beaker from his bag.

"Where did you get the chocolate bars?" his mother asked. "I bought them," he replied. "They're awfully nice," she said, picking up both objects. "And not at all expensive," Frits said, mentioning the price. "I'll have to scour the spots and the dirt off them first," he said. "You mustn't scour them," said his mother, "you'll only ruin them that way, not make them any nicer. Give them to me later, I'll put them in the dishwater, you'll see how pretty they become."

"Nice, is it not?" he said to his father. "A beaker and a plate for Jaap's little Hans, today is his first birthday."

"That's an awfully little plate," his father answered, "who is it for?" "For Hans, Jaap's little one!" his mother shouted. "You must speak a little louder," she told Frits, "that man is deaf as a doorpost." "Is he turning one already?" his father said. "Goodness."

"I'll wrap it first," Frits said, going to the kitchen cupboard to fetch some gift wrap. He returned with a large piece of yellow paper. "But I think I need to scour it a bit before I do that," he said. "Just listen to me," his mother replied, "give it here, I'll put it in the dishwater."

Frits took the plate and beaker to the kitchen, sprinkled scouring powder on them, held them under the dripping tap and scrubbed both with a wet rag. After he had rinsed both objects, he saw that they had become dull of tint and were covered in scratches. "Bloody hell," he said, drying them off and taking them back into the room.

"You see!" said his mother. "Now you've gone and ruined them. That's because you're such a pain, you never listen to anyone." "Come, come," Frits said, "they still have an attractive sheen to them."

He packed the presents, placing the beaker on the plate, a bar of chocolate on both sides and an apple stuffed into the beaker's mouth. "I wanted to give you something for him too," his mother said. "Wait, I'm going to put a few lumps of sugar in a sachet." She gave him a handful of white cubes in a little orange bonbon sack, which he stuck into his coat pocket.

The dry street glittered. "It's as though the paving stones are filled with tiny pieces of glass," he thought. Following the route he had taken on Sunday evening, he passed the storehouses at the start of the canal. At number seventy-one, the door opened the first time he rang. At the top of the stairs he discerned a female form. "Joosje, congratulations!" he shouted up to her. "Thank you, Frits," she called back once he was halfway up the stairs. In front of the coat stand, he shook her hand. A faint light was burning at the other end of the hall. When he looked up at the ceiling, she said: "The one above the stairs here is broken, but this way there's enough light."

He followed her in. They walked down a bare, uncarpeted hallway and entered a broad room with four chairs arranged around a cylindrical heating stove, all illuminated by a tall floor lamp. An old lady was sitting there, knitting. "Isn't Jaap in?" he asked, after greeting the woman. "He has a meeting, and after that they were going out to dinner, I believe," Joosje replied.

He sat down, placed the present on the table and handed her a pair of scissors, which he had seen lying on the mantelpiece.

"Oh," she said, after opening the package, "that is awfully nice, terribly kind of you. And the chocolate too." "And an apple," Frits said. "That is lovely for the little fellow, isn't it?" the old lady said. "Aren't you cold?" she asked Frits. "Come, sit a little closer to the fire." "I'm fine, thank you, only my feet are cold," he said.

"Let me show you what else he got today," Joosje said. Standing, she fetched a few objects from a table in the corner. Her light-blond hair was trimmed high at the back, to a point above her plump, rosy face. The hem of the dress she wore hung a good deal higher on the front, because of her round, protruding belly. She showed him the presents: a wooden locomotive, a lorry, undergarments, an embroidered bib and a picture book. "The book he got from Auntie Stien," she said. "It won't mean much to him yet," the old lady said. Frits leafed through it, looking at the illustrations: a cow, a horse, a pig, peacocks, a dog and a turkey. He put the book back down.

"A turkey like that won't mean much to him, I'm sure," he said, "a ridiculous bird with a mass of red flesh on its head. Has the birthday boy gone to bed?" "He's asleep already," Joosje said. "And do you think Jaap will be long?" he asked. "I have no idea," she replied.

"Probably drinking himself into a hole again," Frits said, smiling. "Jaap doesn't drink; he doesn't, does he?" asked the old woman. "As long as it costs him nothing, he's willing enough," said Joosje. "Oh no, Jaap doesn't drink," the lady said.

"It has been a very long time since I last had a drink," Frits said. "How long?" Joosje asked, opening the damper at the bottom of the stove. "At least a month," he said.

"It is a bad thing, a great deal of misery comes from it," the old woman said. She held a newspaper open in her lap. "It's very unhealthy; it destroys the body."

"In fact," Frits said, "that is not true. One must not drink regularly, but getting good and drunk once every few months is actually good for you, doctors say these days. Modern science has it that the body needs to be thrown out of equilibrium from time to time, it needs a good poisoning." "Oh yes, modern science," the lady said. "When I have been drinking," he said, "I feel tipsy, of course. The next day I have a hangover, there's nothing to be done about that. But the day after that, on the third day, then I feel good! Then it is as though I have been reborn."

He fell silent and glanced at his watch. It was a quarter to eight. He rubbed his hands together and shuffled his feet. "Still, I believe you're feeling a bit cold," the lady said. "Is it cold in here?" asked Joosje. "No, I don't think so," he said, "it is only my feet. My shoes have rubber soles." "Are rubber soles that cold then?" the old woman asked. "They are when you have sweaty feet," Frits said, "then you have to place your shoes behind the stove each night and hang your socks over the pipe. In fact, you need to wash your feet every night too, but that is so much work. In the summer, it's even worse. Then you absolutely have to wash them, otherwise the smell is unbearable. For months, I sprinkled steatite powder on my feet in the morning; it helps a bit, yes, it does help." "Hush," Joosje said, "I hear little Hans. No, it's nothing, I think."

"That is a problem," said the old lady, "I'm pleased I don't have that." "In the summer, the most comfortable thing is to wear sandals with no socks," Frits continued, "then all your problems are over." "Are your feet very cold at the moment?" she asked. "Oh, nothing serious," he replied. "It is never that bad, not so that you cannot warm them again, I've never had that. It's a matter of nutrition as well, of course."

"Do you really think so?" the old lady asked. Joosje poured them coffee. "Oh yes," said Frits, "if one takes cod liver oil every day—I've started doing that of late—one never need fear having cold feet." "Auntie Stien, you take a lot of milk in your coffee, don't you?" Joosje asked. "Yes, please, my dear," she replied. "It is most definitely true," she said, "that we consume various kinds of poisons each day. Things like coffee and tea, for example, which are very normal beverages. You shouldn't take them at all, in fact, but still you do."

"Yes," Frits said, "we would be better off if we lived according to a natural diet. But it is also quite a chore to gather that kind of food and prepare it. It makes more sense to eat the way everyone else does. But that a vegetarian diet is healthier, I am firmly convinced of that." He looked at his watch, which showed a quarter past eight. "Jesus, how am I going to get out of here?" he thought, breathing deeply without making a sound. "It is a fact that eating too much, eating late at night and eating a great deal of meat is harmful," he said. "Oh, is that really so?" Joosje asked.

"Just look at America," said Auntie Stien, "nowhere is there as much cancer as there is there." "That," Frits said, "is because they eat food that is poorly prepared, drink a great deal of alcohol, consume extensive dinners and hot sausages in their cafeterias and make excessive use of seasonings."

"Cancer is really quite common, isn't it?" Joosje asked. "It is a typical disease of the elderly," he replied. "It used to be that not so many people died of it, but now that we live so much longer on the average, more people get it. Cancer is the cause of most deaths." "I didn't know that," said Joosje.

"It is a quite marvellous disease," he continued, "I have read fascinating things about it. It is a parasitic cell, it appears out of nowhere and never stops growing. Right through everything. From one organ to the next. Straight through the intestines. Gruesome, incurable, grand."

"How can you talk like that?" said Auntie Stien, shaking her head. "And the pains of cancer are something fierce," Frits said, "simply indescribable. It is one of the most stupendous of diseases."

"That's what that Mr Overland had," said Joosje. "In his stomach. But it progressed rather quickly. He had it, and his family knew what it was. Within four months he was dead. It must have been terrible for him. Those were people who camped close to us, in Castricum. His wife drowned in the sea." "The hand of fate," Frits said.

"I'm not so sure," Joosje said, picking up her knitting. "She went swimming alone, at night. Later they found her clothes on the beach. She had four little children; the eldest was seven. They told them that their mother was not coming home any more and that she had stayed in the sea. People who were visiting, I believe it was the Velzeners, heard what the eldest said to his little brother. He says: The sea said, you just come with me, you're a worthless old thing anyway. So if the sea ever dries up, maybe she'll come back then, but otherwise she never will."

"Quiet," she said suddenly, "I hear the baby." She disappeared through the sliding doors and came back with a crying child on her arm. His face was pale and sleepy. She sat down and tried to calm him. At last she succeeded.

"Oh, poor little fellow," the old woman said. The little boy looked at her inquisitively. "Couldn't you get to sleep?" she asked. The child burst into tears again. Joosje felt the child's nappy, took it off and, after hanging the wet one over the kettle on the fire, replaced it with a fresh one.

The doorbell rang. "Perhaps you'd better answer that yourself," Frits said. "You'll know who it is, whether they should be given the brush-off or not." Joosje handed the little one to Auntie Stien and went to the door. A few moments later she came back with a woman who looked very much like her. The woman shook Frits's hand hurriedly, and clamped Hans's little hand in her plump fist. "It's your birthday! Yes, it is! Did you know that!" she said. Then, after taking a seat, she began searching through her bag. It was, Frits noted, ten minutes to nine. He looked at the ceiling, which was covered in old, shabby ornamental leafwork.

70

Finding what she had sought, the visitor unwrapped a little silver beaker and handed it to Joosje. "It's real silver," she said, "it is real silver." "How lovely," Joosje said, continuing to peruse the gift. "It's real silver, I polished it till I weighed an ounce," the visitor said. "Show it to Frits," she went on, "he'll be able to tell."

"Yes indeed," Frits said, "it is real silver." He looked at the hallmark stamps on the side. "Very nice, very heavy. A lovely, extremely lovely gift. It should actually have an inscription on it." "That's what I said, isn't it?" the visitor asked, "or didn't I? I thought of it only too late, but I'll have it done." Joosje placed the beaker on the table. Auntie Stien picked it up and looked at it.

"Well, it's happened a fourth time now, Mother, that someone mistakes you for me," Joosje said. "Jaap told me he had spoken to someone who had been invited to Uncle Leo's party. And they said: I met your wife there as well. But I wasn't even there. That's what Jaap told them, and it turned out that he thought you were me."

The visitor blushed, opened her mouth a little and said: "Yes, remarkable isn't it?" "Mrs Mosveld," said Frits, "the first time I saw you, a few years ago, I thought you were your husband's daughter." "What an evening," he thought, "what an evening. When is it going to end?"

"How long ago was that?" she asked. "When was that?" Her brow was furrowed and she was leaning forward. "I don't know exactly," he said, "perhaps five years ago, or six." "No, that was four years ago, in Hilversum," she said quickly, waving

71

her hand. "It was at the summer cottage. Don't you remember, that that was four years ago? No longer than that."

Auntie Stien followed the conversation by turning her head from one speaker to the other. The little boy suddenly began bawling. Joosje shifted him on her lap, picked him up and ran her hand over his head, but the crying did not stop. "Give him to Uncle Frits for a moment," Frits said in a facetious tone. Joosje handed him the child, but it screamed only louder and began kicking its feet. Its moist little hands fought to push him away. Frits handed him back. "Look," Auntie Stien said, "look at your pretty present, look at the pretty beaker." She raised the silver beaker up close to the baby's face. The child struggled to reach the shiny object, seized it then in both hands and went through the motions of drinking.

"Aw, look at that," Auntie Stien cried out, "he's thirsty. Are you thirsty, lambkins? Yes, he's thirsty, the little fellow." Joosje stood up, dropped her knitting onto her chair and poured some milk into the beaker from a saucepan that was resting on the stovepipe. The little boy drank greedily. "You see, that was it," Joosje's mother said. Frits saw that Joosje had thrown down her knitting so hastily that three stitches had dropped from one of the needles. He slipped them back on carefully, pushed the needles a good way through and stuck them into the ball of wool.

After it was finished drinking, the child began crying again. "It is, in truth, a terrible little monster," Frits said. "The nerves have developed all wrong. It probably doesn't have long to live." "Don't say such ridiculous things," said Joosje. "The head is bound to become distended as well," Frits went on. "It is growing all crooked, like a plant to light, mark my words." "Oh, he's just talking to hear himself speak," said Joosje's mother.

Suddenly the child grew quiet, and they saw that it had fallen asleep against its mother's breast. Joosje carried him gingerly back to bed.

When she returned, she poured them more coffee. "How is Father doing?" Joosje asked. "A nasty flu," her mother replied, "I have it too, in fact, but Father's in bed with it. Did you hear what happened? Father is terribly upset about it. Two illustrations were printed incorrectly in the world encyclopedia. No, not with the wrong captions, but in an illogical order. Eight thousand of them were printed that way. The question now is whether they will print the next twenty-two thousand that way, or go back and correct the first ones. If they don't, there will be different versions of the same edition. You do know, I take it, that Anna is getting married on the Friday after New Year? But I'd best be getting home, I am not feeling very well either."

She left, and a silence descended for a time. "It is now twenty minutes to ten," Frits thought, "if one subtracts the minutes by which my watch is running fast."

At that same moment they heard the downstairs door open and someone climbing the stairs. "That will be Jaap," Joosje said. "I'm glad you're back," said Auntie Stien, as a skinny young man in a blue hat entered the room. "Well, what have we here," he replied. "Then I suppose I'll be going," the old woman said, "at least nothing has happened to you." While Joosje was leading her to the stairs, Frits shook the young man's hand and said: "My warmest congratulations on your son.

73

I hope the present proves in some way useful." He pointed to the table full of gifts.

After laying his hat and overcoat aside, the new arrival settled down in Joosje's chair. He had a thin, pale mouth, bony fingers and a narrow skull with indentations at the temples. The wispy, light-blond hair on his head had become so thin at the front and top that one could see the bluish skin right through it. "Well, my good Frits," he asked with a smile, "how are things? A cigarette? A cigar? Always up for that, right?" He proffered a box of thin cigars. They both lit one.

Joosje came back in. "Jaap, haven't you seen the present Frits brought for Hans?" she asked. "Mercy me, no, how could I have forgotten, quite reprehensible of me," said Jaap, barely containing his laughter. "Mr van Egters, I extend to you my sincerest apologies." Joosje handed him the saucer. "Well, would you look at that, and a beaker, and chocolate bars, my goodness." "And an apple," said Frits. "And an apple," Jaap added.

"I'll be damned, but it's Tuesday today, isn't it?" he asked, after the present was back on the table. "The most miserable day in the week, after Monday, but it is in fact a Saturday, for tomorrow is Christmas."

"I find Friday the most pleasant day," Frits said, "for then one has the prospect of Saturday." "And I enjoy Thursday most," Jaap replied, "for then one has the prospect of Friday."

"We could go on like this, I fear," Frits said. He shivered, rubbed his hands together and tapped his feet. "I think I'm coming down with something," he said, leaning back in his chair. "I've

74

been working on the same premise for the last few days," said Jaap. "Have you been staying inside, then?" Frits asked. "Oh yes," Jaap answered, "our tap is still broken. Every morning I lug water from downstairs all the way up those steps. That's enough for me. Then I feel no need to go outside any more."

"But doesn't the office send a doctor to examine you?" asked Frits.

"They do," Jaap said, "but it's a normal doctor with a practice of his own. All you have to do is count the hours: first he has his charity patients in the morning. Then he makes his neighbour-hood rounds. When he's done with that he eats lunch at home and then goes in to see his private patients. Which means he can get here no earlier than three thirty. At three o'clock I climb into bed and read something pleasant. At three thirty, when I hear a car door slam, I know what that means. By the time he comes in I'm asleep, and Joosje wakes me." "And what has he said so far?" "He's only been here once," Jaap said, "so what could he say? You can be as healthy as anything, but if you say 'I feel terrible' and you're lying in bed, what can a doctor like that say but: see how you feel in three days' time. Am I right?" He leaned back and ran both hands simultaneously over his hair.

"You've become even balder," Frits said, "you're getting extremely bald. Are you still massaging it? You told me recently, as I recall, that you massaged your scalp."

"I put paraffin oil on it," Jaap said, "that's an excellent remedy. I massage it with paraffin oil." "What a filthy mess," Frits said, "but then you have to wash it afterwards." "No, of course not, I wouldn't do that," Jaap replied.

75

"I often ask myself," Frits said, "what it is that causes baldness. It's something that occurs almost exclusively among men. While at other spots on the body, the hair just keeps on growing."

"The roots on the scalp die off," said Jaap. "That's a real pearl of wisdom," Frits said, "I knew that already. That is like saying: it will not rain, as long as it remains dry. On occasion I have thought that it comes because the skull grows larger and the skin is stretched quite tightly across it. That restricts the flow of blood. Could that be it?" Jaap said nothing.

"It goes faster all the time, doesn't it?" Frits went on. "There is no stopping it, is there?" "I'd like to inform you," Jaap said, running his right hand over his scalp, "that in the last month or two the hair loss has ceased. There are cases in which the hair becomes very thin, but no longer becomes any thinner: such a case am I."

"In the long run though you go bald anyway, just like everyone else," Frits said. "That is inevitable. Could it be," he went on, "that it has something to do with your heart, with the blood vessels? You have a rather weak heart, don't you?"

"To be frank," Jaap replied, "when I climb the stairs, it goes 'hee hee hee!' down here." He pointed to his left breast and made a hoarse, squeaking sound. "When that happens you do not hear it, but I do." "Isn't that something like high blood pressure?" Frits asked. "No," Jaap said, "that is what *you* have. My blood pressure is too low." "What exactly are the symptoms of excessively high blood pressure?" Frits asked. Looking at his watch he saw that it was nearly ten o'clock; he stood up and began pacing back and forth.

"When you bend over, you feel a tightness in your head," said Jaap. "Yes, that's exactly what I have," Frits said. "Even when you tilt your head to one side, or lower your chin to your breast, it hurts: everything is stiff. Isn't that right?" "Yes," Frits said.

"Pressure on the eyelids is intolerable. It produces pain. When you sit too close to the window, the light hurts your eyes."

"All that is the case with me," said Frits. "Well, bully for you, my boy, congratulations," Jaap said pointedly. "I'm sure you'll tough it out this way for at least a few more years." He grinned. Joosje poured them all more coffee.

"Still, it is precisely these things that enrich our lives," Jaap said. "The ill and the poor in spirit. When I see a wooden leg or an old woman with a cane with a rubber tip on it, or a hunchback, it makes my day."

They both laughed. "Or those wonderful lumps," Frits said slowly, in a pensive tone, "those huge pink potatoes that grow on someone's head, completely free of charge, or behind their ear, in lieu of a pencil." He shook in his chair, so hard that the floor rattled. For a moment, both of them were out of breath. "You should try caressing a hunchback's hump sometime," Jaap said, coughing, "it drives them crazy."

"You also have," said Frits, "that fellow with the peg leg, on the bridge. He sits on the ground and blocks your way with that leg. You almost trip over it; then you have no choice but to give him something."

"A blind man is also a wondrous thing," said Jaap, "with one of those dogs." He hiccupped with laughter. "Pay no attention to me," he shrieked, "me and my dog, pay no attention to me, for I am blind." "It is a glorious thing," he went on. "But the loveliest of all are the ones with a face mutilated by fire. No nose and moist eyes in a socket without lids. That is truly something grand."

"Stop it, the two of you," Joosje said, "with that nonsense." The doorbell rang. "What a ridiculous hour," she said, and went to answer it. "I believe I hear more than one voice," Frits said, when the sound of conversation in the hallway reached them.

Joosje came into the room in front of the visitors, her gaze fixed glassily on the ceiling and her lips forming a little o. Following right behind was a man of about thirty-five years with a protruding belly, accompanied by a woman with closely cropped hair. After greeting everyone, they sat down. Jaap said nothing.

"I suppose we've walked in on a lively conversation?" the man asked. He had, despite his spectacles, a boyish face; his dark-blond hair was parted casually on one side. A smile was frozen on the woman's face. "We are welcome, aren't we?" the man asked. "Joosje, are we welcome?" "Oh well, of course," Joosje said, reddening. "Listen to this," he said, "of all the stupidities." He leaned over to Frits, whose chair was next to his, and said: "Allow me to rectify an omission. My name is Wortel. Arend Wortel." Frits clasped the warm, heavy hand. "That's it," he thought, detecting a faint odour of gin, "he's had a few too many."

"We were," the visitor continued, "at the home of a niece, a married woman. We had to go to another room and I said to a young lady: could I offer you my arm? That's only polite, isn't it? And do you know what she says? She says: Why would you do that, are you having trouble standing up on your own? Well, I became angry. And everyone else got angry at me. Don't ask me why. Then I said: In that case, we shall be going. Then we shall be going. Then we thought: we'll stop by and see Jaap. We are welcome, aren't we, Jaap? Otherwise we shall be going."

Jaap said nothing. The man looked around, coughed and said to Frits: "I don't suppose I could borrow a hundred guilders from you for a month, could I? You do have sufficient liquidity, I take it?" Jaap could barely contain his laughter.

"What do you think of that?" Wortel went on, "they simply ran us out of the house, in fact. That's the long and the short of it. And for what?" "My guess is that you went up to one of those girls and squeezed her tits," Jaap said. "No, oh no," said Wortel. "You were there, Nora, was it anything like that?" "Oh no," the woman said flatly, the smile still pasted to her face.

"Are we welcome?" he asked Jaap. Jaap said nothing. "What time is it?" "It is ten past eleven," said Frits.

"Then we shall be on our way," Wortel said. He gestured to his companion and they disappeared quickly into the hallway, with Joosje right behind. Jaap and Frits remained seated and silent, until they heard the two descending the stairs. "Strange things are afoot," Jaap said with a smile. Frits stood up and wished him a good night.

"And all the best with your health," said Jaap. "Saturday evening is still on; I'm counting on it. I will stop by most probably before then. I am welcome, aren't I?" Saying these final words, he pounded his fists against belly and chest and feinted like a boxer.

Frits picked his way down the half-darkened stairs. Arriving at the bottom, he heard Jaap call out after him: "I am welcome, aren't I?" The voice cackled with mirth.

"In any case," Frits said aloud, having reached the pavement, "it's still freezing hard enough at night." At the far end of the canal he saw that the river was covered with a layer of ice. He took off at a trot to warm his feet.

The light was on in the living room. His father was seated at the table. His eyelids were red, as though from excessive rubbing, and there was a smudge of dirt on his right cheek. He sniffed loudly now and then, to rid his nose of mucus. "Look," he said, when Frits remained standing hesitantly in the room, "here it is." He pointed to a passage in a book with a black binding that lay open on the table before him. "The rights accorded to the counts of Egters date from as early as 1384," Frits read. "What is this all about?" he thought. "Very interesting, extremely interesting," he said, "I'll have a look at that tomorrow." "That is not enough," he thought. "I will examine it closely tomorrow," he added. The radio, he heard then, was still on, for suddenly a voice said: "Our station break has come to an end. You are listening to the 'Dr Jazz Quickstep'."

Frits left the room. "I need to stop thinking," he repeated to himself over and over as he brushed his teeth and undressed. He hopped into bed. "I still have those sugar cubes in my pocket," he thought. "Now rest, a rest most complete." Shortly afterwards he fell asleep.

He awoke to a cry, followed by a noise as of something falling over and voices. He jumped out of bed and hurried into the living room, where he turned on the light and opened the sliding doors. His father was sitting straight up in bed and looking at his mother, who was weeping, rocking back and forth and pressing her face against the pillow again and again. She had a handkerchief stuffed halfway into her mouth and was uttering little cries. "That's something new," Frits thought. "I'll fetch you some water," he said, took a glass from the sideboard and brought it back from the kitchen in a wink. At his repeated urging, his mother drank a sip. "You go on," his father said, "your mother is having a nervous…" "He can't remember the word for it," Frits thought. He closed the sliding doors again and went back to bed. "These are the days given to us under the sun," he said aloud in the darkness. Twenty minutes later he fell asleep.

"We are in the country," a voice said. He was standing at the side of a road between pastures. After walking on a bit he came to a country estate, with a tall metal fence and a drive of white gravel. Right across from it, on the other side of the road, a huge chessboard had been set up on the verge. "They make things far too complicated," he thought, "besides, there are no chess pieces." The board was a good ten feet from corner to corner.

"Come over here," a gardener shouted. Frits pushed open the heavy gate and walked up the drive. "Look," the man said, "we are laying out all kinds of things here." He pointed to flower beds. There was also a series of lawns, bordered by climbing ornamentals which, for lack of a wall or tree, were crawling over the grass. Upon closer examination he saw that these were not flowers at all, but cunningly woven woollen fibres, of the kind children use to weave lanyards, drawn tight as though on a loom. Then he grew afraid. He turned to run, but stepped into the herbaceous border of a lawn and his feet became entangled. Finally, he worked himself free, but heard the danger approaching: a slowly rattling, shuddering sound as though from a steamroller. He fled onto the road, but the terrible thing followed. Looking back repeatedly he saw nothing, yet knew that if he should pause to rest for a moment, it would appear around the corner. He raced into a little house, but a woman's voice cried out: "Hold on, what have we here?" "Quiet, quiet!" he shouted. But the voice went on shrieking loudly.

Then he heard the danger rattling up off the road and heading directly for him. It burst into the house and he, in a last-ditch attempt, ran down a set of winding stairs to the cellar. He leapt, half stumbling, down the steps, but the thing behind continued its pursuit, slowly at first, then faster and rattling ever more loudly.

The further down the twisting stairs he raced, the slighter his lead became. Then he saw the cellar floor. He stumbled and fell. Everything went black. "Am I welcome?" a voice said.

He awoke, his face wet, opened his eyes and squeezed them shut again and again, then raised himself onto one elbow, sitting half upright for a few minutes, before daring to lie down once more.

IV

WHEN HE AWOKE that morning at a quarter to eight, his first thought was: "It is Christmas Day." On the window he saw no frost flowers. "Perhaps the thaw has set in," he thought, then rolled over and slept until eight thirty. "Don't go on lying here for more than half an hour," he thought when he awoke again. Yet he fell asleep once more and awoke only at twenty minutes past the hour of nine, when his mother opened the door and said: "Isn't it about time you got up? I'm going to put on the eggs."

He raised himself on one elbow, but lay down again and pulled the covers over his head. He breathed the bedroom smell of his body between the sheets, and thought: "Would that smell the same to anyone else?" Ten thirty came. "Now I really must get up," he thought. At five past eleven he slid back the blankets.

After washing and shaving he took his clothes under his arm and went to dress in the warm living room. On his plate lay an egg. "It would have been better if you hadn't boiled it already," he said to his mother, "then I could have done it myself. Now it's cold."

"I had no idea you would stay in bed for so long," she said. His father came in wearing his coat; he had a heavy shawl over his arm. "We're going for coffee at the Geitenkoois'," said his mother, draping the shawl over her shoulders.

Once they were gone, Frits cut the cooled egg onto four slices of bread and ate them. He cleared the table, then walked back and forth in the room for a time. The radio was playing quiet organ music. After ten minutes he turned it off and went into the side room. "Carelessness, wastefulness, stupidity," he said as he turned off the gas fire, which was burning high.

Across the street, water was dripping from the gutter onto the pavement. "How can that be, it hasn't even snowed," he thought. "It's been such a long time. I didn't want to lend him that jumper. Now it is only going to smell of Joop, I said." He whistled through his teeth and said to himself: "At the birthday party, now I remember. That little girl, the precocious one. I wish I were a stone, she said, then I wouldn't have to live. It startled everyone out of their wits. She had read that somewhere, or heard it, of course."

The doorbell rang. "God help us," he mumbled and went to open it. "Is Frits van Egters at home?" a voice asked, stammering halfway as it spoke his name. A tall man in a grey hat came up the stairs. He had a pale, bloated face and his head seemed not so much to rest on his shoulders, as to hang in front of them. "If back and shoulders did not prove normal on closer inspection, one would say he was a crookback," thought Frits.

"Do you have a moment?" asked the visitor, fluttering his hands nervously, "could I speak to you for a moment, Frits?" "Of course, Lande," Frits said. "There's no one else at home, by the way, so do come in."

84

"It's rather serious," said the man, taking off his hat. The top of his head was masked in the middle by thin wisps of hair. "Is it convenient to talk here?" he asked, once they were sitting across from each other in the side room. "Yes, certainly," said Frits, "I am all ears. Do tell. I have plenty of time, but first I need to know what it is about."

"Well," the visitor said, "didn't you say to me once: Maurits has a criminal bent, beware of that? That is what you said, isn't it?" "Oh, well," said Frits, "criminal. Criminal, yes, perhaps I did say something like that."

"The reason I've come to you," said Lande, pulling out a pipe which he scraped clean with a pencil above the ashtray, "is because I need to be sure."

"Get to the point, for God's sake," Frits said, "tell me first what is going on. Like a newspaper report. First a brief summary of the whole thing, then the story at length."

"All right," Lande said, "an hour and half ago the doorbell rang. My wife opened it. She said: It is Maurits. I thought: what's he come for, on a Sunday morning? He had two books with him, ones I had lent him and asked about on a few occasions. I asked: did you come all this way just for that, to bring back those books? He said: No, I had to be in the neighbourhood anyway.

"I had just washed my hair and it's always so brittle then, I use brilliantine on it. I had the little tin of brilliantine—do you use brilliantine?"

"No," Frits said, "go on."

"Well, I had put that tin on the stove to soften it and we both looked at it and we talked about brilliantine. I put some of it on my hair and went to wash my hands in the kitchen, because they were greasy. As I was standing there, I suddenly thought: I should let the tap run and suddenly go back into the room. But I didn't. My wife was up in the loft. Instead I dried my hands and, as soon as the water was turned off, went back in quickly. Maurits was standing there in the room, looking a bit awkward, and I thought I saw him rummaging a bit in his coat pocket, his right pocket. And he said right away: Lande, I really must be going, I'm in a bit of a hurry. He'd been gone for less than a minute when I went to the sideboard and looked in the tin box I sometimes keep money in, money I've put aside. For the last few days, two hundred-guilder notes had been lying there, beneath a notebook."

"And now they were no longer there," said Frits. "And what did you do then?"

"First I asked my wife about it and she was sure too, that they had been there. I had not put them in my wallet, I looked again to be sure. Then I went to his house. He wasn't there. But his father, he was at home."

"And what did he say?"

"I said: Duivenis, I need to talk to you alone, right now. It is serious. It is about Maurits. After I went in and told him the story, he said: I shall ask him about it, and if he did it, he will tell me."

"I find it quite meritorious of you, to keep me informed of the facts," said Frits. "I suppose you will now wait and see?"

"And if he tells me that it is not so," said Lande, "what must I do then? Can I take that for a certainty? Do you think he is capable of such a thing?"

"Yes," Frits said, "I think he is quite capable of that. I think he is capable of much more too. And I also know a great deal more."

"What, what is it then?" asked Lande.

"I am not going to tell you. But I urge you to stick to your guns. He has that two hundred guilders and he must give it back. And should he refuse, I would definitely not hesitate to report it to the constabulary."

Lande pulled a conical pouch from his pocket, filled his pipe from it, and lit it. "We shall see," he said, and began buttoning his coat. "Strange things are afoot," Frits said with a smile, "this certainly won't do your nervous condition any good. How is it with that tightness in your jaw?"

"It had been getting better, the last few days. Do you notice anything about my manner of speech now, Frits?" "It is a bit agitated," said Frits, "but the pronunciation is normal."

The other man stood and left. "I trust you'll keep me informed," Frits said as he showed him out.

Once again he extinguished the gas fire, which he had lit for his visitor, and turned on the radio in the living room. A man was speaking about cultivating flower bulbs at home. On the other frequencies, too, he found nothing that appealed to him. He left the radio on an English channel, with the volume low. The whine of violin music was faintly audible. He spat into the stove and watched as each blob formed a brown blister on the coals for several seconds before evaporating. When puckering his cheeks produced no more saliva, he stood on his toes and passed water into the stove, but was startled by the loud plop and

87

the cloud of fine ash that came rushing out of the hopper. He sat down on the divan and looked at his shoes. For ten minutes, he remained sitting like that. "That vapour in the room gives off a mean enough stench," he thought.

Far away, in the distance, he heard the puffing of a train. "And so our hours pass," he thought. He took the skin on the back of his right hand between his teeth and tugged on it. Then he went to the back room, where a mirror hung beside the corner cupboard.

"This is a reasonable mirror," he said aloud. He combed his hair, first over his forehead, then straight back, and after that in two halves down the middle. Taking a copying pencil he drew a thin moustache on his upper lip. He whistled the French national anthem, stamped greasy fingerprints on the mirror with his right hand and went back to the radio; a Dutch station was airing the news. "You are listening to 'The King Football March'," the announcer said when the news was over.

"What I should do now," he thought after turning off the set, "is bolt the door, roll around on the floor, shouting 'oh! oh!' the whole time, then take an iron bar and smash all the windows. When the upstairs and downstairs neighbours come and kick in the door, I'll go into a swoon. And then I'll be off to the institution." "Cheerie-choop-choop-falderie," he sang quietly, "cheerie-choop-choop-faldera."

A woodlouse was making its way across the wallpaper. He took a match and struck it so close to the bug that he was able to press the match head against the insect at the moment of ignition. It shrivelled and fell to the floor.

"A painful yet swift execution," he said aloud. "Pity is to be spurned. Still, it is a sin," he continued, raising his index finger, "for I have killed a living creature."

He heard someone entering the hall. "Is this the private torture chamber?" asked Louis Spanjaard as he entered. "Is this the department of spontaneous combustion? Or is that your own stench I smell?"

"I could say: it's your own upper lip you're smelling," said Frits, "but I will tell you. I spilled some water into the stove."

"My, my," Louis said. He was wearing no overcoat, only a leather jacket. "What are you up to?" "I was poring over my sins," said Frits. "Very good," Louis said, "you certainly picked the right day for it." "Has the thaw set in yet?" Frits asked. "Hardly," Louis said.

"As a child," Frits asked, "did you kill insects so cruelly as well?" Louis did not reply. "Do you know what I did? When I would see one of those big spiders, the ones with a little body and those incredibly long legs—daddy-long-legs, I believe they call them—I would cut off those legs to see what they would do then. Outside, I actually buried frogs alive. Did you do that too?" "I don't recall," Louis said.

"When a wasp entered the house," Frits went on, "I would take a knife from the drawer and follow it until it landed on a window. Then I would sever the thorax from the abdomen, a delicate operation. In the part you have cut off, the stinger keeps bobbing up and down, a peculiar sight. And the front half can still fly a bit." Louis was silent.

"You know," he said, more quietly now, "I also caught little fish and kept them in an aquarium. I had a green spoon that I used to fish them out. I would lay them on a dry surface and watch carefully to see how those fish died, simply because I felt like it. I also burned a great many spiders."

"Do say, do say, Mr Egters," said Louis. "What am I going to talk about now?" Frits thought. "Weren't we going to the pictures, Louis?" he asked, taking the newspaper with the cinema advertisements from the rack. "There's a good one on at Princeps. What time is it? One thirty-five. There is a showing at a quarter to two and one at a quarter to four. A quarter to two, we won't make that one, not any more. We could go together now, though, and get tickets for a quarter to four. *The Seventh Veil*, that can't be too bad."

"We can take the tram, can't we?" Louis asked, reading aloud the title of the film. "Let's walk there, and come back on the tram," said Frits. "And then do that the same way later on, that's more economical."

"Might it be possible to eat with you and your family this evening?" Louis asked, as they were making their way into town. "Yes, of course," said Frits.

There was a crowd at the cinema. Frits purchased two tickets for up front, the only row that wasn't sold out. "At least that's cheap," he said, slipping them into his wallet. As soon as they turned their backs on the box office, they saw the tram approaching, ran to the stop just in time and quickly arrived back at the house.

Frits's parents were at the front door when they got there. Once they were inside, his mother, after pacing back and forth between kitchen and living room for a few minutes, asked: "Frits, what did you do with the attic keys?" "I haven't had them, not at all," he replied. "Didn't you bring down any coal while we were gone?" "No," he said.

With Frits looking over her shoulder, she searched the windowsill in the kitchen, then the table and the counter, then she looked on the mantelpiece in the living room and in the bookcase. She sank down into a chair beside the stove, chin in hand. "No one leaves this room," said Frits. Louis, who was sitting beside him on the divan, poked him in the ribs. His father was standing at the window, examining a book.

"I think I know," she said suddenly, "I do believe I left them in the scuttle, on top of the coal. I believe so. That means they're in the stove. Take a look, see whether they rolled to the bottom of the scuttle."

Louis snorted loudly. Frits looked in the half-emptied scuttle. "Righteous be his name," he said under his breath, "his arm is mighty." "No," he said more loudly, "they are not in there."

"What now?" she asked. "Rye bread with treacle," he replied, "then they'll come out in a jiffy."

"The stove will go out soon," she said. "Go down to the Tintelers' and ask whether we might borrow their box of keys to try." He and Louis went out of the door, returning a little later with a round, blue tin. "Help yourself," he said, placing it on the table. "We must be off." They left. "The streets are getting slippery again," said Louis, after they had walked for a bit. "To be sure," said Frits. They did not speak again until reaching the cinema.

"Not even remotely what I had hoped," said Frits as they shuffled out after the film. "It goes to show how little one should rely on the taste of others." "Oh, it wasn't that bad," said Louis.

Seated in the tram was a man dressed in black, with big, grey boots. He wore a bowler and had all manner of things pinned to his chest: medals, tokens, leaden seals from butcher's sausages, Belgian coins with a hole in the middle, a variety of chains. "The thaw has set in, people, people—the thaw is coming fast!" he shouted in a flat voice. "It is thawing to beat the band, people, listen to it thaw! It's raining hot water out there, people, watch out!" Having said this, he laughed a loud, slobbering laugh. The passengers stopped talking and looked at him. "Yes, people, I could tell you a thing or two," he shouted with a smile as Frits and Louis alighted.

When they got to Frits's home, his mother said: "Not a single one of those keys fits the lock; I borrowed some coal from Hennie instead. We'll have to wait till Friday before I can ask the housing association for another one. I'll let the stove go out tonight." "Those keys will be completely warped anyway, if they fell in there," Frits said.

"What are you up to this evening?" Louis asked once they were seated at the table. "I think I shall go to see Walter Graafse," Frits said. "You mean that fellow with the potato head? That fabulist, that pathological liar?" "Yes, that's the one." "Who is this about?" Frits's father asked. "About someone else," Frits replied.

After the meal, as they were walking down the street together, Louis said: "That was a fine dinner. I never have any complaints about the menu at your house." Arriving at a large metal clock next to a junction, they said farewell.

Frits walked on for ten minutes through a busy area. Then, turning in a southerly direction, he passed through narrow streets and came at last to a canal lined with big trees. He climbed a set of high, steep steps with a set of iron banisters on both sides, and rang the bell. A dog barked, he heard a thumping on the stairs, and the door was opened at last by a short, plump young man dressed in brown. Brushing his hair back from his forehead, he said: "Sir Frits, do come in. Do come in." Frits followed him.

After traversing a long corridor, they climbed the stairs and came to a room that was heated by a gas fire. The room was full of cabinets, tables and racks, all littered with electrical material—lamps, cords, magnets, transformers, meters and coils. The only light came from a bare bulb on the ceiling.

Two people were seated beside the gas fire: a young man with a thin moustache, dressed in grey battledress that was unbuttoned at the top, as was his shirt, and a fat, black-haired girl. "This is Albert," Walter said. "My darling sister, of course, requires no introduction." He passed out cigarettes all around. When he opened a door, a dog leapt into the room. "Did that animal just hop out of a cupboard?" Frits thought. It was a black and white spotted dog of medium size. The animal tried to lick Walter's face right away, but when he shouted "Down! Knock it off!" the dog raced under a table and lay down. "It's a troublesome creature," Walter said. "Not long ago we had seven slabs of gingerbread cooling on the windowsill, and he ate them all. So I held his paws against the gas fire, you should have heard him screech! But it taught him a lesson. Didn't it, Foks?" He grabbed the animal's front paws, but the dog began yelping loudly, struggled free and ran away.

"Come and see what I've bought," Walter said then, leading Frits into one of the front rooms. The young man in uniform followed them. When Walter turned on the light, Frits saw in the middle of the room a piano of unusual format; like a baby grand, but with keys narrower and fewer than on a normal piano. He tried a few of them. The notes were sharp and penetrating, like the strings of a guitar. "It sounds like a clavichord, or whatever you call them," Frits said. "Is that what it is?" "No," said Walter. "It's not a clavichord. That's what they called it at the auction house, but it's more like a spinet. I believe, in fact, that this is the intermediate form between the spinet and our modern piano." "The sound is very pleasing," said Frits, "what did you pay for it?" "A hundred and twenty-five guilders." "Not bad," Frits said.

The young man in uniform pulled a chair up to the instrument and leafed through a book of music that was standing ready. He used his index finger to count the keys, hummed a few notes and began to play. "Amazing, how lovely," Frits whispered. "What was that?" he asked when the music was finished. He saw no title on the sheet. "A partita by Bach," Albert replied. "I play it on guitar too, because there's an arrangement for lute as well."

"Use your heads, for God's sake," said Walter's sister, bursting into the room. She took the music book and closed the lid on the instrument. "Wonderful, light-brown wood, that," Frits thought. "Try to show a bit of sense," she went on, "you know

94

what's going on upstairs." "But she can breathe her last without our assistance, Klara," Walter said.

They returned to their chairs by the fire. "What is going on upstairs?" Frits asked. "Klara limps when she walks," he thought. "Our upstairs neighbour's wife is dying," the girl said. "I'll go ask how she is, then I'll tell them right away that the music was an oversight by one of our visitors. Otherwise it's just too shameful." She limped off and Frits heard her climb the stairs, rather hurriedly. "So what's wrong with the woman upstairs?" he asked. "Completely finished: pneumonia and consumption," Walter said. "But she's in no hurry about it. Care for another smoke?" "No, thank you," Frits said, stubbing out his cigarette. "And you, have you come up with any new and grand inventions?" Walter said nothing. "Do you remember telling me, in our last year at school, that you could fabricate a magnet in your room so powerful that the doors of passing cars would fly open? Do you know that I believed that back then?" "It was true, too," said Walter.

"What was that fellow's name, the one whose house we went to for that afternoon of chess, in Cementwijk?" Frits asked. "Hans Houting?" "Yes, I'll be damned, that's the one," said Frits. "Do you remember that he had a length of inner tube filled with sand, like a kind of sausage? He took it with him when he went downstairs at night to pee, on his own, as a sort of club." "I don't remember that," said Walter.

"I remember lots of things," said Frits. "You always had an ashtray or a dish full of flies, which you had damaged, but that were not dead yet, they just lay there wriggling their legs." "That was not only back then," Albert said suddenly. But he fell silent again right away. "Have you ever heard from your parents?" Frits asked. "Damn it," he thought, "what a thing to ask." "No," Walter said only, with a brief toss of his head.

After that no one spoke. They listened to the muffled footsteps on the floor above and heard Klara pick her way down the stairs. "They didn't hear the music, fortunately," she said, sliding her chair up closer to the fire, "they were at the back of the house." "How old is that woman?" Frits asked. "Fifty-six," Klara said. "She's still quite aware of the things around her. She speaks very quietly, though. They gave me a cup of tea, and suddenly her daughter said: She's saying something. They went over to the bed and put their heads down close to her mouth. She said: The doorbell is ringing. She was right. But no one else had heard it."

"That's right," Frits said, "the dying have very sharp ears, right up to the end. During the death struggle one must be very careful what one says, because they can hear everything. I read that somewhere. It is important to make the agony—that is what it is called, it has its own nomenclature, like any disease—as bearable as possible for the patient. To open the windows for fresh air and to stay close to the deathbed. What is wrong with your foot, anyway, Klara?" "I fell down the front steps outside," she said, fingering her left ankle, "it's still swollen, but the pain is almost over, as long as I'm careful."

"In any case, they're in no hurry upstairs," Walter said. "This has been going on for three days already, I've stopping believing that it's ever going to come." "It sounds almost as though you can't wait," said Albert.

"I want to move in up there," Walter said. "The rooms are much lighter than down here. The landlord thinks it's fine." "Why didn't I stay at home tonight?" Frits thought. He sat up straight: "It is, in fact, a good moment to die," he said. "I for one would make sure I was in the ground before the thaw came, otherwise the churchyard is so sodden. Time waits for no man." "But still, not before one's time has come," said Albert. "I believe there is some truth in that," Klara said, starting to comb her hair.

"I was walking down Riembaan yesterday," Albert said. "A man tried to jump onto the tram, onto the rear platform. That is so stupid. He missed and fell under it. You know how it goes, women screaming, a throng of people gathered. But it turned out well enough. The tram had stopped quickly, it wasn't going at full speed yet. They pulled him out from in front of the wheels; his clothes were torn and dirty and his spectacles were broken. The frames were crumpled, the lenses had fallen out. A very strange sight, because his face was untouched, only a few bumps. He was still all in one piece and he just stood there, white as a sheet, and said nothing. Then I saw the conductor walk up to him. So the conductor stops in front of him and says: Well, well, what did you think you were doing, will you tell me? And he slaps that man twice across the face, one slap on each cheek. And then that fellow suddenly starts weeping and cries out in a very peculiar voice: I wanted to get on the trolley!" He imitated it in a high, whiny voice. All four of them laughed. "I wanted to get on the trolley!" Albert cried out again.

"I always hop on and off the tram too," Walter said. "It's a matter of luck. Fools and babies, you know. Do you remember Wim Barneveld? The one with that massive head of hair?" "No," said Frits. "You don't? Oh, I thought differently. He's completely bald these days, did you know that?" "How could I?" Frits asked. "Oh yes, it's absolutely true. I ran into him about four months ago, he's a pilot. I hadn't seen him for six years. We went somewhere for a beer and I kept thinking: there is something about his face. Then he took off his aviator cap and his whole head was bald, so completely that you didn't even realize right away that there was not a single hair on it. No eyebrows, no lashes either. A hair disease. I had noticed something strange already, while he was still wearing that cap, but I didn't know what it was."

"What does that have to do with anything?" asked Klara. "We were talking about being reckless, weren't we?" Walter said. "Well, this Barneveld fellow was stationed at Soesterberg for a while. They used to go out barnstorming over the Veluwe, he told me. Flying very low in the valleys and then pulling up at the last moment before each hill. He said that sometimes you came back with pine branches on your struts. They flew under the bridge at Nijmegen too."

"It's five past nine, in any case," Frits thought. Upstairs, something fell to the floor. "They drop things all the time up there," said Walter, "they're rather dull folk." "They are very decent people," Klara said.

"The downstairs neighbours told us," Walter went on, "about when they moved in up there in the winter of forty-four. They had twelve sacks of coal. That was enough, they reckoned, to keep two stoves burning the whole time." Frits burst out laughing. "By January there was no coal left; all they could do was stay in bed, they got out only a few hours each week, whenever they had a coupon for sugar beets or something. But it didn't kill them." "Well then, things are starting to look up for you now," said Albert.

"I'm afraid I must be going," said Frits. "I have to stop by somewhere on my way home." "Take one more cigarette, for the road," said Walter, reaching out and placing one between his lips. The dog accompanied the two of them down the stairs, but halfway there Walter grabbed the animal by the scruff of the neck, placed his shoe on the tip of its tail and stepped on it hard. The dog gave a yelp, which turned into a long howl. Walter raised his foot and they continued down; the dog, still yelping, raced back up.

"Be sure to come by again, when you have the chance," said Walter, when they got to the front door.

Frits picked his way down the front steps. The street lights were mirrored in the icy canal. He stamped his feet, closed his collar tightly and walked on with his head bowed. The hands of the clock on the front of a bank read eighteen minutes past nine.

When he got home he found his father lying on the divan, while his mother sat at the table, leafing through the day's news. "You're home early," she said. "Yes," he said, "I was planning to stop and see someone else on the way back, but they weren't at home. Let's see if there is anything on the radio." "There was a nice play on, just now," she said. "Oh," he asked, "what was that about?" "Well," she said, "it was about the olden days in England, no, in Ireland, about the lords and the landowners."

The radio had warmed up. "Now, the Ramblers continue with 'Sensation Number One'," the announcer said. "Pa-rah-pa-pa-paw," his mother said, when the song began, "hideous."

"You should really try to follow jazz music," Frits said. He was seated in a chair close to the set. "Can't you turn off that noise?" his father asked, sitting up. "No," said Frits, "you should try listening, then you would hear that it is not incoherent noise. The orchestra provides the rhythm, the saxophone plays the melody and the improvisations."

"But it doesn't have to be that loud," the man said, turning down the volume. Then he lay back down. Frits took the knob between his fingers and turned it up slowly again, bit by bit, at those points where only a soft drumbeat could be heard.

"I'm going to bed," his mother said suddenly, "I have no desire to stay up any longer." She disappeared into the back room and closed the sliding doors with a loud bang. "It is not clear whether that bang was so loud by accident, or with intent," Frits thought. His father stood up and walked back and forth before the bookcase, coughed, cupped his chin in one hand, opened his mouth, but said nothing.

The radio started in on a waltz. Frits turned it off, tiptoed out of the room and into the side room, where he lit the gas fire and sat down at the writing table. He heard his father pacing in the living room. It was ten o'clock. He unbuttoned his shirt, slid his hand under his singlet and ran his fingers across his chest. Pulling up both shirt and singlet, he looked at his belly, a crease in which was formed by his seated position, and poked the little finger of his right hand into the navel. He sniffed at the finger and wiped it on his handkerchief.

Shortly afterwards he heard from the other room the sounds of the sliding doors opening and the lamp being turned off. He went to the kitchen and was just about to start brushing his teeth when he heard voices from the bedroom. He went to the hall and stood beside the door. His mother was speaking in rapid, keening volleys of words. Whenever she stopped, Frits heard the grumble of his father's voice. Then they fell silent again, only to go on the next minute. Suddenly it sounded to him as though his mother was sitting straight up in bed and holding back her weeping, for he could clearly hear her voice, louder than before. "Never," she was saying, "never in your life have you thought about anyone but yourself, and you have never, ever considered whether—" Frits hurried back into the kitchen. "I hear nothing," he said, closing his eyes, "I hear nothing. Nothing is what I hear." He closed the door and brushed his teeth hastily. When the voices grew louder, he chanted to himself. "Boom, boom, boom, boom!" he sang, his head filled with a heavy buzzing.

Turning off the kitchen light, he moved noiselessly to his bedroom. "Now I've forgotten to put my shoes and socks behind the stove," he thought, "tomorrow I'll have to wear those clammy things again. Wait a minute, tomorrow is Christmas too."

"Hearken unto the message of Christmas," he said aloud. "The saviour is born unto us. He died upon Golgotha, racka-chacka-chack, ding-dong." Crawling into bed and pulling up the covers, he thought: "The bells should really be rung at midnight, that would be glorious." He felt his eyes grow moist, seized the sheet between his teeth and fell asleep.

He awoke at three o'clock with a heavy feeling in all his limbs and a pressing urge to pass water. After relieving himself, he fell asleep while rubbing his feet together.

He dreamt that he was on the first floor of a large department store. While wandering about he felt an increasingly powerful urge to urinate. He went to the Gents, but workers there were repairing the masonry. On the ground floor, the water closets were blocked off by a barrier of planks with a sign reading: "Out of order". He took the lift to the second floor.

Here he was stopped at the door to the lavatory by a salesgirl, dressed all in white, who said: "You are not allowed to use this, you have to register first."

On the third floor he could find no toilet at all. He trotted up the stairs to the fourth, the topmost floor, and raced to a corner of the store, but there he found only a grey door with a square, green sign reading: "Emergency exit. To be opened only upon alarm. Unauthorized breaking of the seal is punishable by law." Beneath the sign, the word "Gents" had been crossed out with a diagonal daub of paint.

As he was hurrying down the stairs again, the loudspeakers suddenly shouted out: "The store is closed. Customers still on the premises must report to the management and pay a fine." The floor he was on was empty, only members of the staff were still walking around. He was standing in the furnishings department, beside a table displaying vases. He picked up one of them, took it behind a partition, urinated in it until it was full and then put it back. The urge had not abated. Cautiously he filled vase upon vase, large and small, until all of them were full. When there was nothing left to fill, still he could not stop, and he had to pass water on the floor. So he sneaked, micturating as he went, from one department to the next and down the stairs.

As he descended the final flight, his path was suddenly blocked by a row of saleswomen, standing hand in hand, from banister to banister. "All is revealed, I must hide myself," he thought and ran back up the stairs, just ahead of the scream-ing group in pursuit. On the third floor he crawled beneath a pile of carpets, but heard someone shout: "Don't forget to look in the rug department." Tossing his hiding place aside he raced to the top floor. The urinating had stopped. He made his way to the emergency exit, opened it and found himself on a balcony. There was no fire escape. "Be sure to look behind the fire door," he heard, closer now. Below, straight beneath him, a train was passing. "We'll jump for it," he said, calculating distance and height, and leapt and crashed onto the roof of a railway carriage.

He succeeded in climbing into the train and took a seat in an empty compartment. The train began going in circles, at a terrifying speed. He felt himself grow nauseous, as on a wildly spinning ride at a carnival. Suddenly someone sat down across from him, someone who looked at him probingly and wore a black hat, with a brim at least two feet wide. "It's a dog," he thought. When the creature opened its coat, he saw that it was true. The skin of the belly was punctuated by a row of yellow buttons, as on a jacket. When he looked at the face, the dog's head changed into that of a pig. "I know about it," the monster said, "I am well informed. Don't try to fool me." As it spoke, the head grew a beak. The figure leaned towards him slowly. He awoke.

It was six thirty. Once again he felt a strong urge to pass water, but did not leave the bed. "Don't doze off again," he thought, "above all, not that." He pulled the pillow away from under his head. "I need to find a position uncomfortable enough to keep me awake," he said to himself.

"I know, let me think about all kinds of things," he thought. A story came to mind that a schoolfellow once told him. How a ten-year-old boy had chopped off his father's head while he was taking a nap on a bench in their garden. The case was described in a pedagogical textbook that belonged to his friend.

The boy's action was prompted by curiosity. There was no hatred or murderous rage involved, said the book, which Frits remembered looking at, only the child's curiosity at what it would be like with the head off.

Then he remembered a newspaper report from a few weeks back, telling of how a little boy had crawled into a cream centrifuge at a dairy plant and how a friend of his had turned on the machine, resulting in sudden death. "It was the centrifugal force," he thought, "it causes the blood to curdle." He examined the shapes that the light from the street lamps in front of the house threw across his bedroom ceiling.

The text of a news story he had read the summer before was one he still knew almost by heart. A farmer had asked his hired man to toss him a pitchfork from the other side of the wagon. When the farmhand did not do this quickly enough, the farmer climbed onto the edge of the wagon and peered over the top of the load, at the very moment the fork came flying. The tines penetrated his eyes and he fell off the wagon, dead.

The clock on the wall ticked loudly. "The strangest accidents happen down south," he thought. His mother had been shocked when he read aloud to her the account of a mishap, which had taken place in a farmyard. Two children were playing with an axe and a chopping block. "Put your hand down on the block," said the one, and the other did just that. "He'll pull it away," thought the boy holding the axe. "He won't really chop with it," thought the other. They were both wrong. The hand was still connected only by a thread, and had to be amputated.

He almost dozed off, but shook his head forcefully a few times back and forth. "As long as we don't fall asleep again," he thought, "or that beast will come back."

He recalled how his brother, when he was nine years old, had awoken three nights in a row, screaming, after a recurring dream. A monkey was chasing him and trying to crush him against the kerb. It resulted in a wild pursuit around a block of houses. Just as he had gained a bit of a lead, a wolf came from the other direction. There the dream ended. After the third night his mother asked the doctor for advice. He recommended that, as soon as Joop awoke, they plunge his head into cold water. When he awoke the next night screaming again, his father held his head down in a bucket of water. The dream never came back.

By the time he was finished reflecting on this, it was ten past seven. Each time he almost dozed off, he raised his head again with a start. That went on until seven twenty-two. "It should be fairly safe now," he thought, "if anything happens, it will be light when I wake up." He fell asleep and dreamt no more.

V

A T NINE O'CLOCK, by full daylight, he awoke. "The second day of Christmastide has broken," he thought. "It goes almost without saying," he said aloud, having viewed the sky above the rooftops, "that the day will be clear and cold. I am not going to lie around too long." At twenty past nine he got up.

As he was washing at the tap, his father came into the kitchen, fully dressed, to keep an eye on the kettle already under a head of steam. "Good morning, my boy," he replied to Frits's "morning". He laid three eggs in an empty saucepan, put the pan on the fire and poured into it the boiling water from the kettle. "What are you doing, for heaven's sake?" asked Frits's mother, entering in her pink nightgown, "are you boiling eggs? You do that by putting them in the water, once it has come to a boil. This isn't cooking eggs. Now the water is off the boil and you have to wait for a few minutes for it to heat up again. This way you never know when they're ready." "You won't forget to put on your white woollen singlet, will you, Frits?" she asked. Then she walked on to the water closet.

At the start of breakfast, no one spoke a word. "Things are off to a roaring start," Frits thought. His father sighed each time he took a slice of bread. "As though raising and retracting the arm were a form of heavy labour," thought Frits. His mother kept her eyes on her plate and poured some tea. "What kind of weather do you think we'll have, Father?" asked Frits. "Not too bad," the man answered, glancing out of the window.

As Frits watched how his father slowly distributed the peeled egg over his bread and then, not knowing what to do with the shells still in the palm of his hand, made clumsy, helpless gestures, he thought: "I have to do something." "What are you waiting for?" his mother asked.

He stuffed his own, unpeeled egg into his mouth, closed his lips around it and began to make clucking noises through his nose, louder and faster all the time. Wide-eyed, he looked back and forth from his father to his mother, then let the egg fall to his plate. His mother smiled, but his father looked startled, wrinkling his face like someone squinting into bright sunlight.

When the meal was over, his father got up and went to the hall. Frits heard him take his coat from the stand, walk into the side room and rustle through his papers. Then he heard him come back into the hall, carefully open the door to the stairs and close it behind him quietly. "He is gone," he said. "Let him have his fun in Utrecht," said his mother, "why should I care?" As she spoke the last two words, her voice broke. "I am certainly not planning to spend the whole day here on my own," she said, suddenly weeping, "I am going to The Hague."

"No one is stopping you," said Frits, "The Lord shall be a lamp unto thy feet. You're right."

She gulped, coughed, removed her spectacles, wiped her eyes and put the spectacles back on. Then she cleared the table and put on her coat. "Does this coat look funny with this hat?" she asked. "God preserve us," Frits thought, "what a combination." "Cheerful, simple attire," he said, "it suits you well. Muted and in no way extravagant." Picking up her leather handbag, she walked into the hall. "When do you expect to be home?" he asked. "I don't know," she replied hoarsely, without looking back.

"What are we going to do now?" he said aloud, after she had closed the door behind her and disappeared around the corner. "Let us make of it a day well spent. We will let ourselves be discouraged by nothing. Rather, adversities, both large and small, shall ennoble us." He stood with his back to the wall and drew a line in pencil on the wallpaper above his head. "One metre seventy, at the very least," he said. "It is getting awfully cold in here," he thought, peering into the stove. There was no fire to be seen and the metal was cold enough to place his hand on the grill. "We'll just have to empty it," he said. He fetched the dustpan from the kitchen and began scraping the contents onto it with his hands. After he had progressed a bit, the ash and embers became too hot for him to continue. "Still, it all has to go," he said. He fetched a milk can full of water and emptied it into the stove slowly, through a hole in the cap. Whenever the cloud of steam became too dense, he waited for the hissing to stop, then went on. A sourish smell filled the room. He dug out the steaming, black chunks of coal and found at the bottom, just above the grate, two crossed keys; the bits were misshapen and the shanks had fused together. The outermost coat of metal peeled away like a dry scab. He put his find in a little cardboard box and placed it on the table. Then he built a new fire and looked into the flames through the opened slits in the loading door. Little tufts of smoke blurred and spread through the room. "It looks," he said quietly, turning on the radio and stepping up to the window, "as though the sun is coming through." "You are listening to Bach's cantata for the Second Day of Christmas," the announcer said.

Frits tuned the radio to the clearest frequency, ran into his bedroom, came back with his tin of tobacco and, seated on the divan, rolled a cigarette so quickly that he was able to light it at the very moment the erratic noise of tuning instruments had ceased and he heard the tapping of the conductor's baton. "Now I am happy," he said aloud and grinned.

The concert commenced with a prelude for violin and trumpet. "As long as no one rings the bell now," he thought, leaning forward and peering through the mica pane at the sparks and flames.

After the cantata came three arrangements for soprano, violin and organ. When these were over, the announcer said: "Until a quarter to twelve you will hear The Luna Ensemble." Quiet, slow waltz music began. He turned off the set, closed part way the vent at the bottom of the stove and stretched. "I'll go out for a little walk," he said.

Outside the sunlight had palled to a grey glare. He took a deep breath, sucked in his stomach and followed the river in the direction of the city. After a while he turned down a broad street and walked slowly, glancing at each shop window he passed. "I won't take the tram," he thought, "that is a saving. Besides, I'm not going anywhere." Turning right, he came to a broad square. He was getting ready to cross it when a young man came up, paused beside him and said: "Van Egters." "Well, well," Frits said with a smile, "so you are still with us." Neither of them moved to pull a hand from a pocket.

The fellow was somewhat shorter than Frits, and his left eye socket was covered by a black, oval patch held in place by a dark cord around his head. His nose was pointed, his mouth marked by thin, stubby lips and his facial complexion by an unsavoury pallor. Curly yellow hair grew sparsely on the top of his head. The grey overcoat he had on was too short and too widely tailored.

"I suppose you're going home?" Frits asked. "I was just on my way into town." "That is a diplomatic way of saying: I don't hold it against you that I have run into you," the other said. "I suppose you could say that, Maurits," said Frits.

"In any case, you've played another nasty trick on me, Egters," the man said. "God forbid! Whatever have I done?" Frits asked. "Yeah, damn it, Lande and that crone of his at the door."

They stood grinning at each other. "Let's go for a cup of coffee," said Maurits, "you have time for that, don't you?" "Well, if it doesn't take too long," Frits said. "There's somewhere I have to be this afternoon." "I know a quiet place to sit on Zonsteeg," Maurits said. They went down a crowded thoroughfare, crossed two canals and entered a café along a narrow alleyway. A radio behind the bar was murmuring softly. They sought out a quiet corner and sat down at a table with an orange reading lamp. Frits ordered coffee.

"So what is the story?" he asked. "Why did you swipe that money? Did he get it back?" "Yes, man, damn it, of course he got it back," Maurits said, "but only after you shot off your big mouth again." "All right, we will get to that in a bit," Frits said. "So why did you pinch it? Because you couldn't resist?" "I've hit rock bottom," Maurits said with a grimace. "I've hit solid rock bottom." He leaned back. "I'm penniless. I spent too much and I still have so many payments to make." "But what about the criminality?" Frits asked. "Is there no money in that any more?"

"You must be joking, I live in utter respectability, I haven't lifted a thing for weeks," said Maurits. "In fact, I'm studying very hard, I plan to take my bachelor's next year already." "So what got into you, to make you take that money?" Frits asked. "Any fool would know that it could be marked." "All that moaning and groaning," said the other, "you shouldn't have gone off blathering. And then that old hag, out to make a ruction on the stairs, that was all I needed. She said that you had said that I had a criminal bent, that you knew much more and that you considered me capable of anything. That's no way to talk, damn it." "I never," Frits said. "Come now, don't try to kid me," said Maurits.

"I will tell you exactly what I said," said Frits. "I said you were a person who experienced moments of weakness, and that they should understand that. And you know very well that I am not the kind of person who says: I know much more than that. I'm not the kind of gasbag who would say something like that. I say: I know this or I know that, or I say nothing at all. My having said: I know much more than that, well they dreamed that up themselves. People always try to hoodwink you; you should know that by now. They send up a balloon, to see how you react."

"And not that I was capable of anything? Or that they should take care? Or that I had a criminal bent?" He slurped back saliva as he spoke.

"What nonsense," said Frits, "what a load of twaddle. I said that you were weak and that you did not hold the property of others in particularly high regard. But criminal—the word never crossed my lips. They were only trying to get your goat. What I said was: God only knows what a person will do, one can never know beforehand. That's true, isn't it? Everything is in His hands." They laughed.

"Besides," Frits went on, "if I had wanted to do you in, I could easily have done so." Maurits leaned over closely now and pulled back his lips, revealing his gums. "Have I ever told anyone what happened there on that canal? Or about that telephone? I don't talk about that. Never, to no one." "Damn," Maurits said, placing his right hand on the table. "Stubby fingers, gnawed nails," Frits thought. "You had better keep your mouth shut," said Maurits, "you talk too much." "Come now," Frits said, "I know what I'm saying. Don't worry. Besides, I have a great respect and fondness for you." Maurits grimaced.

"Do you know what that reminds me of?" Frits said suddenly. "Of my grandfather, who's dead now, the old fart. He told me once, very gravely, that a man had told him something and made him promise never to breathe a word of it to anyone. That man was already dead, my grandfather said. And I asked him: so what was it, exactly, that he told you? And he said to me: I can't tell you, I promised."

They grinned. Maurits ordered two coffees. "What do you actually think of me?" he asked, when the waiter had removed the empty cups. "You know very well," Frits said, "that I hold you in high regard. Your acuity is amazing, incisive, but unfortunately you have chosen the road that leads to destruction. Prompted largely by feelings of humiliation and a lack of self-esteem, which is what produces the hatred. A textbook example."

"And what about my face?" asked Maurits. "A keen face," Frits said. "If you started wearing spectacles, rimless ones and flat at the top, you would have a fantastically hard-bitten, penetrating face. That eye of yours will always be a burden, of course." Maurits fell silent. "Have you read that book by that American writer, with the fellow from the garage who had only one eye?" "No," Maurits said, leaning his chin on one hand. "The fellow had an empty socket," Frits said, "but never covered it. Pus ran out of it. And always whining about how he could never get a woman. But he had only himself to blame. A neat patch over it, a clean face, that was all. You have only yourself to blame."

"And what about my hair?" Maurits asked. "Well, you're starting to go bald at the corners," said Frits. "Not at all," Maurits said, running a careful hand over his coarse but thinly grouped hairs. "I've started having it massaged lately. That makes it grow like mad. I've notice that, that more of it is coming in. Can't you see?" "But you rub some kind of goo on it, grease or something," said Frits, "that's awfully bad for it.

You shouldn't use anything on your hair except for water. That has been proven." "Do you think that's really true?" Maurits asked. "You can put as much energy as you like into your hair," Frits went on, "but if you smear greasy filth on it, it won't help. It plugs the pores, the scalp becomes inflamed."

"I've been thinking about what you said, about those spectacles," Maurits said. "But I never know whether you are pulling my leg. I can never figure that out." "I do pull a leg now and then," said Frits, "but about those spectacles, I mean that." "And what was it you said again?" Maurits asked. "Spectacles with no rims," said Frits, "oval lenses. The earpieces attached directly to the glass, and each lens flattened on top; a good gleam to them, you'll see that I'm right." Maurits was silent. "Let's get out of here," Frits said. He paid the bill. On the way back, they took the same route they had followed there.

"Those waiters earn a mint," said Frits as they picked their way along a narrow stretch of pavement, "that's a good job to have at the moment." "I used to have an evening job, helping out in a bar," Maurits said, "at the Clivia." "Is that a fact?" Frits asked. "That's news to me. When was that?" "Until last week," said Maurits. "You have to work awfully late then, don't you?" Frits asked, "but it pays wonderfully." "Yes, that's true," said Maurits, "but it's horrible. One evening this big, fat fellow was in there again, drunk as a lord. He was short of breath, I could tell. So I ask him: would you like some ice? He says: Yes, on my head. Everyone laughing. So I took a bowl of it and dumped it on his head. They all laughed till they split, but I caught hell. You can't keep that up."

"And where does your money come from these days?" asked Frits. "Petty crime?" "You and your crime," Maurits said. "But if you happen to come across something that's not nailed down, you don't leave it to fend for itself, do you?" asked Frits.

"At home I've got a nice coat you could buy," Maurits said. "Do you have a moment?"

"Wait a second," said Frits, feeling around in his coat, "I've still got that sugar." He pulled the orange paper from his pocket, shook out a few sugar cubes and offered one to Maurits. They walked on, sucking on the sweets without talking.

"I already have a good coat," said Frits. "And besides, it seems rather risky to me to walk around town wearing a coat that I cannot call my legal and indisputable property. I could hardly say: I bought and paid for it myself, from the firm of Maurits Duivenis, tailors. What kind of a coat is it? Where did you get it? I'm awfully curious."

"Traded it without consulting the former owner," Maurits said. "I had a raincoat that was awfully old and tattered, covered in stains. I traded it in at a café on Weststraat. For a nice, heavy gabardine. A stroke of misfortune for that fellow, of course, when he saw that old rag of mine hanging on the stand." He burst out in giggling laughter.

"But when it comes to bicycles," Frits said, "I must warn you against that anew. There are really too many risks involved. They can put you away for a year."

"But tell me, in all earnest," asked Maurits, "what do you think of me?" "I shall always follow your exploits with great interest," said Frits. "I continue to hope that you will get far in life. But the fact of the matter is, you can't keep anything to yourself. When we used to walk to school together in the morning, even then you used to tell me everything. About that cupboard, I've kept my mouth shut about that. And that fire in the underground bike shed, that too. And about that handcart. It's not a problem as far as I'm concerned, but you never know what other people will do." "But I don't tell them nearly as much as I do you, either," said Maurits.

Close to Frits's house they bade each other farewell with a wave of the hand. Frits closed the door to the hallway and bolted it, added coal to the stove and sat down by the window. He kept getting up and walking to the kitchen for a drink of water, then sitting down, looking out of the window and getting up for a drink again. "The sun has lost a good deal of its strength already," he thought. It was two o'clock.

He rolled a cigarette and, unable to locate his lighter, lit it with a match, then started a fire in the heavy glass ashtray. He added matches, wads of paper and fallen tulip petals to the blaze, until the smoke rolled through the room and the flame was as high as his hand. With a rapid movement he placed the hot ashtray on the stove, waited until all the combustibles had been consumed, then put an end to the smoke by laying a book atop the ashtray. "That is that," he said, opening a window. The smoke rose quickly up the wall; he watched the trails of vapour and ash as they went. After closing the window, he went into his room and remained standing before the bookcase. "Today would be an excellent opportunity to arrange things in here," he thought. Until a quarter to four he remained seated on the bed, shivering and leafing through book after book.

He grew hungry, got himself some bread in the kitchen and examined the store of goods in the pantry. He opened a tin of salmon, ate the contents with a tablespoon and stuffed the empty tin beneath the rubbish, all the way at the bottom of the bin. Then he ate half the kidney beans that were lying on a plate, took three slices of cheese from a paper wrapper and ground them slowly between his teeth. After that he raised a bottle of milk to his lips and took six big gulps. "Still, this is hardly what one could call a meal," he thought. He took a chunk of lard from a tin, melted it in the frying pan and dipped bread into it which, sucking air through his teeth to temper the heat, he devoured in huge bites.

Then he went to the fire, sat down and began to think. "I want to see a Christmas tree," he thought. "Viktor has one, I'm sure of that." He remained sitting for a few hours, and turned on the radio. On the medium wave he found nothing to his liking, the long-wave band was filled with static, but on the short wave he found a Polish station playing martial music. He leaned back on the divan as darkness fell. "That's what I've forgotten," he thought, went into the kitchen and boiled an egg, hung the saucepan, nice and clean, back on its hook and, after eating the egg, threw the shells into the fire. "I can't show up at Viktor's any earlier than seven," he said aloud.

Entering the hallway, he turned on the light, examined his face closely in the mirror and squeezed out a few blackheads and a small pustule beside his nose. "The pores are wide and coarse," he thought, "the hairs are bristly, to be sure, but too far apart. That is why I cannot grow a moustache."

When he returned to the living room, a woman was speaking on the radio. He ran through the frequencies, then switched back and forth only between the short and long waves, slapped the side of the set and turned it off. He combed his hair, brushed his teeth and left the house. It was a quarter to seven.

Following the river past Louis Spanjaard's door, he crossed the bridge and rang the bell at a tall house on the far side, with two towery extensions. A woman's voice came through the speaking tube, then an electrical mechanism clicked and the door opened. He climbed three broad flights of stairs, past windows of coloured glass, and was met at the top by a young man with a ruddy face, curly black hair and spectacles. He had on a corduroy jacket and was rubbing his hands together. "How are you this evening, Commander Frits?" he asked. "Come further. It's damned cold out here."

They entered a room lined with bookcases. A heavy carpet covered the floor. The room was heated by a pot-belly stove. "Shall I turn on some more lights?" he asked. "No," Frits said, "only a waste of electricity." A reading lamp with a white shade was lit on the mantelpiece.

"How is it going?" the young man asked, "how are things at home?"

"Very bad," Frits said in a cheerful tone, "very bad, Viktor. Let us call a spade a spade. Let us, when something is bad, say: bad."

"I see," said Viktor. "In a word: bad. And how are your parents?" "A very shrewd question," Frits replied. "Rather like asking, when there's a thunderstorm: what's the weather like at the moment? No, no, that's a lame comparison. In any case, miserable."

They were sitting close to the stove, which Viktor poked up with a length of wire. "Yes, I'm listening," he said. "It gets on my nerves," said Frits. "I'm only waiting for them to hang themselves or beat each other to death. Or set the house on fire. For God's sake, let it be that. So why hasn't it happened yet? But let us not despair. All things come to those who wait."

"I see, I see," said Viktor, staring at the floor.

"Affliction cometh forth," Frits said in a solemn tone. "Everything cometh forth, gradually, nice and slow, but it cometh. Porridge for dessert every evening. My mother puts the sugar bowl on the table. With a little spoon in it. For a level bowl of porridge you need, say, three spoons full. But listen to this. Are you listening?" "Yes, of course," said Viktor, "I am all ears."

"Pay careful attention," Frits said, rising to his feet. "Everyone takes sugar from the pot with that little spoon. What does my father do? He digs out the sugar with his own dessert spoon. Still clean and unused, I'll admit, but it drives me mad to see it, I'm going crazy! I feel like bing, pow, hitting the roof. Lord God Almighty, does that make sense to you? Or not?" He sat down again. "Tell me honestly."

"I understand completely," Viktor said, "it is difficult. To be truthful, I recognize that. I think your parents are fine people. They stand head and shoulders above a great many others I know, by reason of their goodness. It seems to me—"

"But everything cometh forth," said Frits, "one huge, demonic extravaganza. I only wish that I could stir it up, fan the fires. Lessons in disembowelment. If things have to come that far, then let it be quickly. Am I keeping you?"

"Oh no," said Viktor, handing him a box of tobacco. "Roll one of mine. I don't want one." "Still, I hope," said Frits, sliding his chair up closer and leaning over, "that I will come home one day and find him hanging neatly, like a fine side of beef, in the doorway. Between the sliding doors. That would be any easy spot to place hooks for a pair of gymnastic rings. Bestow this upon us, oh Lord. What a world."

"What does he do with his tie? What about that?" Viktor asked. "His tie, you mean his necktie?" "Yes, what does he do with that?" "When he is at home all day," Frits said, "he doesn't wear one at all, no, he spends the whole day without it. What are you driving at?" Viktor stared into the flames. "Well, sometimes, he'll put one on, but then he stands before the mirror for half an hour, tugging at it and adjusting it. What does that mean?"

"When someone stops wearing a tie," said Viktor, "or spends a long time picking one out and a long time tying and adjusting it, then he is not in a good way."

"That diagnosis is news to me," Frits said, "top-notch. But the fact that someone is not in a good way was already known to me. It offers no new insight. How are your studies coming along?"

"I have an exam this month," Viktor said. "I truly don't understand," said Frits, "how you could choose such a senseless subject: classical languages. How the hell did that happen? Why not law or medicine? How do you stand it?"

"That, I believe, is something to which you will never reconcile yourself," said Viktor with a smile. "My day will be complete," said Frits, "when you pass your bar examinations and argue your first case. There can be no doubt about it, you will end up doing law, mark my words. Sooner or later that is what it will be."

"Viktor, are you two coming in for tea?" a woman's voice called out. They crossed the landing and entered a large room with light wallpaper. The unpainted wooden chairs were upholstered in grey wool. In the corner by the door was a black piano, in the corner across from it a playpen with a child sitting in it and rocking back and forth. "Lidia, Herman, both in good health, I hope," said Frits, shaking hands with a young woman with big eyes and a tall, thin young man.

They sat down at a low table and drank tea from blue bowls. The woman took the child out of the playpen. "Here's Joost," she said, "that's right, here you are!" She sat down and placed the baby boy on her lap. "The head is too large," Frits thought. The way the child's wispy hair hung in a wreath around its skull gave the impression of a bald spot in the middle, while the skin on its neck was wrinkled. The little face was wry and oldish. The child went on rocking back and forth in a pendular motion.

"Hello, Joost!" Frits called out a few times. "A year and a half and more," he thought, "but he still doesn't respond to his own name." Lidia put the little boy down on the floor, on his feet, but he dropped immediately to hands and knees and began crawling slowly. Close to the window, the child tried to pull itself up on the cover of the divan. "Are you trying to get up there?" she asked, lifting him onto it. The child sat rocking the whole time without a sound, keeping his gaze fixed on a blossoming potted begonia on the sill. "So, now you're sitting pretty!" Lidia cried. The child dropped to all fours, crept to the window and grabbed the red blossom, which broke off right away.

"Whoa!" Frits shouted. "Hey!" Lidia cried loudly and walked over to him.

The child dropped the flower and began to cry. Even after Lidia had picked him up, he went on bawling. Frits retrieved the flower and stuck it into a vase of tulips, so deeply that a tiny bit of stem touched water. "Time for bed, Joost," Lidia said, and left with the child on her arm.

"Let's retire to the other room," Viktor said. "Herman is quiet this evening," Frits said, once they were back in Viktor's room. "You left the light on in here."

"Yes, I always do that when I'm in the next room," said Viktor, "it's such a fuss, trying to find the plug and socket in the dark."

"It's taking on highly interesting forms, Herman's boy's palsy," Frits said, "it's wondrous to see, the way he shakes and shakes. Do you think he goes on shaking like that at night, while he is asleep? An aunt of mine—well, she's not my aunt at all, we only call her that—has a white dog with the same thing. It fell into the water once, while it was recovering from distemper, and that has never gone away. Its forelegs shake all the time, it can't walk straight on them." Placing his hands on the floor, he gave a demonstration. "Only when the dog falls asleep does the shaking slow, and finally it stops completely."

"I think it's a phase he's going through," said Viktor, "he will grow out of it after a time."

"Let us hope so," said Frits, rolling another cigarette from Viktor's tin, "but madness is never far away. One little defect in the construction, one screw loose and the whole mechanism grinds to a halt. God's handiwork is great." "Let's hope not," said Viktor, "for that is a terrible thing."

"Have you ever seen one of them?" Frits asked. "I don't mean a moron, with one of those skulls big enough for two and an idiotic gleam in his eye; no, I mean a cheerful lunatic, that's a glorious thing. Haven't you ever seen that man in a top hat who walks around in the city?" "No," Viktor said.

"He sings, after his own fashion," Frits went on. "Well, as a matter of fact, not a lot of sound comes out. People give him money, but that's not why he does it. When they lean out of the window and throw it down to him, he leaves it lying in the street. It is truly a sight to behold. I had no idea at first that the man was insane. The children torment him no end. I was coming down Alkmaarsestraat one time and they were throwing potatoes at him. When I walked past he said: Sir, I am a famous singer, but they don't appreciate you until they carry you out between six planks. That sounded very good, but maybe he taught himself that from some book, or maybe someone else said it to him. That would be a pity."

"Or that idiot on Tessel," he continued, "remind me to tell you about that later. Six or seven years ago, in our neighbourhood, there was a big, husky fellow who walked around all the time shouting moo! Children followed him and yelled at him, but always from a distance, because it was a frightening thing. You can imagine: I see him walking along the canal and he comes to an open window. A housemaid is getting ready to stick her arm out to shake a duster, and at that very moment that head appears and shouts: Moo! Very deep, bellowing, like a huge, dangerous cow. I've never seen anyone come unglued like that girl did." He coughed with laughter. "You know how he got that way? The man was a concert violinist and he had already become a bit peculiar, a bit different. He was a good violinist too. And he thought he was world-famous. But he wasn't. One day he imagined that he had received an invitation from America, for a concert tour there. He and his wife left by ship. During the crossing his wife jumped overboard, out of desperation, and drowned. When he came back, he was completely, stark-raving mad."

"You know," Viktor said, peering into the fire, "that I grew up in Haarlem before I moved here. Acquaintances of ours there have a son who is not completely retarded. But he's slow and peculiar, and he's also two metres six. Loony as he is, though, he's also a mathematical genius. He's been on the radio any number of times. He can calculate anything: multiplication, division, the most impossible figures. He works at an office, in the bookkeeping department. The bookkeepers get bored sometimes, and one day they decided just for fun to see if they could pick each other up. And then that boy lifted his boss—a bald little fellow—like a baby, with only one arm." He poked at the fire. "What were you saying about Tessel?" he asked.

"That's right," Frits said. "Years ago I was camping on Tessel. In Oude Schild, I think it was, there was a man who ate paper." Viktor barked with laughter. "He ate paper. He always had a wet ball of paper in his mouth. Whenever he found another scrap on the street, he would take that ball out of his gob, poke a hole in it with his finger, stuff the new piece into it and then tuck the whole wad back in his cheek. He sold weather trees. No, wait, I think that was someone else. Or maybe it was him after all."

"What are those, weather trees?" Viktor asked. "Sort of like weather houses, with a little weatherman and weatherwoman, but then a tree. How should I know, I never bought one. It's easy enough to tell for yourself what the weather is going to be like. I do know that we always asked him—but maybe that was some other simpleton—to give us a forecast. We would ask him: What's the weather going to be like, Leen? And he would say: if the weather is warm, you won't catch a chill. Then we'd moan and complain and he would say: Why don't you buy a weather tree? Then you'd always know what the weather will be like. In this extremely weird, hoarse voice." He fell silent for a moment, tapping his fingernails against his teeth.

"Go on, what else do you have for me?" Viktor asked.

"They say such bizarre things," Frits continued. "A doctor once told me that they asked one of the loonies in the asylum: What are you going to do when you leave here? He says: Oh, maybe I'll become an actor, I've always had a flair for that. Or else I'll work for a newspaper, I did that too for a few years. But there's always a chance that I'll pick up my old calling; in actual fact, I'm a teapot."

"God," Viktor said, breathless with laughter, "you're on a roll tonight." "Shall I stop?" Frits asked. The little clock on the desk said a quarter to nine. "You're slow, did you know that?" Frits asked. "It's actually nine o'clock." "Yes, I know," Viktor said. "Why isn't there a Christmas tree in the house?" asked Frits. "I thought about having one at first," Viktor answered, "but then you need candles and all that other rubbish. There's one at my parents' house in Haarlem, I was there yesterday and the day before. Herman and Lidia thought about it too, but the baby is still too little to appreciate it and everything is still so hard to get. So finally they didn't do it."

"We never had one at home," said Frits, "except for when we were very little. Not after that. They thought it was nonsense. But it's not. It is a tree, and that tree is in the house. That in itself is something special, something unusual. Then you have the candles. A candle is something you almost never see, except for in the cellar, or for when the lights go out, but there they are, in that tree, and they're burning. Imagine that. Burning—"

"Frits, Frits," Viktor said. He looked at Frits's face, then added quickly: "No, by all means, go on. You're absolutely right. I know very well what you mean."

"Damn," Frits said, "you think I'm jabbering. Well, all right. Perhaps I am." He sighed. "What?" he said. "Is that coming from upstairs?" They heard a loud, steady knocking. "That's Joost," Viktor said. "He's awake. He sleeps for a bit, then he's awake for the rest of the night. He bumps his noggin against the headboard of his cot. A few hundred times, then he pauses for a bit, then starts in again."

"It sounds as though the carpenters are working late," said Frits. "Mark my words, that child is deranged. Completely deranged, that's the long and the short of it. The St Vitus boogie-woogie, poltergeist syndrome, general feeble-mindedness."

"Do you feel like having a sandwich?" Viktor asked. The knocking continued. "That sounds good," said Frits. "I thought, just a little while ago, that you were about to say something. About Rageman, or something." "Hagelman," Viktor said. "All right then, Hagelman," said Frits, "who is that?" "You don't know him," said Viktor. "That was in Haarlem too. The man went crazy. He went to the doctor. The doctor wanted him to explain everything. He told him that a beast had entered his house, a mad beast." "A colleague, as it were," Frits said.

"He started chasing it," Viktor continued. "Over highways and byways. Then suddenly, he told the doctor, sitting in the middle of the woods he saw a little devil. He picked it up and petted it and said: You're a lovely little devil. And then, doctor, he said, then I knew that I had found it. Yes, the doctor said, but I have spoken to any number of people who have found it, and they had to take a rest for a long, long time. You need to take a rest as well. Come back on Thursday—that's right, I think it was a Thursday—at one thirty." "Wonderful," Frits said. "Just listen to that pounding up there."

"Wait, wait," Viktor went on, "we're not there yet. He came back that next Thursday at noon. The receptionist said the doctor wasn't in. What, Mr Hagelman said, at the appointed hour the doctor is not in? This is the appointed hour! Of course, the receptionist said, but your appointment is at one thirty. In any case, amid all that commotion, Mr Hagelman claimed that one thirty was too late. All right, the nurse said, then you just come in at one. Ah, of course, Hagelman said, of course! One o'clock is the golden mean. I will return at the golden mean. He talked to the doctor till he turned blue, but the doctor couldn't make head or tail of it. A few days later, Hagelman's wife calls the doctor: Doctor, my husband is in such a bad way, I'm afraid something terrible will happen. The doctor goes there and sees the man—this was in the middle of the night—with a bucket, tossing water on the children in their bedroom. They needed to be baptized, he said. Those children, there were three of them, they thought it was all in fun. It was a warm night, by the way."

The knocking above their heads stopped.

"Then the doctor knew," he went on, "that things were completely out of hand, but it wasn't that easy to get him into an institution. The fellow was still quite lucid in some ways. But he had a friend he listened to unconditionally. The doctor said: It truly would be the best thing, I will call Mr Perel—that was the friend—and you will see that he also thinks that would be best for your health. What? Hagelman says. Talk to Perel about the thread? We can't do that, that's out of the question. In any case, they finally convinced him. He's home again now, that man, he seems to have recovered a bit."

"Viktor and Frits, would you like to have a cup of coffee with us?" they heard Lidia call out. "If you insist," Frits said. In Lidia and Herman's parlour a gramophone was playing. "This is a damned good tango," Viktor said, "listen carefully. In a few seconds he's going to say: 'highs in the low sixties'." The four of them listened until the music halted and the singing voice spoke a few words quickly in Spanish. "You're right, I heard it," Frits said laughing. The doorbell rang.

"Who could that be?" Herman wondered aloud. He went into the hallway. They heard him shout down the speaking tube and open the door. Within a few moments a black-haired girl in a dark-red cloak came into the room in front of him, followed by a small, gaunt young man in a thick blue overcoat. "Good evening," the young man said, panting. They placed their scarves, a handbag and gloves on the table. "I'll come right to the point," said the young man, without looking at the others around the table. "Could we stay here tonight?" A silence descended. They all lowered their eyes. "I'm afraid that won't be possible," Herman said. "I have guests; they've already gone to bed. And Frits van Egters, you know him, don't you"—"pleased to meet you," said Frits; "pleased to meet you," the visitor said—"he is spending the night as well, so there's really no room." Lidia pressed her heel down on Frits's foot.

"You could stay in the alcove for fifteen minutes, Piet," Viktor said. "Couldn't he, Herman? Then we'll just turn up the volume for a while."

"I see," said the young man, "that's unfortunate. Come along, Irene." He gathered their accoutrements hastily, his hands all atremble. Then they left without a farewell. "Good riddance," Herman said after no one had spoken for a minute. "That's been taken care of."

"It's time for me too," said Frits. "But with all of this we still haven't had our sandwich," Viktor said quietly. "Forget it,"

Frits said, "it doesn't matter. It's ten past ten." "No," Viktor said when they had arrived in the hall, "we'll have a bite to eat." Going to his room, he made a few cheese sandwiches. Frits ate two of them, pacing back and forth with his coat on. "What are you reading these days?" he asked, stopping by the writing table and picking up a little book with a grey cloth cover. "That's one you should really read," Viktor replied, "you would definitely enjoy it."

"*The Small-time Neurotic: A Handbook for Better Living*," Frits read. "You can borrow it," said Viktor. Frits closed the book and stuck it in his coat pocket, took a deep breath and said goodbye.

On the street outside he looked at the paving stones, which were covered in delicate crystals of ice. The air felt moist, a light wind was blowing from the north.

"This could be the freezing point," he thought, "it's possible."

Arriving home, he entered the house without a sound. His parents' coats and headwear were hanging on the stand. There was no light from the living room. "The turtledoves have come home to roost," he whispered. In the kitchen he found traces of a hot meal: a frying pan with a few fried potatoes and a pan of porridge. The gravy in the meat pan was still warmish. He dipped a slice of bread into it and ate it in four bites. Then he went to bed.

He fell asleep quickly and awoke at six in the morning. "I did not dream," he thought. "This will be a workday." After passing water he promptly fell asleep again. He found himself once more in Lidia and Herman's big room. Lidia had laid her left leg over an armrest, so that her thigh was exposed. As he looked at it the skin grew drab and chapped, and blue veins arose all over it.

Lidia became aware of his gaze, but remained seated. "Take a look across the street," she said.

He went to the window. "I don't see anything," he said. "Where is Herman?" he asked, turning around. Herman had disappeared. "Take a good look across the street," Lidia said. He strained his eyes and suddenly it was afternoon outside. He saw that the river was only a few metres wide. Across the street, at the first-floor window of a large house, a boy dressed in a blue jersey and grey shorts was doing a handstand on the sill. The sashes had been removed from their tracks.

Again and again, the boy let himself fall from the window with a flourish, but caught himself each time at the last moment, pulled himself up and started all over again. On the street below a girl stood, looking up and calling out to him over and over, but Frits could not make out the words.

"He does the same thing every day," said Lidia, who had come to stand beside Frits, "can you imagine how it gets on our nerves?" "Yes, I can imagine," said Frits, "it is a terrible thing to have to watch."

He awoke, saw that it was five minutes to seven, and fell asleep once more.

VI

ON FRIDAY AFTERNOON the clouds were so heavy that the office lights had to be turned on at a quarter past three. Frits gathered scraps of paper from his desk, blew away the cigarette ash, then leaned back in his chair. "Were it only Saturday already," he thought, "then this weather would put me in the right mood."

"At elementary school," he said to himself, "the sky sometimes grew so dark on Saturday morning, an hour before the bell, that they had to light all four lamps, those globes. On Saturday, an hour before school was over. What made that so wonderful?" "Or the last day of school, before the summer holidays," he thought, "when a downpour came, or thunder, just before the bell rang. There was no greater happiness. Why? Strange."

He bit a corner off a piece of stationery, chewed on it and spit the wad onto the floor. "Now think," he mumbled, "what was it I was going to do tonight? Of course, we're going to the pictures, the *divertissement* of our century. The Lantern, two seats for the late-evening showing. We'll take Viktor along. In fact, life is not all that complicated," he thought. "Modern science is a boon to mankind."

At twenty past four he packed his briefcase, hung his coat over the back of his chair and waited for five minutes. Then he arranged everything on his desk in careful order, put on his coat and shuffled quietly out of the door. In the corridor he picked up the pace, but without stepping loudly, and so arrived in the foyer, where with a push of a button he summoned the lift and made his descent. As he left the building he began to hum. There was barely a breath of wind. He cycled past the cinema to pick up the tickets, took an easterly detour on the way home and, at the bridge, rang the bell of the house with two towers.

"Who's there?" came a man's voice through the speaking tube. "Viktor Poort, you old gasbag," Frits called out, "come downstairs on the double. And make it quick. This is Frits." "I'll look if he's here, but I don't think so," the voice answered. A few moments later another voice called out: "Commander Frits, knock and it shall be opened unto you. Come on up." "No, you come down," Frits shouted through the grillework, "before it's too late. I'm in a hurry." The door swung open and Viktor came down the stairs.

"I have seats for a quarter past nine at The Lantern," Frits said, "and pricey, it cost me a bundle. You're coming along, right?" Viktor turned up the collar of his jacket. "Well," he said, "I—" "You stand there like an old woman with an ingrown toenail," said Frits, "who won't answer the door because she's too afraid of catching a cold."

"There's so much I have to do later this evening," said Viktor, "I don't think I'll be able. To be honest, I was thinking about stopping by your place after dinner, for half an hour or so." "Come now," Frits said, "I've got tickets, I paid good money for them; what a waste."

"You'll get rid of that ticket," Viktor said. "It's awfully kind of you, but I can't. I have to stay at home, for all kinds of things. But I was thinking, after dinner, of coming by for bit. But I'm not absolutely sure."

They said goodbye and Viktor went inside. "The evening is going to be a complete shambles," Frits said, "that much is sure, that is eminently clear. No reason to doubt that for a moment." He cycled home at high speed, put his bike in the storage cupboard and entered the house without removing his coat.

His father was sitting by the fire in his dressing gown. Spanning the armrest of his chair was a green plank from the cupboard, on which he had neatly arranged a number of books and papers. He was writing. Over the gown, around his waist, was a leather belt. When he looked up Frits saw that there were red spots on his forehead and cheeks, which he had rubbed with ointment.

"Well, well," he said, "you've made yourself quite at home here. Next time you go to the beach, be sure to put a towel over your face. The sun can be quite beastly." "What was that?" his father asked. "I asked where the scorched face came from," said Frits. "Come again?" his father asked. "Those raw spots, where did you get them?" Frits asked, pointing at his own face. "Oh," the man said, "I used a washcloth this morning, but didn't realize how hard those things are." "I believe," Frits said, "that you accidentally used the scouring pads known and loved by millions."

He sat down by the radio, put his hand out to it, but withdrew it again. He went to hang his coat in the hallway. "Has mother gone out?" he asked once he had returned. "She's doing a little shopping," his father replied. The clock said ten past five. "Can you believe this weather?" Frits asked, peering up at the sky. "I'd say snow is on its way," said his father.

Frits went to the kitchen and turned on the gas beneath the pan of meat. Then he bolted the door to the stairwell and rummaged through the cupboard. "Nothing," he murmured, "no articles of worth." He leaned on the windowsill and looked out over the gardens. "It's that stupid dog of Aals's," he said. Filling a glass of water at the sink, he emptied it, after quietly opening the window, onto a fat brown dog that was sitting before the neighbours' garden door. The animal leapt aside, shook itself and began to bark. He closed the window.

Suddenly he heard a rattling and a pounding at the stairwell door. He turned off the gas, moved the pan to the back of the range and opened the door. "When are you going to stop that idiocy, bolting the door all the time?" his mother said, coming in with a heavy bag of shopping, which she unpacked in the kitchen.

He went to the living room and sat on the divan. A few minutes later his mother came in as well, looked into the fire and said: "I forgot to check for the newspaper. Would you go take a look?" "It hasn't come yet," Frits said. "Yes it has," she said, "ages ago." "There's no need," said Frits, "that's impossible." "All right, then," she said, "if you're too lazy to get up." "What is it now?" his father asked. "Nothing," they replied.

Frits went down the stairs, found the newspaper in the box and brought it up. "It fell through the slot just as I got there," he said. "The clock is no longer running fast, I see." His father held out his hand and said: "I'll take that." "You stick to your work," said his mother, taking the newspaper from Frits. She sat down at the table, got up to fetch her reading glasses from the sideboard, sat down slowly again and opened the paper.

Leaning against the table, Frits looked at the reddened fingers clutching the pages. "You read like a woman," he said, "you don't move your eyes, you sway your head back and forth. That's horrible, because the columns are so narrow." "What did you say?" his father asked. "I thought I saw a name that I recognized," Frits said, looking at the paper, "but I believe I was mistaken." He sat down on the divan, pushed the curtains aside, nibbled on his fingertips and looked outside.

"Why did that sudden darkness and rain provide such a sense of exhilaration?" he thought. "I need to figure that out." "In fourth class, at the start of the summer holidays," he told himself, "we went home and I was given an empty, wooden box that had been used to hold chalk. I was standing in the hall, waiting for the rain to stop, because I had no coat with me. And I kept sniffing at that box. It was the smell of wood, fresh wood, of resin and of chalk. That much is clear, those are the facts. But how does it fit together?"

"I know," he thought suddenly, "it's simple. The final hours of school had to be sombre, in order to make the transition to days of freedom that much sharper."

His mother had set the table and was bringing in the evening meal. There was raw lamb's lettuce, potatoes, fried onions with gravy, kidney beans, and semolina pudding for dessert. They began eating without a word. "Quick, quick," Frits thought,

137

"say something." "Don't you think this weather is peculiar?" he asked his mother. "It's horrible, dark as it is," she replied. "Still, it's not as cold any more, at least not that humid cold. It's definitely not as cold any more. In the kitchen it's all right. Normally the gravy is already hard when I've turned it off at four or five. But now it was still lukewarm."

His father mixed the lettuce with the potatoes, mashing it with the back of his fork, and stirring everything together with the onions. "God, all-powerful, look upon our deeds and tribulations," Frits said to himself, watching the hand that moved the fork steadily up and down. He felt his face grow warm. "The mashing of a meal prepared with care is considered an affront to the one who made it, Father," he said, looking at his mother. She lowered her eyes. "What?" his father asked slowly, with a smile. "I didn't hear you." "No," Frits said as his mother fixed her gaze on him, "it was something else." "Did I tell you," she asked, "that I have a new key to the attic?" She stood up, went to the sideboard and showed him a key with a newly filed bit, which she had taken from the tea tray. "Very good," Frits said. "I had to hand in the old one," she said, "to show they weren't lost. It cost one guilder." "That is a fair price," said Frits.

When the pudding was served, she placed the sugar bowl on the table and waited. His father took some with his dessert spoon and sprinkled it over his plate with a tired movement. Frits felt an itching on his feet, hands and at the back of his head. "Why doesn't he wear a shirt?" he thought. "No tie, all right, if it can't be otherwise. But why not a shirt? Why doesn't someone who understands such things explain it to me?" He leaned forward, the better to see how a bit of V-necked vest stuck out from beneath the blue, sleeveless jumper: the top button was in plain sight. An oblong depression was visible at the base of the throat, below the Adam's apple.

"Tonight I'm going to The Lantern, for the late showing," he said once the meal was finished. "What's on there?" his mother asked. "*The Second Face*," he replied, "I've heard lots of good things about it. You have a bit of food on your lip." She wiped her mouth and began clearing the table. "It is still early enough for even the first showing," he thought. "Now I have two hours to kill. No cause for despair."

He went and sat by the fire. His father stood in the corner beside the window and stared outside. On the floor in front of the stove were little scraps of potato. "Wait and see whether she calls me in to dry the dishes," Frits thought. He heard his mother turn off the gas under the singing kettle, run water in the basin and place the rack on the counter beside the sink. When he heard the first object being lifted from the sop and placed in the rack, he leaned forward a bit. "Just a little longer," he thought, "she's probably going to dry them herself." His father began pacing back and forth.

"Frits, could you come and help with drying?" his mother called out. He stood up, inhaled sharply through gritted teeth, and as he left the room bumped into his father, who was standing at the bookcase closest to the door. "Was that the doorbell?" he asked. "No," Frits shouted. In the kitchen he quickly dried the plates, cups and saucers. "There's not much washing-up this evening," his mother said.

When he was seated by the fire again, he smelled his hands. "We are imperfect creatures," he said to himself, "I should have rinsed them afterwards." "The smell of my fingers, of the dish-cloth, is nothing," he thought. "A person's breath is worse. The odour of spent ether expelled regularly by the lungs. That was well put. You have different varieties." He used his little finger to root behind his molars. "You have," he thought, "breath like the odour of mouldy old overcoats that have been cooked in vinegar. Assuredly so. Then the breath of someone who has eaten too many hard-boiled eggs. But the worst is the smell of someone who has been fasting for a day. That is like spoiled milk or like the bark of a tree that has lain rotting in the water. Indeed. Five past seven."

He went into the hall, turned on the light and looked in the mirror. "Deliver me from baldness," he said, pushing back his hair and examining the hairline. "It is a gruesome infliction." He stopped and listened. "It makes the head look old, shiny and distasteful," he thought, "that is the truth. But even worse is when the bare skin is cracked or covered with little bumps." "What I do know," he said aloud, following the movements of his lips in the mirror, "is that warts are worse. Warts, what is a wart? Let us provide a good, insightful description. Why else did I go to school, if not for that?"

He went into the side room and lit the gas fire. "A wart," he said, pacing back and forth, "is a fleshy, entirely unrooted protuberance that tends to appear on neck, cheek or chin and which produces pronounced disfigurement. Good, very good."

He sat down and began digging about in his ear with a pencil. "Now for the varieties," he said, "of which there are two. The first appears, dear listeners, in the form of a low, flattened hill, hirsute, in grey or brown contrast with the skin. The second variety, however, and I suggest, ladies and gentlemen, that you make careful note of this, is fructiform, like a tiny pumpkin or cucumber, and nourished by the body through the thin stem by which it is attached." He stood up from the writing table and asked: "Any further questions?"

"Which is worse?" he thought. "Belching? Or speaking with one's mouth filled with bread, so that moist crumbs go shooting in all directions?" "This concludes today's lecture," he said aloud. "Ladies and gentlemen, I wish you a pleasant evening."

He closed the valve on the gas fire, turned off the light and crossed the hall slowly. When he entered the living room, the radio was on. "If you turn it on," he said, "then at least tune the damned thing. It's between channels. Don't you hear that scratching and crackling?" "Shit in their ears, the two of them," he mumbled, adjusting the set. A cowboy song was ending. "There is a Jan who lives in Laren and one in Deventer too," the announced said, "both of whom are celebrating their birthday today. Jan in Laren receives best wishes from Pollie and the Buning family. Jan in Deventer from everyone in his family. I won't be playing 'The Snowy Road' for you, but I believe you'll be pleased to hear the 'Why Not Tango', am I right, Jan in Deventer? After all, you've just come home and are feeling chipper again."

"It's already almost eight o'clock," Frits thought. "Viktor will be popping by." "Did you see the announcement, Frits," his mother asked, "about the death of the Everts' baby?" "No," Frits said, "it had been taken to the hospital, if I'm not mistaken. How old was it?" "Four months," his mother said. "Terrible, isn't it?" "Oh," Frits said, "I'm not so sure. Perhaps it would have gone soft in the head, or developed a propensity to scabies. No use to anyone. Good riddance to bad rubbish." "You're mad," she said. "All appearances to the contrary," Frits said, "you are wrong about that." "What is it now?" his father asked. "Oh, he says that it's all just as well that the Everts' child is dead," said his mother. "No," Frits said, "that's not what I'm saying at all." "Don't pay him any mind," his father said, "he's only blathering."

"Our final request this evening is for 'Grandfather's Clock', as performed by Tulleman," the radio said, "for all personnel at the radio relay in Rotterdam and for Mrs Blijding in Hilversum." Frits squeezed his left cheek in time to the rhythm of the song. "I need to think things through clearly," he thought, "I need a chance to think things through."

He went into the hall, stood before the door leading to the stairs, then suddenly put on his coat. "I'll drop by, and get Louis to go with me," he thought, "leave in good time." He left the house without a sound.

From the riverside he saw a light on in Louis's room. He rang the bell. "If you're quick about it," he shouted up the stairs, "you can come along to The Lantern." A light on the landing was turned on and he saw Louis standing there, wearing a blue shirt. "That won't be possible, I'm afraid," he shouted back, "I have a visitor. Viktor is here." "Of course," Frits mumbled to himself, "I should have known." "Then I'll try to palm it off on someone," he shouted back, pulling the door closed. "The day is void, and the evening without form," he mumbled. "There's still one chance left. Let's stop by Jaap's."

He took off at a trot and turned down the canal lined with warehouses. At number seventy-one he saw Jaap and Joosje carrying the pram down the outside steps.

"I have a seat for a quarter past nine at The Lantern," he said after greeting them, "but I believe you have other plans." "That's right," Jaap said, "we're on my way to see my parents. That's more or less the same direction, though. Will you walk with us?"

The pram hobbled over the granite paving stones. "One seat only?" Jaap asked. "Who was the other person?" "You don't know them," Frits replied, "they fell ill." "But you can get rid of it, can't you?" Jaap asked.

"Oh yes," Frits said, "it's just that you never know who will end up beside you. For all you know, it could be a lip-reader."

"What's that?" asked Joosje, "a what?" "A common lip-reader," Frits answered. "I believe I sense your meaning," said Jaap. "You have two sorts," Frits said, "as is so often the case. You have the extroverts, who laugh and explain things to those sitting beside them. Those are truly terrible." "Yes," Jaap said with a grin. "But the second category is much worse," Frits went on. "Those are the ones who read the subtitles out loud. Aye-aye, Jesus Christ, what an abomination. When you have

143

one of those beside you, you are in for it. And don't think for a moment that you can do anything to stop them. Don't even bother to say anything: it is not for lack of goodwill; they simply do not understand what you mean. You can say loudly to those in front and behind you: he has to keep up on his reading, otherwise he'll forget how, but that doesn't help. Impervious as alabaster they are. You can start screaming until the lights go on, but then the whole cinema will come down on you. So don't even start."

"My," Joosje said, "does it annoy you that much? I never really mind." "But I do," said Frits. Jaap and Joosje turned right. "See you tomorrow," said Frits. He headed down a long, narrow street and reached the cinema post-haste. The doorman was just setting a large sign, reading "Sold Out", on the pavement outside. Frits entered the foyer, and saw that it was full of people waiting. He pulled out his tickets and was looking around when someone tapped him on the shoulder. "He moves in mysterious ways," he thought, "it is Maurits." "I run into you at the least opportune moments," he said. "I'm trying to get a ticket," Maurits said, "do you know where I can get one?" "I have one left," said Frits, "I would rather have sat next to something more interesting, but it could be worse. One fifty-five." "May God protect me," Maurits said, "you have money to burn, I believe." He paid and accepted the ticket with the reservation stub. "You're getting your money back, and first-rate company to boot," he said, "what more could one hope for?"

"Didn't your girl feel like coming along, Frits?" he asked after the usher had shown them to their seats. "She can't stand films like this," Frits said. "Well, I'll be," Maurits said, "so you actually have one?" "You're better off having one who doesn't want to go to the cinema than not having one at all," Frits replied. "You have none; and I don't believe you ever will. But then you are truly repellent. How terrible that must be. What a fate."

"Goddam it," said Maurits, "what about my looks? What do you think of my appearance?" "It is not what one might call particularly conducive to relations with the fairer sex," Frits said, "but I know some who are in an even worse way." Coloured blocks of advertising appeared on the screen. "I've never seen this woman of yours," said Maurits.

"The whole point is that you are incapable of consorting with the other sex," Frits said. "It seems to me less than wise after intercourse to kick the girl out of bed so forcefully that she becomes lame, or at least limps about, for two days afterwards." Maurits laughed.

"You talk just like that doctor," he said, "in that French film, in… I can't remember what it was called. But you have far too good a memory for the things I tell you. Do you go around blabbing about that to everyone?" "That depends," Frits said.

The newsreel began. When the lights went up again for a moment, Maurits said: "But honestly, how do I look?" "Oh," said Frits, "you look normal; base as the next man. In any case, women don't care about looks."

The lights went down slowly and the main feature began. "This is the real thing," Frits thought when it had been going on for five minutes.

After the show, the two of them walked slowly down the street together. "Just one seat left, sir," Frits said in English, lifting a finger. "That was a good one, extraordinarily so." "You have to turn left here too, don't you?" Maurits asked. "We can walk up together." "There's no getting rid of you," Frits said, "I can tell that already." Maurits was silent. "Do you know what occurred to me just now?" Frits continued. "That you'll never benefit from those stereoscopic films. You'd simply see all those bits of colour thrown together." "Let's see how far I can go," he thought. "It is a terrible thing," he said, "having only one eye."

"The new kind of stereoscopic film, the one they're working on now, can be watched without spectacles," said Maurits. "Yes," Frits said, "but you need two eyes to perceive depth. I feel that one should call things by their proper name. Or is that a sensitive point with you? Feel free to pour out your heart, I am prepared to hold your soul up to the light like a rotten egg. Tell the doctor everything. The soul's deepest yearnings." They crossed the bridge. "If you have only one eye, that makes you a sadist, of course. Tell us a bit about that."

"I never know whether you're joshing me," said Maurits. "You make a lot of fuss, but you're digging for something. And I'm always stupid enough to talk."

"We are here at the microphone, dear listeners," said Frits in a squawky voice, "in the study of Mr Maurits Duivenis, the celebrated blabbermouth. Mr Duivenis, could we ask you a few questions?" "Does this anger you?" he asked then, in a normal voice. They followed the ground-brick path along the riverside. There, where pools of black water had gathered on the ice, ducks huddled. "Who would you choose as your victim?" Frits asked. "Age, gender and nature of bodily harm: please, do tell."

"I'd like to strangle little boys in the woods," Maurits said slowly, "simple as that." "That's too insipid," Frits said, "and not particularly original. And perverse to boot." He burst out laughing. "Did you hear the one about the man who went to the psychiatrist? Doctor, he says, I'm having an affair with a horse. Is it a mare or a stallion? the doctor asks. And the man says: Doctor, what do you think I am, abnormal!?" Maurits did not laugh.

"Come, come," Frits said, "you're rather subdued this evening. How do you stand with regard to inflicting burns with a lit cigarette? That appeals to you, doesn't it?" "What makes you think that?" asked Maurits. "I'm just trying to help out, that's all," Frits said, "and who would be your candidate of preference?"

"We'll be at your place in a minute," Maurits said, "why don't we stop at a café?" "Too late for me," Frits said. They were silent for a few seconds. "Or is the blade more to your liking?" he asked. "Yes," Maurits said quietly, "I need to see a little blood on each wound. Walk up with me." Two streets before the canal on which Frits lived they turned right, then left and then right again, and climbed the steps above a butcher's shop. "The old folks are asleep," Maurits said, "so don't make any noise." He opened the outside door and climbed the darkened stairs ahead of Frits. At the third-floor landing he said: "Watch out for the tub of coal. Stay to the right." He fumbled at a lock, then suddenly stumbled forward. "Damn," he whispered, "I was standing there fiddling with it, and it was open the whole time." In utter darkness he led Frits into a room, closed the door and turned on the light. "Now don't go saying: the odour of human habitation," he said. "That's as old as the hills."

They were standing in a small, square room with dark paper on the walls. There was a folding bed, two chairs and, across one corner, a writing table. The walls were hung with printed poems and a mask of papier mâché. "Sit down," Maurits said. Neither of them spoke. "What, in fact, is the purpose of this seance?" Frits thought. Maurits connected a few extension cords, turned on a standard lamp with a red linen shade and turned off the ceiling light. "Do you still have that overcoat in stock?" Frits asked. "It has been converted into currency," Maurits replied. "Unfortunately I cannot offer you a cigarette." "Is there somewhere I can take a piss?" asked Frits. "Be a bit quiet," Maurits said. "No, you can't go down the hall. That makes too much noise."

He took the chair from the writing table and slid it quietly into the middle of the room, across from Frits. They spoke in subdued voices. "Let's not make this session too long," Frits said. "It is almost midnight."

"Do you know the Knip boy?" Maurits asked. Frits nodded. "With those long nails and that hair that is too long? I'd like to get him sometime."

"What are your objections to his person?" Frits asked. "At school I always found him to be a normal, innocuous nothing. Do you see him often?" "He borrows notes from me, from time to time," said Maurits, "he lives close by, on Boomstraat."

148

"I know. But what detriment has he caused you?" "Nothing, friend, nothing at all," Maurits replied. "Is that a problem?" He grinned. "He annoys me."

"Now we must enter into specifics," Frits said, "and describe the desired actions with clarity and insight. Imagine: he has been taken prisoner. What then? I am the doctor."

"Bound on a table, naked," Maurits said, pursing his lips. "On his back or on his stomach?" Frits asked. "You have to tell me, it's for your own good." "On his... on his... back of course," Maurits said slowly, peering at Frits. "Is that all right?"

"Excellent," Frits said, rubbing his hands. "It's really very chilly in here. Go on. You are applying the knife. What will it be, gagged or not? I mean: imagine it were in a cellar, where no one else can hear." "Let him scream," Maurits said, "yes, let him scream." He sank into a reflective pose.

"Fine," Frits said, "and then what?"

"It needs to be a short knife, like a woodworker's," Maurits said; "a long handle and a very short, but very thin... uh..." "Shank," Frits supplied. "Yes, half a centimetre is more than enough. First the point against the skin, push gently and then, not too deep, start carving."

"Quite impressive," said Frits. "Where do you cut, and how? Do you want to leave flaps of skin, truly lay it to waste, or only clean, normal cuts, not too deep and not too long?" "Just that," Maurits said, his eyes on the floor. "Where do you cut him?" "On the arms, legs and in the face." "Good," Frits said, "not mutilate a given body part?" Maurits slid his chair forward. "What do you mean?" he asked, bringing his face up close to

149

Frits's. He was panting. "I've gone too far," Frits thought. He looked tensely at Maurits, at the way he was leaning into him. "Your breath is almost not repellent," he said. "Do I stink?" asked Maurits. "You should try eating orange peels," said Frits, "that's the thing."

Somewhere in the house a clock struck once. "We are not finished yet," said Frits. "Imagine that no one would ever find out. How would you kill him then? Strangulation? Or beat him to death? You are going to kill him, aren't you?" "Of course," Maurits said, sticking the fingers of his right hand almost completely in his mouth. "First a beating. A few hours at a stretch. Let him come to, from time to time. Then strangle him. With my hands."

He leapt up, came and stood right before Frits, leaning over him for a moment. "Indeed," he thought, "I have gone too far." He did not move. "When I was about three," he said to himself, "I would hold my hands in front of my face when I was afraid, and shout: I'm not here. That, at least, is what my mother always says. I need to remain seated. Show no signs of fear."

"What do you think?" asked Maurits, sitting down again. "Am I normal?"

"It is always risky to inform the ill of their condition," Frits said, "it is not proper to tell someone: you have the galloping consumption. Bye-bye!" Maurits twisted his face into a smile. "Your soul is in anguish," Frits continued, "but you are not mad. It is a form of sadism, but healthy and harmless. A very different thing from that merchant on Market Square. A stick with a rag."

"Who's that?" Maurits asked. "The fellow has a stand selling pickled goods," Frits said. "He is an epileptic. When the spirit enters him, he always bites his tongue and injures himself. So he has a wooden stick with rags tied around it. When he feels a seizure coming on, he says: Uh! argh! grrr! Then he takes that stick between his teeth and falls over backwards." His voice was hoarse with laughter. Maurits grinned along with him. "Wait a minute!" Frits shouted, "hand me that stick, would you please? I'll be with you in just a moment, madam."

"I must be going," he said. Maurits showed him out, leaving the door to the room and the stairs open until Frits had finished his descent.

"The sky has gone clear and high," he thought once he was outside. The stars gave off a penetrating, blue light. He stamped his feet and, after passing water against a tree, walked quickly in the direction of home.

While hanging his coat on the stand and trying to stuff his scarf into the pocket, he felt something large and hard. "It's Viktor's book," he murmured, pulling it out. He went into his room, dropped on his back onto the bed and began leafing through it.

"Our Inner Animal Kingdom" was the title of a section on page one hundred and ten. "I know a woman, said Dr Janet," he read, "in whom the words she hears outside herself are repeated on the inside. Echoed. Mimicked. As though she had a monkey inside. I know another, in whom the inner voice, unrequested and to the point of distraction, speaks the names of all the things the eyes see. That is a stone. That is a tree. That is horse manure. Just like a little boy who, out walking with his father, keeps reporting his perceptions. Stone, Daddy. Tree, Daddy."

He leafed on. "Janet: the gentlemen will surely remember," he read, "the case of the lady Oem, whose cat had died. I can, to my great satisfaction, report that her recovery is complete. Thanks to a remarkable course of treatment which I, in this case, applied. My treatment of Miss Oem consisted of giving her a new cat."

He sighed, tossed the volume onto the desk and paced quietly back and forth. Then he took the mirror from the wall, sat down on the bed and examined his reflection. "Frits van Egters," he said, "I have seen you looking better." He sat down at his desk and inspected his teeth, fingered two steel crowns in the upper jaw and said: "White gold." Then he opened Viktor's book at page two hundred and sixty-two and read: "There is a story about a man who was walking at night down a long, dark corridor by the light of a candlestick in his hand. He thought in fright of how ghastly it would be were his light to go out, and in his fright at the thought of actually seeing that light disappear and finding himself in utter darkness, he began panting heavily and blew the candle out."

He closed the book and remained sitting with it in his hand for some time. At last he laid it atop the bookcase, undressed, placed the mirror on the floor and looked at his naked form in it, as though in a pool of water. "I am a cone, or a funnel, if you will," he said. Then he climbed into bed.

It took more than half an hour for him to calm his thoughts. The bed began to move. "That's annoying," he thought. "Knock off the nasty jokes," he said, "or I'll give you a thumping, indeed I will, that's what I'll do." Soon enough, however, he realized that he was in a car, moving at a clip down a muddy road full of puddles. "I mustn't doze off in broad daylight," he thought. Suddenly he realized that he himself was the driver and that no one else was in the vehicle. "How far have I driven already in my sleep?" he thought, struggling grimly with the wheel. The car swerved alarmingly. He tried to reduce speed, but found only pedals that made him go faster.

"It's going well at the moment," he thought, "but the end of the road is coming up." Having roared through a bend, the vehicle suddenly hit a hole and flipped, yet he crawled out of it unharmed. Before him on the road, two large omnibuses were lying on their sides. Everywhere he heard the screams of the injured. Coming closer he saw that people were trapped beneath one of the buses: at various spots, their intestines had been squeezed from their bodies. Their eyes bulged so far from their sockets that they hung down over their cheeks. He felt nauseous.

"How many people have been killed?" he asked a driver in a blue uniform. "No one has died," the man replied, "only two are badly injured, we need to clean them off well, so we can see what is wrong." "And what about them?" Frits asked, pointing at the crushed bodies, "why isn't anything being done about that?" "Do you really think that's necessary?" the man said with a smile. Suddenly he vanished.

Two of the injured were being rinsed off in a ditch beside the road. When all the dirt had been removed, they proved to be unscathed. "Now pull those folks out from under there," Frits said, but no one listened. He reasoned for hours with various people in the crowd, to convince them that help was needed. Darkness began to fall. Finally, he found fifteen men who were willing to help. "Now I have no strength left," he thought. He could barely bend over. While one group was lifting the bus, others pulled the victims away. Intestines and eyes withdrew slowly back into the bodies. "It's not the kind of weather for an outing, anyway," said the driver in the blue uniform.

He awoke; it was four o'clock. "I need to empty my mind entirely," he thought and, with a few deep breaths, his body relaxed and he fell asleep again.

VII

W HEN HE ARRIVED HOME at two thirty that Saturday afternoon, the fire was out. On the table lay a note that read: "Dear Frits. I don't know where Father is. I have gone to Annetje's. I will be home around eleven. There is pea soup, and you can take a piece of meat if you like. Just fry some potatoes along with the onions. Until then. Mother."

"Excellent," he said, "sweet restfulness." He stood for a few minutes, listening to the silence of the house. A break had appeared in the clouds: pale sunlight fell over the rooftops and onto the mat in front of the stove. "This afternoon is perhaps worse than others," he thought. "I have four hours to go till evening."

He entered the back room and began searching through the drawers of a tall, antique cupboard. In the topmost, between some books, he found a little block of pinewood covered in erratic, twisted grooves. "Joop brought this home with him," he thought, "it is an animal that has gnawed its way through all those little tunnels." He looked at it closely, sniffed it, tapped it against the back of his head and put it down. Still searching, he found an abacus and a pair of tiny brown baby shoes, which he placed side by side on the palm of his hand.

"It is cold," he thought, tossing the objects back from where they came and closing the drawer. In the next one he found some old letters. On a light-green postcard he recognized his own hand. "Dear Mother," was written on it in pencil, "I have arrived safely. The weather is dry. This afternoon we are all going to the beach. There is a man here who has a duck decoy. He has a dog that can sit up, with a pipe in its mouth and a cap on. Very amusing. When you stand atop the dune in the middle, you can see the sea in front and behind you. We have already gathered straw for beneath the canvas tent. I don't know what else to write. Goodbye! Frits."

The date was written at the top: 15th July, with no year. "East Vlieland," he read on the postmark. "That was in nineteen thirty-six," he thought, began to crumple up the card, but thought better of it and put it back among the letters. He unrolled a paper scroll, bound with a red ribbon. "List of Gifts Frits wants from St Nicholas" was printed across the top in big, clumsy block letters. Beneath that was a summary: "a pea-shooter"; "a thing that buzzes through the air, that goes up"; "a real saw (not a toy saw)"; "all kinds of sweets" and "a book like the one Frans has, about the black bears".

"That buzzes through the air," he thought. "Yes, I remember." "A kind of toy," he said to himself, "a little propeller with four blades of tin that one can make fly with a twist of two fingers and the thumb. Well put."

He rolled up the page into a thin stick, held both hands ready to snap it in two, but instead put it back, after retying the ribbon, and closed the drawer with a slam. When he went into the front room, the sunlight had left the floor. He lit the fire without using newspaper, by sprinkling the tinder with paraffin oil, and laid a hand on the stove now and then to monitor the rise in temperature. Then he rolled a cigarette and straddled a chair, the backrest between his knees.

"It was night-time," he said, "the pitch blackness of night." "I could of course turn on the radio," he thought, "but whether or not it is wise is open to question." He turned on the set.

"You are listening to Schumann's Romance number two," the female announcer said. Frits waited and let the cigarette smoke drift through his fingers. "Listen, listen," he thought when the music had started. He put the cigarette down on the flue cover, pinched the bridge of his nose between ring finger and thumb and breathed in with wide-open mouth. "So is it," he whispered.

When the piece was over, he turned off the radio. After sitting still for ten minutes, he got up. "If I don't want to be drowsy this evening," he thought, "I should take a little nap right now." He went to his room and lay down on the bed, sat back up halfway to remove his jacket, and listened to the blood pounding in his head. "I should get up," he thought, "and fetch a blanket from the cupboard. But I cannot force myself to sit up straight. I don't have the strength." From outside, the sound of children at play reached his ears. "When I was seven," he thought, "I cut grass on the lawn with a normal pair of scissors and saved it in a paper cornet. I'm lying here like a sick man." Gradually he dozed off.

He heard a class of schoolchildren singing the song "This old man, he played one, he played knick-knack on my thumb".

Then he was walking across a vacant site where children had built forts and dug holes. The weather was sunny and warm.

He came to a canal where a sand barge lay at anchor. Workmen were lashing it behind a tug. He stood on the bank and saw that, in the sand that filled the hold to the very rim, a grave had been fashioned, like a raised bed for garden cress or radishes. It was marked by a cross of sticks with some of the bark still on them, but bore no name.

Slowly the tug, which had built up a head of steam, began to move and the barge slid away. He started shouting, but no one heard him. The ship with the funeral cross slipped further into the distance. He began to weep.

When he awoke at five thirty, the pillow was wet with tears. He got up, went into the kitchen and prepared his dinner.

Using a fork, he ate the cold, clotted pea soup from the pan, waiting until the onions in the frying pan were hot, then spread a few spoonfuls of onion on four slices of bread and ate them, blowing away the heat. With half a bottle of milk and a packet of powder he made custard, but added too much sugar, so that the taste of it made his cheeks pucker. "I forgot the meat," he thought, and looked in the pan. "Breaking up the layer of lard is too time-consuming," he said to himself, "and I don't have the patience to let it melt. I can't stand here and wait for that."

When he had turned off the gas, his father came home. Frits heard him hang up his coat, panting loudly, enter the living room and then return through the hallway to the kitchen.

"Is Mother home?" he asked, standing in the doorway. "She has gone to Haarlem, I believe," Frits said. "Is there anything to eat?" "We can set the table," Frits replied. He set the table in the living room on two sides, placed all that was left over in dishes and heated the gravy.

"Help yourself first," his father said, once they were seated. Frits took some of the onions and fried potatoes. His father helped himself to the rest, began to eat, but then saw Frits's portion and, using his fork and knife, ladled half his helping onto his son's plate. Frits did not speak. When they were finished, they remained seated without a word. They had not touched the meat. "Away, away from here," Frits thought.

"I'm in a bit of a hurry," he said, "I have to go. Would you put the pans and plates in to soak? Otherwise the food will cake to them."

He put on his dark-blue suit and dabbed his face with cold water. Peeking cautiously through the living room door he saw his father sitting, bent over, his head resting on one hand. He crossed the hallway, threw on his coat and, his hand already on the knob, shouted: "I'm leaving! See you later!" From the room he heard a mumbled reply. He descended the stairs quickly and hurried around the corner.

Within fifteen minutes he had reached Jaap Elderer's house. Jaap was still at table. "Would you like some pudding?" Joosje asked. "A nice fresh bowl of pudding, Frits my boy," said Jaap. "No, thank you," Frits said, "I have just eaten. Have I perhaps arrived a bit too early? It feels rather cold to me in here."

"We let the fire go out," Jaap said. "As an economy measure. But then that door needs to remain closed." He rose and kicked the door to the stairs, which was open, shut with a loud bang.

"Darling," he said to Joosje, "when you come in with this, that or the other thing, do be sure to close the door behind you. A draught is wind inside the home." "A draught is wind inside the home," he repeated, turning to Frits, "am I right?"

"Yes," he replied, "a draught is wind inside the home. You are right. But the definition is not reversible. That is a foul omen. I mean: wind inside the home is not of necessity a draught."

"I'm not sure about that," said Jaap, pushing away his empty bowl. "Once again, you are splitting hairs. What else could wind in the home be, if not a draught?" "Just imagine," Frits said, "a room with doors and windows that are closed tightly. But there is a vent open. Through it a gust of wind enters now and again, blowing the papers off the table. Gusts. But not a draught. Or beside an open window. The wind breezes through it, yet it is not a draught. But very much wind in the home." "You are right," Jaap said, "I'll give you that. Do you know what a draught is? A draught is wind that passes through the home. Have a cigarette." "That's more like it," said Frits. "What time are we leaving?" "In half an hour," Jaap replied.

"Is it slippery out?" Joosje asked. "Slippery?" said Frits, "why would it be slippery? It would have to rain first, and it is not like that at all." "First rain, then frost," Jaap said, "that makes it nice and slippery. Sprinkle generously with sand and powdered ash. We count on the public's cooperation." He began to hiccup with laughter and tilted his head to one side. "People need to give each other a leg up, don't you think, sir?" he asked, rubbing his hands together. "I have an acquaintance who is an Esperantist."

The bell rang; a few moments later Viktor came up the stairs. He was wearing a skating cap. "Welcome, baron," Frits said. The four of them went out of the door. "Are you leaving little Hans all alone?" Frits asked as they were going down the stairs. "Yes, of course," said Jaap. "That's the best thing for a child: as much love and as little care as possible." "And what if there is a fire?" Frits asked. "Then that is *force majeure*," said Jaap. "The child will suffocate before the fire reaches him. It is not such a big deal. People make far too much fuss about it. As long as there's plenty of smoke. That thick, greenish kind."

"The four confederates," Frits said as they walked outside. "Shouldn't we actually be making plans to go to Kastrikum again this summer? But not in one of those cottages: we need to go camping."

"Then you die of cold," said Viktor. "Camping, that is a grand thing," Frits said, "I've gone camping often. Jaap, don't you think so?"

"It is pleasant enough," said Jaap, "but nothing to get excited about."

They walked along the river to the centre of town, passing a number of busy junctions, and arrived at a large square, where they climbed a set of stone steps beside a café. Jaap pressed a white doorbell, then pressed it again. The broad glass doors opened. "Are we the first?" he shouted up the stairs. "No, not the first," a fat little man shouted down to them. With the light at his back, they could make out only his silhouette.

"Here," Frits said to Jaap as they climbed the stairs, "I have twelve guilders on me. I'm not spending a penny more. You are handling the cash tonight, aren't you?" Jaap folded the banknotes and placed them in his pocket.

They came to a broad, empty foyer, where they wrote their names in a book on a little table. "Who is this gentleman?" asked the man who had opened the door for them, pointing at Frits. "That is Mr van Egters," Jaap said, "he is my guest this evening."

Then they entered a wide room, the largest part of which was taken up by a dance floor. Its bare white walls were painted with whimsical drawings. There was no one there; in the corner was a cloakroom where, under glass, in a case, sandwiches were on sale. A girl took their coats. They returned to the foyer and turned left into a bar area, where three men were seated around a table. A grey-haired lady was writing in the corner.

After greeting the others, they looked for a table. "Good evening, Arnold," said Jaap. "Mr Elde," replied the man at the tap, who was holding a bottle up to the light. He had a fat, shiny face and wavy grey hair. Jaap ordered four sherries.

"Still, I tell you, there's a system to it," said one of the three men, who wore his spectacles on the tip of his nose. He ran a hand over his bald head. "They sit around with lists, whole pages full of numbers. They spend all day calculating. And it works, that's the crazy thing about it." The two others laughed. Frits listened closely. "No, in all seriousness," the speaker continued. "When it has landed on red six times in a row, there's a much greater chance that the next time it will be black. You need to realize: they spend all morning making notes. Not playing, just taking notes. That requires quite some discipline, not to start

162

playing. Then they see—let us say—then they see that number eighteen has almost never been touched. That afternoon they put their money on eighteen. And they win."

"That's nonsense," said one of the other two, a man with thin, curly hair. "When it has landed on black ten times in a row, then there's just as great a chance that it will be black again next time. That wheel doesn't know what it has been landing on, now does it?"

"Damn," said the first man now, "that is what I thought too. But you should sit and watch them. They're calculating the whole time. It's enough to make you dizzy." The lady stopped writing, removed her spectacles and looked at the speaker.

"That woman," Jaap whispered to Frits, "earns a living from gambling alone." "That is no minor achievement," Frits said.

"I was in Monaco," said the third man of the three. He had a puffed face and beady little eyes; he was still wearing his thick, green greatcoat. "There was a fellow there who put his money on the number of his cloakroom ticket, as soon as he walked in. He kept at it for a while, never anything but that number." "And?" the lady asked. "He won."

"Jesus," said the man at the tap, who had been leaning over the bar, listening. "I know what I'd do. I'd keep turning in my coat, taking a number every time, and winning every time. And go out for a spin around the block every tenth time, to put it all in the bank." Everyone laughed.

"Can just anyone get into the casino there?" asked the man with the thin, curly hair. "Yes, if one looks fairly respectable," the man in the green coat replied. "It would have been tough for you, but I could have introduced you as my guest." He fell silent for a moment, then went on: "One time I was wearing my pullover back to front, you know what I mean, without a tie. But they wouldn't allow it, a fellow came up to me right away. I went to the Gents and took it off, put it back on the other way around. But of course I didn't have a tie. They didn't say anything about that, though, that didn't matter. It looked much more ridiculous than before, of course, but they didn't care about that."

"Three shots and a sherry," Jaap shouted. When their drinks came, he had Frits and Viktor raise their glasses in a toast and said: "*Ad fundum.*" Jaap and Frits emptied their glasses at one go, but Viktor started coughing. Joosje took little nips of her sherry and was silent. "You're not saying much," Frits said. He looked around the bar. The barman was filling a large pot-belly stove. "Actually," Frits said to Jaap, "this place is awfully bare. They could at least have put up some wallpaper." "That yellows too quickly, from the smoke," said Viktor. "Come now, is that such a problem?" Frits asked. "Then you just paper it again." Jaap held out his cigarettes. "My father," he said, "spent fourteen years in a room with two different kinds of wallpaper." "What?" Viktor asked. "Yes," said Jaap; "his father, my grandfather in other words, had said: Let's paper the room a bit more nicely. He wanted to do it himself, on the cheap. He bought paper, mixed the glue, and started in on a Sunday afternoon. But when he had finished half the room, he was so exhausted that he put it all away again. We'll go on next week, he said. But he never did. It stayed that way until they moved, fourteen years later." "Shall we have another?" he asked. "Not me," Viktor said. Frits and Jaap rose and ordered shots at the bar, which they dispatched at a toss. Then they returned to their chairs. From the foyer came the sound of voices. A moment later a sturdy-looking man with a huge head of hair came in, accompanied by a thin woman in a green velvet dress. "Look, look, Dirk," Jaap called out, "over here." The two sat down at the table. "It's awfully dead in here," the man said. "If I'd known, I would have come an hour later. I need something to drink." "Two coffees," he shouted, then laughed shrilly. "Do knock it off," said the woman, "I don't like it at all." "Marie," he said, "now don't cross me." The coffee was put down before them. "Someone just told me," he said, "about a fellow once who was sentenced to die. He's going to be decapitated, he has to lay his head on the block. So he leans over"—he demonstrated by lowering his head to the tabletop, his hands on both sides— "and do you know what the headsman says? Get your mitts out of the way, that could cost you your fingers!" He slapped the table repeatedly. "The gospel truth," the man at the tap called out. "Oh," Dirk said, "they really are on the ball around here." "You just wait and see," the man shouted back.

They heard a rumbling on the stairs. A dozen guests entered, one after the other. They heard the sound of a gramophone starting up on the dance floor.

"What time is it?" Viktor asked. "Mine says going on eight thirty," said Frits. Those who had just entered moved to tables of their own. "Marie, look, there's Owl," the sturdy-looking man said, got up and went to the foyer. The woman followed him.

"Let us have one more," Jaap said. He and Frits drank a quick shot at the bar. "And one for Viktor," he said; he placed a third shot glass gingerly on the table. Viktor drank with a grimace. "Now don't go spoiling things," Frits said. "We have no need of nasty faces like that around here. Watch out, otherwise we won't take you camping." "Frits wastes no time making plans," Viktor said. "Can't we simply go abroad this summer?" "I've never been across the border," replied Frits, "except when I was about seven, across the German border, to pick blackberries."

"You remember those two cousins of mine, don't you, Dolf and Ab?" Jaap asked. "The ones who drove you around on that carrier bike?" Frits said. "One of them threw that rubbish into the classroom that time, are those the ones?"

"Yes, exactly," Jaap said. "They used to go camping too, every year; they called it 'trekking'. They had office jobs and they lived in Haarlem. They still do, actually. They would leave on Saturday afternoon, and arrive at our place around dinnertime. Then it was always: come now, stay and eat with us. Fine, they would stay and eat. By then it was dark out: well, I think we'd be better off leaving in the morning. Fine, so they spent the night. On Sunday morning they packed all the things they had unpacked the night before: bananas, eggs, the primus stove, whatever else it may have been. Then everything was ready, but it always turned out that one of them had a flat tyre. So they would carry the bike back upstairs and fix the flat on the balcony. My mother, she just let them muddle about. Around noontime they were finished: well then, stay and have a sandwich. The bananas, bread, eggs and primus stove—they always packed that on top, of course—were all unpacked again. And around one thirty they finally cycled off. First they would go to Blaricum. They had a grandmother living there, a sweet woman. They would arrive late in the afternoon—because they'd stopped for a rest somewhere—and stay for dinner. You know what, they would say then, it's too late to go on now. Grandma, they said then, we're going to put up the tent back there. Behind the house was a little stand of trees, I should have said that before. The grandmother—she died a few years back—couldn't stand the thought, of course: sleeping in a tent! She would say: no, don't sleep in one of those things, you'll catch your death of cold. She made beds for them on the floor and they slept there in the house. The next morning, they got up none too early. Then they would go into conclave. With big maps. They could go here, they could go there. A whole itinerary. To the Ardennes." "To the Ardennes!" he repeated, barking with laughter. "But they had unpacked everything the night before, of course; the tent too. And Grandmother would say: I believe the weather is taking a turn for the worse. So they spent the rest of the day there, looking at the maps a bit, peering at the sky: we'll wait and see. The next morning it was raining. A fine drizzle, but enough to keep them from leaving. They stayed inside. Their grandmother was pleased as punch, of course, simply to have the grandchildren, and they sat around all day, just talking. When the weather was bad they couldn't leave, and when the weather was good they couldn't either, because it could always take a turn for the worse."

167

He paused for a moment and lit a cigarette. "Help yourselves," he said, laying the packet on the table. "So then what?" Frits asked. "Well," Jaap continued, "those six days—they had six days' holiday—were over soon enough. It went the same way each year. But you mustn't think that those fellows got bored or that their holiday was ruined. On the contrary. Come along, it's time for a refill."

"Four shots," he said at the bar. "Both *ad fundum*," he said to Frits. They emptied both glasses immediately and in succession. "It seems to me," said Frits, "that Viktor is hardly in the right mood. And Joosje is rather quiet." "Joosje," said Jaap, "just takes it all in. She sees more than you might think. Viktor, he is a serious fellow. Extremely serious. But I am very fond of him."

"I have to piss," Frits said. "Then in tandem," Jaap replied. They crossed the foyer and the dance floor to the urinals. "The crowd is starting to pour in," said Jaap as they walked back to their table. Dozens of visitors were waiting before the cloakroom. People were already dancing in the hall. "It tastes God-awful going down," he said, "but once it's inside it is frightfully delicious."

"Well, Viktor," Frits asked once they were seated, "are you in a serious mood tonight? Mr Jaap tells me that you are the serious type." "I'm amusing myself greatly," Viktor replied.

"You'll join us for another shot, won't you?" asked Jaap. Viktor followed the two of them to the bar. It was crowded and they had to wait.

"You are studying," Frits said once they were seated again, "but what is science? It is absolutely nothing." Viktor smiled.

"Consider if you will," said Frits—"will you forgive me, my lady, if I broach a subject that may command little interest on your part?" he asked Joosje—"consider if you will that they, with all their science, have not yet succeeded in making even a single, common grain of sand." He rubbed his fingertips together, as though letting sand run through them. "They are unable to do that."

"Quite right, sir," Jaap said. "This table is brown. But do you also see it as brown? You call the colour that I call brown, brown as well. But it is perfectly possible that you see brown in the same way that I see blue. Work that one out, if you can." He laughed, made as if he were spitting into his hands, and thumped Viktor on the chest. "Am I right?" he asked. "Have you heard the one about the man who went on holiday all alone?"

The room around them grew fuller. "He was carrying on with a girl he'd met at the hotel where he was staying. This evening he goes to bed with her. There is a knock. A telegram is slid under the door. He reads it: wife gravely ill, urgent, immediate return requested. He folds it up again, licks the seal and pastes it together neatly, then places it on the shelf above his bed. He climbs into bed and says: Won't I be shocked in the morning!" Viktor burst into loud laughter. Frits and Joosje smiled.

"There is a great deal of affliction in the world," said Frits, "that much is certain."

"Time for a drink, wouldn't you say?" Jaap asked. He fetched two glasses of sherry, for Viktor and for Joosje, then went with Frits to the bar. They emptied their glasses and walked together to the urinals. When they returned, arm in arm, Joosje said:

"You two mustn't go wandering off like that, I can barely hold on to your chairs any more. They keep asking about them."

Frits leaned forward, hands on the table, looked at Viktor and asked: "Do you forget a great deal?" "That depends, Frits," he replied. "We need to talk," Frits went on, "I need to talk. Let us talk about something." "I have no objection," said Viktor. "Let them say whatever they like about you," Frits continued, "but you are a decent person." "Don't exaggerate," Viktor said.

Jaap had his arm around Joosje. They were talking quietly. "Exaggeration or no," said Frits, "the truth will out. You know, Viktor, are you able to forget things? Do you remember that weird business of mine, that very weird business back then? You do still remember that, or don't you?" "Yes," said Viktor, "I still remember." "Good," Frits said, "but still, you've forgotten it completely. You have forgotten, haven't you? You don't remember any more. Even if you wanted to, you couldn't remember it any more." "Absolutely," said Viktor.

"Good," Frits went on, staring at the table. "Am I keeping you?" "Not in the slightest," said Viktor. "Perhaps I have told you this before," said Frits, fingertips pressed together. "It was in March of forty-five, or in February. I think it was February. Once a week, an old man came to eat at our house. Each Saturday, I believe it was. He came a couple of times. And then he did not show up. On Wednesday we heard that he was dead. An acquaintance had gone to visit him. He opened the door and the two of them sat in his room. Then his chest began to hurt, and suddenly he was dead." "Yes, I heard about that," Viktor said. "Mrs Schaapskooi," Frits continued, "once asked my mother whether we couldn't have a lady, who lived alone, over for dinner. Yes, that was no problem. Three times a week. She was a very skinny little woman. She carried a cane. We were having wheat. Soak it for a few days and then cook it thoroughly, it's quite tasty. She ate a healthy portion of it and then needed to lie down on the divan. She said: I'm feeling a bit woozy. Then she left. When she got home, she fainted on the stairs. She developed a fever right away. The neighbours fed her water with a teaspoon. Through her teeth. The next morning she had lost consciousness completely, and a few hours later she was dead. They found cupboards full of linen that had never been used. And money, stocks and bonds."

"Goodness," said Jaap, who was now listening in. "Those were the people who ate at your house, am I right?"

"Then they asked us to feed a sixteen-year-old boy. Yes, my mother says, but only if he came every day. He was a tall, dark boy. Very thin. He was afraid to talk. The first day, he sits down at the table. My father says: Wim—his name was Wim—we had two people who ate with us before, an old man and an old woman. Yes, sir, the boy says. They both died, my father says, and the idea is that you don't die on us. The boy turned bright red and said: Yes, yes, of course not. He didn't know which way to look. After dinner he just sat by the window. In the kitchen, my mother asked me: why is he sitting there like that? I told her: the boy was brought up well. They taught him that, when you eat at someone's house, you don't simply get up and walk out after dinner. Then she said to him: Wim, you may go if

171

you like. Goodbye, ma'am, goodbye, sir, he says, and he was gone. The next day one of his younger brothers comes to the house. He said: Wim is ill. There goes number three, my father said. The brother stayed for dinner: that way they didn't have to waste a meal. But the next day Wim had recovered. And he ate with us every day for the duration. When the packages came floating down out of the sky, their family received an extra one, because there were seven of them. Later, in the summer, Wim brought us lettuce from their garden, they had an allotment. And when my brother's stove cracked, Wim's father—he is a blacksmith—welded a hoop around it. Very thick, very strong. For free, he wouldn't accept payment for it. Disinterested assistance. Am I boring you?"

"No," said Viktor, "decidedly not. Go on. I am listening."

"You see," Frits said, "had it been up to me, they would not have eaten with us. I was always telling my mother: you're insane. Before you know it we won't have anything left. You shouldn't do it. That's the way I was. That is the way I am. Isn't that despicable?" Viktor pursed his lips and shook his head slowly. Jaap had risen to his feet and was standing a few steps from the table, conversing with a tall, skinny man.

"When it was over," Frits went on, "we still had dozens of pounds of wheat, kilos of beans and peas. But it is the fear. That is the worst of it."

"You are not particularly cheerful this evening," Viktor said. Frits looked at his watch. "At the tone, the time will be nine thirty," he said. "There will be a brief, thirty-second intermission, after which our programme will continue."

Jaap came back. "We'll have another one," he said. "And then we shall take a piss," said Frits. They drank, went to the lavatories and on their way remained standing beside the dance floor for a moment. All the tables there were occupied as well. The gramophone was playing a foxtrot. Many of the visitors stood and talked on the floor itself, so that the dancers had difficulty making their way without colliding.

"You do know, don't you," Frits said when they walked on, "that everything could be entirely different?" "I haven't had the opportunity to make a study of that yet," Jaap said. They stood humming before the porcelain urinals. When they came back and were seated in their chairs, Frits said: "In China, when one saws wood, the main motion is not pushing, the way it is with us, but pulling. When one drives a screw there, one turns it to the left."

"There are many strange things afoot," said Jaap. "Come and sit here," he called out to the tall man to whom he had been talking only minutes earlier. The man looked for a chair, took one that had remained unguarded for a moment at a nearby table, and sat down with them.

"Herbert Witlijn," Jaap said. "No need to shake hands. So tell us, how are things?" The man, who looked to be a few years past thirty, wore a brown chequered suit with a grey shirt. His face was sallow, with dark eyes that looked, at the corners, as though they were inflamed with moisture or fatigue. His black hair was pomaded and parted down the middle. He drummed with two fingers on the tabletop, without replying.

"Do you people believe," Frits asked, "that it is right for one to live in moderation?" "You're always asking such deep questions," Jaap said, "you really should stop that."

"My sincerest apologies," said Frits. "I would not want anyone in this company to find me an annoyance." He held out his hand to Jaap, then bent over and laid his head on the table. "That noggin of yours takes up far too much space," Viktor said.

"Mr Lijnman," Frits said then, addressing the thin man, "are you not of the opinion that eating meat, if not a sin, should in any case be denounced as being unhealthy?" "I have reservations about that," the man said, "but I will give it some thought." Frits peered at the man's mouth, from which a tooth was missing.

"Give it some thought," he said, rapping his knuckles quietly on the table, "give it some thought. That's what they all say. But that won't get us anywhere."

"What is he talking about?" Joosje asked. "Eating meat won't kill you, in any case," Viktor said. "I am familiar with your stance," Frits went on, shaking Viktor's hand now. "It is a view that elicits respect, but which is nevertheless—despicable. Because what is it you are saying? You say: will they eat no meat? Fine. For the vegetarians, steamed mackerel will be placed at their disposal." Filling his cheeks with air, he exhaled.

"Yes, indeed," Jaap said, "there is much room for improvement when it comes to our nutrition. A great deal. Very little attention is given it. But whether the eminent Dr van Egters is right, that is the question facing us this evening."

"I would like to hear the opinion of our honoured guest," said Frits. "Mr Lijnman"—he placed his hand on the wrist of

174

him to whom he spoke—"what are your views on nutrition?" "Say something, at least," Joosje said quietly. "Listen," said the man, "any number of years ago, at the newspaper, we organized a contest for young people between the ages of something and something. With lots of prizes. A quarter-page announcement on Saturday evening. The assignment was to write an essay on any subject. The winner would receive training as a journalist."

"You approach your point by means of a detour," Frits said, "but that is no objection. What you have to say, that is what matters."

"There was a boy from Groningen, or from Drenthe," the man continued, "who won and came to work at the paper in Amsterdam. He had a room and ate in town, in cafeterias. He worked with us for about nine months, then he fell ill. That happened a few times, in fairly rapid succession. Then he would recover for a few weeks. Then he fell ill again. And about six days later, he died. The doctor said then that what killed him was eating in cafeterias—always that same, badly cooked food."

"That is quite something, what you're telling us there," said Frits thoughtfully. "I am a layman, but I can tell you right now that the cause of death was salt. Salt is the kidneys' ruin. Things take place around us. Yet we barely notice them. We have ears but we hear not, eyes but do not see." He scratched his head. "Isn't it about time we left?" Joosje asked Viktor quietly. "In a bit," he replied.

"Let's have another," Jaap said. Arm in arm with Frits, he went to the bar. "It is awfully crowded in here again," said Frits, after they had emptied their glasses. He took a drink along for the tall man and placed it carefully on the table. He had the sensation that all the guests were screaming at the top of their lungs. "They do scream frightfully loud here," he said. "I believe the women scream loudest of all. Would it truly be so hard for them to make a little less noise?" He tried to take a few steps, but lost his way entirely and remained leaning against the wall, close to the door, beside a blinking slot machine. Through the smoke, which stung his eyes, he tried to make out the people in the crowd. Someone laid a hand on his shoulder and said softly: "Don't you worry your head about it, lad, everyone here is feeling exactly the same way." Frits turned and saw a man with a wrinkled face standing before him. "Thank you kindly," he said, and shook the stranger's hand. Then he went back to his table.

"We must remain friends for ever," he said, leaning and resting his head in his left hand, "isn't that right, Jaap? And Viktor? The two of you are dear to my heart in equal measure." "And you, sir," he continued, speaking to the tall man, "you I do not know, and therefore it would be wrong to expect any commitment from me. But nothing would displease me more than to have you think that I am pressing for an estrangement. Far from it." He shook the man's hand.

"This gentleman is a thinker, Herbert," said Jaap, "as am I. But Mr van Egters is a thinker by calling." He leaned his head against Joosje's breast. Viktor studied the ceiling.

"I know very well," said Frits, "that you, Viktor, you are feeling annoyed no end. But you are a man of comportment. I can appreciate that. I am in the right mood." "Now in all seriousness," he said to Joosje and Jaap, "is it not so that most people think too little on those who have died, who have left this earthly bourn? God sees all things."

The tall man, it seemed, spotted an acquaintance in the crowd. He stood up and disappeared.

"What does your watch say, Frits, my boy?" asked Jaap. "It is a quarter past ten," Frits answered. "Yet still we must keep in mind that God is the beginning and the end of all things. Eating meat is sinful."

"That seems to be on your mind lately," said Viktor. He was cleaning his nails with a stub of matchstick.

"It is not only that," said Frits. "If only that were all. But they eat copiously. As God is my witness. They eat fresh white bread in the late evening hours." "Who?" Joosje asked. "People in general. Our fellow citizens," Frits replied, leaning back. "They drink coffee in the late evening hours. Everyone knows that is the body's demise. And the soul is damaged."

"The soul is damaged," said Jaap, sitting up straight. "Don't misunderstand," Frits continued. "This is not intended as a rebuke. But I see it. All those whose eyes are not sealed and who look around them must see it."

"Not everyone is equally acute," said Jaap. "That which for us is too simple for words is, for another, a formidable temple of wisdom. Take that cousin of mine, Uuk, for example. You've met him, haven't you?" "Oh yes," said Frits, "a fine, upstanding fellow. Beyond reproach. As are all your acquaintances. Simple, industrious folk. I say that without insinuation, believe me." "Of course," Jaap said, wiping the ash from the table and continuing: "Uuk is certainly not a stupid fellow. But not long ago he let someone palm off a copper ring on him for fifteen guilders." "You're jesting," Frits said. "Tell us more," said Viktor. "Someone who said he was a seaman and that his ship was leaving in an hour and a half," said Jaap. "That he was not allowed to take gold on board."

"First one laughs," said Frits, "but it is a hideous thing. One human being cheating another. In full sight of the Creator."

"He is a very strange fellow. Not dumb at all," Jaap went on, "but there are some things he doesn't understand. He's walking down the street, someone taps on the window. He goes in right away. It was a whore, of course, but he thought she was calling him in to chase away a mouse or to help her move a cupboard. Wonders never cease."

"We have made a mess," said Frits, pointing at the tabletop. "We are very uncouth." "Let's go watch them dance," Jaap said, "we might learn something."

They got up and elbowed their way through. Viktor was in front; Jaap, Joosje and Frits followed in single file. They forced their way to a corner of the dance floor and sat down on a long bench along the wall.

"We are too old to take part in this," said Frits. "The decline of Western civilization. Still, it is wonderful, being young."

"Shall we have another?" Jaap asked. "No, better not," said Frits, "wait a bit." "A cigarette then," said Jaap, offering his around.

A lady sat down at a grand piano, not far from them. The gramophone stopped and the couples on the dance floor waited. "Come on," people shouted. "This is that old cowboy song

'Don't Fence Me In'," said Jaap, when the pianist started in. He bobbed his head and neck like a bird at water. "When I was little," Frits said, "I could never stand piano music. A human being is a sensitive creature." Jaap was leaning against Joosje now and had stopped moving.

"Listen," Frits said to Viktor, putting an arm around his shoulder. "Am I too grave?" "Gravity from time to time can do no harm," Viktor answered. "Do you believe that science offers any significant meaning?" Frits asked. Viktor remained silent.

The pianist started in on another melody. "I know this one," said Frits, "this is 'Give Me Five Minutes More'. A delightful tune." He leaned forward and bounced his fists on his knees to the rhythm. "Every man has his story," he said, "but it is seldom an important one."

"Have you met Boomgaard?" Viktor asked. "He knows a lot about philosophy." "Boomgaard, no," said Frits, "not a familiar name. I'm afraid not." "No?" Viktor marvelled. "He is a lecturer, but he also teaches secondary school. Classical languages. At Berends Gymnasium. He's been there for about six years now. You went there, didn't you?"

"That was before my time," said Frits. "How old are you, exactly?" Viktor asked. "You almost have to have met him."

"Twenty-three I am now," said Frits. He stuck his index finger in the air. "But don't forget," he said. "I left school in fourth class. Not because I was too stupid, though."

"Oh, I beg your pardon," said Viktor. "Far from it," Frits went on. "But there is nothing worse than shirking the truth. Listen closely. You will understand. If anything is unclear, you are at liberty to ask me. Debate is permitted. Tickets on sale at the usual outlets and at the door." He put his arm around Viktor's waist, leaned back against the wall and gestured with his right arm.

"Perhaps it is of no importance to you," he said, "perhaps you say: what difference is it to me? Perhaps my fate leaves you cold. But remember that God sees us all. He holds the firmament in the palm of his hand." "Yes, go on," said Viktor.

"It doesn't matter to me if you are not listening," said Frits, "although it would cause me great sorrow to know that. I arrived in the first class at Berends Gymnasium. That whole year, on all my reports, I received a ten for Latin. That is a fact. One can consult the primary sources." He raised his head and exhaled loudly. "Subsequently, Dr Poort," he said, "I went to the second class. Things went well. Not badly at all. A few days before the end-of-year report, I took to my bed. Sick with fear that I might not move up. Everyone thought I was mad. Perhaps that was true. I moved up, but with one failed subject, algebra. If this is boring you, do say so, I wouldn't like to be a burden." "Oh no," said Viktor, "go on, I find it quite interesting to hear." "So it does interest you?" Frits asked. "That is marvellous. Sympathetic interest is one of the best qualities of man, this weird and wonderful denizen of the earth." He shook his head pensively.

Jaap, leaning against Joosje, sat watching the dancers with eyes half-open. "So then it was three," Frits said. "Just like in the nursery rhyme. Simple, and yet, or perhaps precisely for that very reason, touching. I'm not keeping you, am I?" "Not at all, please continue," said Viktor.

"Then it was three, as mentioned," Frits went on. "Then I failed French and mathematics, both subjects. And I did not move up." He looked at Viktor. His interlocutor said nothing. "I had to resit the exam. During the summer holidays, an acquaintance helped me. But the exam never took place. Remarkable—fickle is the hand of fate. Do you believe in God?" "No," Viktor said, "I've told you that before." "All right, then," said Frits with a dismissive wave of his hand, "that need not prove an obstacle to mutual understanding." A dancer stepped on his toes. "Clumsiness, but perhaps without malice after all," he said. "The exam didn't happen?" Viktor asked.

"No examination," said Frits. "A few days beforehand, the headmaster announced that the grim situation, with the onset of war, formed an obstruction to an atmosphere of peaceful study. Not badly formulated. You are able to follow me thus far, I take it?" "Superbly," said Viktor, "your account is so clear and succinct."

"In other words," Frits supplied, "all those called upon to resit an exam would move up without having to complete it. That, of course, included me. And so I arrived in the fourth." "We are making progress," Viktor said. "Jaap is almost asleep." "Let him sleep," said Frits. "In the fourth. At the end of the year I had failed English, mathematics and chemistry." He counted it off on his fingers. "Chemistry was a five, that was not too bad."

"Listen, brother," he said emphatically, "for here it comes. I had to repeat the exams, in both mathematics and English. And I resat them both. You know, Viktor, that I have a high opinion of you; that I have a great fondness for you. That is why I am telling you this, so that you might understand. During that summer holiday, I did nothing." "Nothing?" Viktor asked, "what do you mean?" "Nothing, absolutely nothing," Frits said. "Note well: it is not difficult for a man to talk about that which is evil or despicable, only about that which is ludicrous. I read that somewhere." He burped, leaned forward slightly and went on: "I did show up for the resit. Do you understand? Can you picture it?" "Not very easily," said Viktor.

"Can you imagine," Frits said with emphasis, "the heart of one who goes to an exam in the simple, sober certainty of failure?" He opened his mouth, bit down slowly on his lower lip and closed his eyes. "What am I waffling about?" he said. "I am detaining you. I am boring you. I am annoying you. That is the truth of the matter. But you have listened to me. I appreciate that." He seized Viktor's hand. "What an evening," he said. "A memorable evening."

"There is one more thing," he continued. "When the new school year began, we received a letter at home from the headmaster, asking whether it was true that Frits van Egters—your son, Frits van Egters—had quit school. And whether he could have written confirmation of that. I had already dropped out, but the school had received no formal notification. That is all. I thank you for your kind attention." He took a deep breath and pursed his lips. "Lovely, isn't it, the English waltz?" he asked, watching the dancers. "Calm, civilized, stately."

"Come now, Jaap, you're not in your own bed yet," said Viktor, reaching behind Frits and poking Jaap. He sat up straight, snapped his fingers and said: "Last round. One more for the road." The four of them went to the bar and all four of them drank. The music from the gramophone seemed louder to Frits than it had been all evening. In front of the counter, a few guests were swaying to the music.

"Do you know what it is?" said Frits, who found himself unable to stand in one spot, "when I've had a drink I start fluttering, but I never leave the ground. On the ground I remain."

"I'm not well," Jaap said, "I need to sit down." They returned to the ballroom, where their seats on the bench were still vacant. Jaap sank down onto it, almost recumbent. "That is not a good thing," Frits said to Viktor, pointing at Jaap. "The boy's feeling poorly. But he has only himself to blame. One consumes too much and suffers the consequences. But think for a moment of all the suffering for which none are to blame. God alone sees it." He grabbed Viktor by the arm and said: "When you have only one eye, then night falls every time you wink. Have you ever considered that?" Jaap stood up and walked toward the lavatories. "We'll go together," Frits shouted. He followed him and passed water. Standing at the sink, Jaap gagged several times, then vomited. "Out with the bad, in with the good," Frits said. "You go on," said Jaap. "It is time to leave," Viktor said when Frits returned. "Jaap is regurgitating," he replied.

"Who has the money?" Joosje asked. "Jaap does, in his pocket," said Frits. "I'll be right back." He saw, when he entered the lavatory, Jaap standing at a dusty little window that was open a crack, breathing in the cool air from outside. "We're leaving," he said, "will you pay?" "Here's money," Jaap said hoarsely, pulling a little bundle of banknotes from his pocket.

Frits went to the cash desk and said: "I have come to pay for Mr Elderer." "Twenty-eight guilders," the man at the tap shouted to the waiter, who was examining his notebook. The banknotes added up to only twenty-five guilders and fifty cents. "Hold on to this," said Frits, laying the money on the table. "Twenty-eight guilders, you say." "Excluding the tip, that is," the waiter said. "Yes, I realize that," said Frits, "I'll go and get it. You hold on to this."

He walked back into the dance hall. Viktor was standing with the coats over one arm. "We'll have to drag him," he said, pointing at Jaap, who, supported by Joosje, was emerging from the lavatory. They helped him into his coat. When they had put on theirs, Viktor and Joosje held him up on either side. Like that, they descended the stairs. Frits remained close behind.

"To the trams," said Viktor, once they were outside. "We can still catch one, easily." "Could you keep me informed of the numbers?" Frits asked. They crossed the square and stood waiting on a corner.

"A lovely evening," said Frits. "Do you too go in search of the world's misery? Do you also enjoy strolling through graveyards of a Sunday afternoon? Most people never think about a thing."

"Here's the eight," Viktor said. "That's yours." "May you all be permitted a safe journey home. My best wishes accompany you," Frits shouted, climbing aboard the tram. Smiling, he staggered to the front. With every lurch of the tram he had the sensation of being lifted from the floor and slowly settling back again. He stepped onto the front platform. "Calm down, everyone," he said, "there is no need to crowd." He pulled out his wallet, examined the contents slowly, removed a one-guilder note and held it up to the driver. "What is this?" he asked. "A guilder," the man said. "I couldn't tell," Frits said, "but it's yours." The man took the banknote and put it in his pouch. "At least that is taken care of," Frits said, bumping into the closed door. "I have an urgent request. One would do well to warn me when our vehicle reaches Danis Square." He tried to whistle, but no sound came out.

"This is it," said a lady in a green hat. "Thank you very much," Frits said, "your kindness is exemplary." A man gave him a hand as he climbed down.

He crossed the tracks and walked towards a group of three policemen. "Good evening, gentlemen," he said, "I hope you are doing well. The fact of the matter is that I have had a few beverages, but not quite too much, which means you have no reason to detain me. I have had a few, but not quite too much. How delightful." "Go on with you," one of the policemen said, "move along, and get some sleep." "Wise counsel," said Frits, "I thank you sincerely." He walked up to a telephone kiosk and made moves to pass water against it. "You can't do that," the same policeman said, "there is a urinal over yonder." He pushed him away. "Of course," said Frits, "you're quite right. Highly incorrect, what I was doing. I hope you will accept my heartfelt apologies." He turned the corner down a broad street, leaned for a few moments against a shop window and addressed a man who was passing by with a lady on one arm and holding a bicycle by the handlebars.

"Excuse me for bothering you," he said, "but do you happen to know the way to Schilderskade? As long as I'm headed in that direction. It is a matter of finding the right way. Once I know that, it will all go automatically. I have had just a bit too much. It is wrong, but there is nothing to do about it now."

"Walk with us," the man said. Supporting him on either side, they walked on. Frits looked at both their faces. "Could I be mistaken?" he asked, "or are the two of you our esteemed neighbours?" "Yes, we are," said the man. "Then you are the curtains halfway up," Frits said. "That's right," said the lady. "And what was the name again?" Frits asked. "Visser," the man said. "A name without guile," Frits said with emphasis, "an honest name. We see each other every day, but pass each other by, while we should actually be brothers. You are rather devout, am I right? I have had too much, that is sinful. It is bad. I am a bad person. But God sees it."

"Then you should not do it," the neighbour said. They arrived at Frits's house. The man took out a pass key and opened the street door. "I thank you with all my heart. You are good, virtuous people," Frits said. "Go to bed straight away," the woman called out after him.

He climbed the stairs slowly, paused to rest before the door on the landing, then staggered inside. When he felt the heat, he grew dizzy. He tried to open the living room door slowly but, without meaning to, struck it loudly with the flat of his hand.

"Good evening, good evening," he said. His parents were seated at the table, reading. He went in, tossed his coat on the divan, then held himself upright on the edge of the table.

"Good evening, dear father," he said. "Good evening, dear mother. Good evening, dear parents." Letting go of the table, he plumped down into a chair. "So…" he said, tapping his forehead with his index finger.

His father looked at him with a smile of amazement. "How much did you drink, for God's sake?" his mother asked, "where have you been?" She stood up. "Look and make sure he hasn't lost his money," she said.

"I know," Frits said. "I have had too much. God sees everything. His eye is not only on me, his eye is on each and every one of us. The end of days is near. I couldn't have had more than seven or eight." His father came over to him, withdrew his wallet from his inside pocket and looked in it. "No," he said, "there's still thirty-two guilders in it." He placed it on the bookshelf.

"Would you like some bread and cheese?" his mother asked. "No," he said, "I shall partake of nothing more. Purify the body. Christ, behold thy soldiers. And so it happened. It is bad. I have done you, my parents, a great injustice. Great sorrow and injustice. It is loathsome. But God sees us all. I am going to bed. To sleep." But he remained seated. His voice descended to a murmur and his chin fell to his breast.

His mother began removing his shoes. With the help of his father, she undressed him and led him to bed. There he remained sitting upright. "Few there be who appreciate your goodness. I see it. Should I behave as though I do not, that is mere appearance. But should you think, Mother…" "Yes, mouse," she said. "Should you think that I do not see it," he continued, "realize then, that God's eye rests upon the two of

187

you. He sees you. He sees your righteousness." "Hold your arms back for a moment," she said. "Why should I do that?" he asked. "You need to put on your pyjama top," she replied. "Of course, you know what's best, what is right," he said, sticking his arms in the sleeves.

"I am going to throw up," he said suddenly. His father, who had been watching from the doorway, ran and came back with a bucket. "Leave me," said Frits. "It is revolting." He vomited four times, spat mucus and then dropped onto his back, panting. His parents' faces slid back and forth and now and then rose to the ceiling. He coughed, pulled the bedclothes over his head and felt himself spinning in a dark space with walls that were, wherever he touched them, wet. The movement slowed and he was able to stretch out. Then he sank into the deep.

VIII

S UNDAY MORNING at eight thirty he awoke with a mouth
dry as cork. The first thing he remembered was lying
on his bed the day before, to rest, then realized that this was
Sunday. It was not until then that the course of the previous
evening came back to him. He raised himself onto one elbow.
Only after making chewing motions did moisture return to his
mouth. The inside of his head felt as though a fluid were under
pressure there: the tension extended all the way to the back of
his neck. He was thirsty.

"The best thing," he thought, "is to get up immediately, wash
my face, brush my teeth and rinse my mouth thoroughly. Then
go out for a breath of fresh air. Don't eat a thing, and drink water
a little at a time." Then he fell asleep again. A few minutes past
nine thirty he awoke once more. "How very attentive, to hang
the watch up like that," he thought. He raised only his head, but
had to let it fall back from the pain, which arose in the throat
and behind his eyes. "Those clothes have been tossed down sloppily," he thought. From the intensity of the light and the colour
of the sky he tried to determine what the weather was like, but
reached no conclusion. Lying on his back, he raised his knees
and, in the dim light he admitted by holding the bedclothes aloft,
examined his chest and belly, which he had bared.

Then he climbed out of bed, went to the toilet and from there to the kitchen, where he drank water from the tap. "Incredible, what a stench," he said as he entered the bedroom again. "You only notice it when you've left for a moment." He opened the window a crack and crawled back into bed. "It all depends on the will," he thought. "Where that is lacking, everything comes to a halt."

He remained supine, his eyes fixed on the wall, until eleven. "It's not so easy, getting up with the window open," he said aloud. Squeezing his eyes half-shut he tossed off the blankets and went quickly to the kitchen. He hawked loudly into the sink and began washing himself. "The body is gravely damaged," he mumbled, peering into the round shaving mirror.

His mother came in, put two plates and two cups on the counter and asked: "So, has the young gentleman woken up a bit?" "Yes," Frits said. She went back to the living room. After washing his face, he felt unrefreshed. While shaving, he cut himself in two places: beneath the nose and on the left side of the chin. "It's not actually cutting," he thought, "more like shaving off the top layer of skin. It has been scraped off." After rinsing and drying his face, he dabbed at the abrasions with a styptic pencil. As he waited to see whether the bleeding would return, he looked out over the gardens at the rooftops.

"No two roofing tiles are exactly the same colour," he thought. "My vision is sharp. What would it be like if it had rained?"

He dressed, but could not find his shoes and socks. He walked slowly into the living room, sat down by the fire and asked: "Mother, have you seen my shoes? I can't find my socks either." "In your room," she answered. "I don't think so," he mumbled, going to his bedroom and looking around. "They're not there," he said as he came back into the living room. His father entered from the side room. "Good morning," Frits said. "Good morning, my boy," the man answered, sitting down on the divan and opening a book from the pile he had brought with him. "They are there," his mother said. "Well, I don't see them anyway," said Frits. "Then I'll look," she said, hurrying to his bedroom. He heard her rummaging about for a moment. "Who knows?" he mumbled to himself.

"Here you go," she said, coming back and tossing him first the socks then the shoes, one of which landed on his left foot. "Goddam it," he said, "throw things at someone else's foot." "What is it now?" his father asked. "No, nothing," Frits said. "A trifle." He smiled.

"There's bread for you in the cupboard," his mother said. "Thank you," he said. She turned on the radio. "No farm report, no horticultural news, no bad music, no shooting off at the mouth," Frits said. "No waltzes by Strausz, no illustrative music. Let only the very best shine through. Display taste, faulty taste if need be, but progressive." "This is giving me a headache," he thought.

"You're not alone here, you know," she said. "You should think about other people sometimes. It's about time you started taking others into account." The radio set had warmed up and started making sounds. "I am so alone and keep thinking of you," a tenor sang. His father turned the volume down, but not completely off. One could hear singing, but that was all one could make out. "This way, the music is stifled," Frits thought. He approached and ran through the frequencies. At last he turned the radio off.

"So," his mother said, "did the young man have a good time last night?" Frits did not answer. "I suppose you were out with Jaap?" she asked. "Was he drunk as well?" "Drunk," he replied. "Stop nattering, would you? Drunk. Backward provincials is what the two of you are. What do you know of drunk, for God's sake?"

"Oh no," she said, "don't try to tell me you weren't drunk. Your father and I had to carry you to bed." Frits closed his eyes for a moment. "What difference does it make?" he said. "It makes all the difference," said his father with emphasis. "It means that you can't control yourself."

"I'm a bit cold," said Frits, coughing. "What stinks so terribly?" he thought, and sniffed at his hands, his pullover, his coat sleeves and tie. It all seemed to give off the same sour, disgusting odour. "Am I imagining things?" he thought, then stood up and sniffed at the curtains.

"Watch out!" his mother shouted. "Don't go wiping your nose on the curtains! Have you gone completely mad? That's what hankies are for!"

"It still seems a good deal easier to me," he said, "to blow my nose in my handkerchief. As long as I have a handkerchief, there is no need to fear for your curtains." "Oh yes," she said, "I can tell that from the chairs."

"That is another matter," said Frits. "That which is solid must be removed by hand. It can't be done with a handkerchief. And the bottom of a chair is the best place for it. Besides, wherever you go, if you feel around under the chair the pieces of dried snot fall to the floor." "Stop it, would you?" she asked.

He breathed in through his nose, in short, sniffling bursts. "It is vomit that has remained in the sinus cavity," he thought. "A portable stench." Despite the fire's heat, he shivered without pause. Behind his eyes he felt a feeble, pressing pain. He took the big armchair, turned it with the seat towards the window and slouched down in it. "All in all, it is dreary," he thought, "most dreary."

Gradually he sank into a regularly broken slumber that brought him no relief. One o'clock came. "What frequency are the news reports on?" his mother asked. "There are none," he answered. She searched, but found no Dutch-language station, and turned off the set. Silence fell. His mother was at the table adding up little piles of change, and his father, who had spread himself out on the divan, had stopped moving.

Frits relaxed his muscles to the full, let his head fall to one side and held his eyes half-closed to the bright light. Finally, he fell asleep. He did not dream, but heard monotone voices going up and down. After awakening he remained sitting motionless for five minutes. Then, turning his head, he saw by the clock that it was almost two. He got up and began walking slowly back and forth.

"Why don't you go out for a bit?" his mother asked. "Is Father asleep?" he asked. He saw the man lying on his back with his eyes closed. The book on his stomach moved up and down with his breathing. "I would rather go to see someone,"

Frits said. "Aimless walking, I don't feel much like that." "So go to Joop and Ina's," said his mother. "But don't forget, they're not at the house on Overwater now. They've gone to Ina's mother." "Have they run through all their coal already, then?" he asked. "No," she answered, "but they go there so often on Sunday that now they spend Saturday night there too. It saves them stoking the fire again."

"That is what we'll do," he said, pulled on his coat and left. Turning right he followed the river, passed the southern train station, then headed east along a dike. On his right the city ended. Close to the horizon he could see mist hanging over the fields. "Good eye," he said to himself. "Local mist, later in the form of drifting banks of cloud. No precipitation to speak of. Temperatures ranging from freezing to slight thaw. A westerly wind. How do they do it?"

He entered a new area of low houses. Close to the bottom of a dead-end street that emptied out on the fields, he rang the bell of a second-floor flat. "Hello, Frits here," he shouted up the stairs when the door was opened. "It's the old man," he thought. A grey-haired man was standing at the top of the stairs. "Oh, Frits," the man said. "You and I are the only ones here, I'm afraid." "To turn and go away would be awfully rude," Frits thought. "In other words," he said, climbing the stairs, "I have disturbed your afternoon nap." He shook the man's hand. "How are you, Mr Adelaar?" he asked. "Fine, fine," said the man in a deep voice. "Do come in."

He let Frits go first. They came into a light, modernly furnished living room. The windows looked out upon a stretch of allotment gardens. "Shall I sit here?" Frits asked, pulling a chair away from the table. "Yes, yes, do sit down," the man said. He himself took a seat in an armchair across from the fire, next to the piano. On the mantelpiece Frits saw a loudspeaker, the front covered in dark-red fabric. It was emitting a soft murmur. In one hand the man held a knob attached to the top of a little Bakelite box. Two wires ran to it, one connected to the loudspeaker and the other to the wall socket beside the radio set. "That is how he turns the sound up or down," Frits thought, "without having to get up."

"Is the family not at home?" he asked. "No," said the man, laying a book face-down on the table. "The three of them have gone to see *The Abduction from the Seraglio*." "And you had no desire to go along?" Frits asked. "Well," said the man, "that's for those who like that sort of thing. No, I didn't." "It's really very lovely," said Frits. He looked at the man's head. It was angular, but with a thick chin. The grey hair, which grew only at the front and sides of the skull, lay in lank strips across the bare scalp. "He's growing quite bald," he thought. "That won't take more than a couple of years." He removed his tobacco box from his pocket and asked: "Would you like me to roll one for you, Mr Adelaar?" "No, no," the man answered, "smoke one of mine." He tossed an opened packet of cigarettes on the table. "English," Frits thought. He lit one.

"Last Sunday they went out too," said Adelaar, "to that Shakespeare performance, that—" "*Twelfth Night*," Frits said. "By the New Company. That is truly fantastic." "Have you seen it?" Adelaar asked. "No," Frits answered, "I haven't had much time the last few days." "Oh," the other replied. "But I've spoken to quite a few people," Frits said, "of very good taste. No, it must be an extraordinary performance. They change scenes with the curtains open. Stagehands in period dress come on, while a different backdrop is slid into place. Meanwhile a female dancer performs to the tune of Renaissance music at the front of the stage, near the footlights, to divert attention. It is cleverly done. It is worth one's while."

"Yes, oh yes," Adelaar said, "there are marvels to be seen in this world." "Going bald is not necessarily a scourge," Frits thought, "but when you have such blue skin on your scalp, it can never be anything but a horrible sight."

"If you permit me, how is your health?" Frits asked. "Are you feeling better?" "Easy, I still take it very easy," said the man in a voice so low that Frits could make out only the last three words. "What is it like outside?" "The weather?" Frits asked. "Oh, it's not very cold. I wouldn't say that. The air is rather humid, but there is not much wind. You should go out for a walk, the weather is perfect for it. Don't you go out on your days off?" "No," Adelaar said, "no. No, we don't do much of that." He craned his neck, listening closely for any special announcement from the loudspeaker, and said: "This morning there was a hare in the back gardens here." "A hare?" Frits asked. "Yes," said Adelaar, "I saw it twice this morning. Twice, when I went to the window."

"Where could it have come from?" Frits asked. "Are you sure it was a hare? Couldn't it have been a rabbit that had escaped from its cage?" "No, Frits," the man said, "I know a hare when

I see one. A rabbit hops around a bit, but it's actually more like walking. A hare leaps in great bounds. A hare is also much longer and thinner." "That's delightful," Frits said. "It doesn't take much to amuse some," he thought. They fell silent. He looked around the room. Atop a tall antique cupboard lay a big old bible with gleaming copper locks. On the wall above the piano was a colour print of a woodland path in autumn. "I've been here eight minutes already," he thought. "That is courteous enough."

Suddenly Adelaar leaned forward, listened intently and adjusted the knob that was lying in his lap. "You are listening to film news and topics by W.J. den Tuin," the announcer said. Adelaar quickly straightened something in his chair, arranged a few books on the table and crossed his arms when the speaker began.

Frits looked outside. "Those are the gardens," he thought, "and those are the fields. That is the mist, the haze. And this is a house, in which people live." The voice babbled on. "Today the sunlight seems like it is coming through frosted glass," he thought. The whole time the radio commentator was speaking, neither of them said a word. Frits adopted an expression like one listening, his ear directed towards the loudspeaker, but did not allow the words to sink in. When it was over, Adelaar said: "Well, now we know that much." "I do have the impression," Frits said, "that the man is talking through his hat." "No," Adelaar said, "he has a good eye for things." "Do you go to the pictures often?" Frits asked. "No," Adelaar replied, "no." He had turned down the loudspeaker again. Of the piano music playing at that moment, only the powerful chords were audible.

"Wouldn't you like another cigarette?" he asked. "I never smoke that rubbish." "I have never understood," said Frits, taking a cigarette from the packet and lighting it, "how anyone can smoke a pipe. It always singes my lips." Again, a silence descended. "How do you happen to know so much about that," he asked, "about rabbits and hares? Have you spent a lot of time in the woods?" "You don't see hares in the woods," Adelaar replied. "Oh, well I…" Frits said. "We often went to that patch of wild land, out by the fen," the man said in a growl that was hard to understand. "Yes," he said, "catching salamanders. But they can crawl out of anything. At home I had a whole terrarium, with a little pond in it. Oh, I tell you, it was a fine arrangement. And angry, when you couldn't find them any more."

"I'll be off now," Frits said. "I'm taking my afternoon constitutional." He stood up and shook hands with Adelaar, who remained seated. "Don't bother, I can find my way out." He glanced at the title of the book lying on the table: *The House by the Side of the Road*.

Passing through the front room, from where he had entered, he stopped before the barometer that was hanging beside a large grandfather clock. When he tapped against the glass, Adelaar shouted: "It's busted!" The needle of the barometer showed a storm on its way. "Lost its marbles, more like," Frits said, and went down the stairs.

"If it wasn't so tiring for the feet, we could take a long walk," he thought, pulling the door closed behind him. He followed the same route back. "He holds loud and soft on his lap," he said to himself. "Nothing is so horrible but that there is something even more hideous."

When a few drops of rain began to fall he quickened his step, but the squall blew over. Arriving home, he found his mother dozing in the armchair. He looked at her and said to himself, moving his lips silently: "I feel miserable today. But let us pause and look around. Some people are punished severely from the very start: they are born as women. Frits van Egters, sage. Page eighty-two." "I'll be damned if I'm not growing awfully weary of that stench in my nose," he thought. He shivered.

The bell rang. After he had opened the front door, Joop and Ina came up the stairs. "Did you two come here straight from the theatre?" he asked. "Yes indeed," said Joop. "How was it?" "Mediocre," Joop replied, "very mediocre." "I stopped by this afternoon and saw old man Adelaar," Frits said. "I thought I would find you there, but oh no. The family was out. The only one home was the old duck himself. A good man. A soul that has had its wings clipped. He holds loud and soft on his lap." "What?" Joop asked. "You know what I mean," said Frits, "he holds that radio control in his lap. He turns it up and down with that. All wisdom, all readings, everything our ether brings forth is delivered to his door. Such convenience." "Ina, doesn't your father ever go out on Sunday?" his mother asked. "No, no," Ina replied. "He is up to date on all the films," Joop said. "He knows them all, but he hasn't seen one in years." "Where is Father?" he asked.

"Oh, he's gone out for a little walk," his mother said. "Joop," Frits asked, "what has happened to your hair? I've never seen it so thin. One now sees clear as a bell that you are going bald." "I washed it," Joop answered. "A mistake," Frits said. "Washing destroys the roots. It's a pity, but now the hair loss will run its course even faster." He heard the hall door open. "There you have him," said his mother. "Do you have anything to smoke?" Joop asked. Frits began to roll a cigarette.

When his father came into the room, his mother said: "It really is cold out, just like I said, isn't it? I knew as much. Your face is all flushed. I'm glad I didn't go along. I'm sure it would have made my head ache." His father shook hands first with Joop, then with Ina. He placed a chair by the fire, sat down, pulled his pipe from his jacket pocket and stood up. "He is looking for his tobacco," Frits thought, and peered with his eyes almost closed at the man patting down his pockets. Then his father stepped over to the table and reached for Frits's tobacco box. "Hey!" Frits cried, pulling the box towards him. "What is it?" his father asked. "Oh, help yourself," Frits said quickly, pushing the box away again. "Fine, then I won't," his father said. "What is wrong with you? How petty can you be?" He sat down again without touching the box. "Pitiful," he said with an angry grimace, "not even able to share something like a normal person." "It's not that," Frits said. "Everyone is free to roll cigarettes from my tobacco. But when they pull out a pipe, I kick up a fuss. They only have to fill a pipe once or twice and it is all gone." "And what would that matter?" his father asked. His face was still twisted in a grimace. "It doesn't matter," Frits said, "but I don't want that. Rolling tobacco does not belong in a pipe. I roll cigarettes for everyone, as many as they might want, but when someone comes along with a pipe, I feel that it is being wasted. It is the same at the office. They can always roll one from my tobacco, but when they show up with a pipe, I say: no." "I think that's abnormal," his father said. "I have many bad traits," said Frits. "One of them being niggardliness. Reconcile yourself to it. Some people are virtuous, others are not. One is better off having nothing to do with most of them." His father left the room, his face still twisted in anger.

"Why don't you let your father fill his pipe with your tobacco?" his mother asked. "What difference would it make?" Frits did not reply. He went to his bedroom, stood at the window and looked out through a crack in the curtains. "From outside, no one can see me," he thought, "I'm standing here like a spy." He remained standing like that until his mother called him to dinner. They started with soup. "It's horrid," he thought, "my parents slurp when they eat. I must have heard that a thousand times before; why do I notice it only today? It is the worst kind of slurping." "Mother, don't slurp," he said. "Why, does it bother you?" she asked.

"Anything new and interesting?" his father asked Joop. "No, no," he replied. "No, no," Frits said to himself, "no, no, nothing new or interesting." They lapsed into silence.

When the soup was finished his mother put potatoes, gravy, meat and a raw endive salad on the table. Frits helped himself twice and ate quickly. "The crisis is abated," he thought, "the poisons are leaving the system." He and his father were ready for their dessert at the same time. "I know for a fact," he thought, "that he is going to use his fork to dish up more. Look, look." Gritting his teeth, he watched as the man speared three potatoes from the platter with his own fork. "That is unclean," he thought, "a violation of every precept. But we stand powerless."

His mother came in with five little chocolate puddings in teacups. She emptied them onto a dish, one by one. "It worked," she said. His father began eating his pudding before the others had been served. "Let me flee," Frits thought, "I'm sure I can come up with some excuse."

When his mother had cleared the table, he put his box of tobacco on the table and asked: "Father, would you like to fill your pipe?" The man did not reply. "You are most welcome to it, Father," he said. "A pity that I have to leave." "But where are you going?" his mother asked. "Well," he said, "we shall see." "So you don't know where you're going yet?" she asked, "but you say that you have to leave." "The one does not necessarily rule out the other," Frits said. "One may need to leave, without having to go anywhere. Those are the cases in which one must go away from somewhere." "Stay and have a nice cup of tea," she said.

His father had taken a chair by the fire and was warming his hands. Joop and Ina were sitting beside each other on the divan.

"Joop," Frits said, "there's no need to tell you, of course, that you will be bald in no time. But have you ever stopped to think about what you will do once things get to that point? There is a very real chance that it will start falling out in the middle too. That you will develop an actual bald spot. That is a true

202

defacement. Then you look just like an old man. As long as it only grows thinner at the front, it is not such a problem. But when the real baldness comes, have you thought about what you will do then?"

"No," Joop said smiling. "Various methodologies have been advanced for combating it," Frits said, "but that is all quackery; science, in such cases, is virtually powerless. But there are means to disguise the void. That is not something I have learned from any book; you could have known it yourself, but you refuse to look around you."

"I see nothing, go on," said Joop. "Listen," Frits went on, "when the bald opening becomes awfully large, you can take the hair on the sides, which you first allow to grow quite long, and comb it across. Comb it up, over the top and towards the middle." "Shouldn't I put pins in it?" Joop asked. "Bah," Ina said. "No, you must plaster it down well with some sort of pomade," Frits continued. "I admit that a coiffure like that runs counter to the Western European fashion of our age, but it does hide the baldness completely."

His mother stirred the tea in the pot. He looked at his father, who was engrossed in a book. "One also has those," he said, "who lose more and more hair at the front all the time, with growth only at the back of the head. They let it grow long there. When they go to the barber they have him trim it a bit on the sides, but not at the back: they have a whole thicket growing down their neck. They believe that it does not matter where the hair grows, as long as they adhere to the prescribed quantity as a whole." He finished his tea and laid his chin in his hands.

"How about if I go by and see Bep Spanjaard?" he said to himself. "I haven't done that in weeks. If no one is at home, Jaap and Walter are not far away." He went into the hall and put on his coat, stuck his head through the doorway and said: "Good evening." "Don't make it too late," his mother called out. In the kitchen he drank a few big gulps of water and left.

Outside, a few drops of rain fell now and then, driven by weak gusts of wind. "It is a fairly dark night," he thought. "We just might get some heavy showers. But the air is brisk. I am feeling much better."

He followed broad thoroughfares to the centre of town and, just before reaching a square, turned right into a dimly lit alleyway; there he walked slowly, perusing each doorway on his left, until he reached a house where the second-floor windows were brightly lit. On one side the house was adjoined by a warehouse, on the other by an office building: a long, white sign on the front read "Insurance". "Between these two," Frits said quietly, "this is it." He pulled the handle of the doorbell. "Who's there?" a woman's voice called out. "Van Egters, Frits," he said. "Who's there?" the voice repeated. "It is me, Frits," he shouted. "Which Frits?" "Frits van Egters," he shouted, "friend of Louis, of Frans and Bep. An old acquaintance." "Oh, well then why don't you say so?" he heard the woman say, less loudly now. The door opened.

"You are definitely of a suspicious bent, Bep," he said, climbing a narrow, steep set of stairs. "Am I there yet?" he asked loudly as he reached the first-floor landing. "No, one more," the voice above him said. He climbed on and arrived at a landing where a door stood open. "Yes, come in," the voice called, and when he reached the threshold a young woman of thickset stature came to meet him. She was dressed in a loose-fitting gown and wore her dark-blond hair in a roll around her head. Her complexion was fresh, as was the skin on her arms, which were bared to above the elbows. "It is too bad about the teeth," Frits thought, "they could be a bit comelier. But she is certainly a sweet girl." He shook her hand and said: "You are faint-hearted, I notice. Fearful? Mild neurotic disorders?"

They entered a deep room which stretched from the front to the back of the house, with windows at both ends. The old, wood-stained floor was covered in part by a rush mat. Wicker chairs were arranged around a white table, and to the silk-plastered walls a variety of photos, frameless, were stuck with paper mounts. The bright ceiling lamp shone from behind a plate of frosted glass.

"Fearful? Yes, fearful," the girl said, giggling. "Just plain scared. Someone rang the bell last night at one o'clock." "Aha," said Frits. "Have a seat," she said. Frits sank down into one of the wicker chairs. "So the doorbell rang," Frits said. "And what was it?" "I don't know," she replied. "I was too afraid to move." "You could have looked out of the window?" Frits said. "No, no," she said. "Did they ring the bell again after that?" he asked. "No," she answered, "not after that."

"Listen, Bep," he asked, "do you live all alone in this house? What is downstairs?" "Yes," she said, "downstairs is the work-room, upstairs is the attic." "And the houses next door? Who is there at night?" "Next door? No one. That is a warehouse"—she pointed in the direction from which Frits had come—"there is never anyone there. And that"—she turned around—"is an office. People are there only during the day." "So you are here all alone?" Frits asked. "No one downstairs, no one upstairs. No one on that side, no one on this side. And it is night. Boo-hoo-hoo. My, my. Do you make sure there's a valid token in the electrical meter whenever darkness falls? Just imagine if the guilders were used up or a fuse blew. Total darkness. Oh, help, help." He puckered his lips and said slowly: "Oo-hoo. Hoo. Hoo."

"Be sure to help yourself to some cookies," she said, placing a tin on the table. "I could never live in a house all alone like this," Frits went on. "Hoo. Darkness, night, voices, inexplicable sounds." "Knock it off," Bep said. "Of course," Frits said, "you are, by nature, highly strung. But you do hear strange, inexplicable sounds. Am I right?" "Yes," Bep said. Her expression was frozen in a laugh, but no sound came out. "When I was in the kitchen last night," she said, "I was sure that I heard someone in the living room. Someone sitting down in a chair."

"Ah, there you have it," Frits said slowly, in a subdued voice, "now we are making progress. One is in the kitchen and someone enters the living room. He sits down in the wicker chair. You hear it clearly: first the sound of someone pulling up a chair, then the cracking as their full weight is committed to the seat. You walk slowly, in deepest dread, down the hall, towards the room—" "Yes, exactly," said Bep, "that's right." "Very carefully, all atremble, you peek around the door," said Frits, "but there is no one there. Am I right?" "Yes," she said.

"And those footsteps in the attic, you hear those quite often as well, don't you?" "All the time," she said, nodding vigorously, "all the time." "And you don't dare to go for a look, not when you're alone in the house," he said. "Boo. God only knows what it could be." "No, no," she said.

"Still, it is dangerous to live on one's own," he went on. "You could be murdered in your bed at night. You think there is no one in the house. But how certain can you be? How do you know that someone hasn't crept in before closing time? I find it very plucky of you, that you dare to be here alone at night. Even if there were two of you, you would not be completely safe. Like that old couple in Haarlem." "Watch, now she's going to ask: what was that about?" he thought.

"A couple in Haarlem?" Bep asked, "what was that about?" "What do you mean?" Frits asked. "You said something about old people, the two of them, something happened," she said.

"Oh," Frits said. "Nothing that out of the ordinary. A burglar came through the toilet window. The old woman saw him. He struck her on the head, at least twenty times, with a chisel, until she told him where the money was. They went to the money and then the old man came in. He tried to put up a fight. But he was seventy-seven years old. The burglar stabbed him, until he fell to the floor. A little later he was dead. Then the fellow took the money and was gone. The woman tried to sound the alarm. But too late. I don't know whether they ever found the culprit. The only thing is—oh, well, perhaps I'd better not talk about that."

"Yes, tell me," Bep said. "I almost forgot my tobacco," said Frits, taking his box out of his coat pocket and rolling two cigarettes. "The fat one is for you," he said, "one must not forget one's manners." A sudden series of cold shivers ran through him, and he felt his left eyelid tremble. "A nasty thing, how long the feeling sticks with you," he thought.

Bep took a few deep drags of her cigarette and blew the smoke out slowly, bit by bit, in little clouds. "Remarkable," he thought, looking at her legs, "that she wears no stockings, even in December. Dark flesh, imbrued with blood." "What was it, then?" she asked. "Come, tell me."

"It was the blood," Frits continued. "The old man was dead; all life had left him. And the woman they took to the hospital. Because that's not particularly helpful, you know, twenty blows and stabs with a chisel. But then the burglar. He must have been covered in blood. They were able to follow the bloody tracks for eight hundred metres through town. It must have been dripping off him. Hideous things. I swear, that's the way it went."

"And if it didn't happen that way," Bep said, "you would have come up with it yourself. From what I hear, you can't do without such things."

"The devil take me," said Frits, "it is a delight to me each and every time. Those reports like: child killed by exploding grenade. Glorious. Deferred suffering from the war. That is always a joy. They always start off so cosily, those reports." "The seven-year-old son," he said in an impassive voice, "of the Karels family, agriculturalists in Breda, attempted on Wednesday afternoon to dismantle a small anti-aircraft shell with a claw hammer."

He clapped his hands once, softly. "I'll wait till you've blown off steam," Bep said.

"It always ends," he went on, "with: he will have to do without his left hand. Or: the child breathed his last on the way to the hospital. Or: the boy shuffled off this mortal coil. Well put, don't you agree? Shuffled off this mortal coil. Here we see a poet at work." He clicked his tongue. "Another lovely one is: a six-year-old playmate, who was watching from a little distance, was struck by shrapnel in the stomach and legs. My, my. Hideous things. And so young, those children. Wonderfully poignant."

"Would you like some coffee?" Bep asked. "There's milk on the stove." "A bit early for coffee," Frits said, "but nice, yes. Please." She went into a little alcove to one side, separated from the living room by a floral curtain. Soon she came back with two cups of coffee. "Did you remember to wipe the dredgings off the rim?" he asked. She did not reply.

"How is your leg?" he asked, once she was seated. "Does it still itch so badly?" "The last few days, almost not at all," she answered. "Let's have a look," Frits said.

She stuck out her right leg and turned it so he could see the inside. A trail of brown and dark-red spots ran from the ankle almost to the knee.

"Advancing steadily, I see," he said. "Is it still festering?" "No, oh no," she said. "That doesn't prove anything," Frits went on, "the suppuration has probably internalized. The pain will only come once the bone membrane has been damaged. At least you have time left till then." "Oh, you," Bep said. She pulled down the hem of her gown. "Of course, why not, go right

209

ahead and dismiss all serious counsel," he said. "But the day will come when you will need a little chair"—he rocked from side to side—"to shuffle from door to door, just like that man who comes by every year. You remember him, don't you? He had no legs, or almost no legs. No, his legs were paralysed. He went from door to door selling pencils in his chair, wrenching it from one leg to the other. I am the man, who comes by every year. Didn't you see him in your neighbourhood?" "No," said Bep.

"Then you missed a great deal," Frits went on. "Are you still seeing the specialist? What does he do, what does he say? Cold-water massage?" "Oh, come on," she answered, "he prescribes that grey ointment. That makes it itch even worse. He says it needs to erupt." "Do you think that will get rid of it?" Frits asked. "No," she answered, "I don't know. He always says: Oh. Well, my. I've asked him so many times: Doctor, what is it? Then he says: If it must have a name, it is related to eczema."

"Talking, they're good at that," said Frits. "Enough to drive you into the arms of a quack. That costs you not only your money, but your nerves as well. But sometimes it helps. Why haven't you seen a good wonder doctor yet? A competent layer-on of hands?" He slapped his thighs. "The Koo-way methodology. I feel good. I still feel good. I feel better. Oh, I'm already feeling so much better. I'm already better than I just was." "I wonder if this will work," he thought.

"On Monday I went to a fellow like that," Bep said, smiling. "Bingo," Frits thought, "just as I suspected. Bull's-eye. A flower in my buttonhole." "So you actually did," he said. "Where was that? Did you have to wait long?"

"On Vlierstraat," she said. "Zaber, that's his name. The two of us went. Nutty people in the waiting room. You'd die laughing, if you heard those stories." "Who went with you?" Frits asked. "Lies," she answered. "I went in, we went in together." She pushed back a strand of hair that had fallen over her forehead. "That man asked: are both of you here for treatment? No, I said, only me. Then he wanted me to look at him. I couldn't help laughing. He says: You have a problem with your leg. Let me see it. He looked at it and then I had to look at him again. He said: There is something you are afraid of. What is it? I said: I'm not aware of anything. A whole lot of questions, then he said: You are afraid that it is tuberculosis." "Of course," Frits said, "that's the most likely thing." "I had no idea," Bep said. "He asked me: do you have faith in me? We couldn't help laughing the whole time. If necessary, yes, I said." "Very good," Frits said, "and then he started feeling your leg."

"No," Bep said, "he ran his hands over it, but never actually touched it." "A true gentleman," said Frits. Bep held her leg out again and used both hands, palms face down, to make caressing motions from top to bottom. "And afterwards, each time," she said, "he flapped his hands, as though they were wet. You should have heard it. His knuckles cracked something fierce. Like he was slapping his hands against a cupboard." "And the two of you sitting there, laughing the whole time," Frits said. "We almost died laughing," she continued, "and he went on with that for at least ten minutes. The man must be exhausted when he gets home." "Did it help?" Frits asked. "I don't know," she answered, "but when I left, I noticed that it had stopped itching."

"*Voilà*," said Frits, "and then came the bill. How much did he charge?" "Two fifty. But first he asked very politely whether I could afford it." "Well, how about that," Frits said, "for ten guilders the whole thing will be ancient history. He pinches you on one side and the consumption goes flying out the other. Gangway! The triumph of modern science. Will you keep going back?"

"Why not?" Bep said. "I went to see my mother. She said: If it helps, keep going to him. Fine by me, as long as she's willing to pay." She squeezed her leg and drew it back again.

"That is how superstition enters the world," Frits said. "In Dordrecht you once had a very famous uroscopist. My aunt told me about her: it's a true story. The woman became very wealthy. As a girl, she had worked as a whore in Rotterdam. She had a coach and a driver and a page in livery, who showed the people to their seats in the waiting room. She would hold the piss over a flame in a glass retort and tell you what was wrong with you. She gave them herbs, the same herbs to every patient, but they only found that out later on. One day a farmer came to her. He was from Dubbeldam, I believe. He brought a bottle full of his old mother's piss with him. The woman says: She is recovering, she'll be better within a few days. Ha, yes, that's exactly what she said." "This is another of your nasty stories," Bep said.

"No, let me go on," Frits continued. "So she says: She'll be better soon. But within a week the old mother was dead. Do you know what that farmer did then? He filled a bottle with pig's piss and went to town. He goes to the uroscopist, but the lady doesn't suspect a thing. Holding the retort over the flame, she says: 'Wonderful, she's making good progress.' Then that farmer kicked up a huge fuss, it must have been something to behold. The newspapers got wind of it too. She had to sneak out of town and they smashed all her windows. Wonderful." "I am feeling pretty lousy," he thought. "If I don't get to bed too late, I'll be fresh in the morning."

"Have you seen *The Green Pastures?*" Bep asked. "It's that race film, isn't it?" Frits asked. "No, I haven't seen it." "Do you know whether it's any good or not?" she asked. "Yes," he replied, "I've heard many good things about it." "Because I'm going tomorrow evening," Bep said. "Where is it playing?" Frits asked, "it's not on anywhere at the moment, is it?" "No," she said, "it's a special midnight screening at The Lantern. At eleven thirty. A benefit for the Free Podium." "Oh," said Frits, "I'd like to go too. How much is it?" "A guilder," Bep said. "Do you think I can still get a ticket?" he asked. "I still have to pick them up," she answered, "then—yes, that's two—yes, I can do that. Come by here tomorrow night. We'll all be here."

"Who?" Frits asked. "Eduard, Louis, Jaap and Joosje," she answered. "Oh, good," Frits said, "shall I give you the money right away?" "No," she said, "we can do that then." They were silent for a time. "There's still some work I need to finish," Bep said. "I have to develop a few prints for tomorrow." "Yes," Frits said, rising to his feet, "I must be going anyway." He walked over to a bookcase and took down a toy rabbit from against the wall on the top shelf. He held it in his hand. It was made from coarse, light-brown wool, with a white belly. Resting it on his arm, against his chest, he said: "Sweet, isn't it? Sweet little rabbit. He's sweet. It always brings tears to my eyes, every time I see it." "You think he's nice?" Bep asked. "You can borrow him. Would you like to take him?" "Can he stay at my house for a couple of weeks?" asked Frits, petting the animal. "I'd like that." He placed it on the table and buttoned his coat.

"Does your mother have enough coffee and tea?" Bep asked. "I'm not sure," Frits replied. "As you know, our family is characterized by great thrift." "What is going on?" he thought. Bep got up, went into the alcove behind the floral curtain and, when she came back, laid a package of tea and a bag of coffee beans on the table. "Take that with you," she said. "What is this about?" he asked. "Did you borrow something from my mother?" "No," she replied.

"I wouldn't dare claim that I understand a bit of it," he thought, stuck the packages in his pocket, tucked the rabbit inside his coat, close to the armpit, and left. It was raining. "Still only a quarter to nine," he thought, glancing at his watch.

At home he opened the door without a sound, closed it quietly behind him and remained standing. "So what do you want?" he heard his mother say in the living room. "If I only knew what you wanted. But you don't want anything. You yourself don't even know what you want. You say that I harp at you. But I never say a thing. This morning I asked you: Do you comb your hair with that little nailbrush? Aren't I allowed to ask that? Do you have to answer back: do you mind? And you

214

looked as though you felt like strangling me. You feel threatened. Do I threaten you?"

A brief silence descended. Frits opened the door again, backed silently into the hallway, closed the door carefully and then opened it again with a great display of noise. Then he slammed it shut and walked into the room, humming. His mother was sitting in the low armchair by the fire; his father was at the table. Both of them remained silent when he came in and wished them a good evening. "Not good," he thought, "not good at all. Quick, quick."

"When was the first time you saw a film, Father?" he asked. "What?" asked his father. "Do you remember," Frits asked loudly, "when your first saw a film?" "Yes, yes," the man said, exhaling a deep sigh, "it was at the travelling carnival, as a young boy. Living pictures, they called them back then." "That wasn't a motion picture, though, was it?" his mother asked. "You didn't have films back then, did you?" "How would you know?" asked his father, his face wrinkling in irritation. "I don't believe a word of it," she said. "Well then, don't believe it," his father said.

"Did it actually move, or was it a slide show?" Frits asked. "No, of course not," his father replied, "it was a film. A bit artless. And the pictures were quite shaky." The angry expression on his face vanished. "The constables chasing a gang of smugglers. And shooting. Pow!" He moved his right hand as though firing a pistol. "I thought it was wonderful. It made quite an impression on me." "Without any sound," Frits said. "That's right, without sound," his father said. "Will I be able to come up with another question?" Frits thought. "No, I can't." "I'm

going to bed a bit early," he said, "I need to be fit tomorrow."
His eyes closed, he walked out of the room slowly. He put the
two packages in the kitchen cupboard. The rabbit he took with
him to his bedroom, where he placed it on the bookshelf.

With a careless gesture, he tossed his clothes over the chair
beside his bed. "No time for all that folding and hanging,"
he mumbled. Once in bed, he thought: "I didn't brush my
teeth. I need to get up again." He tried to sit up a few times,
but was unable to rise. "I'll count to twenty," he thought. At
twenty-four he hopped to his feet and went to the kitchen.
After brushing his teeth, he dropped his underpants and,
holding the shaving mirror between his legs, examined his
crotch and, pulling a thigh aside with his free hand, his anus.
"Very distasteful," he mumbled. "If you saw a photograph of
it, taken from below, you would hardly believe it was human.
Oh, oh."

Hanging the mirror back in place he returned to his bed,
but could not sleep right away. "That's what you get, when you
go to bed early," he thought. "It doesn't help, because sleep will
not come. It makes you nervous as hell. Besides, I need another
blanket. I have to get out again. Fetch one from the cupboard."
He rocked back and forth, striking the wall with his fist now
and then, and fell asleep only forty minutes later.

He was in a canoe, paddling across a large, calm lake. The
sky was overcast. There was no wind, and the water's black
surface was smooth as glass. "The water is rising," he thought.
More and more water entered the canoe. He stuck his hand
in it, then felt the water outside the boat. "A nasty sign," he

thought, "the water here inside the boat is much colder than that on the outside. It is different water. Where is it coming from?"

He paddled as hard as he could. "As long as I can see the shore," he said aloud. The water in the bottom of the boat rose and reached his legs and thighs. "I'm lost," he thought. The water continued to rise, the canoe sank deeper and deeper and the sky grew dark. No matter how hard he paddled, the canoe moved more slowly all the time. Finally, the water reached the rim of the little boat.

He stopped paddling. "As long as I don't move, it will stay afloat," he thought. At that moment, in the distance across from him, he saw a wave approaching in the dusk, high as a house. "A wall of water," he thought, "it is the storm surge."

The suction drew the water around him steadily towards the approaching wave: he could tell by the clumps of debris, leaves and blades of straw drifting past him faster all the time. A constant thundering sounded from the distance. "The current hasn't taken me yet," he thought, "I have to try." He turned the canoe around and started paddling, but made almost no progress. When he looked over his shoulder, the swell was already very close: a fine cloud of spray floated across the crest. In the roar one could clearly make out the spattering of foam and the groan of the mass of water as it fell.

He awoke, but no clear thoughts came. Before he could recall the full content of his dream, he fell asleep again. It was three o'clock.

IX

ON MONDAY AFTERNOON, when he took his bicycle out of the shed after office hours, the front tyre was flat. Standing by a street lamp he turned the wheel slowly and discovered a tack jammed into the rubber. He removed it, felt in his coat pocket until he found a stub of red pencil, and drew a line across tyre and rim. "I know how it will go," he thought. "I'll put it in the storage cupboard and forget about it. I won't get around to it. On foot it is then, for the time being."

The air was filled with a fine mist. Here and there on the pavement were puddles from the rain that had fallen that morning. "This is mist," he said to himself, "that is getting ready to turn into rain. It is rain that is almost heavy enough to fall." Walking along, he ran his hands from time to time over his coat, which was becoming wet.

"The end of the year is approaching," he thought. "I am here, walking through town, through the mist, on my way home, as darkness falls. These are the final days of the year." He followed the pavements, lifting the front wheel carefully at each kerb. "Still, this the right weather to do some thinking," he mused on. "At this atmosphere, one discovers one's true worth." He began singing to himself softly, half humming. Arriving at the front door he thought: "There is no single, valid reason why this evening should be a failure. I have a suspicion that it will succeed. An evening, the course of which is fixed beforehand, cannot possibly be a failure. The point is to imagine nothing more of it than can reasonably be expected, that's all."

When he came into the living room, his mother said: "You're a bit later today." She was sitting at the table, writing a letter. "Yes, a little later," Frits said. "A touching solicitude surrounds me," he thought. He looked at her, how she held her head and how the pen moved across the lined paper. "One must not be unreasonable," he thought, "they are people too, God's children." He was just about to start humming when she asked: "What about this horrible, wet cold? It cuts right through everything. There is nothing worse than that soaking-wet chill."

"Oh," Frits said, "it has its advantages. The frost is gone. It's quite possible that it won't freeze again for the rest of the winter. Wet, of course, but when you make sure you're wearing a coat, that's no bother." "It always makes my head ache so terribly," she said. Frits went to his room, remained standing before the bookcase and took the toy rabbit in his hand. "Symbol of beneficence, beast of atonement," he mumbled, holding it up to his cheek and looking in the mirror. "Not an appealing face," he thought, "I have a sick soul."

When he heard someone come through the door to the hallway, he recognized his father, after listening for a moment, by his footsteps and the way he breathed as he hung up his overcoat. "He sired me," he thought. "Let me view him charitably." He patted the rabbit, making dust rise, then put it back in its place and went to the living room.

"Hello, Father," he said as he came in. "Hello, my boy," the man answered. He was sitting by the fire, poking at a molar with his finger. "One may think whatever one likes," Frits thought, "but one must never be unreasonable." He went to the kitchen, drank water slowly from a ladle, and looked out of the window.

Facing off in the gardens below, separated by the fence, were the downstairs neighbours' brown dog and the white keeshond belonging to the people next door. "A unique opportunity," he thought, filling a bowl with water, but then emptying it again in the sink. "It provides no real cheer," he said aloud. "I won't do it."

He went into the side room, lit the gas fire and observed how far the valve could be closed before the flames died. "A silly waste of time," he thought. His mother called him to dinner.

He ate mechanically of the red cabbage, potatoes, beets and the porridge. When they were finished, his father pulled out his pipe, felt at his pockets, put the pipe away and from the bookcase took down a box of cigars. As soon as Frits saw the box in his hand, he asked, his eyes fixed on the table: "Would you like to fill your pipe with my tobacco, Father?" "No, that's fine," the man answered with a smile. He offered Frits one of the little cigars.

No one spoke as his mother cleared the table. As the table grew barer, Frits felt tension growing within him. "Now I must ask a question, with discernment and feeling," he thought. "But first a few words to sharpen the hearing."

"Abadida didonkolo bolde netsowan intedus, Father," he said, "igatedo bewank dedestel." "What?" the man asked, leaning over to him. "Father," Frits asked, "how old were you when you went to work at the factory? Significantly younger than is allowed these days, wasn't it?" "That should keep us talking for fifteen minutes or so," he thought. "After that, I'll see what I do."

"The factory?" his father asked. His forehead wrinkled in a frown. "I was twelve. In the weaving mill." "Did you go to work with the weavers right away?" his mother asked. She folded up the tablecloth. "I thought you worked in another part of the factory first." "No, of course not," his father said, pursing his lips as though against a cold wind. Slowly his features relaxed again. "Father," Frits asked, "what time did you start work then, and what time were you finished?" "From six thirty," the man replied, placing his hands on the table and lacing his fingers, "until seven in the evening." "This isn't quite the tenth time I've heard this," Frits thought. "Were you allowed a break?" he asked. "Yes," his father answered, "from noon to one thirty."

"Aha, I see," said Frits. "Ask him about the bench now," he thought. "It's almost impossible for me to imagine," he said, "a twelve-year-old boy in a factory, amid all those terrible machines. That would drive a child mad, wouldn't it? If something was out of reach, well, you couldn't get to it, could you?" "Here comes the bench," he thought.

"They brought in a bench for me," his father said, using his hands to indicate breadth and height. "Uh-huh." He looked straight ahead, pursed his lips, made a little tent with his fingertips and said: "When I stood on that bench, I could reach everything." His eyes opened a bit wider and remained fixed on the curtains.

"No," Frits thought, "the fun and games end here. Hear ye, hear ye."

"When you come in," his father said, "the whole factory hall is still dark. Only a few paraffin lamps are lit. At six thirty the big drive shafts, up at the top"—he lifted his arms—"start to turn. Slowly at first. Then the lights go on, gradually." "Just like at the theatre," Frits said, "when the curtains are raised. Then it gets lighter and lighter, but you can't see that they're increasing the current the whole time." "What you see," his father went on, "what you see is that long shaft with all those gears, as long as the whole factory, starting to turn"—he made a tumbling motion in the air with his hands—"and then the lights come on, and then it begins."

"Is it a roaring sound or a rattling sound?" Frits asked. "Everything is drowned out, right?" His father nodded. "What I mean is: is it only the zooming, the roaring that drowns everything out, or is it the rattling of all those machine parts taken together?" "A fairly stupid question," he thought. "It's both," his father answered. "You can't be heard above it. You have to speak in sign language, with your hands." Leaning his temple against his right fist, he ran his free hand through his hair.

"How long did you work there?" Frits asked. His father did not reply. "Father," he asked again, "how long did that go on? How long were you there?" "Five years," the man answered, probing at his molars with his thumb.

Frits got up, went to his bedroom and remained standing at the desk. He stubbed out the cigar, which was only half consumed, and laid it in the penholder atop an inkpot. "I mustn't leave too late, but also not too early," he said to himself. "Not so that I give myself the feeling: I got there first, too early, out of boredom. And also not: I'm showing up at the very last moment, because all I care about is the film. No, halfway through the evening, between eight and nine. That's the best time." Rolling a cigarette, he said out loud: "All our goods are packed by hand, not touched by a finger, now isn't that grand." He picked up the rabbit, kissed it on the snout and sat down with it on the edge of the bed. "You are my sweet, good rabbit," he said aloud, "and that's that. Don't you pay any mind." He felt tears coming to his eyes, wrapped thumb and middle finger around the animal's neck and bit down on one of the long, stiff ears. "Bah," he said, spitting out little fluffs of wool, and placed it back in the bookcase. After pacing back and forth a bit, he picked it up again and, loosening two buttons of his shirt, tucked it between his vest and his bare chest. He sat down in the chair at his desk, pulled the animal out again, clasped it between his legs at the crotch and stroked its ears. "It's cold in here," he said aloud, then stuffed the animal behind a row of books, turned off the light and went to stand at the window. "Evening has come," he mumbled.

He walked back into the living room. On his way he heard his parents' voices in the kitchen. "That is a stroke of luck," he thought, "Father is drying the dishes."

He turned on the radio without changing stations. The news reports were being read. Even before the voice had reached full volume, he switched stations and listened to an accordionist, who was playing a musette waltz. His mother put her head around the door and asked: "Do you know what the real time is? Will you let us know when the news starts? Father would like to hear the news." "I'll listen for it," he replied. She withdrew. He searched for the first station, kept the volume down and waited until the news was over and the sports results were being broadcast. "Yes, here's the news, Mother," he shouted. "The news!" he heard his mother shout in the kitchen. His father came in, hurried to the radio and sat down on the divan in front of it. "Shoot," he said, "it's already over." "A pity," Frits said, "I was listening to the other station and I waited too long. They always broadcast the news on that other station. When it lasted too long, I tried this one and they were already in progress. You missed the best part of the programme. A waste and a pity." "Hoopla, hoopla, hoopla," he said to himself. "What shall we do now?" he thought. "It is already past eight. The best thing would be to leave and to walk slowly." His father left the room, his head bowed. "There he goes," Frits thought. "Life is not simple." He turned off the radio.

A few minutes later his mother came in with the dishes. "I'm going to Bep Spanjaard's," he said, "and from there we're going to a midnight showing at The Lantern, at eleven thirty." "What time will you come home then, for God's sake?" she asked. "It will probably be around two o'clock," he replied, "be sure not to bolt the door." "One of these days you'll go completely mad," she said. "True," Frits said, "I am already moving in that direction, by leaps and bounds. But don't tell anyone." "Where lies salvation?" he thought. His father came in and asked: "What is it now? What is all this fuss about?" "No, Father," he said, "it is a matter of speaking loudly in order to explain something." "What kind of a film is that, that people have to go to it so late at night?" his mother asked. "It's *The Green Pastures*," Frits answered slowly. "What is it about?" she asked. She was standing in front of the sideboard. His father had deposited himself on the divan. "That is what I shall find out this evening," Frits replied. "Well, enjoy yourself," she said. "Forward march," Frits mumbled to himself. "Double time. Away, away." He pulled on his coat without first grasping the sleeves of his jacket, so they ended up around his elbows. "We'll take care of that in a minute," he said quietly, "but first, out of the door." "Goodbye, Mother. Goodbye, Father," he called out at the living room door, "I wish you a pleasant evening. Should anyone come to visit me, please tell them that Mr van Egters will be home very late; warn them that it could be a very long wait indeed." He closed the door quietly and hopped, holding onto the handrail, down the stairs, three steps at a time.

"The mist has not disappeared completely," he said once he was outside. He sniffed loudly, drawing mucus up his nose, and thought: "If I don't buy myself some more cod liver oil soon, I will definitely catch a cold. But I keep forgetting. I used up the last of it a week ago. The deficiency makes itself known after about eight days." Walking on, he wrung his arms around in his coat to force the sleeves of his jacket into place.

In the alleyway he paused for a moment in front of Bep Spanjaard's house, and looked at the lighted windows before ringing the bell. He heard laughter and loud shouts of something, but could not make out what. The door was opened with great force and slammed against the wall of the stairwell.

"Frits," he shouted. At the top of the stairs stood Jaap Elderer and a young man he did not know. "Oh yes," Jaap yelled, "of course. If we were to say: bah, bah, here comes Frits, that would be unkind." "Fine, thank you, and you?" he asked loudly, once Frits reached the landing, "this is Eduard." Frits shook the stranger's hand. The young man was squat and wore spectacles with thick, dark frames. His black, bristly hair stood out stiffly at the back and sides. His face was round, without an angular spot to it. The eyes were small, the nose short, and his lips were broad and thin. "A person with his looks shouldn't go wearing a bow tie," Frits thought. He looked at the black tie, speckled with white, which hung crookedly at his collar. "What was the name again?" Frits asked. "Eduard Hoogkamp," the young man said in a toneless whisper. "You are a real dolt," Frits said to himself.

The three entered the room together. Bep and Joosje were seated on either side of the potbellied stove. Across from them were two empty chairs. Jaap and the young man who had introduced himself as Hoogkamp each picked up a chair and made room for Frits, who sat down between them on a little bench he took from the corner. "Five little Indians around the fire," he said. He pulled out his wallet, removed a one-guilder note and held it out to Bep. "Here you are," he said, "or was it more than that?" "There is no admission at the door here," said Jaap, "but refreshments are mandatory." Bep took the guilder without a word.

226

"What is the first thing someone will say?" Frits thought. "It's impossible to guess, yet still there's no harm in trying." Everyone remained silent. "Bep hasn't spoken, and Jaap hasn't really either," he thought. "Just a moment ago, right before I got here, someone said something and they're all still thinking about it. That's what it is."

"Well, well, Mr van Egters," Jaap said, "what is the weather like outside?" "Foggy, my liege, my lord," Frits replied. "Aha," Jaap said, looking around with an expression of triumph, "how lovely is the onset of spring, when everything starts growing again. I have already seen the coltsfoot in flower, now we must only wait for the Michaelmas daisy, then we're finished with the whole thing. Yes, yes, allez, allez, oy oy oy, wise words and true, neighbour." "Holy Christ," Frits thought, "I've barely come in the door." "Why don't we actually talk about something?" he said. "If anyone knows of anything, let them speak." "What's wrong, don't you like flowers?" Jaap asked, tilting his head and grinning. "You disappoint me; you disappoint me terribly." "Oh, stop it, stop it," Bep said, giggling. Hoogkamp cleared his throat. "And now I'm stuck here from nine to eleven," Frits thought.

"The miracle of the flowers," Jaap went on, waggling his head back and forth. "When you look closely, the way those stamens and pistils swell!" Lifting his head high he said, in a tone as though reading it aloud: "That is, in fact, a most wondrous thing. Then come the busy little bees…" Bep and Frits burst out laughing. "Oh yes, oh yes," Jaap said, smacking his lips.

"Let's see about a little coffee," said Bep, filling the cups from a green enamelled pot that she took from the stove. "Not for me," Frits said. "Me neither," said Hoogkamp. "You must remember, he was ill only recently," Jaap said. "The only thing to be done about it is to join in," Frits thought.

"The atmosphere here this evening is exceeding stale," he said. "Joosje and Bep are women, they may remain silent if they wish. But Mr Hoogkamp, it is time for you to tell us a story from the annals of life itself." "Now we'll get to hear what a dolt you really are," he thought. "Well, nothing really comes to mind at the moment," Hoogkamp said with a smile. "This is not getting us anywhere," Frits thought. "You are quite right not to accept coffee," he said, "I'm not taking any either." "God help us," he thought, "how awful. Now move on." "Jaap, do tell me," he said, "how things stand with your hair loss." "Jesus," Joosje said.

"It's growing well," Jaap said, running a hand over his hair. "No, that subject is bound to bog down," Frits thought. "Still, go on with it." "I should like to draw a distinction," he said. "I would like to divide baldness into three categories: baldness due to an illness with an indirect effect on hair growth, typhoid fever for example—" "Don't let me forget to tell you that one about the bet," Jaap said. "Then," Frits continued, "we have baldness as a result of a disease of the hair or the subcutaneous fat, and thirdly there is baldness due to old age. And if you ask me, I believe that yours is a case of number two: a hair disease."

"Have you heard the one about the fellow who says to his friend: you're not healthy, I bet you have anaemia?" Jaap asked. "So he says: I bet you have anaemia. No, come on, the other fellow says. Sure as sure can be, the first one says, would you like to bet? They bet twenty-five guilders on it and the second fellow goes to the doctor for a check-up. The first one waits outside. After a while his friend comes out of the office, skipping and dancing"—he spread his arms as though taking flight—"and he shouts: Ha! I won! I have stomach cancer!"

Bep and Frits laughed. Joosje curled her lips in a smile, but Hoogkamp's expression remained unchanged. "When did I hear that one before?" Frits thought. "With another disease in it. It wasn't that long ago. It's all the same thing." "Fine, you can tell us all that," he said, "to divert attention from the crux of it, but in your case it is a hair disease."

"Still, old people don't necessarily go bald," said Joosje. "My grandfather had a full head of hair, all the way up to the end." "And yet, dead," Frits said, "there is nothing to be done about it." "My grandfather is still alive," Hoogkamp said slowly. "He still has plenty of hair on his head too." "Hair or no," Frits said, "once they're past sixty they should all be put down. Painlessly." "Come on, stop it," Joosje said.

"Yes, really," Frits went on, "no misguided leniency. That is foolishness. Old people are a plague. As soon as they have trouble walking, or start to befoul themselves, or complain or make a mess at the table—off with them! A blow to the base of the skull with a length of sturdy pipe and then straight into the lime pit. Am I right, Bep?" "I've never had any problems with old people," Bep said.

"Whether you like it or not," Frits continued, "they are a burden. Mr Hoogkamp, you have not yet reached sixty, but I am sure you have a well-defined opinion on the matter; would you also be willing to say that you have never had any problems with those old encumbrances?"

"We had an elderly aunt who lived with us," Hoogkamp said in an equable tone, as though he had spoken of his own accord and not in response to a question, "and she made sucking sounds when she read." With a wave of the arm he seized a newspaper from the table behind him, spread it across his lap and, his eyes scanning the lines of print, made sucking noises as his lips spelt out the words. "What was that?" Joosje asked. "She did not," Eduard said slowly, "actually read out loud, but she mumbled. Or actually, it wasn't mumbling, it was a sort of…" He rested his chin in his hand and fell silent.

"And what did you do then, Eduard?" Jaap asked. "Me?" Eduard said. "Nothing. It was a real chore for her, that passing away. It went on for more than ten years. She took her own sweet time about it."

"Maybe you're not such a bad fellow after all," Frits thought. "No, old people, that is a lost cause," he said. "My thoughts exactly," Jaap said. "I went to my grandfather's funeral today. That's right, he's off the twig." "The old one, the stingy one?" Frits asked. "Why didn't you say so before? I love funerals. Or are you pulling my leg? Did you actually go to a funeral today?"

"Of course," Jaap said, "you need to understand that I tend not to direct much attention towards my own suffering. It is a sore loss for the family. It's hard for me to talk about it. Leave me alone." He raised his head, shook it briskly, pursed his lips and said: "That poor, poor man."

"No, come on, are you kidding me?" Frits asked. "Was it that grandpa, the one you visited in the hospital a few times?" "Exactly," Jaap answered. "You got the day off," Frits said, "didn't you?" "Of course," Jaap said. "Relatives in the first remove, or isn't that the first remove?" He produced a pouch of tobacco and began rolling a cigarette.

"Was it a fine funeral?" Frits asked. "This is the third time already," said Joosje, "that I'm having to listen to this." "Certainly," Jaap said, "I realize, sweetheart, that it is an ordeal, but try to think of me." Turning back to Frits, he said: "First we went to Voetstraat. A very proper funeral parlour. You come in and there's a book waiting for you to sign. Nicely bound in black, very austere." "Was it a second-class funeral?" Frits asked. "No, third class, but still quite lovely. We sat there for about half an hour, until everyone arrived, then this tall fellow came in"—he imitated the man's walk by twisting his torso back and forth and rolling his eyes at the ceiling—"who said: My name is Horen, I am leading the service today. Will you accept my deepest condolences? Will those present please follow me to the chapel? Then you go in single file to the chapel, like a herd of silly sheep. The coffin is there, in a sort of alcove. Everyone sits down and they play a little tra-la-li-tra-lah-lah on the organ and then, with your hands clasped behind your back, you walk past. It's an open coffin, covered in plate glass. You're supposed to pause for a moment and say something. For example: his suffering is over. Or: He looks so natural. That's always a good one. Although maybe not in this case, because his neck was puffed up even thicker than his head."

231

"How old was your grandfather, then?" Frits asked. "He reached the blessed age of seventy-six," Jaap replied. "With a crust on his scalp, this thick." He held up his hand, thumb and forefinger a good inch apart. "That's rather distasteful, Jaap," Hoogkamp said. "A crust?" Frits asked. "What do you mean?" "Well," Jaap said, "in the hospital they gave him blood transfusions all the time. The blood was lost as fast as it went in, otherwise he would have burst like a balloon; but it seemed to all clot up around his head. A neck almost as broad as his shoulders: this huge crop. And a thick crust on the top of his head, as though it had broken through his scalp and solidified."

"What did the organ play?" Frits asked. "I'm not sure," Jaap said, "you know, I'm not that well versed when it comes to music. When it was over, though, that fellow came back again. Pulls shut a curtain in front of the coffin. So they can drag him away on the other side. He reads a list of names for the cars in the procession. Outside they're standing in two neat rows, hats held in front of their stomachs. I was in the last car and I looked back through the rear window. The doors were barely closed when those fellows ran over to a little Fiat and climbed in, all eight of them. It races off right away. If you didn't know that and you got to the cemetery at Veldrust, you'd think: it's a blooming miracle, the same fellows again, still with their hats in their hands. But they actually raced around the funeral procession at top speed, to get there first. Then you go to the chapel again, at the cemetery this time. Another organ plays and that fellow says: Slowly now… yes! Then they've got the coffin on their shoulders."

"It's amazing that no one else is saying anything," Frits thought. "As though the two of us were here alone." "Did the coffin go down with one of those wooden scaffolds, with a motor on it?" he asked. "Sort of like: bzzzzzz?" "Yes, that's great, isn't it?" Jaap said. "How did they do that in the olden days? Ropes, wasn't it?" "Yes," Frits said. "The trick was to lay the coffin down straight in the hole. Not on its side, and not vertically either. Otherwise it's so nasty for the family. Down at the bottom are two little beams the coffin rests on, that makes it easier to pull up the ropes."

"Don't you think that's a wonderful moment, when the coffin goes down?" Jaap asked. "Now someone else really has to say something," Frits thought, "otherwise I won't be able to stand it any more." "At cheap funerals," he said, "they must have tipped them over sometimes. So that they ended up on their side, or standing on their head."

"Do you people know," Hoogkamp asked suddenly, "that sometimes, when they dig people up, they find them in a different position from the one they were buried in? People who were only apparently dead?" "Is that true?" Jaap asked. "Yes, definitely," Hoogkamp went on, "it's less than one in a hundred, but it does happen." "You're no easy one to figure out," Frits thought. He looked at Joosje and Bep, who had been sitting motionless for some time now, listening. "I can't imagine," he said, "that such a thing could still happen these days." "It can occur when the victim has had a massive electrical shock," Hoogkamp went on. "In such cases, there may be no more perceptible signs of life. Not even with a stethoscope. But if

233

they respirate them artificially for five hours, sometimes the life comes back into them." "I get it now," Jaap said, "if they stop after four hours, for example, then he goes into the box before he's dead. That sounds like fun to me, waking up down below. Where am I? Isn't anybody home?"

"Such a convivial evening," Bep said. "He never talks about anything else," said Joosje.

"There are many people," Hoogkamp went on, "who ask to have a knife plunged into their heart, after they're dead. That's how afraid they are of being buried alive. Corpses have been exhumed that were all doubled up in their coffin. Or kneeling. Trying to push away the lid."

"A losing battle," Frits said. "Where is this headed?" he thought, "it's much worse than I would have expected." "Can they still see that, so many years later?" he asked. "After forty, fifty years, say?" "Twenty years," Jaap said. "If it's not a private grave, with a deed of sale, then they pull you up again after twenty years." "But then your bones are already rotted away from the inside, aren't they?" asked Frits.

"If there's nothing special about the soil, yes," Hoogkamp said. "But you have those strange churchyards in Friesland, and those crypts, where they don't rot." "They turn into mummies there," Jaap said. "No, not always," Hoogkamp continued, "you have two different situations. You have clay graves, which are airtight. Almost nothing happens to the corpse in those. At most a bit of fermentation. The crypts are something else again. The gases that arise during decomposition could escape, but there's something in the atmosphere, some sort of natural gas, that prevents decay. The bodies dry out, but they don't rot."

They were all silent. "So do you have to go back to the chapel then?" Frits asked Jaap. "Or are you free to go wherever you like?" "No," Jaap said, "everyone goes to the home of the deceased. That's where the fighting starts." "Were there fights?" Frits asked. "No, there was nothing to fight over," Jaap replied. "No, this time there was no reason to fight. When my uncle died, last year, there wasn't either. But they were ready for it. If there had been. We had an uncle, and everyone thought he was going to leave something behind. So it was: yes, uncle; hello, uncle and do come again, uncle. Until he died, and then there wasn't enough left to bury him with. Only a few dirty, sucked-out briars. Goodbye uncle."

"You two are certainly good company this evening," Bep said. "What did he die of, your grandfather?" Frits asked. "Internal bleeding. His intestines had rotted away completely," Jaap replied. "And that uncle of yours?" "My uncle? Diabetes."

"Forward," Frits thought, "through the fray." "Oh, but that's an interesting disease," he said. "People who die of diabetes are completely swollen up and full of water. When they're dead, the tissue bursts and it all runs out. That must produce an incredible stench. Someone told me a while ago about a lady—she had died of diabetes—who had to be carried down three flights of stairs. Very narrow stairs. And the coffin leaked. Sometimes they hoist them down too, I've been told, but that must look very strange." "Messrs Plank & Shovel Ltd," Jaap said, "for all your European removal needs."

"Would you two please stop it," Joosje said. "We could always have a smoke," said Jaap. He pulled out his tobacco pouch and began rolling cigarettes. "Like one?" he asked Frits. "No," he answered, "I have my own." He took out his box. Jaap handed one to Joosje and Bep, and Frits rolled a cigarette for Hoogkamp.

"So now we've dealt with cancer and diabetes," Frits said. "Elephantiasis, that's a fine one too," Jaap said. "Then you sit on your own balls, like a hassock. Truly something to behold." Frits burst out in a high, screeching laugh, choked on the smoke in his lungs and hacked. "You know what we haven't talked about yet, or at least only superficially?" he asked, looking at Bep and Joosje, who had not laughed along with them, "the galloping consumption." "Maybe I'm going too far now," he thought. "Too far. It's almost nine thirty."

Jaap gestured to him, pointed at Hoogkamp without the young man seeing it, and shook his head. He spelled out a few words with his lips. "Ill," Frits made out one of them to be. "Ill," he thought, "ill. I need to do something, say something. It needs to be erased." "It is not the dangerous illnesses, but the distasteful ones that are hardest for one's surroundings," he went on. "Don't you agree? The head cheese left by diphtheria in the oral cavity." "Stop it, now," Joosje said, "you two are not funny." "Do you know what's also terrible?" Jaap said, rubbing his hands together. "Ocular genabbi." "Genabbi?" Frits asked. "Can you imagine, I've never heard of that?" "That," said Jaap, "is when your eyes keep popping open and closed, accompanied by a very fine spray of blood." "Oh," Frits said, laughing, "is that what you call it?"

The bell rang. Bep went to open it. They heard someone come up the stairs, leaping loudly from step to step. The living room door flew open with a bang and Louis Spanjaard came in, pushing Bep ahead of him. He was dressed in a dark-blue sailing jumper and grey trousers, the cuffs of which were tucked at the ankles into a pair of white socks. He strode into the room and slapped Jaap and Frits on the shoulder, simultaneously and with such force that each of them gave a little yelp. "There's a chair in the kitchen," Bep said. Louis disappeared behind the floral curtain and came back dragging a chair with a wooden seat; he let the back legs rasp across the floor.

"Have you come here straight from your lodgings?" Frits asked. "No, I was on Tessel, for two days," Louis said. He sat down between Jaap and Frits and jabbed his fists like a boxer to one side and then the other. "Hey, old Eduard," he called out to Hoogkamp. "Lean back," Jaap said, "and try to calm down a bit, my friend. So you were on the island of Tessel. And what did you see there? Come, tell us in your own words."

"I went swimming yesterday afternoon," Louis said. "In the sea?" Frits asked, "that couldn't have been too warm." "Let us cease to be amazed at anything," he said to himself. "It was glorious, oh yes," said Louis. "But I couldn't get my clothes on afterwards. You have to sort of slide them up over your body and then run off behind the dunes, where you try to pull them on all the way. But it didn't work. So I just ran down the road through the dunes until I got to Vester's. I couldn't get them on until I was inside." "What's it like now, the water?" Bep

237

asked. "Pretty cold," Louis said, "but within the realm of the possible. It was lovely this time too."

"Did you go swimming in the sea?" Joosje asked. "No, not that," Louis replied, "who in his right mind would do that? What kind of a fool do you think I am? We were at the public pool. You weren't listening carefully." Bep poured him a cup of coffee.

"I would enjoy that, I believe," Frits said, "but if your heart's not up to it, you would hit the water and die. I mean: if the cold overpowers you and knocks the wind out of you, or you get a cramp, then you are a goner. Because there's no one else on the beach, of course." "Oh yes there were," Louis said, "those little men who mess about on the jetty. They stood watching quite respectfully. I guess they thought it was rather daring of me."

"But if something had gone wrong, not one of them would have come to your rescue," Bep said. "Then you would have drowned," Frits said, "how gruesome. That must be a terrible way to die." "Oh no," Jaap said, "you hear bells, the ringing of bells. And you wash up on the beach of your own accord, all you have to do is be patient." "When have I heard him say that before?" Frits thought, "he's said that before." "What time are we leaving, exactly, Bep?" he asked. "Around eleven, whenever we feel like it," Bep said.

"Where are you people going?" Louis asked. "To the pictures," Frits said. "Midnight showing at The Lantern." "What's on?" Louis asked. "*The Green Pastures,*" Frits replied, "at eleven thirty. We have tickets." "Do you think it's sold out?" Louis asked.

"Yes, I think so," Frits said. "I think so too," said Bep. "Well," Jaap said, "you can try, but you don't stand much of a chance."

"Listen," Frits said, "you can always walk along with us to The Lantern. Without a ticket. And then, when we get to the entrance, you can take leave of us. Then we'll say: Bye! You remain standing outside. Perhaps it will even be raining. Hideous." He leaned forward, turned closer to Louis and went on in a muted voice: "I can't imagine anything more dreadful. Going to visit someone who has a ticket for a film or the theatre. And then walking along with them, and then staying outside, alone. Don't you think?" "Yes," Louis said.

Bep and Joosje began conversing quietly. Jaap scratched his head; Hoogkamp leaned forward and looked at Frits. "You know," he went on, "when I was little I thought it was an incredible treat, whenever we would take a trip. I pitied the people who stayed behind: the porters on the platform, the cyclists and pedestrians at the level crossings. I was going on a trip; I was going to sleep over. They were not." "Hmm," Louis said. "What are we talking about?" Jaap asked. "About childhood," Louis replied. "The gentleman is telling us about his childhood." "Didn't you have that exact same thing, Jaap?" Frits asked, "that you couldn't rid yourself of the thought that—" "Exactly," Jaap answered, "I know exactly what you mean. In fact, I can place myself entirely in the situation. It is a wonder, the things that take place in the mind of a child."

"Piss off," Frits said, "let me finish my sentence. What I meant—don't be such an idiot—is the thought that I could be left behind at the station, by accident. The others, who don't know where I am, go rolling off into the distance. To hash over that thought, again and again, from start to finish, each time…" He looked at the others intently, took a deep breath and went on: "What I mean is: to hold onto that thought. You are all going camping, for a few weeks. The fear that you will fall ill on the day you leave. Or catch the wrong train. To keeping running that over and over again in your mind. That you might lose your suitcase. Then you start pitying yourself, you almost feel like weeping. Didn't you ever have that?"

"Yes, I understand that," Hoogkamp said, "I believe I know what you mean." "You'd do better to keep your trap shut," Frits thought. "Then you go on torturing yourself," he went on, "at the station. Right before the whistle blew, I would get off the train, to take a quick pee. Then I thought: the train is going to leave, it's leaving. If I stand here for another twenty seconds, I'll never get to it on time. And feeling sad, at the same time, because your parents are waiting for you and they're all in a tizzy. I wanted to go back, but I couldn't. I had to stay there in that *pissoir*, even though I was finished. Ten more seconds, then five. And then at the very last moment, as the train was already starting to move, I hopped on board." "Yes, yes," Joosje said. "What does anyone else care about this?" Frits thought. "My mother shouting to the conductor," he continued, "and there I was, completely stunned, beside myself. What's wrong? they asked me then. I was still trembling, a cold shiver now and then. Yes, I remember it clearly still. Do you understand that, Jaap, have you ever had that?"

"I have never experienced that personally," Jaap said, "but I can imagine it." "That's the way it is with you now, Louis," Frits said. "You have to walk along, you do your best at the box office, but there is no seat for you. In the end everyone has gone in and you are still standing outside. Oh, terrible, my God." He felt his eyes grow moist. "Is this normal?" he thought.

"Youth is a glorious thing," said Jaap. "How often have I not"—he looked around triumphantly—"thought to myself: O, to be young once more. Yahoo! To romp and frolic like that again. Where has the time gone? That's right, and it's not coming back." "You're terrible," Bep said. "On your backs," Jaap shouted. "Rub-a-dub, straight up and down! That's right, long strokes makes for bouncing baby boys and girls!"

"I need to leave," Frits thought. "Go outside for a bit, muster my strength." "Bep," he asked, "Violenstraat, is it that way?" He pointed west. "I need to drop off a letter there. We won't be going that way later, will we?" "I'm acting like a moron," he told himself, "I know that it's in a completely different direction." "No," Bep answered, "it's the other direction." "Fine," Frits said, "I'll just go and drop it off, otherwise it will only stay in my pocket." He pulled on his overcoat, which was lying on the sideboard, and said: "You won't leave until eleven, will you? Fine. I'll be back by then."

Once he was outside, he pounded his chest with his fists, spat on the ground and inhaled deeply through his nose. "My head is seriously ill," he thought. "The abscess is spreading." "The soul is covered in countless points of infection," he mumbled. At the end of the alleyway he stopped and looked around. "I still have twenty-five minutes," he thought, "let's walk calmly now." He turned to the right and walked to the central train station, wandered through the concourse, went back out and walked around the building, along the quay. The mist had grown a bit less dense, and a faint wind could be felt.

"The thinking is coming to a standstill," he thought. "All our hope is fixed on the film. Should it be a failure, then the gravity of the situation is incalculable." He followed the same route back, slowing his pace halfway, and entered the alley again. The door to Bep's house was ajar. "For the life of me," he said softly, "I left it open." He closed it quietly behind him and sneaked, treading on only the steps' edges to avoid all sound, to the landing, where he stood at the door and listened. "I am lurking at the door," he thought, "that is how far I've sunk already." He heard nothing. "I could give them a start," he thought, "I could roar and howl here at the door." He rubbed his chin, ran his hand over his forehead and went down the stairs as carefully as he had come. "I won't do it," he said to himself, "I am a grown person." Downstairs he closed the door carefully until it clicked in the lock, then rang the bell. Bep opened it; she was wearing a blue duffel coat. "I'm back," he called out, climbing the stairs loudly. Everyone was sitting in the room with their coats on. "We're off," Hoogkamp said.

"Bep," Frits asked, once they were on the landing, "when you're here alone, you hear sounds, don't you? But do you also hear them when there are others around?" "Not tonight," Bep answered. "The weather is not right for that," Jaap said. "You need a sort of whistling wind." He puckered his lips and made a

242

howling sound. "For the love of God, open up," he whimpered in a high voice and knocked against the banister. "Tune in for part two, next Friday at the same time."

They went outside. "Are you walking along with us, Louis?" Frits asked. "So you can see how we go into the cinema?" "I'm headed in the same direction for a while anyway," Louis replied. When they turned right, he came and walked beside Frits. "If my eyes don't deceive me," Frits said, "the threat of baldness is manifesting itself in your person as well." "I can see exactly," he thought, "how the drops of mist settle on the front of the skull, where the hair is both short and scanty."

Louis said nothing. "This weather," Frits continued, "is not particularly beneficial to your health, I should think. The moisture causes pressure in the head and a ringing in the ears." "I mustn't pester him too much," he thought. Jaap and Hoogkamp caught up and walked beside them. Bep and Joosje followed at a slight distance. Frits looked back. "Very good," he said, "no reason why the women shouldn't walk behind us. It is appropriate that they be unassuming, for they are incapable of logical thought." "If no one else says anything," he thought, "I have no choice but to keep talking."

"Do you suppose so?" Hoogkamp asked. They had already walked a way along a canal and now they crossed a narrow bridge for pedestrians. The iron railings were thick with droplets. "Yes, definitely," Frits replied. "I would like to think differently, if only I could. But it is the way things are. Hold up a road map for a woman to see. Whether you hold it the right way, or upside down, she won't notice. Have you ever come across

243

a woman who could repeat the contents of a radio report? Or quote anything accurately, no matter what the source? They are defective, deplorable creatures." Louis grinned. "I cannot agree with you," Hoogkamp said. "Baa, baaa," Frits said to himself, "Mr Twit, bow tie by birth." "How dismal everything is," he thought. "The streets are aglimmer." They fell silent.

At the corner just before the cinema, Louis kneed all three of them in the backside, in rapid succession, said farewell and turned right. "There are three things," Frits said to Jaap, "that make a person angry. First of all: slapping the back of a newspaper while someone is reading it. Secondly: seizing someone suddenly while they are standing at the edge of a roof or precipice and saying: look out! And the third is, while someone is standing still, to nudge them at the backs of their knees so that their legs buckle forward. There is no one alive who does not become enraged by that. Why that is the case, the jury is still out. But research continues." "But this was not any of those cases, was it?" Jaap said. "This was simply a kick to our buttocks," Frits went on, "but it is related to the third case. I do not know why, but it never fails to displease me." They said nothing more until they arrived at the cinema.

Waiting in the foyer, they examined the photos and posters on the walls. Frits went to the lavatory and, when he returned, began pacing back and forth. "I know already that it will all be a failure," he thought, "but there is no going back. Home at two, consumed with disappointment, broken with misery, dull with fatigue. Sleep tight." He went to stand beside Hoogkamp and said: "I have as yet received no accurate impression of you."

"Come on," he thought, "no foolish qualms." "You seem to me to be a bit of a dolt," he said. Hoogkamp did not reply. The five of them were standing before a large display of photos behind glass. "I am not saying this to be hateful, don't misunderstand me," Frits went on. "It is a matter of sincerity. You just happen to have, as I have noticed, limited intellectual faculties. Must one keep silent about that?" He suddenly felt himself tiring. "What venom, what misery," he thought. "I wish you a great deal of success," he went on. "There are people without personality who go through life with surprising ease." No one spoke a word. He turned to Jaap and asked quietly: "Now that we're on the subject; is one allowed to perform a funeral on one's own? I mean: if you don't have much money to spend, or if you consider it a waste of resources, are you allowed to transport a corpse yourself, on a handcart for example, to the cemetery? And dig the grave yourself?" "I believe so," Jaap replied. "I believe that if the interment itself is in accordance with the law, you may transport the dead person yourself. Acquaintances of ours took their child to the cemetery on the back of the bicycle. The coffin on the carrier. And they dug the hole themselves." "Excellent," Frits said. "Look, the doors are open."

Their seats were in the middle of the cinema. Frits ended up between Jaap and Hoogkamp. When the newsreel began, he closed his eyes. "I am resting my eyes," he thought. "I need to be refreshed when the main feature starts." But after a minute he opened them again and watched the international news: ski races in Switzerland, a big fire in Toulouse, an air crash in the Italian Alps, the launching of a ship at

245

Southampton and a train accident in North America, in the state of Texas. "This shot was taken from a gyroplane," he said to Jaap, "it doesn't shimmy." "A fine piece of work, sir," Jaap replied.

The Dutch news showed skating contests at Franeker, the opening of a bridge across the IJssel, a parade in Tilburg and the unveiling of a war monument in Apeldoorn. The lights came up, and coloured advertisements appeared on the screen. "In fact, I'm sitting here alone," Frits thought. He studied the movement of the dust particles in the beam of light. "How can it be," he thought, "that a person inside a house can see out through the curtains, but not the other way around? There must be a scientific explanation for that." From the corner of his eye, he examined Jaap's face. "Who is he?" he asked himself. "Stupid of him, in any case, to admit a jackass like Hoogkamp into his house."

The lights dimmed again for the main feature. A choir began a slow song; the names of the cast and crew appeared on the screen. "This is the loveliest bit," he thought, "the names and lists. It has started, even though it actually still has to start." "Negro spirituals," he read beside the names of the choir members. The voices, which had launched into a fast hymn now, grew louder. Frits could not understand the lyrics of the American hymns, but at the end of each line he could pick out the words: "Yes, Lord." "Yes, Lord," he repeated to himself. The credits faded and the film began in a Sunday school class for Negro children. The teacher opened the bible and read aloud from the Book of Genesis.

The camera wandered around the room; the children listened, some of them open-mouthed. The teacher, the thick lips in his black face framing each word, said: "Methuselah was the oldest man that ever was. And all the days of Methuselah were nine hundred and sixty and nine years. And he died." "Did everybody get so old back then?" a girl at the front asked. "They were very strong men," the teacher answered. "Did they go down to New Orleans all the time with their mamas?" the child asked. "There wasn't any New Orleans then," the teacher replied, raising his finger. "There wasn't even an Earth. It's a long story. Let's begin at the beginning."

The camera showed the faces of the children from very close up; then the picture retreated, grew vague and vanished. A bank of clouds arose and came closer. "Hallelujah," the choir sang. Slowly the clouds parted and a huge pasture became visible, floating in the air. Hundreds of Negroes in long, white robes and with cardboard wings on their shoulders walked around, talking, eating and smoking. A little boy floated by, seated on a cloud, as if on a bale of cotton. Flapping his hand back and forth in front of his mouth he shouted: "Woo!" and added: "I'm an Indian."

"Yes," Frits thought, "the man who made this had the gift of vision. Praised be his name." He felt his arms and legs trembling, leaned forward, opened his mouth and breathed deeply but silently, his eyes fixed on the screen. "The people are laughing without there being the slightest reason for laughter," he thought, and bit down on his fingertips.

When the film had been going for forty-five minutes, he felt his eyes grow moist. He glanced over at Jaap and Hoogkamp,

247

but their eyes were fixed on the screen. "People who are quickly moved to tears are generally shallow and cruel by nature," he thought. "It is despicable." He blew his nose, gulped and tilted his head to the right. "Let me make sure that no one can tell by looking at me," he thought. He dabbed his eyes with his handkerchief, without rubbing. "There's nothing to be done about it," he said to himself, "it doesn't matter. I'll just surrender to it."

When the film ended with a loud, deep chorus, he quickly wiped his face on his coat sleeve, slid out to the aisle and worked his way out of the door quickly. "I don't want to talk to anyone," he thought. "Peace. Tonight there is peace." Turning up his collar he hurried around the corner, then walked on at a normal pace. "Hallelujah," he said softly.

At home he entered the hall cautiously, keeping his coat on, and went into his bedroom without visiting the kitchen first. "No need to brush my teeth," he murmured, "it is an evening of conciliation." He took the rabbit from the bookcase, placed it on the desk, then opened the left drawer and removed the little white marble rabbit that lay in the left front corner. "The Sunday before yesterday I held it in my hand as well," he thought. "Why am I cursed with a memory full of torments? But it doesn't matter. This evening is delightful. *The Green Pastures*." He repeated the name of the film, smiled, placed the marble rabbit atop the head of the bigger one and said quietly: "Despise not thy brother. Know that God seeth you and looks upon you with favour." He moved both animals so that their snouts touched and then moved apart. "A kiss," he said quietly, "and now make up." "It is ten past two," he thought.

He took off his overcoat, tossed it on the floor, removed his shoes and walked across the coat. "No matter," he said to himself, "atonement has come." Picking up the coat, he hung it over the arm of the chair, along with the rest of his clothes, and climbed into bed. "Tonight I shall not dream," he said aloud, "it will be a peaceful night." He fell asleep quickly. At four thirty he awoke, went to the toilet, climbed back into bed and remained awake for thirty seconds. "I am not having any dreams at all," he thought.

The doorbell rang. He sat up and heard footsteps on the stairs. "Quick," he thought. "I'll go and talk to whoever it is. Otherwise they'll wake my parents." He walked into the hall noiselessly, switched on the light carefully without making it rattle, and opened the door. Two men in dark clothing were waiting on the landing. The man in front held a lantern with a candle in it. "Is this the Egters residence?" he asked. The man behind him was carrying a long, light-brown package. "We have brought it to you," the man said, "he has been found."

Frits took from him the long object, which was wrapped in brown packing paper. It was almost as long as he was, it felt warmish and seemed to move almost imperceptibly. After saying goodbye, the men turned and left. He closed the door and bolted it, then listened, but did not hear them go down the stairs. He began to be afraid. There was a knock at the door and a voice Frits recognized as that of the lantern-bearer said slowly: "Do not forget: what we bring to this house may never leave it again. Consider yourself warned." Then he heard rapid footsteps descending the stairs.

"I know what it is," he thought, "it is the dead man." He tried to put down the package, but could not bend his back. "Now all the horrors are coming at once," he thought, "it is a dreadful punishment." The package grew limp and began sagging at both ends. Using all the strength he possessed, he was able to unclench his hands. The package fell, but the paper remained stuck to his fingers. As it fell, the contents rolled out. He raised his eyes to the ceiling. "No," he said, "don't look." Slowly, though, he could not help but bow his head. On the floor lay the intact body of a young, very slender man in green uniform. The head was a skull, with earth and a dripping, slimy substance in the open cavity that was its mouth.

He awoke with a congested feeling in nose and throat. His watch showed it to be a few minutes past six thirty. "It will come back," he murmured. Each time he seemed about to doze off, he kept himself awake by shaking his shoulders jerkily and knocking together his knees.

X

AT TWO O'CLOCK on Tuesday afternoon, he left the office. A fine drizzle had just ceased. "Unless I am very much mistaken, some real fog is on its way," he said to himself as he stepped out of the door. "The wind will keep up for a bit first, but as soon as it dies down, we are in for it." He walked towards the bicycle shed, but stopped suddenly when he came close to the entrance. "The bicycle is still at the house," he thought. "Man's frailty." He turned and began walking home. Head bowed, hands in his pockets, he moved at a modest pace. "We're early today," he thought, "the hours are like those on a Saturday. In reality, though, it is Tuesday. Tomorrow is a Sunday, but it is Wednesday. When we go back to work again it will therefore be a Monday, but at the same time it will be Thursday. So therefore we can rightly say: the day after tomorrow is Saturday. This illustrates how, with only limited means, one can render simple things complicated. It is not a bad week." He took a deep breath and sighed. "Is it raining, or isn't it?" he said to himself. "There is a situation in which it is raining and one in which it is dry. Between the two there is nothing. Still, minutes go by when you don't know, when you hold out your hand and are not sure. In the face of uncertainty let us say: it is still raining, but imperceptibly so. Yes, that is a good way to put it."

In passing he looked at the display window of a bookshop, at the large model of a fountain pen suspended on two thin wires above the books there, its nib pointing down. "If we were to simply ignore the trifles," he thought, "we would see that things are not so bad after all. Imagine New Year's Eve were to fall on a Saturday? God preserve us. Still, it can happen. Or can't it? Yes, it must work out that way, once every few years."

He cut across a busy square and followed a canal intersected again and again by other canals. At each crossing he made his way across a steep little bridge. "When I am on foot, this is the route I prefer," he thought. "Magnificent," he said quietly, looking out over the water of the canals, "it looks as though the mist is steaming up out of the water. Appearance and reality. Aren't we extraordinarily profound this afternoon."

As he was passing the third canal, someone tapped him on the shoulder. "Well, if it isn't Maurits," he said, after turning around. "What difference does it make?" he thought. "It is New Year's Eve." He lifted his arm. The other grasped his hand immediately and grinned. He had on a long, dark-blue overcoat that fit him well, and new, light-brown shoes. His hair was cut short. "You're wearing your poker face again, van Egters," he said, "even though you have such phenomenal expressions at your disposal. Nice to run into me again, isn't it?" "Well," Frits said, "I can't avoid you completely. So when I run into you, I at least abide by the terms of common courtesy."

"What do you think, exactly, when you run into me?" Maurits asked. "I'm going that way," Frits said, pointing straight ahead, "I have no intention of retracing my steps. If you

252

want to talk, you'll have to walk with me." They stepped off the bridge. "What do you say to yourself, when you see me?" Maurits asked. "I always find it thought-provoking," Frits replied. "You know that I condemn your deeds, but your style of living commands my interest. You are a man of sinful and criminal character, but I feel that I must continue to upbraid you." "Yes," Maurits said, "but do you feel loathing when you see me? What I mean is: what do you say to yourself then? There is that vile face again?"

"Your hand was a bit clammy," Frits said. "Do you know the one about the two farmers?" "No," Maurits said. "Two farmers meet each other on the road," Frits said, "and shake hands. The one says: Have you got a headache, man? Your hand is so clammy. No, the other one says, I just took a piss." Maurits grinned. "Very good," he said, "but I just wish you would tell me for once: do you feel loathing when you see me?"

"I hope you realize," Frits said, "that I in no way underestimate your criminal inclinations. In my politeness there is also an element of fear. I know a great deal about you. I must always take into account the possibility that, in a foul mood, you will stab me to death in some back alley." He examined Maurits's expression. "Let's see how he takes that," he said to himself. "Wait a minute," he thought, "he's not wearing his black patch any more. This one is pink." "By the way, Maurits," he said, "did you throw away that other patch? I suppose you thought that this one matched your skin better, didn't you? You must have thought: from a distance they will think that I do have an eye on that side, but that the eyelid is closed. There can be no

253

doubt about it, however; you can still tell from a mile away: you are a Cyclops, and a Cyclops you will always be." Maurits's expression stiffened. "Does this cause you pain?" Frits went on, "does it wound your soul, when I say this?"

"Goddammit," Maurits said with a grimace, "I had just stopped thinking about it." Coming to the end of the canal they turned left, down a broad street. "Is this the route you usually take home?" Maurits asked. "Your fate is hideous," Frits said, "but that is nobody's business but your own. Each day I feel thankful when I think of what you have been through, and what you must still face. At the moment, that eye is merely an unpleasant detail, but by the time you get to thirty, madness will come pounding at your door. Well put, actually. A lovely mist coming up now, isn't it? Don't you just love this kind of weather?" "Are you serious about that?" Maurits asked. "What do mean, by the time I'm thirty?"

"Oh," said Frits, "I'll explain it to you. And I shall do so for free, no charge. When you are in your twenties and you can't get a girl, you can always tell yourself: I have no desire for that, or: let them keep their distance, or: I lead a simple life. But when you turn thirty, you arrive at the realization that it cannot be anything but that eye. It is not a disorder that can be cured, or a bad habit one can quit. It is that eye, that you can never get back, not even if you saved every penny for ten years. That is the fate that awaits you. Bear it with valour. If one is a bit dull, it need not be such a problem. But if you are a man of keen intelligence, who can penetrate to the cause of things, then it becomes a living hell."

254

"I just wish I could figure out when you're being serious," Maurits said. "Listen," Frits went on, "go home and think about it. Whether I am serious is not the main question. You must first try to determine whether or not what I say is true. And I'm afraid, very afraid, that then you will have to say: yes." "That is very different from what you told me last time," Maurits said. "You have a memory like a steel trap," said Frits, "but last time I was in a hopeful mood. I was inclined to point out a bright side to all things, even the most disastrous. Today I feel obliged to advance the truth." "But you told me all kinds of things then," Maurits said, "what I should look like, how I should dress—"

"And you took that to heart, I see," said Frits, "you are dressed to the nines. It helps a little at the moment, but by the time you get to thirty it won't, not any more. Did you pinch that coat from a shop window? It's so new. And those shoes?" "From the public pool," Maurits said with a grin. "I thought that everyone there turned in their clothes for safekeeping," Frits said, "but don't make me ask so many questions, just tell it to me straight." They crossed a busy junction.

"Well," Maurits said, "I simply go to the pool. It costs a fair bit to get in, so it's not all that crowded. Most people practise at home in a tub." "A crowd would seem to me an advantage in your line of work," Frits said. "No, no," said Maurits, "that's not at all the case. That's such a stupid idea." "Do you actually go swimming?" Frits asked. "No," Maurits said, "I'm afraid of water. I look around a little. I was there the day before yesterday, at this time of year lots of people come in from out of town, places where there are no indoor pools—" "Jesus," Frits said, "if you want me to listen and give you advice, you'll have to get to the point."

"No, there's a reason for all this," Maurits went on. "I mean, those people from out of town are usually dressed quite nicely." "Farmers in the guise of humans," Frits said. "Right," Maurits said with a grin. "There are many among them who are too stupid to put their clothes on hangers and turn them in for safekeeping: they simply leave them behind in the dressing room. The whole trick is to make sure you get lucky in the first cubicle." "How do you do that?" Frits asked. "Man, that's not so hard," Maurits replied. "You hang around by the side of the pool and look around a little. Act as though you think that diving off the board is mighty interesting. They never fall off the board anyway, not even if you stood there for an hour. You keep a good eye on what comes in. If it's someone with decent clobber, you watch carefully to see where he goes." "Aha," Frits said, "so you do have a system. That's wonderful. Without a system, you won't get anywhere. But you have to watch out that the system doesn't get the better of you. That you don't go to work without thinking about it, because then things can go awry. Listen to the counsel of the old and the wise."

"So you watch where he goes in," Maurits continued, "follow him, see which cubicle it is. Then you step into the cubicle beside that. You wait for him to go into the water. Once he's in there splashing around, you slip into his cubicle." "Without being frightened or hesitant, I suppose," Frits said. "It is growing darker," he thought, "there's a downpour coming."

"It only feels strange when you first go in," Maurits went on, "but once you are in there, bent over—the doors are shoulder-height, so you don't have to duck down all that much—you've got all the time you need. You can pick and choose, at your leisure. There's really nothing to be afraid of. That thicko just got into the water, he won't be coming out for a while. No one can see you. To be sure, though, you stay at the back of the cubicle so they can't see your feet, but the doors are close to the floor anyway. You'd think they were designed for it." He laughed and coughed.

"How do you feel at such moments?" Frits asked. "Does your head pound? Don't you have a feeling like: wonderful, he's swimming around there, I can do whatever I like with his clothes? Do you smell them, do you sniff at those clothes?" "Now watch this," he thought.

"How did you know that?" Maurits asked furiously. "How did you know? That's right. Yes, damn it." He lowered his eyes for a moment, then eyed Frits closely and was silent. "Do you drape the clothes over your arm, or carry them in your hand, or do you put them on right away?" Frits asked. "If you do that, you have to leave your own things behind, don't you? Isn't that risky?" "No, not at all," Maurits said, "as long as you don't leave anything behind in your pockets. But I wasn't wearing an overcoat. I had warm clothes on under my suit. So I just put on that coat, and the shoes too—nice shoes, aren't they?—and left my own, simple footwear behind." He grinned. "And there was a wallet with forty-six guilders in it."

"That is a decent haul," Frits said, touching the mist-wet surface of Maurits's coat, "but the only thing to do is sell it.

257

Fancy clothes don't look good on you." "It's not far to home now," he thought, "I have to come up with a few more decent things to say."

"What do you really think about the way I look?" Maurits asked. "You've had your hair cut short," Frits said. "It's much easier to see now that you are growing quite bald at the corners."

"Oh, come on," Maurits said, running a hand over his head, "it's actually started growing again."

"You are mistaken about that," Frits said. "That is mere appearance. You treat your hair with some kind of tonic. That makes it coarser and thicker. Then it looks like there's more of it. But that has nothing to do with growth. In actual fact, that makes the hair loss even worse. When you comb it, whole clumps remain stuck in the teeth of the comb: they are pulled out. For you, total baldness is a matter of four or five years, six at the most. But next year, I mean, yes, next year, you will already have a bare spot in the middle of your scalp. There is only one means to apply in your case, but it is a bit out of the ordinary; you may think I'm pulling your leg." "What will he ask me now?" he thought, "which words will he choose? Will he ask: what do you mean? Or: do you really mean that? Or: come again?"

"Which means is that?" Maurits asked. "I'm prepared to tell you," Frits said, "but not if you think I'm pulling your leg. We must speak in all earnest." "Yes, of course," Maurits said, "tell me."

"You must," Frits said with emphasis, raising his index finger, "as soon as the weather improves—it's too cold for that now—have your head shaved, or do it yourself. That rejuvenates everything on your head." "Goddammit, do I really have to do that?" Maurits asked, running his palm over the back of his head.

"Didn't you know that?" Frits went on. "When the hair has been removed all the way down to the scalp, air can get to the roots. Shaving it thoroughly—shaving is the only way, of course—stimulates them: the skin cools, and in that way the circulation around the roots is resumed. A great many people, whose hair was not growing so readily any more, have tried it. And the results have been astounding." He stopped in his tracks and said: "I have to turn left here, I'm almost home."

"How do you know all that, about hair?" Maurits asked. "Are you messing with me now too? I bet you'd laugh yourself silly if I went walking around with a shaved head. How do you know that?" "It's common knowledge," Frits replied, "but you have to know about it, otherwise your hands are tied. To my disappointment I note that, despite your acuity, you do not ask yourself often enough, in everything you see and do: How? Why? Still, those seemingly minor issues are the most important, the most fascinating. Do you know, for example, why women are afraid of mice?"

"They're not all afraid of them," Maurits said. "I'm referring to the ones who are afraid of them," Frits continued, "and do you know why?" "No," Maurits said, "well, I guess because they think it's a filthy animal that crawls its way up everywhere." "A filthy animal, indeed," Frits said, "but why is a woman so fearful of it that she wakes the whole neighbourhood with her screams?" "I don't know," Maurits said. "They can't tell you themselves," Frits said, "but why is a woman afraid of mice? Stop and think about it. What is she afraid of, unconsciously?" "I'll be damned," Maurits said, "I get it." He grinned. "Do you think that's really it?" he asked. "Is that it, really?" "Exactly," Frits answered, "it is a scientific fact." "Spiders and frogs too, probably for the same reason, right?" Maurits asked. "Yes," Frits replied, "of course it's now clear to you as well why they always climb up on a chair." Maurits grinned. Neither spoke for a moment.

"I've noticed," Frits said, "that you have tried to sell me neither those shoes nor that coat. May I conclude from that that you are no longer strapped for cash?" "That's right," Maurits said, "things have been better for the last few days. I found a purse, not long ago. New, with a hundred and eighty guilders in it. Not bad, eh?" "Doesn't that make you feel depraved?" Frits asked. "The person it belongs to cried all night about it." "It is going to start raining soon," he thought, "I'll make it home just in time to keep from getting wet."

"Maurits, Godspeed," he said, waving his hand. "I'll see you around." He walked off quickly. "I still need to talk to you sometime," Maurits shouted after him. "At least I don't have to shake that hand," Frits thought. "But I could at least have wished him a pleasant evening, in any case, and a happy and prosperous New Year. That was lax of me." "Yes, Maurits, we'll talk soon," he shouted back.

The rain began. He hurried his step. "Rain with moderate gusts," he thought as he arrived at the front door. "It's dry here, let us pause to think for a moment." "So I'll go upstairs," he said to himself, "right. Up the stairs, go inside. What are they going to say? Imagine my father is home alone. He says: Hello, my boy. If my mother is home alone, she says: Well, is that you? If they're both at home, they won't say anything at first. Then my mother will ask me something, whether I closed the door behind me, whether I wiped my feet, something like that. Why? Who can tell?"

He opened the front door, closed it quietly behind him, climbed the stairs slowly and crossed the landing. Right in front of his own door, he stopped. "I could have looked at the coats on the stand," he thought. "Now I don't have a clue. Who is in there?" He closed his eyes. "Both of them," he said to himself. "I smell it, I can sense it. I know it. Inside are the two people who are my parents. Onward."

He opened the door and stepped inside. Beside the fire, his father sat reading. His mother was lying on the divan. He closed the door quietly behind him. "I should say something simple, something normal," he thought. "It is up to me." "Frits," his mother asked in a sleepy voice, "if your coat is wet, will you put it on a hanger beside the fire? Is it raining out?" "Yes," he answered, "but not in." "It's by the sideboard," she said. "Aha," he said, picking up the hanger. He slid his coat over it and hung the hook on the ornamental ledge above the sliding doors. "Look," he thought, "behold, how the light falls in this room. Light is not what it is, more like less-than-total darkness." "What are we going to do this evening, Mother?" he asked. "Who is coming over?" "It will be just the three of us, nice and cosy," she replied. "What is it?" his father asked. "Is someone at the door?" "No," Frits said. "Aren't Joop and Ina coming, Mother?" he asked. "They're going to the Adelaars' this evening," she answered. "It is," he thought, "only a quarter to three, but still this day will fill itself like any other." He pulled a chair over to the radio and turned it on.

"—decision to be made," a flat voice said. "The condition of many playing fields makes it uncertain still whether the Sunday competition will take place. But we will know more on Saturday afternoon; at that point I will discuss with you the opportunities that lie in store for Enschede Boys, Be Quick, Speed and Haarlem First in particular. So until Saturday, dear listeners. I thank you." "You were listening to *Sport Talk*, with Henk Appelman," the announcer said. "For the second time this afternoon, here are the Air Masters. They will kick off with the foxtrot 'Blue Blue, Everywhere I See Your Eyes' by John Fireground, as arranged by Piet Matel and sung by Arie Toleman."

"Hilversum Two," Frits mumbled, twisting the dial to the right. The final bars of a waltz sounded. "Yes, and now we've arrived at a request from Mr and Mrs Frissendonk of Zeist," said an announcer with hurried diction. "They have requested 'Tales from the Vienna Woods' by Johann Strausz. Tales aplenty we've got for you. This record is also for Mr—" Frits switched off the set and stood up. "I'm going to fix that tyre," he said to himself. He went into the kitchen, opened a cupboard beside the sink, pulled out a large tin box and examined the contents. "Cleaning fluid," he said softly, "glue, four tyre levers—more than enough—patches, yes, that's all in order." He set the box down on the kitchen table and went to the landing to fetch his bicycle.

"Frits," his mother called. He left his bike sticking halfway out of the storage cupboard and went inside. "Are you going to work on your bike?" she asked. "Yes, it's about time I did," he answered. "Don't forget," she said, "not to take your bicycle into the kitchen." "No, I was going to do it in my bedroom," he said. "Absolutely not," she said, "if you are going to mess about with your bicycle, go to the attic." "That's too much lugging around," Frits said. "I don't want you doing it down here," she said. "Upstairs, you have plenty of room there."

He walked out to the landing, rolled the bike back into the storage cupboard, went to his room and lay down on the bed. "I didn't put away the tools in the kitchen," he thought. "Why am I lying down? Not to sleep. I need to think. To be sleepy now, I'd have to be old and sick." "This is the way a person lies in bed when they have the flu," he said to himself. "It is winter, the light is harsh and it is about to rain. It is raining already." He fell asleep.

An hour and fifteen minutes later, he awoke. "Why am I lying here, as though I were exhausted?" he thought. "I need to come up with some plans. I need to establish a programme for tomorrow. It is slowly growing dark, and I am just lying here." He got up, went to the window and looked outside. "This is the final day of the year," he thought, "until midnight it is still December of this year. Immediately after that it is the 1st of January. Between the two there is nothing. It's cold in here."

263

He paced back and forth a little and said to himself: "If I lie back down again, my brains will turn groggy." He sat down on the bed, scratched at his temples, slowly sank back and fell asleep once more.

He was walking outside along a narrow road through the open field. It started to rain. He raced in the direction of a large building with factory smokestacks. "It happens every time," he thought, "only when you go out without your coat does it start raining." He turned up the collar of his suit jacket. By the time he reached the roofed veranda at the front of the building he was wet through and through. He shivered. A double door, like that of a garage, opened. In the opening stood a man in a pair of yellow overalls. Instead of a human head, he had the head of a fox. "I bid you welcome," he said, "but pay no heed to my appearance. I would be most grateful if you paid no attention to my head."

"Don't give it a second thought," Frits replied. "Besides, your face is much more sensible than that of most. It appeals to me." "It does not appeal to me in the slightest," he thought.

"You are wet," the fox head said, "good thing we have just fired up the furnace. You will be dry as a bone within minutes. Come along."

They entered a factory hall where huge fires were burning in all manner of furnaces, as well as on the actual factory floor itself. Air was being pumped into them, and the flames roared whitely and spread an enormous heat. Frits remained standing before each hearth for a moment, approaching as close as his skin would bear. "I'm almost burning up," he thought, "but I'm not getting any warmer." Cold shivers washed over him. "It's very good, what you're doing," the fox head said, "no need to remain standing beside any particular fire, just walk along with me; you will dry even as you look."

The further they walked into the factory hall, the lower the ceiling became. Each fire they passed was fiercer than the one before, and each time Frits had to shield his face against the blaze. "Doesn't anyone work here?" he asked. "We haven't come across anyone." The fox head gave him a piercing look. "You may dry yourself here," he said, "but you do not have the right to meddle." "My apologies," said Frits. At last they came to a dusky corner of the hall, where they descended a set of stone steps and entered a cellar. In the middle an enormous fire was burning, the flames were more than six feet high; its light hurt Frits's eyes. Beside the fire was an anvil.

A man in a close-fitting leather suit entered. He was so tall that he had to bend over; he ran one hand over the ceiling as he walked. Over his shoulder he carried a large hammer with a long handle. When he arrived at the anvil and entered the full light of the flames, Frits saw that he had the head of a bear, with round, little ears. The creature raised the hammer and began pounding the anvil. The blows rained down harder and harder. Suddenly, the ceiling lifted a long way. The man could stand up straight, he turned slightly towards Frits and grinned, exhibiting a pair of fangs.

"He's not pounding anything at all," Frits thought, "the anvil is bare. Why is there nothing on it?" "It's not going to remain bare," the man with the fox head said suddenly, staring at him intently.

Every blow the man in the leather suit struck was harder than the one before, the hammer was lifted higher and higher each time, its head grew ever larger. "My head is splitting," Frits thought. Every time the hammer came down he opened his mouth. "Stop it," he shouted, "let me out of here."

"We're not going to harm you," the fox head cried. "This is our blacksmith. He's hammering at the moment, but if you like I can make him dance at the end of a chain. With a whip, if he doesn't feel like it. If it is too noisy for you in here, you may leave." The man with the head of a bear produced a growl and brought the hammer down so hard on the anvil that Frits felt something tear in both his ears: fluid from the openings ran down over his cheeks. The pain in his eyes became so intense he had to close them. Feeling around with his feet, he searched for the steps. "Over here, sir," he heard the man with the fox head call out, "over here." The voice began laughing and shouted: "Over here, sir, we're waiting for you." "No," he thought, "it's the anvil. It's waiting for me. Get out! I have to get out! It is a trap. I am done for."

He had just placed one foot on the bottom step when an icy cold wind almost blew him over backwards. He was able to remain upright, but could not climb the steps. The pounding of the anvil stopped. "Here they come," he thought, "I need to get up the stairs." He tried to move forward, but could not.

His heart beating wildly, he awoke, shivered and sat up. "I didn't pull a blanket over me," he thought, "maybe I have already caught a cold." He stood up and turned on the light. For one whole minute, black spots went on dancing before his eyes. He looked at his watch: it was five thirty. "The chill here is unbearable," he thought, "I'll go to the front room." He went to the kitchen and drank some water. His mother was cooking dinner.

"Where were you the whole time?" she asked. "You need to fetch some coal. The repair kit, the whole mess, you just left it lying there. I suppose you thought the maid was going to tidy up after you? As long as you realize that I would just as soon toss it out of the window as put it away. Next time I'll throw it in the bin." "Or drop it in the stove, you could do that too," he thought. "Teedeetadeetee tom tom," he sang to himself.

He shut the metal box of tools that was still on the kitchen table and slid it back into the cupboard beside the sink. Then he went into the living room.

His father was sitting in a chair by the window, reading a newspaper. "Frits," his mother called from the kitchen. "No," he thought, "full repose. I hear nothing." "Frits," she called out again. "Is Mother calling?" his father asked. "No," he replied, "you must be mistaken." "What?" his father asked. "No, no one is calling," Frits said loudly. "Two times," he thought, "that should do it." He listened closely. "Very good," he said to himself after a few moments, "she's not calling any more." He sat down by the radio.

"Let's look at the guide first," he thought, stood up and rifled through a pile of newspapers on the little table beside the window. "What is it?" his father asked. "Oh, I'm looking for something," he answered. After searching through the newspapers he piled them up again, but bumped against the stack and knocked a few to the floor. "Leave it for the moment," he thought, "I'll look again in a bit, just to be sure. The paper I'm looking for is gone anyway."

As he was searching through the newspaper rack on the wall, his mother came into the room. "What are you looking for?" she asked, "don't toss things all over the place. I suppose that was you again"—she pointed at the little table. "You don't look for things, you just rummage about." "I'm looking for yesterday's newspaper," he said, "for the radio guide."

"Yesterday's paper isn't in there," she said, "don't go tearing everything apart." "So then where is it, yesterday's paper?" Frits asked. "It's not in there either," she said, pointing at the rack, "I was looking at it just this afternoon." "What good is that to me?" he said. "You need to look around," she said, "it's here in the room. Or else you threw it away, or someone else did."

He returned the newspapers, which he had taken from the rack during his search, to their places and walked over to the little table again. He picked up the fallen newspapers, searched slowly through the pile, and went to the window. He opened the long curtains a crack and looked outside. Three people stood talking beside a lamp post. "The evening of the old year," he mumbled, "the night the year is made new." He closed the curtains again and turned around. Suddenly his eye fell on the newspaper his father was reading. He read the date: Monday, 30th December. "There it is," he said to himself, "he has it."

268

"Well, Mother," he said, "it's not here on the table. If you think that I am incapable of searching, why don't you try?" "It's as though the two of you were morons, as though no one in this house has any sense," she said. "Don't you two have eyes in your head?" "What's all this screaming?" his father asked. "Nothing," Frits said, "there is no conflict whatsoever. It is a friendly debate. Later on there will be an opportunity for you to pose a few questions."

First his mother searched the rack, then the pile on the little table. "It's like having six little children around the house," she said, "every bit as much bother." "See? It's not there," Frits said after she had searched through the whole pile. "I'm perfectly capable of looking for something."

"What newspaper does he have there?" she asked, stepping over to his father. She seized hold of a page. "By the life of me," she said. "Sometimes I wonder whether the two of you are all there." "Were you looking for this?" his father asked. "If I could borrow it for a moment, yes, please," Frits said, taking it from him. He sat down in front of the radio again, reached out and laid his hand on the set. "What shall I do first, look at the guide or turn the thing on?" he thought.

"Frits, would you go and fetch some coal?" his mother asked. "It's all finished, the sacks too. There are still a couple of them upstairs, but I want to keep those. Scoop it up out of the box, that's the bit that needs to be finished first. Can you go right now? Otherwise the fire will go out." "No," he replied, "I'm afraid of the dark, you know that. That's asking too much." "There is the scuttle, behind the stove," she said. "Fill it and put a few briquettes on top. I'll think I'll just let it go out later tonight, we won't be getting up that early tomorrow anyway."

"Mother," Frits said, "you know very well that I am terribly afraid of the dark. It's unreasonable to ask me to go up to the attic now." "What is it?" his father asked. "Oh," his mother said, "he's refusing to fetch coal from the attic."

"It's not that," Frits said loudly, "I would be more than pleased to fetch coal. But I'm afraid of the dark. Boo-hoo. You never know what may be lurking behind a door. Am I right, Father?" "Tee-ra, tee-ra, tee-ra," he sang to himself, "boom-see-kay. Old goat." "He's too lazy to fetch coal," his mother said. "As though I haven't been breaking my back all day."

"But what if one is afraid?" Frits asked. "There are all kinds of things up in the attic. Even as a child, it scared me." "What a pain," he thought, "I mustn't stop now." "I don't understand what you think is so wonderful about that play-acting," his father said. His face rumpled in a frown. "My father can make such ugly faces when he's angry, can't he, Mother?" Frits said. "Huh?" his father asked. "I said that it's important to respect a person's notions," Frits shouted. "When a person is afraid, you mustn't force them. That is a well-known mistake in child-rearing."

He picked up the coal scuttle, waved it around, letting it swing low over the tabletop as he did, and walked into the hallway. "Why women are afraid of mice," he thought, "I told Maurits about that. But I forgot to say that elephants are actually afraid for more or less the same reason. They're afraid that one will crawl up their trunk."

He climbed the stairs and crossed the narrow, darkened landing to the attic door. "If there is a monster up here," he thought, "and it grabs me, and strangles me before I have time to even scream, then no one will notice." He opened the door and went in. The outlines of the windows were only vaguely visible; he could make out nothing of what lay on the floor. He felt his way across it. Banging his leg against an old bicycle frame, he cursed and rubbed his shin. "Coal and briquettes," he said to himself, went to a window and listened to the silence.

"If there is someone up here," he said in a whisper, "who wishes me ill, who is waiting with a length of cord to strangle me, then I am a goner." Moving his head slowly from side to side, he looked around, drew his lungs full of air and stood still. "I am afraid," he thought, "but still I enjoy it. I enjoy the fear. How can that be?" He bent down over a large trunk that lay beside him, the contours of which he could now make out, opened it and breathed in deeply. "Odours don't vanish," he said to himself, "it is the same smell."

"In a trunk like this one," he said to himself in a whisper, "two children were once playing, two brothers, aboard a ship. It was a very large steamer trunk, very heavy, with a heavy lid. And deep, it was very deep. Can you hear me? Have you been able to follow me so far? Good. They were playing, they were in the trunk together, and the lid fell shut. They couldn't get out, couldn't lift the lid. After half an hour, people noticed they were gone. They searched for them for an hour. Then someone said that he had seen two children playing in a trunk. The rest is simple. They had suffocated. Yes, people, life is no bed of roses." "I am afraid," he said to himself, "but I won't say that out loud. If he hears it, he'll leap from his hiding place."

He sat down on the floor beside the window, his back to the wall, lowered his head between his raised knees, took a deep breath and peered into the darkness. "He could leap on me now," he thought. "I'm afraid, I am trembling, but at the same time I'm enjoying it. It's like with boiled sweets, when I was a child, those red ones. You suck on them till the roof of your mouth is raw, but it remains pleasant." He clutched the coal scuttle between his legs and clenched his teeth. Shivers ran up and down him. He stood up, tiptoed to the crate of coal and filled his scuttle. Stepping carefully, he left the attic, closed the door and raced down the stairs so quickly that he almost fell twice.

"Here you are," he said, placing the scuttle behind the fire. "What in heaven's name were you doing up there the whole time?" his mother asked. She was sitting by the fire. "I couldn't find the scoop," Frits replied. "I always put it on top," she said, "it's always on top, you don't have to look for it at all." "Well, it wasn't on top," Frits said. "I had to feel around all over the floor. It was over by the window." "Then you're the one who put it there," she said. Looking past the fire at the scuttle, she asked: "Didn't you bring any briquettes?" "No," Frits said, "I have no idea where those things are, if you wanted them you should have given me directions. Briquettes, bring some briquettes with you. That's not enough. As far as I knew, they would be in with the coal. But that's not where they were. I can't go crawling around over the floor looking for them."

"They're stacked against the wall, on the right, beside and behind the blue crate," she said. "If I don't have any briquettes, I can't get the fire lit in the morning."

"Oh," said Frits, who had taken his seat before the radio again, "that's no problem. When I light the fire, it goes very well without briquettes." "Yes, if you happen to have a whole storeroom full of wood," his mother said. She picked up the scuttle and shook a few pieces of coal into the fire. "And now close the lid with a bang," Frits said to himself.

Using her index finger, she wiped coal dust from the rim of the feeder and slammed the lid loudly. "Ow," Frits said in a whisper. "Still, in my opinion, Mother," he said, "you definitely light the fire all wrong. You do it very clumsily. First you take a newspaper. You light it. Once it's on fire, once it's almost burning your fingers, you stuff it into the stove. The lid stays open. Then you toss in cardboard, then wood, and a huge flame goes on roaring out of the opening the whole time. The room fills with smoke. And only after you have tossed in the briquettes do you close it." His father stood up, took a book from the shelf and sat down again in the chair by the window.

"So how would you do it?" she asked, rattling the grate back and forth. "I put everything in the stove first, piled up," Frits replied. "Paper at the bottom, then cardboard, then wood, then thicker pieces of wood, one or two briquettes broken in half, and little bit of coal, a thin layer. There's no reason why you can't put that all in there. You keep everything closed and then light it from the bottom."

273

"I've been lighting the stove for thirty years, maybe longer," she said. "Well then you've been doing it wrong for thirty years or maybe longer," Frits said, "so much the worse."

"What on earth are you two arguing about now?" his father asked. He was holding the book, closed now, on his lap. His mother began setting the table. "Oh no," Frits said, "we're engaged in a discourse with regard to the physics of combustion in stoves." "What?" his father asked. "It is a conversation concerning a principle of nature," Frits shouted. "I don't understand," his father said, "why there must be this snapping all the time." "The skin turns all red at the places where the creases are," Frits thought. His mother brought their dinner. They sat down at the table.

The meal began with soup. Frits tapped his fork against the rim of his bowl, raised the tines to his ear and made a humming sound. "Soh," he sang loudly. He repeated it twice and looked at his father. The man raised his eyebrows. "Almighty Christ," Frits thought, "they're slurping. Both of them are slurping. Now they can still pretend that it is because the soup is hot. Although that is really no excuse. But later on they will keep on slurping, because that's easier. Could it really be easier?" He picked up his fork again, tapped it against his bowl, held it to his ear and sang loudly, in a low voice: "Soh!"

"Sometimes I think you could well doubt your own sanity," his father said. He pursed his lips, producing a half circle of creases on his chin.

"Absolutely," Frits said loudly, "I am a small-time neurotic. It starts with small-time compulsions. And it ends with counting

274

change or saying no." With his right hand he made the motion of quickly counting out change and shaking his head back and forth jerkily. "Then you are well on your way." "It doesn't sound like anything to be proud of," his father said. "You mustn't say that," Frits said, "it's all the rage at the moment." They ate the rest of their soup in silence.

His mother took the bowls to the kitchen.

"There, now we have a little more space," she said when she came back. "More space," Frits said to himself, "space." He served himself from the platters. There were potatoes, canned broad beans, apple sauce and pork. "It seems to me, Mother, that you have once again outdone yourself," he said, "especially the gravy." "Don't go too wild with that, please," she said, "what's in the boat is all there is." "We are dining in particularly great fashion today," Frits said. He took a second helping of potatoes and apple sauce.

"Perhaps it would have been even tastier if the apple sauce was cooled," he thought. He glanced over at his father. "That he leaves his meat on his plate so long is his own business," he said to himself. "It doesn't matter to me. There's a bone in it, I see. Not a big one. You could remove it with a single swipe of your knife and fork. But good God almighty, I know for a fact that he is going to use his hands." "Don't you want some more?" his mother asked. He went on eating quickly, but kept an eye on his father. When the man had finished everything on his plate but the meat, he picked it up and used thumb and index finger to separate the meat and a border of fat from the bone, laid the meat back on his plate, stuck the bone in his mouth, withdrew it with a sucking noise and then held it cupped in his hand. "I wonder if there's a…" he said, peering around. "Fetch a saucer, would you?" his mother said. Frits got up, took a yellow saucer from the sideboard, carried it over on the flat of his hand, then stood beside his father and bowed, holding it out to him. "All-Powerful, Eternal One," Frits said to himself. "I can't believe that this has gone unnoticed in Your eyes. What is he going to do with his fingers now? Impossible to say."

His father pulled out his linen handkerchief. "Aha," Frits said to himself. His father wiped his hands, crumpled up the handkerchief but did not return it to his pocket. "What now?" Frits thought. His father unfurled the handkerchief and blew his nose, then examined the linen closely and put the handkerchief away. "Approved and accepted with no visible anomalies," Frits said to himself, moving his lips soundlessly.

For dessert there was yellow vanilla custard, with layers of *beschuiten*, jam and chocolate sprinkles. "The chill is off a bit now," his mother said, lifting the glass bowl from the mantelpiece and placing it on the table. "It is delicious," Frits said after the first bite, "it could only be a bit cooler. Now it is still lukewarm. That doesn't help the flavour. But still, very tasty."

"When it's too cold, it makes my teeth hurt," his mother said. "Then you need to do something about that," Frits said. "When are you going to the dentist? Father needs to go as well. His teeth are always bothering him too."

"What is it?" his father asked. "I was saying," Frits said loudly, "that the two of you, in fact, neglect your teeth. When are you going to see Mergel again?" "Right," his father said, raising his hand to his face. "Now we are about to receive a glimpse of the pearly whites," Frits said to himself.

His father opened his mouth and poked at the top row of molars. "This is where it is," he said. "The remains of dinner are not a standard part of the tableau," Frits thought. "If he doesn't notice, he will leave them sticking to his finger. But it's also possible that he will suck them off, or wipe his finger on his trousers." "Watch now," he said to himself, "watch out. Red alert."

His father withdrew his hand, closed his mouth, looked at his index finger and wiped it on the edge of the tablecloth. Then he went back to his pudding. "What could be worse?" Frits thought. "I know," he said to himself, "it's when we have bean soup. The stock has been drawn. Gnawing the bones, with a piece of bread. That was a month ago. There was a chunk of lower jawbone in it, with a bit of the lip and bristles still attached. I didn't let on. That was courageous of me."

"Do you know what's really terrible, Mother?" he asked loudly. "It's something Louis told me about. He was spending the night at a farmer's house in Doornspijk. In the middle of the night he gets thirsty—are you listening, Father?" "That first part," his father said, "what was it about Louis?" "I was talking about something really terrible," Frits said, turning to face his father, "that Louis told me. He was spending the night at a farmer's house in Doornspijk. In the middle of the night he gets thirsty and goes to the kitchen, but the pump is dry, nothing comes out. That happens sometimes, you have to pour water into the top of it first. He looks around." "He does what?"

277

his father asked. "He looks around," Frits repeated. "And he sees a glass of water. He drinks from it and, when it's almost empty, a pair of dentures knocks up against his teeth. That's quite something, isn't it?" "Fantastic, the nasty faces the man is capable of," he thought.

"You could have saved that for after dinner," his mother said. "So now we've had the dentures," Frits thought. "What else have we got? Oh yes, the elephant."

"Do you know, Mother, why an elephant is afraid of a mouse?" he asked, "do you know that?" "No idea," she said. "He's afraid that he'll get one up his trunk," he said. "My," she said. "But it's also because his mother was afraid of them too," he said. "Haw haw," he mumbled to himself, "a laugh a minute, pure entertainment."

His mother stacked the dishes and cleared the table. "Even if it's only for half an hour," Frits thought, "I need to get out of here." "Mother," he said, "there's somewhere I need to go. I'll be back at eight o'clock." "Will you come back right away?" she asked. "I have something nice, and there's something else as well." "Well, well," Frits said, smiling, "and what might that be?" "You'll see," she said. "A surprise?" he asked. She nodded.

"Where are you headed?" she asked after he had taken his coat from the stand. "Is he going out tonight?" his father asked. "There's somewhere I need to go," Frits said, "otherwise I'm sure I'll forget about it completely." "Back in a bit," he shouted, and went out.

Stepping outside, he turned up his collar. It was dry and the air was clear; a mild easterly wind was blowing. "I should have worn a scarf," he thought. "I'm sure the weather is taking a turn. The mist has blown away already and the air is drier. That means a light frost, and thaw during the day." He walked along the river and stopped before Louis Spanjaard's door. "Not even a quarter to seven yet," he murmured, looking at his watch. He stepped back and looked up. "The light is on," he said quietly, "he must be home. Fortune smiles on us."

As soon as he rang, the door was opened. "Here I am," Louis called from the top of the stairs, "pleased to see you of course, but I am going out later. If you take that into account, you will be received here in all good grace." "That suits me perfectly," Frits shouted back. "How are you?" he asked on the landing, shaking Louis's hand, "you're not looking any too well this evening, I must admit." Louis was wearing a heavy, dark-blue jumper with a high collar. A few loops were missing from his grey trousers: in two places, the waistband stuck out widely beneath the belt. He was in stockinged feet. They spoke no further until they were in his room, where the oil burner was hissing quietly.

"I was here the Sunday evening before last, too," Frits said to himself. "We start off there where we have finished." He sat down in the chair by the window. "There are no flowers on the panes," he thought, and wiped his finger across the steamy glass. "You definitely look quite peaky, Louis," he said. Louis sat at his table, drumming on a book with his fingers, and said nothing.

"So you won't be home this evening?" Frits asked. "Are you going to your parents'?" "Yes," Louis replied. "I don't see any cats in here," Frits said. "They have stopped coming into the room lately," Louis said. "Frightened, of course," Frits said. "I suppose it could be that," said Louis, his eyes on the floor. "Do you know why an elephant is afraid of mice?" Frits asked. "No," Louis said. "Because he's afraid of getting one up his trunk," Frits said. "Ah, might that be it?" said Louis. They were silent. "What am I going to talk about now?" Frits thought. "Will there be a lot of guests at your place tonight, Louis?" he asked. "Will there be drinks?" "Could be," Louis replied. "If it's too boring, I'll leave right away. I won't stick it out till midnight, I don't believe."

"God preserve us," Frits said, "you are not in much of a mood this evening, I can see that already." With his right index finger he wrote "Frits", mirrorwise, on the windowpane. "Look, Louis," he said, "how quickly I can do that. It's not much more difficult than normal writing." "Yes," Louis said, raising his eyebrows, "in the olden days, everyone wrote from right to left. With their right hand. Until someone noticed that he was rubbing his hand through his own letters. Then they switched to the other way around."

"It won't have gone that quickly," Frits said. "The first one who noticed that was roasted over a slow fire, of course." "Ah, of course," Louis said, "you're right. Do you have anything to smoke?" "Damn, I left my rolling tobacco at home," Frits said. "If another silence descends, we will be in a bad way," he thought. "I'm spending the evening at home," he said, "alone, with my parents." "Whoo-pee," said Louis, "oh, Jesus." "Well, watch what you say," Frits went on, "who knows what misery you will encounter at your parental home this evening. He who laughs last." "Anything is better than just the three of you," Louis said. "That's only a little worse than just two."

"There will be drinks at your place tonight, won't there?" Frits asked. "But you don't touch the stuff, do you? You can't handle it, am I right? Yours is a pitiable fate. Like one of those children born with their heart on the wrong side. Or without a stomach. Madam, your child won't live past the age of eleven. But doctor, is there no hope? No, ma'am, I'm afraid not. The only thing is, you yourself turned eleven a long time ago. You are way past your limit. So you don't drink? Of course that's always good for a laugh, when everyone else has had too much and you sit there being sober."

"I heard a wonderful story about Elseboom," Louis said. He grinned and rubbed his hands together. "You know who I mean? The painter." "Yes, yes," Frits said. "They were having a drinking party at someone's house, during that week when it was so cold," Louis went on. "And he was tanked, Elseboom, to the rim. He needed to take a shit. So they brought him to the toilet. But it was so cold in the house that they were all still wearing their overcoats. He was too." "Were you there?" Frits asked. "No," Louis replied, "but Willi told me." "All right, go on," Frits said. "He sat down on the pot," Louis continued, "pulled down his trousers first, he still had that much sense left, and sat down on the seat, but on top of his coat. He pooped it all into his coat. And then he fell asleep. And stayed sitting there like that. It was so cold in there—the toilet was off in one corner of the house—that the shit froze to his coat. That was the night when it got down to eighteen degrees below zero."

"Goddam me, fantastic," Frits said, clapping his hands. "That is amazing." "They found him with the frozen shit inside his coat," Louis went on. "They put him in the bath, fully dressed, coat and all, and started tossing buckets of water over him. Then the turds came loose. Floated around like flakes in the water." He grinned, making a dispersive motion with his hands. "Grand, quite grand," Frits said, "distasteful, but grand."

"Are there things that you find truly distasteful?" Louis asked. He turned his chair around and rested his feet on the hood of the oil burner. "No," said Frits, "you mean, things that spoil my appetite? No, it would have to be awfully bad for that. What I do find quite filthy is what someone told us at home one time, a nurse. She was helping out with a family where the mother was ill. Three children, three boys, who every evening, after undressing for bed, ate the black stuff from between their toes."

"Wha!" Louis shouted, stamping his feet on the floor, "bah, bah. Yes, oh yes. That's very good." He put his feet back on the oil burner. "Now I truly know nothing more to say," Frits thought. "The Sunday before last I was sitting here too. There is little hope in store for this evening." "Do you know, Louis," he asked, "that your hair is becoming rather thin? There's not much to it any more. It definitely won't be long before you go completely bald." "Do you suppose?" Louis asked flatly. "It seems to make little difference to you, whether or not there is anything growing on top of your head or not," Frits said. "Is it all the same to you?"

"I won't go bald, not for the time being," Louis said. "It's starting to fall out very quickly at the corners," Frits said, "I must be frank. And because you don't have so much hair to start with, I see baldness approaching. But if you don't care all that much, well, all the better. You have bald people who are quite happy. Not that I can imagine that, I'd rather be dead myself, but you do hear of them." "Well, really, I'll never go completely bald," Louis said. "All right, now he's going to run his hand over it," Frits said to himself, "here we go." Louis raised his hand slowly and felt at his forehead and crown.

"What do you use on your hair?" Frits asked. "Nothing," Louis answered. "Well then, what keeps it so slick?" Frits asked. "Water, I comb it with water, nothing else," said Louis.

"Listen, that's exactly it," Frits said, "you put water on it and think that can do no harm. A very common misconception. On normal skin, without any hair on it, water dries up. Like on your hand, or your arm. But on your head, that's something very different. It's like walking around in a wet bathing suit when it's cold outside. The skin between the hairs becomes eroded. The roots as well. A great deal of grime, that would otherwise blow away, remains stuck in the pores." Louis said nothing.

"As of yet, no one actually knows what causes baldness, did you know that?" Frits asked. "They talk about ageing, subcutaneous fat imbalances, skin ailments, vitamin deficiency, aberrant blood pressure, you name it. But they still haven't found a solution."

"Don't you think it might be hereditary?" Louis asked. He was chewing on the stub of a pencil. "I don't think so," Frits replied, "because you very often see people with a thick head of hair in a family of baldies. No, I've looked into that.

It doesn't apply. It's an individual thing." "Do you think it's actually a sign of old age?" Louis asked, tapping the pencil against his teeth.

"Do you know what it might be?" Frits said suddenly. "People go on too long producing children. That's it. You have people of thirty-five, or forty, or fifty, or sixty—I'm not kidding you—who still produce children. If those parents are already close to baldness themselves, then they pass that trait of reduced hair growth on to their children. I believe that must be it. That is the whole problem. Old people go on making children with impunity. That should be stopped." "Sit down and write a pamphlet right away," Louis said.

"No, seriously," Frits went on, "I'm firmly convinced of that. Old people cause a lot of the world's misery. They contaminate our lives. They spread a sour smell in the tram. Like a pot of fruit preserves that has been opened and then forgotten. Everything over sixty should be done away with." "Why not everything over forty?" Louis asked. "You wouldn't hear me complain," Frits said, "but we have to stay humane. Between forty and sixty there are still signs of life."

"Transplanting it from one head to the next wouldn't work, would it?" Louis asked. "I've thought about that too," Frits said. "To take the scalp of a dead person and transfer it to the head of a bald one. Then you would know right away whether it was a matter of something in the blood or something with the skin. Not the blood, I think, because at other spots on your body it keeps on growing like a pine forest. Even your beard goes on growing." "It's about time I left," he thought.

"At the Museum of Safety they have the skin from someone's head on display, the whole thing," Louis said, "in formaldehyde. Torn off by a machine." "After an accident like that, can't they just put it back on quickly again?" Frits asked. "I don't know," Louis replied, "if it got dirty and all crumpled up in the machine, I shouldn't think so."

"And how is your own health, Mr Spanjaard?" Frits asked. Louis remained silent. "Do you know what I think?" said Frits. "I think there's something inside your head. It is growing and swelling. It touches the inside of your skull and the pain begins. Until finally it breaks through, until a blood vessel bursts, at which point it is all over."

"No," Louis said, "I don't believe so. Otherwise they would have seen that on the slides." "Still, I think an operation would be good," Frits said. "Maybe it's somewhere in a recess, or behind a lump of bone. If they would just open it up, there's a chance they might find it. They're awfully clever these days." "If it was my only hope," Louis said, "but as long as they don't say so themselves, we'll just wait and see."

"They admitted a fellow to hospital once," Frits said, "who had fallen head first into the hold of a ship. About eight metres deep. Landed right on his skull. Cracked open completely. Full of fissures. But he wasn't dead. That was highly irregular, of course. So all right, in the hospital they waited for him to die. But he didn't; he simply remained unconscious. Then a professor came along who said: Let me give it a go, I've never seen anything like it. That professor sawed off the entire skull, tidied up the man's brain again, took out all the dirt and blood, put the lid back on and closed it up. And that fellow is still alive. But he has to put in an appearance at a medical conference once a year, to show them his noggin. They reimburse him for the train ticket at least. Incredible, isn't it?" "That was an awfully silly story," he thought, "I'm going to leave." Louis, wearing a pensive look, kept his eyes on the floor.

"Someone told me a real whopper recently, have you heard it?" Frits asked. "It's something you should save for when there are ladies present: it will definitely be a big hit. It's wonderfully pathetic." "Then do tell," Louis said, "that always comes in handy." He raised his head and snapped his fingers. "It really happened, or rather, the person who told me didn't actually say that it hadn't. So it's possible. In any case, a good one for a rainy day. A father is playing with his little child of about eighteen months, tossing it in the air and catching it again. But he misses. The child is lying on the floor. Dead. A trickle of blood coming from its mouth. The father screams at the top of his lungs." "Of course," Louis said, "that is a mighty blow for a father." "The mother hears it," Frits went on, "and comes running in from the kitchen. She looks at the child: a great lamentation. Suddenly the wife remembers the child of a few months old who she had been giving a bath to in the kitchen. She runs back: the child has already drowned. She had simply let go of it in the bath. You should tell that one when there are women around, you'll laugh yourself silly."

"Didn't you tell me that one before?" Louis asked. "No," Frits replied, "you're confusing it with the one about the father who picked up his children by the head. In fact, you told me that one yourself. That it had really happened, that's what you claimed." "Yes, yes," Louis said, "but this one is also very good. Wonderful stuff."

"I have to leave," Frits said, "I promised to be home around eight." He stood up. "I'll walk with you," said Louis. He turned off the heater and straightened the sheets of paper and books on his table. "We're off," Frits said. They descended the stairs in silence. "He is not obliged to say a thing," Frits thought, once they were walking outside. "Why doesn't he have a coat on? But I mustn't be the one to start talking. I can simply collect my thoughts." He kept glancing over at Louis's face. "This day," he said to himself, "was grim. It was a veritable ordeal. But beware, lest we overlook that which must still come to pass. Let us think on what is yet to come, before darkness falls. Hallelujah." He shortened his pace, so that each step came down in the precise centre of a paving stone.

"I will shore up my courage until midnight," he mumbled. "I must persevere till then. There is nothing else for it." "Still, I really should say something," he thought, "but I don't know what. Let me go home. The chill is working its way into every-thing." "Do you enjoy wintertime, Louis?" he asked. "Definitely," Louis answered without turning to look at him, "but I always find it so much colder than the summer. Besides that, though, I have nothing against it."

"This day was empty," Frits thought, "I realize that." "Here is where I turn right," he said, "you're going straight on, aren't you?" "Yes," Louis said, "I wish you a great deal of stamina." He poked Frits in the side. "My best wishes accompany you,"

Frits said. "Let us pause to recall that this is the final evening of the year." He felt his eyes grow moist. "New Year's Eve," said Louis, "good thing you mentioned it." They had stopped. "Perhaps I offended you this evening, with something I said," Frits said. "No, no, not in the slightest," Louis said. "It was most convivial. Highly enjoyable." They shook hands. Louis walked on without looking back. Frits turned right, but after a few metres he retraced his steps, slipped into a doorway and, sticking his head around the corner, watched as Louis walked away.

"So here I am standing in this darkened doorway," he thought, "like a spy. What else am I, if not a spy?" He waited until Louis was out of sight, and sighed. "Once a spy, always a spy," he said to himself. "Peering out from darkened rooms into lighted streets. And so it is." He took off at a jogtrot and, having reached the front door of his house, continued to run in place as he pulled out his key. "Up the stairs," he thought, "at a single go. Don't stop to think." Entering the downstairs hallway at a bound, he slammed the front door loudly behind him and remained standing for a moment. Then he walked slowly up the stairs and into the front hall.

The house was filled with the smell of frying. From the kitchen he could hear the hissing of fat in a pan. "Close the door behind you," his mother said when he came in, "otherwise the smell goes all around the house." "Are you making oliebollen?" he asked. "Apple *beignets*," she replied.

On the kitchen table was a deep bowl with chunks of apple and a plate of batter. Between them lay four peeled apples. She took a handful of chunks from the bowl, dipped them in batter and tossed them one by one into the black stewing pan. "If you do it that way, you get all kinds of shapeless lumps," Frits said, "because those pieces of apple are all different. You should actually have peeled a few apples first and punched out the cores. Then you can slice them into rings. So that you get pastries that look nice too."

"I would, if I had one of those things to core them with," his mother said, "but it's not in there any more. You probably did something with it." "No," Frits said, "there's one here." He opened a drawer under the kitchen cupboard, felt around in it without looking and pulled out an apple corer. "Here you are," he said, laying it on the table.

"I can't work with one of those things," she said. "If it slips, you hurt your hand. I've had that happen." "There's nothing to it," Frits said. He seized one of the apples and poked out the core. "That's the way it goes," he said as he picked up the paring knife from the counter and cut off three slices of apple. "Here you have your rings," he said.

"Yes," she said, using a fork to flip six of the finished *beignets* onto a plate, "but I'm not sure how much batter I have left. I'll make a plate of these first. They're round, everyone likes these."

"Fine by me," Frits said. "You want to make balls of batter with bits of apple in them, like you do with raisins. But then you should do it right. Now there's a thick chunk of apple in each one. That will never become cooked. When you bite into it, you first come across something soft. But the pieces are still hard in the middle. Just like apple sauce that isn't cooked all the way. You need to dice them fine and put a lot of them in each ball of batter. Tiny little cubes. Or else cut them into rings. If you do that, the slices of apple should be thin. The way you're doing it, the pieces stay hard." He took one of the oliebollen from the plate, broke it in two and, with the index finger of the other hand, picked out a chunk of apple that was still hard. "Damn me, that's hot," he said, blowing on the piece of pastry and waving it back and forth, then dropping it on the floor. "Pick that up, would you," his mother said, "I swept in here only this morning."

He retrieved the crumbs and pieces of apple, stuck them in his mouth one by one, made blowing sounds, left the kitchen and went to his bedroom. Turning the shade of the desk lamp towards the ceiling, he walked slowly back and forth, then took the toy rabbit from the bookcase. "Good rabbit, sweet rabbit, of you I'm fond," he said aloud. He set the rabbit on top of his head and, balancing carefully, moved to the mirror. "He may sit on my head," he murmured quietly, moving his lips for emphasis, "he may ride along." "No matter how many plagues are sent our way," he said to himself, "we will never leave each other in the lurch. Afflictions mount. Yet still, the end is not in sight."

He put the animal back where it came from, sat down on his bed, slid aside the curtain that covered the lower shelves of the bookcase and sat there, staring quietly. Leaning forward suddenly, he stuck out his hand and snatched a book from the row. It had a hard, light-blue cover. "W.F.C. Timmerhout," he said aloud, "*France and Classical Antiquity*." He leafed through it, closed it loudly, opened it again, examined the first few pages closely and, at page forty-eight, blew away a dead mosquito he found crushed there. He took a deep breath and, examining the binding, found the middle of the volume, spat between the pages there and slammed it shut. "And this is what young people, mere children really, are forced to read," he said to himself. "I'm not making that up: that is the whole truth and nothing but the truth." "So help me God," he said out loud. He looked at the binding and slid the volume slowly back into place.

"Frits!" his mother shouted. "Take it easy," he said to himself. "I'll let her call me one more time, then I'll go." "Frits!" she shouted again. "In fact, a third time would be even better," he murmured. "Frits, could you come in here?" he heard her shout. "I haven't had my fingers in the cookie jar," he thought, "I'm almost sure of that." He stood up, turned off the light and shouted loudly: "Just a minute. I'm coming." He pounded his chest, sucked in his stomach and went to the kitchen.

"Look," his mother said. She was standing at the stove and pointing at the counter behind her. "Do you mean that bottle?" he asked. On the counter was a bottle containing a dark-red liquid. The neck was sealed with an orange capsule. He came closer. "What is it?" he asked. "I bought a bottle of wine for this evening," she answered, scooping a few oliebollen from the pan. "That's lovely," Frits said. He picked up the bottle by the neck. It had a blue label with a yellow border. "Berry-apple," he read quietly. "Berry-apple," he said to himself, "berry-apple. Help us, O eternal one, our God. See us in our distress. From the depths we call to you. Hideous."

"Mother," he said. "Yes, mouse," she answered. "Mother," he said, "it doesn't really matter, but this is not wine." "Not wine?" she asked, turning around. "The man tells me: Apple-berry, fruit wine. Wine, the man tells me." "Yes," Frits thought, "the man says: Apple-berry, wine. Besides, it's berry-apple. Oh, look upon us. Stretch forth thy hand."

"No," he said, "wine it is not. And it says so on the bottle. Berry-apple. Prepared from the juice of fresh-picked, top-quality redcurrants and reinette apples. It's nothing but juice. With sugar added, let us hope. But it doesn't have anything to do with wine."

"Let me look," she said, taking the bottle from him. Peering over the tops of her spectacles she examined the label, then handed it back. "I can't see a thing," she said, "these glasses are fogged up. I'll take a look in the other room, in a bit." "There's no reason to look, it's not wine," Frits said.

"Then don't open it yet," she said, "I can take it back the day after tomorrow." "No need for that," Frits said, "I'm sure it will taste fine anyway. What did you pay for it?" "The man said: Apple-berry," she said, "wine." "How much did it cost?" he asked. "And that woman said the same," she went on. "He asked her: do you have any of that wine left? Yes, she says, over there." "How much did you pay for it?" he asked. "Three guilders ten," she answered, "including the twenty-five cents for the bottle." "I'm sure it will be good," said Frits, "it doesn't matter much." "And now the moment for tears has arrived," he thought. His eyes grew moist.

"Mother," he asked, laying a hand on her shoulder from behind, "are you sad? Shall we cry together? Shall we be nice and pitiable together?" He laid his face against her shoulder for a moment. "Shall we pause and feel sorry for ourselves?" he asked.

At the last two words, his voice became hoarse. "That man said…" she said. "Now be gone, flee," he thought. "Before it is too late."

He hurried out of the kitchen, closing the door quickly but soundlessly, and went to his bedroom. After turning on the light, he went and stood at his desk. "You who holds the stars in the palm of his hand," he said quietly, "I know these things are seen by you." A tear ran from the corner of his right eye; almost immediately, another one followed from the left. He bowed his head, took a sheet of paper from the corner of the desk and held his face right above it. The liquid gathered at the bridge of his nose and flowed down to the tip. A drop fell onto the paper. He sat down, stuck out his tongue and tasted it, then dried his face with his handkerchief.

"All the world's suffering, swept together in a shoebox," he said quietly. With a sound like a sob, he sniffed up the mucus in his nose and leaned back. "You good woman," he mumbled. "Wine. It was wine, that man said." "Of all the things that happen, this is the most hideous," he said to himself. "It is like when I was little. I still remember that. She bought two doggy heads for the two of us, they resembled bicycle horns. Little metal dog heads, with a rubber ball on them. When you squeezed it, it made a sound like barking. One was gilded, the other one was red. One for each of us. But the red one didn't work. She found that out only after she got home, unpacked them and showed them to us. Why don't people die at such moments? She had us draw straws for them. Joop got the broken one, without any sound. But I couldn't be happy with the other one, not after that." He shook his head and frowned. "Buying something expensive," he

293

whispered, "that turns out, once you get home, to be broken or worthless. No greater suffering can there be. It is worse than everything else added up. It is too bad to even talk about. I am trembling. I am all nerves."

"Or flowers," he thought. "Buying expensive flowers that are already past their prime. When the person you give them to waves the bunch slightly, all the petals fall off. You would be better off dead. It is eight thirty."

He went to the living room. His father was lying on the divan, reading. He went to the radio and turned it on. An organ was playing a melody, legato.

His mother came in with a plate of oliebollen. "You two can get started," she said, "I'll be right back with tea." "Aha," his father said, rising to his feet. He sat down at the table. Frits took a seat across from him.

"Maybe I didn't put enough sugar in them," she said, "that could be. I only mixed a little through the batter." She put the sugar bowl on the table, along with three dessert plates. Then she went to the kitchen.

"Eating with a knife and fork would be overdoing it," Frits thought. "Normally, one puts sugar on one's own plate, picks up the oliebol and dips it into that. Wait and see what happens now." He peered through his lashes at his father. The man took an oliebol from the pile, bit a piece out of it, chewed, swallowed and looked at the part that was left.

"It doesn't matter," Frits said to himself, "what must be, must be. It is not so horrible. It is to be expected. One is better off simply taking it in one's stride, as part of the scheme of things." He smiled. "Aren't you hungry?" his father asked. Frits reached out quickly and took a pastry. His father removed the lid from the sugar bowl, pulled out the spoon and pressed the gnawed-off half of his oliebol into the sugar. Then he dropped the spoon back into it.

Frits picked up the bowl, shook some sugar onto his plate and dipped his pastry into that. "You're better off putting the sugar on your own plate first, Father," he said, "otherwise the bowl gets so full of crumbs." "What?" his father asked slowly. He smiled. "You're better off putting the sugar on your own plate," Frits said loudly, "it's more convenient. Otherwise you get crumbs in the sugar bowl. That's not very handy when you're having tea."

"Yes," his father said. He put sugar on his plate and ate the remaining piece of pastry, after having rolled it back and forth on his plate with the palm of his hand, in two bites. "So that's one," Frits thought.

The organ music stopped. "Piet Karwiel concluded this organ concert with a few variations by Franck," the announcer said. "From now until nine you will hear a non-stop programme of Hawaiian melodies." "That is a bit too awful, that whining," said his father when the music started, "why don't we just turn it off?" "I'm particularly fond of it myself," Frits said, "I love the way the strings howl." "We can at least turn it down a little," his father said, standing up and lowering the volume. "That's such a mistake," Frits said, "and one that a lot of people make. Something is playing on the radio, but they need to do something else, or they're carrying on a conversation. So they turn it down.

If you ask me, you should either listen to music or not listen to it at all. If you're going to listen, play it loudly enough. The way you would hear it at a concert." "I am expressing myself very stupidly and sloppily," he thought. "Don't you agree, Father?"

"What did you say?" his father asked. "I consider the radio to be one of the miracles of this modern age," said Frits. His father did not reply.

His mother came in with tea. "Frits, do you have any idea what is on this evening?" she asked. "Where is last night's newspaper?" he asked. "On the table, right in front of your nose," she said, "so don't you go turning the place upside down again." She put cups on the table and poured them tea.

"How do they taste?" she asked, pointing at the oliebollen. "The ones here, on top, are very well fried," said Frits, "seeing as the chunks of apple have gone soft. Did you make any with rings?" "No," she said, "the batter was finished. Isn't there anything else on the radio?" She sat down.

"This is wonderful, I think," Frits said, "let's wait a bit until this is over." They lapsed into silence. Frits opened the paper to the second page and perused the radio guide in the lower left-hand corner. "No," he said, "there's nothing on this evening." "Let me look at that," she said. He handed her the newspaper. "Why they have to use such small print, I'll never understand," she said, putting it back down. "I'll look later, with my other reading glasses." They fell silent once more. All three helped themselves to the pastries and continued eating.

The music stopped. "This is Hilversum One, brought to you by the VARA," the announcer said. "That was the conclusion of today's programme. We are going off the air now and will return tomorrow evening at seven o'clock, on the Hilversum Two frequency. Until tomorrow, dear listeners; we wish you a pleasant evening and—at twelve o'clock you will not be hearing my voice, so let me say it now—a very happy New Year." A crisp click sounded from the speaker, then a quiet zoom. "This is Hilversum, the NCRV," another voice said. "Good evening, esteemed listeners. We are switching now to the Church of the Reconstituted Congregation in The Hague. The service is led by the Reverend K.W. Twigsong."

The radio crackled. For a moment, there was no sound at all. Then there was a popping sound and suddenly the psalmody of a full church blasted into the room. "I almost jumped out of my skin," his mother said. "Let's put an end to that," his father said. "I think it's glorious," Frits said, "it puts you in just the right mood, if you ask me." His father, who had already risen to his feet with his hands on the armrests, sat down again.

"That was a terrible story, there in Papendrecht," Frits said, "with those poison batter balls." "Yes, where did I read that?" his mother said, "two people killed. Horrible." "One of them was only an old woman," Frits said, "a woman close to sixty." His father took two books from the shelf, returned to the table and opened and leafed through them in turn.

"How did that happen, actually?" his mother asked. "Nothing too complicated," Frits replied. "There was something wrong with the baking powder. They mixed a faulty batch at the factory. You're supposed to add only little of that substance that makes the batter rise. But one of the workers did it the other way around:

a bag full of that rubbish and a tiny bit of flour." "Is that really so poisonous?" she asked. "Well, not actually poisonous," he said, "but some people die of it. That woman, who had eaten too much of it, dropped dead as she was leaving the church."

"How long has that custom been around, Father," he asked, "the custom of making oliebollen on New Year's Eve?" "What?" his father asked. "For how many years have people been making oliebollen, do you think?" asked Frits. "Um-hum," his father said.

The singing stopped. The sound of coughing and the shuffling of feet came from the radio. "Let us pray," a cavernous voice called out suddenly. "Quick," Frits said. He jumped at the set and turned it off. Then he sat down again. "The whole trick is to start a conversation and keep it going," he said to himself. When the pastries were finished, his mother took the plate and carried it into the kitchen.

"Did they make oliebollen when you were a boy, Father?" Frits asked. "Are they finished already?" his father asked. "What I was asking," Frits said, "was whether, when you were a boy, back then, whether they also made oliebollen on New Year's Eve."

"Yes, absolutely," the man replied, "in a big, deep pan. Oh yes." He held out his right hand, the palm facing down, and pointed to a pale spot the size of a one-guilder coin, halfway between index finger and wrist. "Here comes the burnt spot," Frits said to himself. "I've never heard it before, of course." "My mother was frying them," his father said. "Something flew out of the pan, with this huge hissing noise." He kept his gaze fixed on the spot and went on: "It was the oil spattering; it landed on the back of my hand."

298

His mother came in with another stack of pastries. She carried the platter with both hands: the bottle of fruit juice she held clutched under her left arm.

"Aha," his father said, looking at the bottle, "and what have we here? Wine?" "It's so-called wine," his mother said. "Is that wine?" his father asked. "That is fruit juice, made from berries and apples," Frits replied loudly, "a fresh, slightly tart beverage. Very tasty after one has eaten greasy things." "What sort of glasses should I use?" his mother asked. "Those little wineglasses?" "Just use the mustard jars," Frits said, "they're the right size."

Moving the platter of pastries, which she had set down on one corner, to the middle of the table, she fetched three mustard jars from the sideboard and tore the capsule from the bottle. "Here's the corkscrew, Frits," she said. Frits held the bottle between his legs, twisted the screw into the cork and pulled. His father leaned over and watched him. "It's in there fairly deep," he said. "Goddammit," Frits thought after two hard pulls, "it's got to come out." He pulled again as hard as he could, working the cork back and forth at the same time. Suddenly it shot loose. "Upsy-daisy," his mother said. His chair rocked back and a dash of juice splashed onto his trousers. "On my trousers," he said. His father stood up, leaning his elbows on the table and said: "You have to clean that off quickly. Wine spots are very hard to get out, if you don't act right away." "Upsy-daisy," Frits thought, "upsy-daisy." "It isn't wine," he said loudly. "Not wine?" his father asked. "Not wine? Then what is it?"

"I was in the shop," his mother said, "and I asked the—" "It's fruit juice," Frits said, turning to face his father. "Juice made from

299

berries and apples. A fresh, tart beverage." He pulled out his handkerchief and wiped the spot on his trousers. "Upsy-daisy," he said to himself, "upsy-daisy." "Goodness," his father said.

His mother filled the glasses and took a sip. "Sour," she said, pursing her lips, "horribly sour." "What?" his father asked. "It's a bit too cold for Mother," Frits replied, "but I actually find that nice." He took a sip as well. "Very good," he said. "There is sugar in it. But not enough to ruin the fresh, sour taste. Just right." His father emptied his glass and was silent. He took another oliebol, stuffed it in his mouth and lay down on the divan. His mother picked up her knitting from the side table and went to sit by the fire. None of them spoke a word.

"We have almost made it to ten o'clock," Frits said to himself. "Soon we will have passed it. Then it is a matter of keeping one's chin up till eleven. After that, in fact, it is finished." He placed his right fist atop his left on the table and lowered his forehead onto it. After five minutes, he sat up straight again. "A conversation that stagnates is a dangerous thing," he thought. "Even if a question is entirely pointless, it is better than no question at all." "Father," he said loudly, "Father." The man looked up. "It is no disaster, to be unhappy," Frits thought, "but how discouraging must it be to know that there is nothing to pin the blame on, outside oneself? The grave yawns, time zooms, and salvation is nowhere to be found. Poor man. The shiver of pathos. Scrumptious pity."

"Yes," his father said. "Father," Frits asked, "were those normal oliebollen, the ones your mother made at home, or was there a special recipe for them there in Twente?" "Pay close attention now," he said to himself, "he's going to give a serious reply to a question that is entirely moronic. I can ask him anything. And I will, too." "No, just normal pastries," his father replied. He frowned, his lips slightly parted. "He was planning to say something else," Frits thought, "but he can't remember what. A thought has almost gelled, but now it's gone and he has to start thinking anew. Quite a feat. No sinecure." His father closed his mouth and lay back down.

"If I say nothing," Frits thought, "perhaps nothing special will happen. I'll keep my mouth shut. See how that goes." In the silence he could hear the ticking of the clock. His mother's knitting needles rattled. "In books and nursery rhymes they always tell you that a clock says tick-tock," he thought, "but that's not true. Not tick-tock, in any case, because those are two distinct sounds." He listened closely. "Tocka tocka tocka is more like it," he said to himself, "but I can't hear it very well right now. I must be patient, wait until she has finished another row, until the rattling stops."

The moment his mother switched needles, he opened his mouth, lowered his eyelids and listened breathlessly. "It's not really a word at all," he said to himself. "Heard correctly, it's teppa teppa teppa, but very quiet. That's not quite it, not exactly, but it's close." "Ten o'clock is the first milestone," he thought, "then it's on to eleven. Once we're past that, the worst is over."

He got up, moved noiselessly to his bedroom, took the mirror from the wall and placed it on the desk, against the wall. Then he took the toy rabbit, laid it beside the mirror and sat down at the desk. "Listen, rabbit," he said quietly. "This evening I want you to pay careful attention. I'm in no mood for jokes or smart talk, not tonight. So don't go thinking you can just listen with half an ear and decide: oh, drop dead." He rattled the desk, causing the animal to move as though nodding. "You show signs of agreement," he said, "but you are not to be trusted." He picked up the animal, tossed it in the air, almost to the ceiling, and caught it again. Then he loosened his belt and zip, placed the animal against his abdomen, fastened his trousers again and tightened the belt. Only the animal's head stuck out.

He inhaled deeply, held his breath, then pressed his belly hard against the waistband. "Now you're feeling the crunch, aren't you, sweet beastie?" he asked. "Well, there's nothing to be done about it."

He slid the mirror over in front of him, leaned forward, twisted the shade on the desk lamp back and forth until the light fell directly on his face, and looked at what he saw. "A complexion full of coarse, unclean pores," he mumbled, "a tired, stale face. A mouth chafed at the corners, where the skin is flaking. Dark bags beneath the eyes. Over forehead and cheeks, a layer of greasy, glistening sweat." "Yes, you just hold your horses," he said, swatting the rabbit on the head a few times. "You can't get out of there anyway. Don't even bother trying. For you I have a very special punishment in store. You will be given twenty-three lashes. If you scream, ten more. Then I'll stick a pin in your rear end and another one in the back of your neck." With his right hand he seized the rabbit's ears and went on: "Then I'll twist your ears. I'll wring them like wet laundry, until a bit of blood drips from them." He let go. "Then I'll make you dance on a glowing iron plate. That is a very harsh punishment indeed, but what you did is so disgraceful, there is no other punishment for it." He clamped his teeth in one of its ears. "There is no escape," he whispered, "because around your neck is a chain, which is riveted to the ceiling. I will heat that plate hotter and hotter, till it glows." He released the ear, petted the rabbit's head and said a little louder: "Now don't cry. Nothing has happened yet. And it won't, not until ten thirty. You still have half an hour."

He looked in the mirror again. "And my hair, rabbit," he murmured, "I haven't looked at that yet." He pressed his shock of hair back flat on his head and examined the hairline from close by. "No, rabbit," he said, "the hairs are still growing well. The hairs grow well. They're still quite firmly anchored, nothing wrong there. If the Almighty is merciful towards me, he will safeguard my follicles for many a long day."

"Teedee tadeedee. Teedee tadee," he sang in something like a hum. "When you don't use anything at all," he said to himself, "when you use no grease, no starch, no colouring, no bleach, no hair powder and no scent in your hair, then you have a major head start. The ignorant are an easy prey for baldness. God grant that it continue growing." He pushed the hairs apart and examined the skin beneath. "A healthy scalp," he mumbled, "but I must start massaging it in the coming years, otherwise it may grow hard and tight. A supple scalp is the sustenance of hair growth."

"Now the cold is rising through my legs," he thought, "it is already up to my knees. Like with a dying man. But it promotes

reflection." Without standing up, he turned off the light by twisting the bulb to the left, and laid his head on the desk. "I must
think," he thought, "and for that silence is needed." "Rabbit,"
he said aloud, "if anyone comes along, tell them I'm not here.
Gone out for a bit. Or rather, tell them I'm taking a bath." He
worked his jaw back and forth. "A cracking sound," he said to
himself. "It is as though the joint is cracking, but it is the desk."

He dozed off, awoke, sat up straight, bowed his head and
then remained sitting motionless. "In a dark room," he thought.
"I am in the dark. I can see everything that happens around me
and yet I myself am invisible." He nodded off again and again,
but each time he almost fell asleep, he sat up again with a start.
"Everything hurts," he thought, "my head is a giant abscess."
He turned on the lamp again.

"Frits!" his mother shouted. "Ah, yes," he said to himself,
"one more time." "Frits!" she shouted again. "That's twice,"
he thought, "but I didn't hear it. One must not forget: I am
hard of hearing." "Frits, where are you?" she called out. He
heard his father say something in a deep voice. "That is thrice,"
he said to himself, "but the fourth time I will certainly hear."
He waited. From the room, he could hear his parents talking
loudly. "Frits!" his mother shouted after thirty seconds. "Yes,
I'm coming," he shouted and stood up. He pulled the rabbit
from under his belt, kissed it on the head and put it back in
the bookcase.

"Where have you been, for heaven's sake?" his mother asked
as he came into the living room. She was still sitting in the chair
by the fire. His father lay on the divan, reading a large book

that he had placed on the seat of a chair slid up beside him. "Father was just saying," his mother said, "that you'd probably gone out. But I said: Then I would have heard him. Where were you? I called you any number of times. For the last half hour."

"Nowhere," Frits said. "I was in the next room, checking something." "It's already well over a quarter past eleven," she said. "A quarter past eleven?" he asked, "quarter past eleven?" He looked at his watch. It showed eleven twenty-two. "I'll be damned," he said, "I was looking for something in a book. I suppose I must have nodded off, or else I was daydreaming."

"It is past eleven," he thought suddenly. "Ten o'clock is behind us, eleven o'clock has come and gone. Long gone. Sing, angels, sing. Almost eleven thirty. Wonderful. Glorious." "This is the same feeling," he said to himself. "Mr Vogel is ill. The last period has been cancelled." He turned on the radio. "How simple things are," he thought. A piano was playing a slow tune. The tones grew weaker and faded. "Don't start twisting the knob back and forth right away," his mother said. "No," he said, "it fades. That's part of the programme."

"On the evening of this day, before darkness falls," a calm, mellow voice said slowly, "we would like to once more enter into the presence of—" Frits ran through the channels. "—have arrived now at the final musical course of our banquet of cheerful New Year's melodies," an announcer said. "You are hearing the Bobbing Nightingales with… 'Sunny Boy'." "Is there really nothing else on?" his father asked once the music started. "This is Brussels," Frits said, "we could try Hilversum One." He turned the knob to the left. "Here we go," he said.

They heard the sound of shuffling feet in a cavernous space. "Probably another church," his mother said. An organ began playing softly. After a few bars the congregation joined in. "Hark, hark," Frits said to himself, "hours, days, months, years." "Listen to that," he said aloud, "hours, days, months, years." "Hours, days, months, years," he repeated to himself, "hours, days, months, years." He turned up the volume. "Can't you turn that down a little?" his father asked. "No," Frits replied, "this needs to be loud. Leave it like this, just the way it is." His heart was pounding. "Hours, days, months, years," he said to himself. "This is the evening. This is the night. It is New Year's Eve. In a little over twenty-eight minutes it will be midnight. I still have twenty-eight minutes. I must collect my thoughts. I must be finished thinking when twelve o'clock strikes." He looked at his father. "Help those who are oppressed and imagine themselves abandoned in this world," he thought. "Old fart."

The singing stopped. After a brief postlude, the organ fell silent too. "Brethren," a high voice said. Frits spun the dial, but did not look for another station. The loudspeaker hissed softly.

"Now I have to say it," he said to himself, "I have to say it. But how? Just a few more moments. I have to. It's still not too late."

"Father," he said loudly, "Father." "Yes, my boy," his father said. He laid a pencil between the pages of the book and closed it. "He is listening," Frits thought, "but I don't yet know what I am going to say. I don't know." His head throbbed. "If I don't speak right away, something terrible is going to happen."

"Father," he said. The man sat up. "Frits is talking to you," his mother said. "Yes, I hear that, obviously," said his father. He grimaced for a moment, causing a row of wrinkles to appear at the spot where nose met forehead. "I can't back out any more," Frits thought. The room rocked back and forth before his eyes, faded for moment, then settled into place. "What is it, what did I say?" he thought.

"Father," he said, "only people can sing. That's curious, isn't it? That singing is something only people can do?" "Lost, all is lost," he thought, "I didn't dare to say it. I said something else. What did I say?" He felt his head grow hot. "Something very different," he thought, "and nonsensical. Idiotic nonsense. A handful of words tossed out. Nonsensical words. The purest blather, neither here nor there. It's ridiculous: birds sing too. What exactly did I say?"

"But birds sing too, don't they?" his mother said. "Help," he thought, "I am lost." "Yes," his father said, "birds sing quite beautifully, I've always thought." "I mean," Frits said, "I, I mean, Father, don't you understand what I mean?" The lamp shrank before his eyes, slid away into the distance and came back again. "No," his father said, "that only people can sing, that's simply not true." He crossed his arms over his chest. "Maybe, if I go on talking," Frits said to himself, "I can distract them." "You mean those birds they catch and keep in cages," he said, "to make them whistle. A canary, I can imagine that, that's one of those tropical birds that can't live out of doors around these parts. In fact, most canaries are born in captivity. They don't know any better." "What am I saying?" he thought, "what am I babbling on about?" "But they also catch thrushes and blackbirds," he went on. "And all kinds of other birds, I don't know, that live in the wild. They put them in cages." "It's your purest nonsense," he thought. "There is no way out of it." He felt the blood rush to his ears. "I need to sit down," he thought. "A chair." He pulled a chair back from the table and dropped down onto it. "Could it be that they didn't notice anything?" he thought.

"Yes," his mother said, "in the countryside you see that so often. A blackbird, or a lark, in a cage in front of the house. What's the charm in that? I can't understand it." "Dearest, best among women," Frits said to himself. "Wine. Apple-berry. Berry-apple, actually." "I started off talking gibberish," he thought, "could they have forgotten what I said first?" The throbbing in his head diminished slightly.

His father slid his legs off the divan and sat on the edge. "When I was little," he said, "when summer came, my father and a few other men would go out catching finches. That was a real occasion." He scratched his chin, broke wind and went on: "They would go out on Saturday evening and wouldn't come back till Sunday morning, around nine o'clock. With a whole heap of finches. They sold them."

"I am delivered," Frits said to himself, "the conversation has moved on from a nonsensical start." "Is it true," his mother asked, "that they actually blind finches? Is that true?" "Oh yes," his father said, "they blinded them, that makes them sing better; at least that's what they claimed." He parted his lips, gritted his teeth and said: "I remember seeing my father do it. He took a glowing knitting needle and burned their eyes out." Resting his chin in his hand, he looked at Frits. "Father," the boy thought,

"Father." "Are the oliebollen already finished?" he asked. He pointed at the empty platter. "Father said: Let's eat the rest of them," his mother said, "Frits won't be back that quickly. I told him: let's not. Well, it happened anyway. Your father has them in his stomach. Shall I make you a sandwich?" "Oh no," Frits said. "What did you say?" his father asked her. "I said," she shouted, "that you ate all the pastries, including his." "Yes," the man said. "Those pastries," he said suddenly, turning to Frits, "I believe I ate your oliebollen too. Didn't I?" "No, that's fine actually," Frits said. "They would only be hard and chewy in the morning. I don't want any more."

"How about a little wine?" his mother asked. "It is juice," Frits said to himself. "Berry-apple." "Yes, I'd love that," he replied. "The bottle is still half-full," she said while she poured. "It will be good for a pudding," he said, "you can use it to make a good sauce for semolina pudding."

"You won't forget the radio, will you?" she asked. "It can't be long now." He looked at his watch. "Four minutes," he replied, "going on three now, that's three minutes. A little over three minutes." He pulled his chair over to the radio and began running through the channels. "—we bring you 'The Policeman's Holiday'," a voice said. "After that there will be a pause of about thirty seconds. You will hear the seconds ticking away; at ten seconds before midnight you will hear the sound we announcers know so well, signalling the full hour: a brief, clear tick."

"Sort of a strange song to end with, don't you think?" Frits asked once the record began. "Time to fill the glasses, then," his father said. His mother poured. She spilled some. "Apple-berry,"

Frits thought. "Berry-apple." The music stopped. The seconds ticked. "Grr-tock," they heard suddenly. "Here it comes," Frits said. He shivered.

"Seven, eight, nine," he counted off to himself. The slow tones of the overture began. Then two counts of silence. The chimes rang. Outside the sirens roared. "Happy New Year, dear," said his mother, taking his father's hand. "Happy New Year," he said. They kissed. "Happy New Year to you, Mother," said Frits, once his parents had let go of each other. His mother took his arm and pulled him to her, kissed him once on the cheek and once on the side of his neck. "Happy New Year," she said. He kissed her on the corner of the mouth. While she was still holding him tight, he stuck his hand out to his father. "Happy New Year, Father," he said. "Happy New Year, my boy," the man said, gripping his hand and pumping the arm up and down forcefully.

As soon as Frits was released, he raised his glass. His parents followed suit. They held them together, carefully clinked each other's glass and drank. "Apple-berry," Frits thought. "It is finished." His parents sat down. The radio started in on a march.

"I'm going out to take a look around," he said. "I need to be outside for a bit." He threw on his coat and rushed down the stairs. In front of the house he stopped. "First I need to take a piss," he mumbled. He stepped up to the wall and made water against a drainpipe. More and more sirens and whistles mixed with the din. Closing his fly, he looked up. Halfway across the sky was an opening in the clouds, where the stars sparkled brightly. To the south, a rocket traced a green trail; it climbed, slowed, fell and extinguished halfway to earth. "That's one of those flying suns," he thought, "four cents apiece." Passers-by, who had stopped to watch the rocket, walked on.

He raced across the quay to the river, turned left and walked quickly, leaping from time to time, along the bank. There was almost no wind; the water's surface was marked only by faint ripples. Two boys on a bike, dragging three large tins behind them on a string, passed him at high speed. Occasionally one of the tins bounced high in the air. "Very good," Frits said to himself. On the far side, right behind the first row of waterfront houses, three red rockets shot up in rapid succession. "It's not really red," he thought, "more like a light purple. Like the silver foil around the chocolate towers when we were little." At their apex the rockets spattered apart into white stars that died out after a few seconds.

"Let us walk on," he said to himself, "wish some people a happy New Year."

On a covered barge along the far bank he made out a few silhouettes. "It's fairly light out," he thought, "are those the street lamps or is the moon up there somewhere? It must be behind a cloud, because I don't see it." The figures on the barge were stooping over something. Suddenly he saw a flame rise up between them, at the level of the deck. First it flared white, then grew brighter and changed to a dark green. The flame grew, changed shape and became a globe. The faces of those standing around it became clearly visible. "Bengal fire," he thought. "It looks like there's moss growing on their faces. You can see even the individual stones in the walls."

The glow lasted for thirty seconds, reached full strength, flickered and then died out slowly. The sirens and whistles stopped, one by one. He looked around. Two young boys were standing a few steps away from him. They were wearing black raincoats. One was a head taller than the other.

He took a few steps in their direction. They leapt away immediately. "They're afraid," he thought. "They are afraid of me; eight years old or so." He cleared his throat and asked: "So, gentlemen, are you allowed out so late at night?" "Yes, sir," the biggest boy replied, "it's New Year's Eve." "So it is," he thought, "they speak when spoken to, because one has to say something back, even to the stupidest questions." "Still, it's dangerous, you know," he said, "with the bogeymen out and about." "There's no such thing," the little boy said, "and besides, there's two of us. I'd hit him on the head with this stick." He produced a thick length of tree branch from under his raincoat.

"He says that was cold fire," the bigger of the two said, pointing first at his companion and then across the river, "but that can't be, can it, mister?" "Cold fire does not exist," Frits said, "there's no such thing." "See!" the big boy said to the little one. They turned suddenly and ran off. "A common misconception among the young," Frits said to himself. "The belief in cold fire. They believe that fireworks and sparks are made of cold fire." He moved close to the water and picked his way along the granite revetment. "This is more or less the spot," he thought, "where Louis walked into the water. That was a good eighteen years ago. He wasn't paying attention. His father suddenly heard a splash behind him."

He crossed the bridge with the stone balustrade and speeded up to a trot. "First we'll wish Jaap a happy New Year," he thought.

On the far side he ran along the water's edge, quickly rounded the corner onto the canal lined with warehouses, sped on to number seventy-one, skipped up the front steps and rang the bell. "Eleven minutes," he said aloud. "How about if I shout something cute. German police!" "That's once," he thought after waiting for half a minute. He rang again, hopped down the stairs and slowly headed back the way he had come. "Of course," he said to himself, "they've gone to Jaap's parents. Taken the child along. Very wise. Or else they left it at home, in the hope that there will not be a fire."

"There is nothing going on tonight," he thought, "it was only a bit of noise. In London everyone rushes out into the streets. In Moscow they fire cannons and set off huge fireworks over the whole city."

He followed the route back along the river and rang the bell at the house with the towers. "Viktor is bound to be at home, at least," he said to himself, "and he won't have gone to bed yet either." "Who's there?" a woman's voice called through the speaking tube. "Frits," he shouted back, "is Viktor home?" "I don't really have to wait," he thought, "he's not here anyway. Otherwise he would have opened the door himself." "Viktor has gone to his parents, to Haarlem," the voice answered. "Fine," Frits shouted back, "tell him Frits van Egters says hello. He knows who that is. I'll come by soon, to wish him a happy New Year. Goodbye, Lidia."

He sauntered back across the bridge. "I still have one chance left," he thought, "that's Louis. I suspect that he got home about an hour ago." He remained standing at Louis's door for a few

313

minutes. "I'm not going to ring yet," he said to himself. "It's freezing, but no more than half a degree below zero. Everything is cooling down. The street, the trees and the walls have to become cold first. They go on radiating heat for a whole day. Now I'll ring the bell. Almighty God, see me in my distress. This is the final door."

He pushed the button, held it in to the count of five and waited. "No one," he said. "No one." He rang the bell again, stepped back and remained standing before the portico. "Not home, the imbecile," he murmured. "Here I stand." He started walking home.

"From the depths I have called to you," he said to himself, "but my voice was not heard. Berry-apple. Now am I going home. Eternal and only God, our God, I am going to my parents. Look upon my parents." His eyes grew moist.

"Eternal, only, almighty, our God," he said quietly, "fix your gaze upon my parents. See them in their need. Do not turn your eyes from them." "Listen," he said, "my father is deaf as a tradesman's dummy. He hears little, what he does hear is not worth mentioning. Fire a cannon beside his ear for a joke, he'll ask if there's someone at the door. He slurps when he drinks. He dishes up sugar with his dessert spoon. He takes the meat between his fingers. He breaks wind, without anyone having asked him to do so. He has the remains of food between his molars. He does not know where the guilder is supposed to go. When he peels his eggs, he does not know what to do with the shells. He asks in English whether there is anything new and interesting to report. He mashes together all the food on his plate. Everlasting Lord, I know that it has not gone unseen."

A group of six girls came by, walking side by side, arm in arm, sometimes running, sometimes slowing to an amble. "He spills ash when he empties his pipe," he whispered once they had passed. "He mislays postage stamps. Not on purpose, he actually mislays them. You can't find them, and that's all that matters. He wipes his fingers on his clothes. He turns off the radio. If I play around with the fork, he thinks I've gone mad. And he spears things from off the platter. That is unclean. And he often goes without a tie. Yet great is his goodness." He remained standing and gazed out over the water. "See my mother," he said quietly. "She says I should stay at home, nice and cosy. That I should wear the white jumper. She makes oliebollen with the wrong pieces of apple. I will explain that to you sometime, when the occasion arises. She lights the fire and fills the room with smoke. And she melted the attic keys. Almighty, everlasting, she thought she was buying wine, but it was fruit juice. The sweet, good woman. Berry-apple. She moves her head back and forth when she reads. She is my mother. See her in her immeasurable goodness." Using his sleeve to wipe a tear from the corner of his right eye, he walked on.

"A thousand years are as one day unto you," he continued, "and as a watch by night. Behold the days of my parents. Old age approaches, illnesses possess them, and there is no hope. Death approaches and the grave yawns. In fact, it's not even a grave, because they'll be put in an urn: we pay for that in weekly instalments." He shook his head.

"See them," he whispered, "for whom there is no hope. They live in solitude. However they cast about, they touch only emptiness. Their bodies are prey to decline. He does still have hair on his head, a whole thatch of it. No, bald he is not. But that will come."

He had reached the front door. "Peace," he thought, "it is over. There is peace. Sublime good cheer abounds." Head bowed, he went in, quietly climbed the stairs and crossed the landing slowly. In the living room his father was standing by the fire in his underwear. "Good evening," Frits said. "So, my boy," the man answered. "How could anyone develop a paunch like that?" Frits thought. "A pregnant manservant." "All-powerful God," he said to himself, "behold this. What do they call underwear like that, with shirt and pants all of a single piece? A union suit, I believe." He took a good look at the garment. At the rear, by the lower back, was a long vertical split that stood open. "I can see his crack," he thought. "The crap flap is open." "Lord almighty," he said to himself, "look upon him: his crack is showing. Look upon this man. He is my father. Keep him from harm. Protect him. Lead him in peace. He is your child."

"Frits, is that you?" his mother called from the bedroom. He entered. She was lying in bed. "Was there anything going on outside?" she asked. "Not much," he said, "a few rockets."

His father entered from the living room and climbed into bed. He reached over to the reading light, which stood on a chair beside the bed, and turned it off. "Don't stay up too late, will you?" his mother asked. "I am going straight to bed," Frits replied. "Good night." "Don't trip over the cord," she said. He left the room, stepping high, turned off the light in the living room and went to brush his teeth in the kitchen. Suddenly he stopped, the toothbrush still in his mouth, and spread his arms. He strode to the mirror in the hall and stood before it. He removed the toothbrush from his mouth.

"I live," he whispered, "I breathe. And I move. I breathe, I move, therefore I live. What could possibly happen? Calamities, pains and horrors may come. But I live. I can be confined, or visited by gruesome diseases. But still I breathe, and I move. And I live." He walked back to the kitchen, finished brushing his teeth and entered his bedroom.

"Rabbit," he said, cradling the rabbit on his arm, "your punishment has been revoked, in view of your resounding accomplishments for the cause." He placed the animal on the desk, closed the curtains and began to undress. When he was finished, he drummed his fists against his chest and ran his hands over his body. He pinched the scruff of his neck, his stomach, his calves and thighs. "Everything is finished," he whispered, "it has passed. The year is no more. Rabbit, I am alive. I breathe, and I move, so I live. Is that clear? Whatever ordeals are yet to come, I am alive."

Drawing his lungs full of air, he climbed into bed. "It has been seen," he murmured, "it has not gone unnoticed." He stretched himself out and fell into a deep sleep.

Amsterdam, Sunday, 18th May 1947

317

PUSHKIN PRESS

Pushkin Press was founded in 1997, and publishes novels, essays, memoirs, children's books—everything from timeless classics to the urgent and contemporary.

Our books represent exciting, high-quality writing from around the world: we publish some of the twentieth century's most widely acclaimed, brilliant authors such as Stefan Zweig, Marcel Aymé, Teffi, Antal Szerb, Gaito Gazdanov and Yasushi Inoue, as well as compelling and award-winning contemporary writers, including Andrés Neuman, Edith Pearlman, Eka Kurniawan, Ayelet Gundar-Goshen and Chigozie Obioma.

Pushkin Press publishes the world's best stories, to be read and read again. To discover more, visit www.pushkinpress.com.

═══

THE SPECTRE OF ALEXANDER WOLF
GAITO GAZDANOV

'A mesmerising work of literature' Antony Beevor

SUMMER BEFORE THE DARK
VOLKER WEIDERMANN

'For such a slim book to convey with such poignancy the extinction of a generation of "Great Europeans" is a triumph' *Sunday Telegraph*

MESSAGES FROM A LOST WORLD
STEFAN ZWEIG

'At a time of monetary crisis and political disorder... Zweig's celebration of the brotherhood of peoples reminds us that there is another way' *The Nation*

THE EVENINGS
GERARD REVE

'Not only a masterpiece but a cornerstone manqué of modern European literature' Tim Parks, *Guardian*

BINOCULAR VISION

EDITH PEARLMAN

'A genius of the short story' Mark Lawson, *Guardian*

IN THE BEGINNING WAS THE SEA

TOMÁS GONZÁLEZ

'Smoothly intriguing narrative, with its touches of sinister,
Patricia Highsmith-like menace' *Irish Times*

BEWARE OF PITY

STEFAN ZWEIG

'Zweig's fictional masterpiece' *Guardian*

THE ENCOUNTER

PETRU POPESCU

'A book that suggests new ways of looking at the world
and our place within it' *Sunday Telegraph*

WAKE UP, SIR!

JONATHAN AMES

'The novel is extremely funny but it is also sad and
poignant, and almost incredibly clever' *Guardian*

THE WORLD OF YESTERDAY

STEFAN ZWEIG

'*The World of Yesterday* is one of the greatest memoirs of the twentieth
century, as perfect in its evocation of the world Zweig loved, as it is
in its portrayal of how that world was destroyed' David Hare

WAKING LIONS

AYELET GUNDAR-GOSHEN

'A literary thriller that is used as a vehicle to explore big
moral issues. I loved everything about it' *Daily Mail*

FOR A LITTLE WHILE

RICK BASS

'Bass is, hands down, a master of the short form, creating in a few pages
a natural world of mythic proportions' *New York Times Book Review*